VISIONS VI

Books from Lillicat Publishers

Visions Series

VISIONS VI

GALAXIES

EDITED BY

CARROL FIX

LILLICAT PUBLISHERS
USA

VISIONS VI
GALAXIES

Hubble Deep Field
Hubble Space Telescope · WFPC2

1996 - mankind's deepest, most detailed visible view of the universe.
Credit: R. Williams (STScI), the Hubble Deep Field Team and NASA

CONTENTS

STEPPING STONES TO ETERNITY

The *Visions* series tells the story of how humanity must ultimately venture outward from our tiny home and explore the Universe.

Visions: Leaving Earth, the first volume, describes our first faltering steps to rise from Earth's surface and build homes in space.

Visions II: Moons of Saturn confirms humankind's success in leaving Earth and building homes in the other planetary systems circling our sun-father Sol.

Visions III: Inside the Kuiper Belt proclaims domination of all that dwells within the solar system—from our Sun to the outermost reaches of the Kuiper Belt and into the Oort Cloud.

Visions IV: Space Between Stars astounds us with the infinite possibilities of adventure and danger far from any suns or planets—in the cold, dark regions of deepest space, where dark matter and nebulas of celestial gases abide.

Visions V: Milky Way leads us to explore our own galaxy. Although vast and unreachable with current technology, the Milky Way is but a tiny point in the Universe. We must first learn about our own home galaxy before we can explore further outward to other galaxies.

Visions VI: Galaxies follows human progress into other galaxies. Humankind survives to spread across the Universe, making distant galaxies and planets into a home for a race destined to seek horizons ever more far away.

The final volume, *Visions VII: Universe,* will open the doors to incredible possibilities for the race called *Human.* We will venture into realms where what seems impossible becomes fact.

Our vision is limitless.

INTRODUCTION

Visions VI: Galaxies moves us beyond our own provincial area of space and into the broader perspective of multiple galaxies. With hundreds of billions of galaxies in the Universe and hundreds of billions of stars in most galaxies, the possibility of habitable planets other than our Earth is a certainty. When humankind spreads outward, as it must in order to survive, communication and interaction between galaxies must also reach unforeseen capabilities.

Life in a distant future, where moving between galaxies is accomplished with ease, will be different . . . yet in many ways the same. Human interaction is a constant—love, hate, trust, fear—emotional qualities of life cannot change. Or can they? What will future humans be like? For that matter, could our cousins already exist and be waiting for us to contact them?

These stories provide exciting and original ways of viewing the future of humankind and the fellow beings we may encounter. Humans, aliens, and technology come together in another fascinating journey through the realms of the *Visions Series*.

Carrol Fix
Editor
Lillicat Publishers
October 16, 2016

"If you know your enemy and you know yourself, then in a hundred battles you will never be in peril."
~SunTzu, The Art of War

OLD SOLDIERS

Bruce C Davis

HASTINGS CLOSED HIS eyes as the shuttle hit the atmosphere. This was the part of space travel he had always hated, whether it was the violent pitch and roll of a combat drop, or this gentler falling sensation of a commercial reentry.

It had been a long trip out from Tau Ceti base. Three jumps and nearly a month of total transit time to reach this backwater world at the end of one of the Andromeda Galaxy's spiral arms. By the time he returned home to Earth, he'd already be almost a year beyond his retirement date. He'd get full pay and benefits for the extra time, as well as a stop-loss bonus, but that wouldn't make up for breaking his promise to Peg. He hoped she'd understand. She'd once been a Consortium Marine herself. Orders were orders, even for old Lieutenant Colonels who should have been put out to pasture after the Draki War.

The shuttle leveled off and slowed as it began its final descent. Hastings opened his eyes, but the windowless isolation compartment was as bland as it was empty. The curving bulkhead glowed with a shifting pattern of soothing pastel colors. The acceleration couch was covered in fine leather, or at least something that felt like leather. Soft music played over small speakers in his headrest.

Grieg, he thought. It was light and pleasing; a soothing melody.

At least they make the solitary confinement comfortable, he thought with a touch of bitterness. *Anything to keep the beast tame and tractable.*

With a muted roar, the shuttle slowed to a hover before touching down with a soft bump. Almost immediately, the hatch to the main passenger compartment opened and a short gray-skinned Hanqui stepped through. The hatch closed quickly behind the toad-like alien and Hastings caught only a glimpse of the other passengers as they started to climb, crawl or slither out of their own seats.

The Hanqui executed a passable imitation of a human salute, despite its stubby arms. "I see you, Lieutenant Colonel James Hastings," it said in croaking but understandable English. "I trust the reentry was not too uncomfortable for you. If you would be patient for a few minutes more, I will conduct you directly to Customs processing and we will avoid the queues at the regular entry port."

And avoid being seen by any of the gentlebeings waiting in line, Hastings thought. *It would not do to frighten the tourists.*

He returned the salute and gave a croaking bark of greeting and respect in the Hanqui's own language before replying in English. "I see you, Joqui Garluff. Thank you for your concern. The ride was far more comfortable than many I have experienced. I am at your disposal."

Garluff had been his *guide* for the entire trip out, always there whenever Hastings changed ships or transited a jump point. He knew the Hanqui's real job was to reassure the various other races of the Five Galaxy Consortium, whose areas of influence they transited, that the human was properly supervised at all times and would not commit murder or mayhem as he passed through their space.

Hastings smiled. For all that, Garluff had been polite and companionable enough. At least the Hanqui didn't quake with fear or recoil in disgust when he was in Hasting's presence.

"Have you any last minute advice for dealing with my hosts," Hastings asked, more in the way of making conversation than because he expected any useful information.

Garluff grunted in what Hastings recognized as a sign of approval. "The Gorsk are a young race and prone to excitability. They are somewhat provincial by Five Galaxy standards, living as they do out here at the end of the Wormhole Jump Chain. They have had limited contact with other Consortium races and none with Humans. You will be the first of your race to visit here, perhaps the first to meet any Gorsk face to face. Do remain aware of that as it may color future relations with your own people."

Hastings nodded, knowing that Garluff would understand the gesture. "I studied their history and physiology on the trip out. What I mean to ask is, do you have any insight as to why the Gorsk sent an urgent request for a field officer to come out here to the end of the intergalactic road, literally and figuratively, without any explanation."

"Alas, no. As I said, they are a young race and prone to excitability. Your superiors must have thought the request had merit."

Hastings shrugged. "If my superiors know anything more than I do, they didn't see fit to tell me."

"Whatever the issue, it must be significant. A being of your experience and ability is not dispatched from Tau Ceti without due consideration."

Hastings laughed. "You overstate my importance, my friend. I am just a soldier."

"Not so," croaked Garluff. "Your handling of the Haven Crisis showed superior courage combined with a deft sense of cultural diplomacy."

"And a willingness to crack a few of my fellow humans on the head in order to get their attention. Those tactics are unlikely to work with the Gorsk. Why would any Consortium race, even a young one, intentionally invite a visit from a human soldier?"

"I do not know," said Garluff. The Hanqui stepped aside and the hatch slid open. "Shall we go and find out?"

Government House, the Consortium equivalent of an embassy, housed representatives of many of the various races in the collective. Even this far out from the Five Galaxies administrative center, more than twenty races maintained a presence in the huge complex. Human representation was lacking, but there was a series of spaces dedicated to the Hanqui delegation. Garluff showed Hastings to a small suite near the main Hanqui office that had been made available for his use.

"The Gorsk are most insistent that you meet with their Security Minister immediately," Garluff said after he had shown Hastings the room and the lavatory arrangement. "I explained that you would be fatigued from your journey, but they are quite anxious to see you. As I said, a young and excitable race."

"No, that's OK," said Hastings. "I want to get this out of the way. Give me a few minutes to get ready."

Garluff bowed and withdrew, and Hastings lifted his space bag up to the bed. He drew out his Marine uniform, a heavy leather belt and holster, and an old .45 caliber Colt semiautomatic pistol. He dressed methodically, donning the uniform, the accompanying collar devices and campaign ribbons. He buckled on the belt and holster, slid a magazine into the Colt, checked the safety and holstered the weapon.

He stepped out into the corridor and found Garluff waiting for him The Hanqui stared at him as if he'd never seen him before. For the first time, Hastings sensed fear in his official minder.

He sighed. "I still see you, Joqui Garluff," he said. "The uniform changes nothing."

"I see you as well, James Hastings," said Garluff thoughtfully. "Perhaps for the first time."

They exited the Government House garage in a covered ground car also with opaque windows, Garluff sitting in the front with the Gorsk driver, Hastings in the back, a glass partition separating him from the forward seat.

The car stopped after a short time and the door next to Hastings hissed open. He got out into another enclosed garage, this one considerably darker and damper that the one at Government House. Garluff bustled up, his earlier fear forgotten, or at least better concealed.

"This way, Colonel," said the Hanqui.

They entered a lift tube and ascended rapidly for what Hastings estimated to be at least ten floors. The lift opened and Hastings walked forward into ruddy sunlight. Floor to ceiling windows faced the lift giving a panoramic view of Karf'El, the capitol city of Gorskaka. Hastings had little opportunity to take in the sight before Garluff steered him to the left where a tall Gorsk with a black carapace and a complex black braid regarded him with cocked head.

Its mandibles clacked and Hastings translator whispered, "You are the Killer?"

Hastings drew himself up. "I am Lieutenant Colonel James Hastings, 5th Battalion, 13th Regiment, Consortium Marine Corps."

The Gorsk bleated softly through its axillary sacs and repeated, "But you have killed sentient beings?"

Hastings sighed. *Always the same.* In the entire Consortium, only humans seemed to be capable of taking sentient life. The other races were all militant pacifists. Some were so incapable of taking another life that they used no animal products and didn't even kill animal pests. Humans were the anomaly in the ranks of spacefaring species. *Well, humans and Draki,* thought Hastings. *But we Humans made them extinct, which earned us our reputation for ruthlessness, even if the rest of the Consortium breathed sighs of relief when the last Draki ship was destroyed.*

Hastings drew himself up to attention and recited his record in the format the Consortium Council required. "I am James Hastings, Human of Earth, currently residing on Tau Ceti 4. I have personally caused the deaths of 76 sentient beings under combat conditions. I have given orders directly resulting in the deaths of 12,473 sentient beings. I willingly participated in the destruction of the Draki fleet which destruction caused the deaths of an estimated one million, two hundred and seventy thousand sentient beings. These deaths were sanctioned by the unanimous vote of the Consortium Council but are on my responsibility and conscience alone." *And may God have mercy on my soul.*

The Gorsk nodded, a Human gesture it had obviously practiced. "We have need of your services, James Hastings," it said through the translator. "We need you to take the life of a sentient."

"No," said Hastings, a little too loudly. "I am a soldier, not an executioner. Do your own dirty work, or let the poor bastard go if you can't do it yourself."

The Gorsk hissed slowly. "You misunderstand. We are holding another soldier, one deemed too dangerous and hostile by both my government and the Consortium Council, too be kept safely in captivity. That is why you have been dispatched to this place. Your race has taken upon itself the obligation to protect the other member races of the Consortium from random violence and the threat of war. This duty is required of you under that obligation."

"A soldier? Another human? What has he done?" demanded Hastings.

"Not another Human," said the Gorsk. "A Draki."

"Impossible. The Draki fleet was destroyed at Celebrim in M46. The last ships were hunted down over six Standard years ago. All the rest committed suicide before they could be captured. Draki never allow themselves to be taken captive."

"Nevertheless, said the Gorsk. "A Draki is currently in a secure isolation room not thirty meters from here. It was found in a stasis capsule that drifted into the path of one of our trading vessels. It was brought here before the capsule was opened and its contents known. We immediately placed the Draki in confinement. It was injured, but we have treated those injuries and it has healed satisfactorily. Now we require your assistance in killing it."

Hastings laughed at the irony of the Gorsk curing a Draki's injuries, only to demand a Human be dispatched to kill the thing afterwards.

He drew himself up to attention. "You will show me this Draki. I wish to interview it."

The Gorsk official's axillary sacs fluttered in agitation. "Whatever for? It is safely secured in an isolation room. We have various toxins that can be introduced into the air it breathes, or there are small ports in the walls through which you may discharge a weapon. Why speak to it?"

"Because it is a sentient, damn it. It deserves the dignity of knowing who is killing it." *And I am curious,* he admitted to himself.

The Gorsk pulled a small disc from a pouch near one of its legs and spoke into it with clacking and hissing mandibles. It apparently received a reply, for it looked again at Hastings and said, "As you desire. Follow."

It led Hastings and Garluff through a set of double doors into a long corridor lined with gray metal. To Hastings it looked like hull armor. At the end of the corridor was a windowless hatch with a central wheel coupled to heavy metal rods that slid into recesses in the doorframe. The Gorsk entered a code on a keypad next to the wheel then spun it, releasing the hatch. It swung inward. Inside was a small chamber, like a ship's airlock. On the opposite wall was a second similar hatch, also held closed with heavy metal dogs.

"The code to release the inner hatch is green-red-green-white-blue," the Gorsk said. "You will not open it until the outer hatch is properly sealed. If the Draki should attack you, speak the word 'Emergency' in your own language. The air will be evacuated from the inner chamber, subduing the Draki. You will be extracted before permanent damage occurs."

"Right," said Hastings. "That sounds like fun."

He waited as Garluff and the Gorsk exited and secured the outer hatch. He entered the code and spun the wheel. He drew his sidearm. The inner hatch opened and he pushed it inward.

The Draki sat in a corner, facing the door. It rose slowly as Hastings entered, its feline eyes narrowing as it took note of Hastings' uniform and the gun in his hand. Hastings read the patterns of its fur and the three notches in its right ear.

"So, the plant eaters have sent a Human to do what they could not," it said. "Do you clutch that pathetic weapon out of fear, or do you intend to shoot me right now?"

"I am Lieutenant Colonel James Hastings, 13th Consortium Marines, and I have too much respect for the prowess of the Zebu Clan of the Draki hoard to insult a Prime by appearing in his presence unarmed."

The Draki grunted and folded its powerful arms, sheathing its claws. "You at least have manners. I offer you Guest Rights, James Hastings. I would seal the pact with food and drink, but as you can see, my current den lacks both."

"I accept," said Hastings slowly holstering the Colt. He bowed. "May I know the name and family of my host?"

"I am Rask D'An, Prime of the Third Zebu Cohort." He spread his arms and roared. "I welcome you to this den."

"The Third Zebu were feared fighters. My unit faced them at Second Kattoria. You killed many of my lads and nearly overran our position with your final charge."

Rask D'An bowed. "The Thirteenth Marines are known for their valor. If not for your air attack, our charge might have succeeded. Never had we seen such close coordination."

"So, how do two old soldiers, such as we, find ourselves in this place? How did the Gorsk capture you?" asked Hastings

D'An shook his shaggy head, the Draki equivalent of a shrug. "I was in the lead cruiser at Celebrim. The bridge was breached and I was injured. The stasis capsule of my command chair deployed but the guidance system failed. I was six years in stasis before these plant eaters found me." He rumbled deep in his throat. "They spent days repairing the damage to my body, and now they have sent you to kill me."

Hastings nodded. "By their standards they are doing the right thing. I am not sure I will comply with their request."

"You must. If you do not, they will simply send another, perhaps one with less courage and etiquette." The Draki sighed. "I do not fear death, James Hastings. I welcome it. I am the last of my clan. This is the end of the hunt. "

"End of the road," muttered Hastings. The Draki cocked his head. "We say, 'the end of the road' when there is no longer a reason to go on."

"I would ask two things of you, Human. The first is an honorable death, on my feet, facing my slayer." Hastings nodded. "Second, an answer. Why do you Humans do it? Why do you fight like demons, die like Draki, to protect the plant eaters? You are predators, like the Draki. Such as these Gorsk are your prey, yet you debase yourselves preserving them. Why?"

"Do the Draki have sheepdogs?" Hastings asked.

"I do not understand."

"No," said Hastings. "I thought you would not. Long ago in human history, so long in fact that no one knows when, Humans allied themselves with a species of pre-sentient pack hunters called dogs. In exchange for a share of our food and the warmth of our hearths, dogs joined us in our hunts, guarded our fires and became our companions. Over generations we bred and trained them to perform many tasks. A particular type of dog learned to guard sheep–herbivores that are useful and docile but stupid. The sheepdog is a predator, but it will guard and protect its flock, with its life if necessary, because that is its job, because that insures the future of its offspring and buys them a place at the human table."

"So you willingly become pets?" asked D'An. "Servants to these dirt eaters?"

"The sheepdog not only protects the sheep, it guides the flock from pasture to pasture, keeping the strays close to the group," said Hastings. "We see ourselves doing the same thing with the Consortium; guiding, influencing, directing the Council to new goals."

D'An was silent for a moment, then he rumbled even more deeply, over and over. Hastings realized he was laughing.

"You mean to herd them. To prey on them so slowly and quietly that they will not realize their danger," he said.

Hastings remained silent.

Finally, D'An stopped laughing. "Thank you, James Hastings. You have made the end of this hunt most enlightening. I am ready to die."

Hastings looked into the Draki's eyes, a challenge which caused an involuntary snarl. He drew the Colt from his belt and stood regarding it for a moment. "End of the road," he said.

He reversed the weapon and held it out to D'An, grip first. "I see you, Rask D'An."

The Draki took the weapon. "I see you, James Hastings," he said quietly.

Hastings turned his back and entered the code to unlock the hatch. He swung it open and passed through, closing and dogging it behind him. He opened the outer door of the lock and was just reclosing it when he heard the muffled report of a single gunshot.

Bruce Davis is a Mesa AZ based general and trauma surgeon. He finished medical school at the University of Illinois College of Medicine in Chicago way back in the 1970's and did his surgical residency at Bethesda Naval Hospital. After 14 years on active duty that included overseas duty with the Seabees, time on large grey boats, and a tour with the Marines during the First Gulf War, he went into private practice near Phoenix, Arizona. He is part of that dying breed of dinosaurs, the solo general surgeon. He also is a writer of science fiction novels. His works include the YA novel Queen Mab Courtesy, his military science fiction novel That Which Is Human, and the Profit Logbook series, including Glowgems For Profit, Thieves Profit, and Profit and Loss. His nonfiction memoir, Dancing in the Operating Room, is a glimpse into the life and training of a Trauma Surgeon.
The Website: www.thatwhichishuman.com
The Blog: www.dancingintheor.wordpress.com

Deep in the Andromeda Galaxy, a young Earthling slave learns about friendship, love and the true meaning of family.

SHIDEE

W. A. Fix

They had been coming to this spot since before Rickie was born. Howard felt like it was their spot and refused to even think about arriving and finding it occupied. Luckily, in nine years they never saw another person. He and his ex-wife, Shelley, found it while looking for a place to pick blackberries, during Shelley's "canning" phase. A year after Rickie was born, and canning a thing of the past, they changed the outing from blackberry hunting to a weekend fishing trip. Then three years ago, when Rickie was five, Shelley stopped coming with them. It was great to spend the time together and reconnect, but Howard understood how the "guy's weekend," as Shelley called it, was really more about giving *her* a free weekend.

It was late July, mid-afternoon, maybe two or two-thirty—that's what he told the cops later—the sun sparkled on the creek like a million stars in a night sky. A light breeze agitated the bushes growing along the creek bank, creating a slight rustling sound that gave the scene an amazing level of peace. Rickie reclined on a boulder that was connected to the bank by three half-submerged rocks that Howard and Shelley had placed as stepping stones years earlier. The handle of Rickie's fishing pole was wedged into a crack in the boulder, clearly created for that purpose, and the fishing line stretched lazily to mid-stream, mooring a red and white bobber. His son was dressed in a pair of cut-off jeans, a straw hat and flip-flop sandals. Howard smiled and thought, *Christ, if Mark Twain had seen this, the book would have been called*

15

Rickie Dawson. The sun was hot and Howard could see pink starting to show on Rickie's chest and legs.

"Hey buddy, did you put sun screen on?" he called from his chair on the bank.

"Nah, I'm fine," said Rickie.

"Yeah, and tonight you'll be whining about a sunburn. Hang on, I'll get it." Howard sat his beer on the ground then pushed himself up using the arm rests of his lawn chair. "I'll be right back."

He walked the thirty feet to the campsite, pulled back the flap on the tent and went inside. He found the tube of spf50 and headed back to the creek. When he exited the tent he noticed Rickie had left the rock, the pole still in place with the bobber beginning to show interest from below. Thinking his son had simply gone into the bushes to take a whizz he went back to his chair and waited.

"Hey buddy, you better hurry up, I think you've got a bite." Howard watched the bobber begin to bounce up and down then completely submerge. "You've got a fish on, Rickie. You want me to take it?" He stood and threw the sunscreen into the chair. He walked toward the stepping stones then stopped and looked around.

"Rickie . . .? Where are you, son?" He waited several seconds then said more forcefully, "Come on guy, stop screwing around. Where are you?" Still no answer. He walked to the area that they used as a toilet. There were no fresh signs. Howard began a frantic search around the camp, in the water, and on both sides of the creek. Nothing.

"Okay, son, this isn't funny. Please . . . Come out now." He looked at the sun and realized he needed to get help soon. His voice clearly racked with panic now, he yelled, "Rickie, I'm going to find help! If you're hurt stay put, we'll find you! I love you, son, and I'll be back as soon as I can!" He ran to the SUV and was speeding toward town within seconds. As he drove, tears ran down his cheeks and he kept glancing at his cell phone for any signs of service bars and faster access to the police.

Two hours later, the local Sheriff had a helicopter searching the surrounding area. Ten Sheriff's Deputies combed the area around the camp for what remained of the daylight. The search continued for three days, using hundreds of volunteers, professional trackers, and scent dogs. Then the night temperature dipped to thirty-eight degrees for two straight nights and, considering the way Rickie was dressed when last seen, the sheriff announced the mission had changed from rescue to recovery. Nothing was found. No scent trail. No tracks. No DNA. Nothing. Ever.

Howard was devastated. He found solace in large quantities of alcohol and he blamed himself. He knew Shelley blamed him, her parents blamed him, and even his own parents treated him differently. He knew it was all his fault—it had to be his fault. When the Sheriff came right out and asked him if he had anything to do with his son's disappearance, he had to say, "Yes."

Kolank was the Gray home world and Rickie knew all about the Grays from TV shows back on Earth. It had been a while, maybe four Earth years, but he smiled to himself remembering how he had loved those shows with the creepy gray stick figures with oversized heads and large black eyes.

The trouble was, the producers of those shows had it wrong. They were not stick figures. On the contrary, Ricky knew from experience and many beatings that they were muscular and extremely strong. The signature gray skin was actually a tight fitting space suit that covered light purple, almost white, skin. The oversized head with its huge black eyes was a helmet with dark shields for a slightly larger than human head and wide set almond shaped eyes. The eyes were all black, but only half again larger than his own. The helmet had a very small slit that was simply a speaker for vocal communication and not an actual mouth. Their nose was easily three inches wide, with large nostrils set flat on the face and half an inch above a very wide mouth. Rickie hated that mouth, with its wide, dark-purple lips that hid razor sharp, shark-like teeth. Whenever Rooz, Rickie's owner, smiled he wanted to run. He didn't run, but he sure wanted to.

"Reeekee, stand here," shouted Rooz from fifty feet away. He pointed to a spot at his side. Rooz and another Gray–Rickie still called them Grays, even though they were purple–watched him closely as he jumped to his sandal-covered feet and dashed to the spot indicated. Both Grays were dressed in brightly colored robes with long full sleeves. Rickie slid to a stop and stood with them in the Kolank Saa slave market, where at least a hundred other Grays milled around looking at or selling stock. There were two breeds for sale; humans, and a pale yellow-green reptilian race with a wide strip of multi colored feathers flowing over the head and down the neck all the way to the middle of the back. While watching the crowd, Rickie had seen only one other human in the market.

"Walin Shidee will examine you," said Rooz.

Rickie hesitated and Rooz slapped the side of his head, almost knocking him off his feet. Rickie righted himself, controlling the anger that flashed through him. Carefully keeping his expression neutral, he retook his position, then unzipped the one-piece coverall and allowed it to drop to the ground. He stepped out of it and moved in front of the Gray identified as Shidee. He took the standard inspection pose with feet at shoulder width apart, arms held to the side and away from his totally naked body, and fixed his gaze in the distance, while forcing his teeth to unclench. Shidee stepped forward and separated the shaggy mane on Rickie's head, ran his purple hands over dirt-crusted shoulders, and squeezed his arms. The Gray said, "Bend," and Rickie leaned over at the waist. Shidee spread his butt cheeks for a brief instant and then said, "Up." Rickie raised back up and the Gray's hand found each of his testicles, pulled his penis to its full length, then traveled through a small growth of hair and pushed on his stomach. Rickie tightened his stomach muscles until they were rock hard. The Gray tilted Rickie's head back and then forced his mouth open, looking at both upper and lower teeth. He lifted the eyelids of both eyes, allowed them to drop, and finally stepped back. He looked Rickie up and down several times, deep in thought.

"Nomwa Rooz, how many times have I told you that you lose money by not taking care of your stock? This one stinks and insects are in its hair. You should have bathed it before coming here. The teeth are beginning to rot and the muscle tone could be much better. I would pay more if I didn't have to fix your negligence. I will pay you three thousand deet for it."

This was the first time Rickie had ever heard one Gray chastise another Gray for anything, let alone poor treatment of a slave. He sneaked a glance at this new Gray.

"Three Thousand! I will not be robbed! This one will be a breeder and worth three times that. Look at it, the females will be standing in line if you let them." Rooz paused in thought, then said, "No. I will take no less than five."

Shidee stepped back in front of Rickie and quietly said in perfect English, "Do you speak Earth English?"

Shocked, Rickie staggered half a step backward and for the first time, glanced into the Gray's eyes then quickly away. "Yes, sir," he whispered, also in English. Rickie had never heard a Gray speak anything but Kolankig and a small grain of hope rose within him.

Shidee spun him around, not allowing Rooz to see Rickie's surprise. He pointed to the four ownership tattoos on Rickie's right shoulder. "Look at that, four owners in two Kolank cycles. That tells me this one is trouble. You've probably tried to sell it several times and can't. I'll give you four thousand. That is my final offer and you better accept quickly." He paused and looked around. "I see another human over there, maybe I'll go talk to its owner."

Rooz waited a little too long to answer. Shidee turned and started to walk away. Rickie's heart sank.

"Wait! Wait," said Rooz. Shidee turned back and Rooz pleaded, "It resisted training and its other owners lacked the patience. It no longer resists. I will take four and a half thousand but I won't make anything."

Shidee turned and walked away again. He was almost to the other human when Rooz, defeated, said to Rickie, "Go get him. Tell him I accept his offer."

Elated, Rickie ran to Shidee and said, "Please stop. Nomwa Rooz has accepted your offer."

"Good," said Shidee. He turned and they walked back together. Shidee produced a hand held brand from his robe and placed it on Rickie's shoulder below the other tattoos. The instant he touched the skin Rickie felt an electric tingle and a new tattoo appeared. Shidee entered the amount of the purchase, then Rooz touched the tattoo with his own brand, certifying the transaction. That was it. The money was transferred and ownership of Rickie was registered to Walin Shidee.

His new owner turned to Rickie. "You are now my property. Put the clothing on and wait for me where you waited earlier. I will come and get you after I speak with the owner of the other human."

Rickie put the coveralls on and ran to the exact spot where Rooz had called him. He watched Shidee talk with his former owner, and then walk to the other human's Gray. Shidee spoke with the Gray for a brief moment then turned and walked toward Rickie.

"Follow me, we must get you cleaned and your teeth fixed." They left the market, turning onto the city street and after a short distance, entered one of the many store fronts that lined the sidewalk. As he entered, Rickie skeptically looked around and was reminded of a pet shop on Earth.

They waited only a moment before a Gray approached Shidee. "It is good to have you return, Walin Shidee." Then, scowling at Rickie, "I can see it will it be the same as always?"

"Yes, but this one also needs work on its teeth. Fix them and do not remove any. I have business in Kolank Riddo. Deliver it to my estate when you are finished. I will tell them to expect the delivery in . . . two cycles?"

"That will be plenty of time."

Shidee touched his brand to Rickie's tattoo again. "Payment will be made as services are rendered."

Finally, he addressed Rickie, only now he spoke English, "Do whatever they say. The procedures may be uncomfortable but they should not be painful. They will not harm you, and the same will apply at the estate. Do not disappoint me. Do you understand?"

Rickie looked up and into the dark eyes, saying in English, "Yes, sir. I understand." Shidee acknowledged the shop keeper then turned and left the store.

Two of the feathered reptiles entered through a door behind the proprietor. The Gray spoke softly to them then waved them away. Rickie had dealt with the lizards many times before. They seemed to be okay, just not very smart. But he couldn't get over the fact they were, well . . . lizards. They understood every word of Kolankig, but, they had no lips or vocal cords to speak the language and communicated using elaborate gesture and signing with their three-fingered hands. One of them walked back through the door while the other touched Rickie's shoulder and pointed. Rickie followed the first lizard into what was clearly a grooming room.

One of the lizards unzipped Rickie's coverall, and helped him remove it. The creature then pointed at his sandals, indicating they should be left with the clothing. On one side of the room was a shallow raised tub that stood a little above Rickie's knees. Water was flowing over the top and into drain channels around the base. Both lizards pointed at the tub, so Rickie stepped into the water and sat for a moment on the edge before slowly sliding into the luxuriously warm water. He usually got sprayed off with cold water from a high pressure hose or was walked into an icy stream. This was heaven. One of the lizards dipped a pan in the tub and poured the contents over his head. It repeated the process a few times and then squirted a clear jell into his hair and massaged it until a sweet smelling foam covered his head. Rickie felt tingling and wasn't sure if it was the suds or the lice in death throes. He didn't care. It felt amazing and he moaned loudly in pleasure. They left the shampoo on his head while they scrubbed his skin with soft brushes oozing rich foam. They scrubbed every inch of him until one of them pulled a spray from above and rinsed him thoroughly. When they indicated, he stood in the tub. Looking down, the water was so dark he couldn't see his feet. They drained the water, then using the brushes again scrubbed his lower body and feet. At one point, it began to feel a little too good and his body reacted. He heard the lizards produce soft hissing sounds that he recognized as laughter. Slightly embarrassed, but unwilling to acknowledge it, he refused to make eye contact with them until they finished his bath by spraying him down again. This time, he thought the water was a little colder than before. They dried him using a wide hose that blasted warm air. Finally, they cut his hair to a uniform one-inch length and vacuumed away the remains.

Grooming completed, they ushered him into another room where a Gray waited. This Gray proceeded to give him the most thorough medical exam he'd ever had, taking samples of his blood, his spit, his pee, even his poop. They laid him on a table and scanned him from head to toe. They looked in his ears, his mouth, his eyes, his nose, his butt, between his toes and fingers. They scanned his head again, this time concentrating on his mouth. Everything happened quickly and with assembly-line precision.

Next, they sat him on a chair and put a helmet over his entire head. Images appeared and he began following them with his eyes. After a few seconds, his vision blurred to near blindness, then slowly began to clear. When it reached normal, Rickie was relieved, but then it continued to clear. When the clearing stopped, he could see with a clarity he wouldn't have believed possible. A piercing flash of light blinded him momentarily and they removed the helmet. Blinking and squinting, his vision quickly returned to the new crystal clarity.

Finally, they took him to a small room with a bed and toilet. He sat on the bed until one of the lizards brought him a large container of water and a bowl of dry food. The food had little flavor but he knew from experience it would be nutritious and all he would get. The water helped to break down the food and it quenched the thirst created by food devoid of liquid. He drank all the water and wanted more. When he finished the meal, he lay down and looking at the ceiling tried to understand the events after meeting

Shidee. Gradually, his eyes closed and he drifted into sleep. He slept soundly and, for the first time in a long time, without dreams.

He awoke sometime later with stomach cramps and an urgent need to get to the toilet. After a half hour, he was exhausted and went back to bed. He was awakened by a lizard entering his room carrying a fresh container of water. Rickie was thirsty and immediately drank half the contents. The lizard waited. After a short while, it tapped the container and pointed at Rickie who promptly finished the contents. The creature exited the room and Rickie sat in a dark room listening to his stomach and bowels churn. His stomach began feeling upset so he lay back down and slept again. Before he knew it, he was rushing back to the toilet. When he finished he felt dizzy and there was a tingling in his arms and legs. He barely made it back to the bed. This time his sleep was fitful with flashes of consciousness. He was being bathed again. He was scanned again. He was at the dentist, only the dentist was a Gray.

When he awoke it was gradual and Rickie fought for the bliss of sleep and lost. He had a pasty soap taste in his mouth. When he ran his tongue over his teeth he found several repairs had been made and a few spots on his gums were very sore.

He was sitting on the bed when a lizard opened the door. It walked in and handed him a stack of straw-colored clothing and a pair of white canvas shoes. The lizard left the room and Rickie stared in amazement at the clothing. He had seen other human slaves who wore clothing and shoes like them, but never dreamed he would ever have them himself. In the stack was a pair of jockey shorts, just like the ones he used to wear on Earth, and a pair of thick white socks. He couldn't believe it. But, when he put on the shorts they felt uncomfortable and he wanted to take them off, but he left them on and then put on the socks. He pulled the shorts away from his crotch several times before sliding the pants up and tying the draw string. Next was a V-neck, long-sleeved pull-over shirt that fit perfectly. The shoes had Velcro-like straps instead of laces and he pulled them a little too tight at first. After adjusting them twice, the fit was perfect. Finally, he stood fully upright and for the first time in a very long time Rickie wished he had a mirror so he could see himself.

The next time the door opened, a lizard stepped in and pointed out the door. Rickie walked out and followed a second brightly dressed lizard carrying a bag over its right shoulder. He couldn't tell if they were the same two as before, and decided he really didn't care. He followed close behind the leader, gradually getting used to the feel of shoes on his feet. They walked out of the shop, turned right, and proceeded through an alley between two very old buildings, emerging on a very active street in the center of Kolank Saa. Rickie could now see things in the distance that had been just a blur before. It all seemed new and exciting and he began to walk with pride and confidence.

The lizard stopped abruptly and pointed to a waiting vehicle with a door open. Rickie cautiously peeked inside. It was empty, so he entered and sat on the right bench seat. The lead lizard entered behind him and sat on the left bench facing Rickie. As soon as the door closed the driverless vehicle rose slightly and moved into traffic. Rickie watched the city flow by and remembered the ride to the camping spot with his dad. He could remember watching his dad's hands on the steering wheel and wishing he was old enough to drive.

Suddenly, Rickie's stomach let out a long and loud growl and the lizard released a short hiss-laugh. It touched its own head with both hands then rolled its eyes and began digging in the bag it carried. It pulled out a container of water and handed it to Rickie then continued digging. It found a sealed package that looked to Rickie like a large candy bar and handed it to him. He opened the wrapper and smelled the contents. It looked and smelled like an energy bar. He tasted it and the flavor exploded in his mouth. It was grains and sweet fruit, all held together by something that resembled honey. It was wonderful and it was gone before he could stop himself.

He drank half the water, sat back, and relaxed. He looked at the lizard who was watching him closely.

"Thanks to you," said Rickie.

Clearly surprised, the creature's eyes widened briefly then it acknowledged Rickie by closing its eyes and slightly bowing its head.

The scenes outside turned from city to rural. The sun was high in a violet-colored sky and gave off gold light with a reddish tint. The light accented a group of clouds with gold lacing around the edges. It all reminded Rickie of a sunset on Earth. Within minutes, there were no buildings in sight and the landscape was very similar to Earth. The plants were different, of course, but the overall appearance was so like Earth it tugged at his heart. He said aloud, "This reminds me of my home. What about your home?"

Again the half closed eyes and bowed head.

They rode in silence a while longer, with the creature watching him intently. Finally, the lizard seemed to come to a decision and began digging in the bag again and produced a small fan of feathers held together by a bright purple ribbon. It leaned forward and loosely tied the ribbon around Rickie's neck. It adjusted the feathers to hang over his chest, hissed loudly, held its hands in the air and then sat back in its seat seemingly satisfied.

Shortly after the feather thing—whatever that was—they turned off the main road and traveled away from the main road on another one, more narrow. After a short time, they stopped in front of a large stone and glass structure. When the vehicle door opened, the lizard got out and waited for Rickie to follow. It then marched him to the building entrance. It stood Rickie in front of a scanner to the right of the entrance, straightened the feather bouquet, and turned Rickie's brand to the scanner. Rickie heard a beep and the lizard produced a brand and held it to the scanner which beeped again. The lizard turned and paused directly in front of Rickie for a brief moment. It looked him directly in the eyes, and then returned to the vehicle and closed the door. The vehicle raised a few inches off the ground then sped away.

Rickie turned back to the entrance that now stood wide open and inviting. He walked through and followed a narrow hallway that opened into a large courtyard. A human woman watched him approach. She had light brown hair with a few streaks of gray shining in the light. Her skin was tanned and slightly wrinkled, but her blue eyes smiled, in unison with soft lips devoid of makeup. She was beautiful, and she motioned for him to come toward her. With a slight British accent, she said, "Hello, young man. My name is Sylvia Finch. We were all very excited when we heard you would be arriving today."

Rickie staggered forward then fell to his knees, tears welling in his eyes. He sobbed heavily while trying to gain breath. Sylvia rushed to his side and, also kneeling, wrapped her arms around his shoulders and stroked his cheek with a warm hand. Rickie clasped his arms around her waist, and held on so tightly he could feel her warmth and hear her heart beat. He couldn't stop the tears.

"It's okay, you're safe now. What's your name, sweetheart?"

"Ri . . .Rickie . . . Daw . . .son," he said between sobs.

Rickie stayed with Sylvia, who waited for Shidee to return. He saw no one else, Gray or Human. The first evening, Sylvia prepared a meal for him. Rickie could smell the vegetables cooking. His first bite was ecstasy. There was no meat, but there was a sweet potato-like root that he loved. There was a leafy salad with a spicy oil as dressing and his normal kibble sprinkled in, and bread with butter. It was amazing and he ate until she finally stopped him.

"That's enough. You must not eat too much. Your digestive tract is not used to this type of food. It will take a while to get used to eating regular food again."

The warning was justified a few hours later, when he urgently asked where the restroom was. When he returned she said, "I'm sorry Rickie. I should have been more careful. We will take it more slowly from now on."

He asked questions constantly, which she answered always the same way, "When Walin Shidee returns, he will answer your questions." They always spoke in English. Sometimes Rickie had trouble remembering the right words and once he used a Kolankig word. Sylvia quickly corrected him saying, "We speak only Earth English here. If you can't remember the correct word, ask. Everyone here understands and will help. Outside this estate you must speak only Kolankig."

Rickie frowned and said, "Everyone? Are there more of us here?"

Sylvia chuckled softly, "There are many of us. Walin Shidee insists on making the first introduction. It is his right and we honor it. He will return tonight and will answer your questions."

Shortly after sunset Rickie was in the courtyard looking at the stars when Walin Shidee unexpectedly walked up behind him.

"Are you well, Rickie Dawson?"

Surprised, Rickie glanced at the Gray then quickly averting his eyes and struck the inspection stance.

"Thanks to you, sir, I am very well."

"Relax yourself Rickie Dawson. Within this estate I do not expect the traditional master-slave protocols. My family and I have long denounced slavery. By Kolankig law I am your owner and it must remain so. It also must appear so to all outside this estate, because many of my race would try to destroy this place if they knew the truth."

Rickie hesitated, not sure of what to do until he heard Sylvia speak. "He is telling you the truth. Relax, and you may look at him."

Rickie looked from one to the other. "I am sorry, sir. I find this very hard. What is this place?"

"This is one of my family's estates. We have two others that are scattered over Kolank. One is in Kolank Riddo, another in Kolank Doro and, of course, this one in Kolank Saa. My father Onsik Walin was very wealthy. He died many Kolank rotations ago and passed the family to me as his first born. My father's father Dellos Onsik, began these estates to preserve your race and also the Mishis." Shidee walked to a chair, seated himself, and indicated that Sylvia and Rickie join him.

Sylvia said, "Would you care for refreshment, Walin Shidee?"

"Perhaps water."

Sylvia walked out of the room as Rickie tentatively sat across from the Gray.

"Mishis? I'm sorry, sir, I don't understand"

"The Mishis are the feathered reptiles."

"Preserve our races? Why would you need to do that?"

Shidee accepted a drinking cup from Sylvia and sipped from it. Sylvia then moved to a chair next to Rickie, handing him a cup as she sat down.

Shidee continued, "The Kolankig Union of Worlds was built upon slavery and to this moment it controls our economy. Almost all of our labor force are slaves. My race is no longer capable of surviving without it. We have, for over a thousand rotations, had a partner race, very much like our own, that has provided us with an endless supply of races for our markets. Virtually all of the slave races have died out. The Mishis, however, are by far the easiest to breed and as a result have become the most dominant of the slave races. Yet we cannot possibly keep up with the demand. Your race is relatively new to us and has only been supplied for the last fifty rotations. About one hundred rotations ago the slave shipments began to slow and have dwindled gradually to virtually nothing. The ship that brought you was the last we have seen. As a result, slave prices have increased dramatically causing our economy to slow to a crawl. Not long ago, Rickie Dawson, I would have purchased you for less than one thousand deet. As you know, I paid four thousand and another one thousand to repair the neglect by that idiot Nomwa Rooz."

Sylvia spoke up, "If I may interrupt, Walin Shidee, the report was clear. Rickie is now intestinal parasite free. His teeth are repaired and the dentin has completely regenerated. His eye sight is repaired and, according to the shop proprietor, best of all, he no longer stinks."

Shidee rolled his head back and made a laugh that sounded more like gargling. "All very good news." He returned his gaze to Rickie and smiled broadly. Rickie had no desire to run. This was a gentle smile that, like humans, incorporated the eyes and was nothing like the leer produced by Rooz.

The smile faded, "As I suspected, you were a very good purchase. I continue your answer. Without an adequate supply of stock for the markets, our economy will soon collapse and with it, our society. Most of my race no longer has the skills to survive the coming chaos. Some think that time is upon us, or within the next two rotations. Within five rotations of the collapse, we believe slave revolts will destroy almost all that is remaining of Kolankig society. Within ten rotations, my race will be gone at the hands of our slaves, and only a few of the surviving slaves will remain. This place will be a refuge for humans. Kolank Riddo and Kolank Dorro for the Mishis."

"What happened to the slavers?" asked Rickie.

"We don't know and for some reason they refused to tell us. Some think they have died or are dying off. Some think they could not morally continue trading in the misery of others. When the ship that brought you departed, we were told there would be no more contact, and that was all. Some of my race wanted to go find them or simply take over their business. We quickly realized we don't have the technology anymore, nor the time to develop it. The distances are too great."

"Why not just take us home?"

"Rickie, even if we had that technology – which we don't – we wouldn't. You were brought from what you call the Milky Way Galaxy and we are in the Fatusat, or by your name, the Andromeda Galaxy. It would take our star's light over one million rotations to reach your home world. No matter what technology brought you here, the place you call home no longer exists or resembles anything you would recognize."

Rickie's eyes filled with tears and Sylvia reached out to grasp his hand, "My mom and dad and everyone I know are gone? Dead?" he asked.

Sylvia said, "I know it is hard, Rickie. But yes, they have been gone for a very long time. They all lived their lives, grew old in the normal course . . . and died. They had children, their children had children and their children's children had children. We were taken out of that world, probably put in some kind of suspended animation and brought here. Without information from the slavers, there is no way of knowing how it was accomplished or how much time has passed."

Sylvia glanced at Shidee who continued. "The number of humans is small compared to the Mishis, but you are prized for your communication ability and intelligence. Generally speaking, the size of the human brain is one quarter larger than the Mishis. Our scientists say the difference is in the cognitive regions and many studies support those findings."

Rickie was confused and looked at Sylvia, "Cognitive?"

"The part of the brain that allows you to figure things out and reason," she said.

"Unfortunately, many of your race have been ruined by their owners," said Shidee. "When a human refuses to submit, an operation is performed that dramatically alters those regions of the brain. The slave owner can then use it for physical labor and in some cases breeding. The human becomes valuable only as a breeder. That was the case with the other human we saw in the market."

"I've seen many who could barely talk. I thought they were born that way," said Rickie. "Rooz said if he couldn't sell me he was going to fix my brain. Can they be fixed?"

"No. Once modified there is no possible way to correct the damage," said Shidee. "You are very lucky to have survived."

"So how many of us are here?"

"There are 1,856 humans including you. Soon to be 1,858," said Sylvia. "We are expecting two births within the next cycle. We also have 100 Mishis here. There are 100 humans at each of the other estates. We are in constant communication with the other two estates. When the collapse begins the humans will coordinate between the three locations."

"What about Kolankig," asked Rickie?

"Very few and all have been with my family for a very long time," said Shidee. "They are here as teachers and to interface with city officials, if needed. The Government does not bother us here or at the other locations, but sometimes they need to be on the land. Far fewer questions are asked if they are dealing with one of us."

Rickie looked at Sylvia, "Teachers? What do they teach?"

"The first thing is how to communicate with the Mishis, and then all the things you would have learned on Earth. Proper English communication, written and spoken. Earth history is a bit of a problem. We have pieced together what we can, as best we can, and have courses that highlight the history of the eighteenth, nineteenth and twentieth centuries. We have another series of the history of Kolank. The rise of slavery and the slavers and the Kolankig Union of Worlds, its rise and pending fall. The soft sciences that deal with or are dependent on the environment, like weather, farming and botany. The hard sciences—mathematics, physics and chemistry and then, engineering which merges it all to solve every day problems that advance society. Everyone that comes here goes through this school. You will begin tomorrow."

Rickie looked surprised and asked, "How long will it take?"

"Five to ten rotations, which is ten to twenty Earth years," said Sylvia. "How long it actually takes depends entirely on the learning ability of the student."

"Wow, that's a long time," said Rickie.

Shidee gargled loudly. "Yes, it is, Rickie Dawson, so, you best get some sleep this night. It seems you are going to need it. However, before you do, come with me." Shidee stood and led Rickie into the next room. He walked to a book case that held several hundred identical, thick books.

"When you have learned to read Kolankig, you are welcome to read these volumes. It is my lineage beginning with the one who first began recording it," he pointed to the top shelf and the first book on that shelf. "To here," and he pointed to the last volume on the bottom of the next bookshelf to the right. "It is the recordings of the first born of each generation of my line. I will finish this volume and that will end my family. You see, Rickie Dawson, I have no first born," Sadness was apparent in his voice. "If you choose to read these volumes it will help you understand my race, perhaps better than we do ourselves." He opened a drawer in the base of the bookcase and extracted a book identical to the others and a scribe. He handed the two items to Rickie.

"Rickie Dawson, you are the first born of your lineage to be on Kolank. You must document your line. It is your family and your responsibility. When your *being* leaves this world you must pass your family and that responsibility to your first born, and that one to their first born."

Rickie had his first mating at the beginning of his third rotation of school. Sylvia was angry with him for not protecting against inception, and every time she saw him found some way to remind him that he would only be seventeen years old on Earth. Far too young to be a father. But when the child was born Sylvia treated her like a granddaughter. Her name was Amie and she was the most beautiful thing Rickie had ever seen. He was overwhelmed with emotions and couldn't identify any one emotion that fit the moment. At one minute he was unbelievably proud, the next sad that he could not share this with his own father. As he watched the infant with Rosa, the child's mother, he felt love so intense he never wanted the moment to end. It finally ended when Shidee rushed into the infirmary smiling and struck Rickie solidly on the back.

"Rickie Dawson, this cycle is a proud time for you. This cycle marks the continuation of your lineage. A momentous occasion!"

Rickie thought about it. Other births were celebrated, but he had never seen the birth of a first born of a first born. He had no idea that the entire estate had been preparing to celebrate the birth of his child. When he walked out of the infirmary with Shidee, half the occupants of the estate were waiting and a cheer erupted. Suddenly the intense pride welled within him again. Some of the women came forward with gifts and toys for the baby that soon became a pile that he couldn't possibly hold.

Shidee arranged for someone to collect the gifts and deliver them to the baby's mother. Meanwhile, every woman present, it seemed, had to kiss his cheek and each man had to hug him or ruffle his hair. The crowd took him to the main courtyard and they sang and danced and played music on hand-made earth-like instruments. They drank beer made from grain. Once he tried to sneak away and return to the infirmary, but he was spotted and dragged back into the fray. Later in the evening, he heard Shidee's laugh and spotted the Gray holding a drinking cup in one hand while trying to match steps in a group dance. Rickie laughed so hard he had to sit down as he watched Shidee dance and, finally, realized that the Gray was the closest thing to a father he had. The party lasted far too long and Rickie awoke the next cycle with his first hangover. Over the next five cycles, every woman that could not attend the party sought him out and kissed his cheek. Eventually, they all must have finished the task because everything started getting back to normal.

Between Rosa and Sylvia, Rickie was allowed only small patches of bonding time with Amie each cycle. They would say, "Go. You need to study. We will watch her." He tried to spend as much time with Amie and Rosa as possible and before long he settled in as a devoted student and father. The couple was not married—slavery virtually eliminated marriage from the traditions of the humans on Kolank. Rickie had his own apartment and found himself lonely when Amie did not visit.

Eventually, he completed his studies. It took him a little over six rotations to complete the school, almost two full rotations ahead of the average. Amie was three and a half rotations old—almost Rickie's Earth age when he was taken from Earth—when Rosa brought her to live with him. Rosa had mated with another male and was again pregnant. Rickie was surprised, and a little hurt, but he never questioned her right to be with whomever she wanted. But, as his first born, Amie would live with Rickie until her tenth rotation or until she gave birth to her first born. They settled into this new arrangement and both seemed happier than ever.

Rickie had proven how very smart he was and it didn't take Sylvia long to choose him to be her assistant when she became the Estate Leader. She complained loudly, however, whenever he didn't bring Amie to work with him and have her playing close by.

On several occasions, Rickie jokingly said, when he saw Amie and Sylvia together, "You only gave me this job to keep Amie close by."

Sylvia would reply, "And it was lucky for you. Now, go do your work. Amie and I have important things to talk about."

One day Rickie announced proudly, "Sylvia, next week is Amie's fourth rotation and she will begin school."

"Yes, I know that." She watched the child watering flowers in the garden. "She is ready." She smiled broadly and looked up into his eyes, "I think she will be finished faster than you."

"I will do everything I can to make sure she does," said Rickie.

Shidee continued to make his trips to the market and Rickie became the new human greeter, in addition to his other duties. Shidee and Rickie worked closely, helping to integrate the new arrivals into the community. He was waiting for an arrival one cycle when his eyes fell on the blossom of feathers that had been hung around his neck by the Mishis when he was delivered. He had not seen another and wondered why. Rickie had hung the feathers on the wall next to his desk in the greeting hall as a reminder to himself that he too had come through this hall. He looked at the outside monitor and saw the vehicle pull to a stop at the entrance. Something made him take the feathers from the wall and arrange them around his neck. He glanced at the monitor again and saw a Mishis and a human, maybe two rotations older than himself, approaching the entrance scanner. The Mishis stood the human in place and waited for a beep. Rickie walked through the door and approached them. The Mishis, surprised, stepped back, then saw the feathers around

Rickie's neck. It stopped and placed both hands on its narrow chest, closed its eyes and slightly bowed its head.

Rickie was confused and said in Kolankig, "I mean no harm. I understand your signs so you may talk with me."

The creature raised its head then made a series of quick hand signs. "You wear the plumage of my father. How did you come by it?"

"He gave it to me over six rotations ago. What does it mean?" asked Rickie in Kolankig.

"It is a symbol of friendship and remembrance," signed the Mishis.

"Where is your father? I hope he is well," said Rickie

More signs, "He is well and I will tell him you asked. The shop owner thinks he is too old to make these trips, considering the hostilities that have occurred recently. This one has been violent, but Walin Shidee seemed to calm it by speaking in its language."

Rickie glanced quickly at the newcomer and saw the distrust in his eyes, "Please, be patient. This is a safe place. He will leave and we will go inside in just a moment," he said in English. He turned his attention back to the Mishis. "We have many Mishis here and have found that your real names do not translate well to our vocal language. What is your calling name?"

The Mishis stood a little taller and, with a slight squint of its eyes, signed, "I am called with Slave 27."

Rickie said, "We do not use that name in this place. May I call your father Friend 1 and may I call you Friend 2."

The Mishis seemed to relax, closed its eyes and bowed its head then signed, "You honor my father and you honor me. I will be called by you, Friend 2. I will ask my father if he approves."

The vehicle began a relentless beeping sound. Friend 2 became agitated and signed, "We have taken too long to begin my return. I must go. What do I call you?"

"My name is Rickie Dawson. Please call me Rickie."

Friend 2 signed quickly, "We will talk again . . . Rickie," then dashed to the vehicle and entered. As the vehicle pulled away Rickie turned to the newcomer.

"You are probably wondering what is going on here. Do you remember your Earth name?" he said in English.

"Walter. Yas, I is wonder," he said.

"Okay, Walter. I see we have a lot of work to do. Come with me."

Shortly after Walter's arrival, Shidee returned to the estate and told Sylvia and Rickie he would not be returning to the Market.

"I fear the collapse is upon us. It is not safe for Kolankig, Human, or Mishis to be out. There is looting and groups are attacking each other. It is as predicted," said Shidee. "I spoke with what remains of our security force. They say they no longer communicate with any of the other Kolankig worlds and only a few of the other cities on Kolank"

Sylvia said, "We are in constant communication with the other estates and they report chaos everywhere. I spoke with the other Estate Leaders and we agree it is time to fortify the boundaries of the estates."

Shidee said sadly, "I agree."

Over the next half rotation Rickie often wondered about the fate of Friend 1 and Friend 2. There were several attempts to enter the estate by small bands of Humans or Mishis. Those groups were not interested in becoming part of the estate. They wanted food or to loot and when they attacked they were put down without mercy. From the information gathered from the attackers, the Kolankig that remained were being systematically eliminated as fast as they were found by Human and Mishis

One mid-cycle, with the sun slightly past its apex, a small band of twelve Mishis walked up to the estate entrance. One of its members reached into a bag it carried over its shoulder and produced a small blossom of feathers suspended by a brightly colored ribbon. It hung the feathers around its neck and approached the scanner. It signed, "May we speak with Rickie Dawson?"

Rickie arrived as quickly as his feet would carry him. When he looked at the monitor he smiled, put his own feather blossom on, walked out the entrance and approached the Mishis. He placed both hands over his heart, closed his eyes and slightly bowed his head.

The Mishis signed, "Rickie Dawson, I am honored for you to call me by Friend 1."

Howard 5 Dawson stood in front of the family lineage bookcase. To the left was the lineage of The Honored Walin Shidee. Five hundred and twenty generations of a race that depended on slavery so much that it could no longer survive without it. Walin Shidee had saved the Human and Mishis races on Kolank.

Howard 5 pulled the first book of the Dawson's seventy-five volume lineage. He opened the volume and smiled. He loved reading this volume, especially the first page, while trying to picture what the beginning must have been like.

"My name is Rickie Dawson. I was born in the year 2012, on the planet Earth, in the Milky Way Galaxy. I am the first born of Howard Dawson and Shelley Greenwald. I remember my mother and father's parents only as Grandma and Grandpa Dawson and Grandma and Grandpa Greenwald. I have tried many times, but I can only remember seeing Grandma and Grandpa Greenwald once. Grandma and Grandpa Dawson lived close by and we saw them all the time. Grandpa Dawson used to tickle my feet and Grandma Dawson gave me sweet things to eat.

"My mother, father, and I lived together for a while and then my mother and I moved away. I don't remember why. My dad and I—I used to call him Dad—sometimes went fishing together and that is where I was taken. I was eight years old and Dad walked away for a minute. I remember him saying, 'I'll be right back.' That was the last Earth memory I have.

"I remember waking up with two Kolankig arguing. Frightened beyond reason, I began screaming and one of them struck me several times until I was unconscious. That happened many times, until I learned not to scream, or yell, or fight my captors. I was taught the Kolankig language with slaps to the side of my head for pronouncing a word wrong or not understanding what was said to me. Needless to say, I was not considered a *good* slave. In my second rotation on Kolank I was told by my fourth owner, Nomwa Rooz, that no more time would be wasted on me. He was taking me to the market and if he couldn't sell me he would have my brain fixed. That was the first time I met Walin Shidee.

I will remember that moment for the rest of my life and I will honor Walin Shidee every cycle for the remainder of his life, and when he is gone for every cycle of my life, and my children will honor him and so will their children. I say this because my lineage exists only because of him and now, with his permission, I append my lineage to his."

Howard 5 Dawson closed the volume of Rickie Dawson and replaced it on the shelf next to Shidee's final volume. He smiled and said, "And we honor you still, Walin Shidee."

W. A. Fix is a retired Information Technology Professional, who, with his wife and three cats, lives in the suburbs of San Diego, California. Several of his works are published throughout the Web. He is a featured author in "The Future Is Short: Science Fiction in a Flash" (volumes 1, 2, and 3) anthologies of flash fiction and he has longer works in "Visions: Leaving Earth", "Visions II: Moons of Saturn", "Vision III: Inside the Kuiper Belt", Visions V: Milky Way, and "Twisted Tails IX: Wunderkind".

As the 21st Century drew to a close, we had finally shucked the stifling rags of primitive superstitions and harnessed the energy of our star.

Driven by insatiable curiosity, we found ourselves occupying planets around our nearest neighbors. Still, the question remained: What might we find if we traveled just a bit farther? Perhaps the better question would have been: What might find us?

GOD SHIP

J. Richard Jacobs

Com chimes sounded and the image of Michael Ranken, Chief Navigator, appeared on her screen. He looked excited and nervous; a look not consistent with his usual, irritatingly calm self. Captain Cho lifted her gaze to the screen.

"Okay, Mike, what is it that's so important you had to interrupt my dinner?"

"Not sure yet. From the data, it's big. Mainly titanium, carbon, some aluminum, and a sort of steel alloy, still unidentified. The surface of the thing is scattering our signals too much to get solid data, but I think it may be a ship and, if it is, it's the biggest damned ship I've ever seen. I can tell you this much about it, though; it's for sure and certain not one of ours."

"How big, and what do you mean by it's not one of ours? The company's?"

"Forget the company. This thing's eight thousand meters long and about seven hundred in diameter. It's all one structure as far as I can tell. Not broken up, though the surface is irregular. Hard to know, exactly, but it's big. Even with a full train, the biggest thing out here is the *Kolmogorov*, and she's only twelve hundred meters with her full train stretched out to the limit. And the *Kolmogorov* is not a third of that diameter across her

41

extended rings. This is one big mother and it didn't come from any company in this planetary system, I can tell you that."

"Are you . . . are you suggesting that this thing is alien?"

"If it's a ship and it's not from this neighborhood, then that's what I'm saying, sure enough."

"If you're right, can you imagine what the people in the Limb Colonies at G Five would be willing to pay just to look at it? We take possession of it and put it in orbit, then we sell tickets to tourists for a hundred thousand a head."

"Salvage is company property. Maybe they give us a bonus, if they're feeling generous, then they sell the tickets. That's if, and only if, the government doesn't step in—and we all know they will."

"Not if the brain in charge doesn't call home to tell them what we're doing."

"Fathead Meninger? He checks with Limb Central to get permission to change his skivvies."

"Yeah, well, it was a nice thought, anyway. Can we snag it?"

"We'll have to get better data than what the nav drones are giving us, but I'd say, yeah. You're really thinking salvage, aren't you?"

"Absolutely. That's what the company does, isn't it? Gliese Consolidated Freight and Salvage, right? It's built right into the name. Besides, if this thing is alien, it seems to me that we're obligated to bring it in . . . no matter what."

"Well, yeah, I suppose you're right. There's a note somewhere in the regs on that. You know, for the sake of mankind and all that crap. Can we snag it? If you consider what *Triumphant* is, we could probably bring Moon Three in if we wanted to, and we're delivering four new spiders for G Six Base Camp that we can modify to get the job done."

"So, what are we waiting for?"

"We'll have to detach our boxes before we go chasing that thing. Then we can intercept and match up in about seven hundred hours. But we can't say whether that tumbling isn't part of its standard flight mode. What if the folks aboard don't want to be snagged? What if there's no one on board and the ship doesn't want to be snagged? What if—?"

"Stop with the what ifs. Can't we work all that out on the fly? We have plenty of time to figure out what to do, right?"

"Well-l-l . . . yeah. But what if it isn't dead? I mean, seriously. If they get all defensive and start shooting at us, the only open options are to duck, dodge, and run like hell. For all we know, even if there's nobody aboard, the thing may have an AI programmed to defend itself against anything that comes close enough. And we don't know what 'close enough' is for that thing."

"We'll find out, won't we? Frank, are you listening?"

"Oh, yeah," a voice said from the com box. Frank Peele, *Triumphant's* expert in all things dealing with the MAGI and automated ship control, let out a small, hollow laugh.

"Any ideas?"

"Not yet. Maggie's still stealing data from Mike's nav system."

"Okay, Frank, get a message off to G Six as soon as you have enough information and ask Meninger if we can get cleared to dump our train and do a salvage job. What's the current TD?"

"Little over thirty minutes one-way, Captain."

"Oh, and Frank, be diplomatic. We don't want Meninger to come unglued."

"Yes, ma'am. Diplomatic Frank, that's me."

"Okay . . . jump on it—ASAP. I'm going to stay here with Mike. Mike, get the numbers running for a hook-up and feed 'em to Maggie."

"Your wish is my command, madame. Truth be told, because of that I'll-have-you-for-breakfast look you've been giving me, I've already done that."

The MAGI automatically transmitted a change of status message to the remainder of the crew.

The station ComBoss barged into Gabriel Meninger's office without asking. He was out of breath and waving a com chip around in the air.

"Mr. Meninger?"

"Who the hell would you expect to be in here? And what happened to decency and ordinary courtesy?"

"I . . . the message, sir. Burst just came in from *Triumphant*. They want permission to separate from their train to do a . . . salvage."

"Salvage? Salvage what?"

"Salvage an . . . um . . . alien ship, they said, sir."

"A what? What the hell have they been drinking, smoking, or whatever? Who's driving the *Triumphant* and when was his last psychological exam?"

"He's a she, sir. Captain Marsha Cho, and her psyche status is up-to-date and ranked A-1 Alpha. She took command of *Triumphant* when it made its last delivery to G Four Orbital Colony Omicron. Before that she was running the Eldridge in the belt mines for Carver Mining. One of their best, according to the Coordinator General at G Four Central. Twenty plus years of experience."

"You tell Lady Cho I said, no. No, wait a minute, scratch that. You tell her I said, hell no. Alien ship. How can they tell it's not just a runaway train from one of the other companies and not worth the time, trouble and added expense?"

"The data, sir. We don't have anything that comes close to matching what they're looking at."

"Oh?"

"No, sir. This thing is huge and, even without their train, they'll be straining butt to catch it. You know the *Triumphant* has the highest Delta-v in our fleet, and it'll take everything they can get out of her to make contact with whatever it is they're tracking."

"All right, let me see what we got."

The ComBoss handed Meninger the chip he'd been flailing. Meninger flipped it over in his fingers, then plugged it into his private system. Data sprang up on the screen on the left side and a graphic display of what the *Triumphant's* long range nav drones were seeing assembled itself on the right.

"Holy . . . Mother of the Universe. What the hell is that? How far is *Triumphant* from the brake threshold?"

"Sixty-five hundred hours."

"Okay. That's good enough for me." Meninger rose from his chair, looked up at the overhead, then began a slow pacing behind his desk.

"Okay. You can tell Captain Cho she has her salvage—if she can guarantee the *Triumphant* can get here in one piece in two thousand hours or less over schedule with whatever that thing is in tow. She is not to abandon the real reason we hired her."

He stopped his pacing, then turned slowly until he was facing the ComBoss.

"Tell her I approved the train separation request, too. After they've dropped their containers, I think it would be a good idea for them to brake their train with one of the big bots. That should be good enough to take some of the pressure off. Can't afford to have those boxes roaring through here with no one on the helm and not be able to catch them. Oh, and make sure they understand that no one is to attempt opening or boarding the damned thing. Follow the book to the letter. Just stop its swing, grab it, and bring it in so the science people can handle it. Got that? Forward what we have to G Five Central, too, or the military will throw a fit and we'll have government all over our ass. We're probably going to have them crawling all over us, anyway. Whatever that thing is, it had better be worth the effort and cost, or we'll all be living in a sewer and eating rat crap for the rest of our natural lives."

Meninger sat and squirmed uncomfortably into his chair. His face was tight.

"Um, wait a minute. Let's make this easy on everyone if we can. Do we have anything available to trap *Triumphant's* train before it makes threshold?"

"Yes, sir. The *Valiant* cleared the repair dock this morning."

"Has it been assigned?"

"No, sir. She's scheduled for a short trial tomorrow, then six weeks in dead orbit."

"Good, she can have her trial on the way to the keyhole. Get the *Valiant* readied to grab the *Triumphant's* train and bring it in. Tell Ms. Cho she's been relieved of responsibility for it and doesn't need to worry about deadlines. Make sure she understands that this salvage of hers had better be more extraordinary than what we've already seen or she'll be looking for other work, and it won't be commanding anything more exciting than a bucket cleaner for the remainder of her career."

Klaus Lundgren was having one of those lousy I-wish-I'd-stayed-in-bed days. Nothing was going right and he could see a transfer of the downward kind wending its way toward him. He was definitely not happy. He took a note board down from the wall and was preparing to leave when one of his com boys called out.

"Hey, Klaus, put an eyeball on this."

"What is it?"

"Top secret data transfer from G Six to Central. Seems the *Triumphant's* going to bring in a load of little green men, or grays, or whatever they call aliens these days."

"What the hell are you talking about?"

"Take a look, man."

Lundgren bent down to see the message on the board. His eyes widened and his jaw fell slack.

"I'll be double damned. Transfer that to Ops Central right away and make it look as if it hadn't stopped here first, but don't purge it from our system so I can take a better look at it, later."

"You're the boss. But this is an A-Class message and if they find out I read it and you kept a copy, I'll be out of a job and I think you're going to bend a lot of noses on your way to prison."

"Let me worry about the noses, just do it—quick." Lundgren stepped away from the monitor and punched in a code on his wrist board. He was smiling for the first time in a week.

"FleetCon," a voice said in his ear.

"This is Commander Lundgren in ComCon. How many Fox Charlies do we have up and ready?"

"Just two. *Antares* and *Schedar*. The other three are in the maintenance bay at M Three."

"Give me the names of the COs on the two ready birds."

"Borg on *Antares* and Fielding on *Schedar*, Commander."

"Thanks," Lundgren said and slapped his hands together. Raymond Borg he knew from the Academy—that would help. Carl Fielding, a slightly more than casual acquaintance, he knew from fairly frequent elbow bending, lie slinging sessions at the Old Earth Inn. Lundgren figured both were approachable.

M Three Command's offices were filled to overflowing with people doing their busy little jobs. Bodies in standard green Fleet Command uniforms scurried purposefully up and down the halls with chip boxes dangling from their fingers. Carl Fielding had never seen the place so active. It was like being inside a brunager hive after it had been rattled by some kid with a stick. Fielding and Borg made a sharp right and entered the office of the Coordinator General, G Five Station.

"Ah, Commanders Borg and Fielding, come in and take a seat," Coordinator General Simmons said. "I'm not going to waste any time fanning dead space with you. One of you is going to volunteer for a fast run to G Six Station, that's one of Consolidated's stations. Part of your Marine contingent will be replaced by a large group of civilian scientists and engineers. Some of them are already here, the others will be arriving in two weeks."

"What's the purpose of the run, General?" Borg asked.

"That's secure information for now. All I can tell you is that this could become the most important run in the history of human existence and we of Gliese 667C have the privilege of making it. Now, which of you is going to volunteer?"

Borg and Fielding exchanged glances, then spoke in unison, "We'll both go, General."

Simmons gave them a stiff, Marine starched collar smile that looked a little painful and chuckled. "That's what I thought would happen. I've already made arrangements and you two will share command of the

Antares. The stragglers will be going out on the *Schedar.* I'm thinking of giving Lanscombe command of the *Schedar.* Any complaints, Fielding?"

"No, sir. Just tell him not to bend my baby."

"I'm going to leave it up to you two how you divide your efforts after your arrival at G Six Station. Your mission objective should arrive at about the same time or shortly after. Full information on the run will be available in your ship's system in a for-your-eyes-only slug that will activate ten days after your departure. After you see it, it will self-scrub, so pay close attention. Until then, keep your mouths shut and your gear packed."

Like all the bars on M Three, the Old Earth Inn was packed to overflowing and the noise, the so-called band was making, shifted automatically to ride comfortably above the human din. Carl Fielding pushed his way through the gyrating mob on the dance floor toward the bar where Lundgren was working on his third gin and tonic.

"Okay, Klaus, what's up?" Fielding said as he pulled out a stool.

"What's up? You're going to tell me. I hear you and Borg are going for a little ride."

"Oh? And where did you hear that?"

"Sources. So, is it true? You guys going to G Six Station?"

"That's classified☐"

"Classified, my ass. If it were classified, how would I know about it?"

"Because you're in ComCon and you put your sticky little fingers in the system, that's how."

"Okay, Carl, you got me on that one. I won't deny it. What if I also tell you I know why you're going? What do you think about that? I'll bet they didn't tell you guys anything about the reason, did they? Security and all that crap, right?"

"No, they didn't and yeah, it's supposed to be hush. So, Mr. Omniscience, why are we going?"

"Huh-uh. I'll tell you that on one condition."

"We'll find out, anyway."

"Not until you're well on your way. Am I right?"

"Yeah, you're right. What's the condition?"

"I go with you."

"What? We can't . . ."

"Yes, you can. You're in charge of who goes. Get me transferred to the com slot. If they ask why, just tell 'em it's because I'm the best there is and that you need me."

"So, you want us to break protocol just to get a preview of what we'll find out anyway?"

"Something like that. Besides, since when is replacing a com officer breaking protocol?"

"It's not something that . . ."

"Okay. Look, Carl, I . . . I really want to go. I mean, this place is driving me nuts and I'm bored senseless. I haven't been on a run in three years and . . . and this thing is big noise. I want to be part of it. Do it as a favor?"

"Frank, does Maggie have everything under control?"

"Maggie always has things under control, Captain. She makes me feel useless. Take a look on your screen. Seventy-five hours to a ten-kilometer stand-off. Maggie also came up with a simple solution to the rotation problem. Want to see it?"

"Yes. Pass it down."

The data showed the thing to be of surprisingly uniform shape. Enough that two mining bots could easily move from pivot center and be anchored at each end on opposite sides. Once in place they could stop the swing with just their standard thruster units with fuel to spare for maneuvering. Maggie had worked out a procedure that would require no EVA until it was time to hook up for the tow. Cho smiled.

Maggie, you're a beautiful machine.

"Captain?"

"What is it, Frank?"

"New numbers from Maggie. The track that thing is on will take it into G Five's orbit. I think it may be a bad idea to try capturing it."

"What makes you say that?"

49

"What are the odds of some random piece of drifting junk being on a path that will take it directly into a matching orbit with the only real population in this system? There has to be a reason."

"You're being paranoid, Frank."

"No, I'm being cautious. Think about it."

"You're saying it was sent here? That it's under control? What?"

"Could be either one or both, Captain. Either that, or it could have detected signals coming from G Five out there somewhere beyond the system and set a course for its fall in. I don't know, but it makes me nervous."

"Is there some mistake?"

"We make mistakes. Maggie doesn't."

"All right. It sounds like it's time for plan B."

"Plan . . . B?"

"We stop the tumbling, then go over and have a look."

"What? Inside?"

"Frank, anything we need to know about the outside of this thing, Maggie can give us. She can't tell us anything about what's inside."

"Yeah, but . . ."

"If it's a dead hulk, we go ahead with the salvage. If it's up and running or there's someone . . ."

"Something."

"All right. If something is inside, we try to make contact. Imagine it, Frank."

"I am imagining it, Captain, and I'm not ready to be something's dinner. Are you?"

"A little overly dramatic, don't you think? Not to mention that paranoia of yours is overflowing."

"Maybe, but what about the orders from Meninger? He said we were to do nothing more than bring it in and the science people would handle it from there."

"Frank, if we take the thing in tow, how long before we arrive at Station Six?"

"Maggie projects eighty-two hundred to threshold plus forty-six hundred to orbit. Why?"

"Because that's over a year and a half, Frank. Right now we're only three plus days away from being able to know what it is. That's why."

"Well-l-l . . . okay, Captain, but I still think it's a bad idea. Who's going over, so I can get their gear ready?"

"Everyone but Mike, so get your gear ready."

"Me? Why me? And why not Mike instead?"

"You said it yourself, Frank. Maggie makes you feel useless, and Mike is certified on all ship functions. He's the only one who can run this ship alone."

"Yeah, great. In case we all get eaten, he can go tell somebody about it. Great."

The visual nav cupula on *Triumphant* was large compared to most ships in the mining service, but it was still a tight fit for three. Dr. Stahlman, a smallish fellow in his early fifties, wore an expression of amazement and trepidation evenly mixed. He stared intently at the tumbling cylinder still some thirty kilometers away. *Triumphant* was closing on it at a mere ten meters per second now and slowing. The thing appeared to be hanging there, stationary and tumbling.

"Look at the size of that thing," he said in a half whisper as if afraid he might awaken something that shouldn't be awakened. "It's a single structure. We could never build something even close to that size. Do you have any idea where it may have come from? Why it's here?"

"Nothing more than what we've told you," Cho said, matching Stahlman's hushed tone.

Peele lowered his binoscope slowly. "It's no wonder we were getting weird returns in the beginning. The damned thing is like a cucumber. There are ten meter blisters all over it. Wish there were more light. Here, Stahlman, take a look."

Stahlman took the instrument from Peele, then raised it to his eyes.

"Hard to tell, but they look like hemispherical pods attached to the outer surface. Wonder what purpose those serve?" Stahlman said, still in a whisper.

"Well, if we're lucky, we'll be finding out in a few hours," Cho said. "What does Maggie have to say, Frank?"

"She's still refining data, but we should have some good images from the IR and radar scans taken earlier. Better than eyeballing through this thing, anyway. Oh, speaking of the scans, there was no response from that whatever-it-is and we've had no EMF of any kind coming off it—it may be a dead derelict after all."

"Bad news, gents," Lundgren said as he came through the bridge entry. It was apparent he'd been too long on M Three as the half g acceleration made his step somewhat labored. "Automated Mayday from the *Triumphant* just started up."

"Change of plans," Borg said. "Any way to know what triggered it?"

"You're kidding. She's a freighter, man. I'd say it's a miracle the company installed an automated unit, what with the way they trim costs on everything. Could be anything from major damage to something as simple as the crew being away too long."

"Have you tried . . .?"

"Contacting them? I'm a ComCon man. It's what I do. With the TD, it'll be awhile before we get any response—if there is one. I already fed the signal into the nav system, just in case you want to go after them."

Borg keyed the com. "Carl?"

"Nav gave me the word a minute ago. Already on my way," Fielding responded.

A moment later, Fielding entered. He nodded to Lundgren on the way through to his seat. "Good thinking, Klaus. Maybe it was a good thing we brought you."

"Told you," Lundgren said, giving an exaggerated wink.

"Well, Ray," Fielding said, "do we go for it or wait for Central?"

"What do you think? I say balls to the wall."

"Agreed. Klaus, anything at all changes in that signal or anything else, you . . ."

"Yeah, yeah, I know. I'm on it."

Lundgren left the bridge and headed back to his station.

"Nav?" Fielding said into the com. "I want course and engine for quickest time to that signal."

Antares locked into the universal docking ring of the *Triumphant* and sealed the connection. Ten kilometers away drifted the alien ship. A boarding team made up of Fielding, Lundgren, two Marines, and a three-man science team made their way through the ring into what appeared to be an empty ship. There were no responses to repeated signals over the three months it took to reach the scene. The Marines began their search immediately, while Lundgren went directly to the MAGI system to extract all the records that might let them know what happened to the crew.

Twenty minutes later, Lundgren's voice came over the com. "Carl, last man in this compartment sealed it and changed the code. Told you you'd need me. Anyway, that was Stahlman, the ship's doctor. I managed to get in after playing with the code for a couple of hours. All of them but one, guy named Michael Ranken, went over to that monster sixty days ago. That means eleven of them are over there and the Nav Officer, that's the Ranken guy, should be here. They haven't returned. The MAGI indicates that Stahlman came back thirty days after they left and stayed here for quite a while, then logged out eighty hours before we arrived. There has been no communication with the MAGI since."

"No record of problems?"

"None, but there's a lot of stuff here the white coats should look at. Me, I can't understand a damned word of it. Stahlman was here tapping the MAGI for all sorts of information about genetic structure—definitely white coat stuff. He's also coded a long message. I'm working on retrieving that now."

"I'll send them over after we find the one who . . ."

"Found one," a Marine's voice interrupted. "In the galley. Looks like a caged cat, sir."

"Caged cat?"

"Yeah. You know, eyes wigglin' like crazy and all curled up in a corner. What should I do, sir?"

"Just keep a watch on him, but leave him alone."

"Aye, sir."

The other Marine drifted by, headed for the galley. Fielding turned to the science team.

"Anyone here know much about psychology?" he said.

A woman in her early thirties, very attractive to his eye, pushed away from the bulkhead and moved toward him. She was smiling at him and Fielding was wondering why he hadn't noticed her before. Her uniform bore the name of Schirmer, Helena. She missed the overhead hand grab and drifted into him.

"Oof . . . ! Sorry, Commander. I haven't been in nograv for a while."

Fielding smiled at her and winked.

"That's okay. It was my pleasure. Are you up on psychology?"

"I've been chief psychiatric officer at G Five Central for fifteen years. Nobody flies unless I say so. Why? What do you need?"

"One of the ship's crew . . . . Never mind. Come with me. Klaus, stay with it. We need to know what happened here."

"Where would I go?"

The Marines moved away from the entry as Schirmer approached. Curled in a ball, Ranken hovered about halfway between the deck and overhead. His head jerked sporadically and a thin line of saliva extended from one corner of his mouth and floated in front of his face. Schirmer withdrew a small cylinder from her kit and fired at the man in the corner. His body tensed, straightened abruptly, then went limp.

"You shot him? Why . . .?"

"Tranquilizer, Commander. We . . ."

"Just Carl, please."

"All right, Carl, there was no way we could get close to him in the state he was in. Who knows what he might have done? He could have injured himself . . . or one of us."

54

"Understood."

She looked intently at Ranken's face, then turned to one of the Marines.

"Take him to the Ring One infirmary. We'll be along shortly."

"So, what do we do with him? He may have important things to tell us," Fielding said.

"We should be able to talk to him in an hour. A little simgrav and some deep sleep should do the trick. In the meantime, we need to work on the MAGI to see what might be there. Your man—Lundgren? —knows the MAGI well?"

"Our ComCon is the best in the system, and he talks to machines like we talk to each other. He's been working on it but he said most of the stuff in it is beyond his understanding."

Ranken twitched, then violently jerked against the restraints. His eyes snapped open. Wide.

"What the hell? Where am I? Who are you? What—?"

"Relax, Ranken. I'm Commander Borg and this is Dr. Schirmer. We're here to help."

"Wanna help? Take these damned straps off. That'll help."

"You were restrained for your protection when you came around," Schirmer said as she began at his ankles. "That's a nasty tranq I used on you and it's not like waking up from sleep."

"Tell me. I feel like a mountain fell on me." He sat up slowly and looked around the compartment. "Military?"

"Yes. Do you feel up to talking? We need to know what happened. Not everything, just why you were sealed in the galley and the rest remained over there," Borg said.

"Not much to tell. Well, yeah, there is, but it's weird." He shifted his position on the table to more comfortably see both of them. "We took station at this thing about three months ago and a month later—I think it was a month. Pretty blurred right now. Captain Cho made the decision to go over. She took everyone, but decided the one to stay behind would be me, which didn't bother me a bit. I didn't want anything to do with it, you know. Sorry now

I even mentioned it to her when it showed up. Have any coffee?"

"Sure," Schirmer said, then motioned to the orderly sitting quietly on the other side of the compartment. "Go on."

"Thanks. Well, everything was fine. I was getting pretty nervous with everyone gone like that for so long, but I was okay. After about thirty days, Doc called and said he was coming back over to talk to Maggie. That made me feel a little better. Somebody to talk to, you know. When he got here, I went to open the inner hatch for him and he just sort of pushed me out of the way, like he didn't want to have anything to do with me. He said it would be wise for me to seal myself in the galley and not to come out until a rescue ship arrived. That's when things got really intense. I asked him why, and he told me they'd been infected. He said he'd rig the distress call. The whole time, he didn't get out of his suit, but what I saw of him through his faceplate wasn't right. I don't know how to explain it. It just wasn't right."

He seemed startled when the orderly handed him the coffee, then settled down.

"What . . . what didn't seem right?" Schirmer said.

"I really can't explain it. Something about his skin. Anyway, he went off to talk to Maggie and I went to the galley, too nervous to spit. Several days later, I was really on the edge of something when he came by on his way to the transfer lock. It wasn't just the skin then; but the eyes. They weren't his eyes. They were the eyes . . . the eyes of something else. Not human. He gave me a thumbs up on the way by and that was it. That is, until you got here. I don't know what I was thinking. All I know is that when I heard the docking ring clamps extend, something snapped. I don't remember anything after that." He moved the cup so the aroma entered his nostrils, then took a long, slow sip. "I'm sorry, but I can't tell you anything more."

Schirmer laid an understanding hand on Ranken's shoulder as Borg rose.

"I have a ComCon to chase down. Thanks, Ranken. I'll be back in a little while, Helena." In one smooth motion, Borg turned while raising his board and shouted, "Carl, on the Bridge. Now."

Before he made it to the door, the general alarm sounded and warning lights flashed.

"Evacuate *Triumphant* immediately. Evacuate *Triumphant* immediately. Automatic separation sequence begins in ten minutes. Evacuate *Triumphant* immediately. Evacuate *Triumphant* immediately."

Borg grabbed the edge of the door and stopped his move into the passage. He keyed the general com code. "What the hell's going on, Carl? Who issued that sep order?"

"I don't know. I was about to ask—"

"I did." It was Lundgren's voice. "You guys have fifteen minutes to assemble all command personnel at the MAGI—better have a couple white coats with you, too—because I'll talk to you then. Too much to do right now. Get everybody off the Triumphant now. I've taken over all control functions. You have no choice. And you know no one can break into my codes, so don't try. If you do, things will . . . go bad."

The connection went dead.

"Evacuate *Triumphant* immediately. Evacuate *Triumphant* immediately. Automatic separation sequence begins in nine minutes. Evacuate...."

The low frequency thrumming of the separation thrusters continued rumbling through *Antares* and acceleration was building up to the one quarter g shutdown. Those gathered in the MAGI compartment were secured in their seats, facing the large screen tucked in among banks of panels displaying seemingly random flashes. Of course, there was nothing random about it. The MAGI was thinking. If the flashing ever stopped, that would be time for concern.

The image of Klaus Lundgren assembled on the screen. He appeared calm. Perhaps too calm for the circumstances. An odd glint filled his eyes. A cynical smirk curled his lips.

"Hello. Here's how this is going to work. I'm going to tell you what I figured out about what's happening to Captain Cho and her crew—me too, I think—over there on that thing, and what it really is. After that I have a couple of requests, then I'll say goodbye.

"They found a way into that thing. They were suited up at first, but the thing determined what conditions they needed, manufactured it, and they removed their suits. Of course, it wasn't necessary, but it made things easier for the little things to do their work. Yeah, I know. What things, right? Hang on.

"What their doctor was doing on the MAGI was trying to find the source of the infection. That's what he called it, because he didn't know any better. They were being affected by something and he, being a doctor and all, thought it was a bug or something like a virus. During his stay back on *Triumphant,* he ran a series of tests on himself and missed the answer that was right under his nose the entire time. He didn't recognize it. He'd been smart enough to seal himself in with the MAGI so it might not spread. At least he did that right.

"Long story short, when I entered their MAGI, I got it, too. That's why the separation and why I made my decision. That thing over there is not just a giant, bumpy dildo. Oh no, it's a lot more than that. Apparently, the folks who built that beast figured out what we did. Interstellar colonization isn't easy, cheap, or quick. The difference is, they came up with a different answer than we did. By our standards, unethical as all hell.

"Rather than scale back and slow down, they did the opposite. They figured out how to do it without committing their people—or whatever they are—and they found out how to do it fast. What the doctor missed is that these are machines. Nano scale fabricators that go in and adjust DNA to suit their plan. Whatever life they find becomes them in the end. It may take a dozen or so generations, but in the end, there they are. That's what the blisters are. I guess you could call them seed pods.

"That's all I know about it for now. I've programmed this ship to self-destruct in twelve days. In ten days it will

58

transmit to you all I could dig out of the MAGI. Put people to work on it right away because I don't know how much time we might have. In the meantime, I'm going over to try talking that monster out of its present plan. If I can't, G Five is its next stop.

"So, about those requests, here's what I want. If what I'm trying to do works, and the people decide to make me a hero," he leaned back and brandished a broad grin, "make sure they use the shots of me when I graduated from the academy. They're the best. The other thing is, I want the Old Earth Inn to name a drink after me. I guess that's about it. Oh, wait." Lundgren squirmed in his seat. He leaned forward until his eyes filled the entire screen and he squinted hard. "Carl. Ray. You know, the one thing that bothers me—I mean really, really bothers me about this? This may not be the only one."

J. Richard Jacobs is an award winning author of science fiction novels and short stories. He has also published a number of anthologies and round robins. Some of his recent short stories and science articles have been published in **Perihelion Science Fiction,** *which he considers the best online hard science fiction magazine around.*

Veya lives in Canyon Falls, a city linked via hyperspace gateways to distant alien civilizations. She wants to join the Nova Guild, the ancient and powerful organization responsible for keeping the gateways functioning, but a tragic event from her past threatens to ruin her apprenticeship and endanger lives.

CANYON FALLS

By

John Moralee

In our arrogance we thought we were the only sentient race in the universe, like cavemen living in a small, dark cave, with no idea that everyone else was outside, living in the light.

Bounded by the speed of light, humankind crawled from star to star in ships that took thousands of years for the simplest journey. We were trapped in the Milky Way by the great distances between the galaxies–until we found the gateways on Terminus, left behind by a long gone alien civilization.

Then everything changed.

We stepped out of our cave.

–Captain Diana Thork, discoverer of Terminus

1763 YEARS AFTER GALACTIC UNIFICATION.

Terminus was always busy on the thirteenth day of the week. That was Market Day in Canyon Falls, when thousands of alien races came to our world, bringing new wares to sell in the lower city.

Dressed in a grey suncloak, hiding my face under its cowl, I struggled to follow my cousin Paulo through the

61

dense crowd, my eyes stinging in the midday suns, wishing I was inside where it was cool and quiet. Paulo was also wearing a suncloak, but his was bright red and blue. Designer fractal patterns shimmered on the sleeves, like a peacock's plumage. In my drab clothing, I was practically invisible, the way I liked it, hiding in plain sight—a sidekick to my more extroverted cousin.

The market was on the east side of Canyon Falls, standing on a vertiginous promontory above the turbulent river fed by the Great Falls. Paulo stopped at every market stall, touching the strange foods with his bare hands, laughing whenever something weird happened, like a fruit tried to bite him. Several alien traders barked at him in their native languages, warning him to keep his hands to himself, but Paulo ignored them. He was afraid of no one and nothing. At eighteen and a new recruit of the Protectorate Navy, he acted impetuously, dragging me along like a little girl, though I was only a few months younger and soon to graduate as a Nova Guild apprentice.

I didn't mind the market on normal days, when local farmers and craftspeople sold their wares, but whenever aliens travelled to Terminus, life became a hubbub of consumer madness. Once every twenty days, the planet orbited the rotating black hole at the heart of the system, powering the gateways to maximum, linking our world through hyperspace to the other galaxies spread far and wide across the universe, allowing trade and tourism, making those days a special event for most inhabitants. For a few hours, the length of time the Nova Guild's navigators could keep the gateways open, citizens rushed to buy new things before the traders returned to their home worlds.

Not me, though.

I hated Market Days because they reminded me of what had happened to my eight-year-old sister, Marila.

One day, during the summer holiday, when I was thirteen, my parents gave me the task of babysitting her. They expected me to play with Marila in our rooftop garden and keep her amused – but I soon got bored and left her to read indoors. For weeks Marila had wanted to see the

Dance of Seven Elements performed by a troupe of Traliad airwalkers, but our parents had never had the time to take her. That morning Marila entered my bedroom and begged me to go with her to see the show. I refused, because I had already seen the airwalkers. I didn't want to watch their show twice. Selfishly, I wanted to stay indoors reading Daphor's poetry, leaving my sister bored and restless. It was a mistake. Without my knowledge, Marila sneaked out of our home and went alone to the lower city.

She never returned.

At the time the local authorities made some inquiries with the alien delegations, but no useful answers were forthcoming. Her disappearance remained a mystery that still haunted me five years later.

To many citizens of Canyon Falls, the area around the market was an exotic wonderland of narrow streets and secret places. To me, it was a dangerous, lawless zone. Moving through the crowd, I was more frightened than excited by all of the strange sights and sounds. My heart was pounding, sweat running down my neck. Something buzzed past my face with green leathery wings. Then something scarlet and wet dripped on my cowl. I shivered despite the heat. My skin crawled. Every part of my body screamed to get out of there. I grabbed hold of Paulo. "Please. Let's leave."

"Try enjoying yourself," Paulo said. "Everything is amazing here. Do you hear that gragio music? I want to buy a unique love song for Min's birthday."

Dust, dirt, and noxious vapours assaulted my senses wherever we went, but Paulo seemed unperturbed by the chaos. Undisturbed by my reluctance, Paulo dragged me onto a rickety walkway leading to a second, temporary market perched precariously over the Great Falls. Traders were selling things illegal on most civilized planets— memory wipers, bi-tek coders, extreme cybernetic augmentations, even slave drones. A big grin formed on Paulo's tanned face, white teeth shining in the harsh sunlight. He grabbed me by my shoulders and turned me in the direction of a display of greasy slug-shaped fruits that smelled like burning rubber and diesel fuel.

"Veya, check these out!"

"No, thanks. They look vile." Each fruit pulsated as though squirming with maggots. "What are they?"

"Kranix plungs."

"Ugh! They look toxic."

"No. They're safe for humans. Ripe ones are supposed to taste like melting plastic, but they make you feel like you're floating on a cloud. I'm buying one."

Paulo spoke a few words to the purple-skinned Kranix lurking in the shadows. The alien's long, multi-hinged jaws clacked in reply. Paulo thumbed the credit tattoo on his wrist and sent eighteen universal credits to the vendor's account. Once the transaction was verified, Paulo lifted a plung to his mouth, biting off a squelchy chunk.

"Oh, wow! It tastes disgusting!" He chuckled and ate some more, grimacing with each swallow. "Yes, it is absolutely horrible!" His pupils dilated as the opiates affected him. His next words were slightly slurred. "I'm getting a taste for this stuff. Want to try it? It'll make you feeling immortal."

"No," I said, pulling away from him. "Why would I want to try something disgusting? I just want to get to the guildhall for my training. My mentor expects me on time."

The guildhall was beyond the market square in the quieter southern quarter of the city, higher up the canyon's side. It had been built a billion years ago by the unknown alien race that created the gateways. The direct route was blocked by a thousand market stalls, selling goods from countless worlds. Ten thousand humans and aliens were crammed into the lower city, eagerly seeking bargains and new experiences. I could hardly see the guildhall's sixteen golden spires over the crowd pushing and shoving me. Someone elbowed me in the ribs. Hands brushed against my robes, trying to touch my breasts or steal something from me. I slapped them away, blushing, loathing this awful place. I was surrounded by perverts and thieves. I cursed my cousin for dragging me into this hell-hole against my will. I would rather have walked the long way over the six bridges.

"I'm going now," I said. "I'm not going to be late. See you later."

I turned away, but Paulo chased me. "Wait! We have plenty of time. Don't you want to buy something from Ransor or Jarik Epsilon? See that memory vendor? It sells genuine historicals."

I saw the high prices and shook my head. "I don't have the money to buy anything. I'd prefer leaving with nothing than buy junk, anyway. Especially from an unlicensed memory vendor. A bad disk could fry my brain."

Paulo rolled his eyes. "I got paid today. I'll buy you a disk as a gift. I know you're interested in galactic history. They might be something old from Earth or Mars or New California. At least look before saying no."

Paulo could be very annoying, but he was right about my passion for history. But I wasn't interested in buying a bootleg memory of someone's birthday party or a wedding ceremony. I would have walked away, but I was feeling light-headed in the boiling sun. I had not been born with the constitution for the summer heat. The stall had a fan and an awning offering shade. For no better reason than to cool down, I browsed the racks of silver-cased memory disks, which had their contents written in Standard Galactic. The disks were categorised by planet of origin, then by subject, then the time of recording. I browsed through rows of Earth material, looking for something interesting, while the vendor studied me from behind a counter.

The vendor was a gangly Karrunian wearing shiny body-armour like a mediaeval knight, only with four arms. Two of the arms were attached to the shoulders, and two smaller ones waved on its head like feelers. A mirrored visor hid its face, but I sensed it looking at me through a dark slit.

"Can I help you?" it said through a translator.

"No, just looking."

"Spicy memories for you." A gauntleted head-hand waved towards a large section marked Erotica. "Excellent value."

My cheeks burned. "No, thank you. I'm interested in historicals."

"Ah! Have them too," the vendor said. "Full-sensory recordings. Be Cleopatra, Queen of Ancient Egypt. Very popular title."

Memory-recording devices had not been invented until the late twenty-third century, so the Cleopatra disk was an obvious fake, as were all of the ones supposed to show events from Earth's early history. The vendor didn't have any genuine Earth historicals, just fantasy re-enactments. I couldn't see anything more pointless than buying a fake memory. I was disappointed. I was wasting my time. I had cooled down enough to move on, but my cousin was browsing the Alien Erotica section. I could see green tentacles on one lurid cover in his hands. I shuddered in disgust. "Let's go."

"Just a minute," Paulo said, taking a dozen disks to the counter. "I'll take these, please."

"Superb choice, sir."

I shook my head and turned away. I didn't want to know what Paulo was buying. It would take a couple of minutes for his transaction. I spent that time idly looking along a rack of disks recorded locally. Paulo was almost done when I spotted a disk entitled TRALIAD AIRWALKERS: DANCE OF THE SEVEN ELEMENTS.

The date of the recording was marked on the disk, the day Marila disappeared.

As I read it, I felt faint and I almost passed out. I stared at it, checking the date again and again. I picked up the disk. The manufacturer information looked genuine. The disk was supposed to contain three hours of unedited memories recorded from the mind of a Traliad airwalker. The troupe had been performing during the time my sister had gone missing. It was too important to ignore. What if the recording showed what happened to her? The disk could contain vital evidence overlooked by the authorities.

I was breathless. I had to have the disk, even though it was expensive. I joined my cousin at the counter. He had promised to buy me something, so I added it to his purchases.

He frowned at the price. "You want *that?*"

I nodded, unable to speak for the thoughts pounding inside my skull.

Paulo shrugged. "Put this on my bill, please."

The vendor bagged everything. Once we were on our way out of the market, the crowd thinning around us, I fished my disk out of the bag. "Thanks. This means a lot."

I wanted to sample it there on the street, but I needed a quiet place and the free time to do it safely. Nobody tranced in public.

Reading the title of my purchase, Paulo looked puzzled. "Airwalking? What's so special about that?"

"Nothing, but look at the date."

Paulo frowned. "Sorry. Don't get it."

"Marila disappeared on that day."

"Oh! Wow." Paulo looked around and lowered his voice as though afraid someone was listening. "Do you think that will help you find her? Is that why you bought it?"

"Yeah, I hope so."

"Don't want to be pessimistic, but you've got to be realistic. Don't get your hopes up. Your sister's probably dead."

"I know," I admitted. "But if there's even the slimmest chance–"

"I understand," Paulo said. "I really hope you find something useful. I miss Marila, too. Let me know what you learn, okay?"

"I will, I promise." We were nearly at the guildhall. I slipped the disk into my suncloak, sealing it in a pocket. Then I decided to have some fun messing with my cousin. "So, you're into alien erotica, huh?"

"What? No! Don't get the wrong idea. I didn't buy those disks for myself."

"Yeah, right. I believe you."

"Really! The guys in my barracks love that sort of alien weirdness. I'll make a good profit selling these disks to Franco or Zeech."

"I understand completely," I said. "You're saying you're *not* a perv, just a black marketeer?"

"I'm an entrepreneur," he said. "You're not going to say anything to Min, are you?"

Min was my best friend as well as my cousin's girlfriend.

"Don't worry," I said. "I won't tell *Min* about your tentacle fetish or your dodgy deals. She's already got enough to worry about just going out with you, cuz."

We said our goodbyes at the stone steps leading up to the guildhall. I watched Paulo heading in the direction of the naval academy, then I ascended into the shadow of the massive guidhall.

Two armoured guards stood motionless on either side of the grand entrance doors, holding ornate shields and gleaming swords. They looked like stone statues, but they would come alive if anyone armed approached.

I removed my cowl as I climbed, revealing my face for their ID check. The guards didn't move, letting me pass. There was more security at the doors, but it was discreet. To prove myself a member of the Guild, I touched my hand to the left door and offered my right eye to a scanner. A micro-needle pricked my palm, taking a blood sample. And a rainbow of lasers pulsed over my retina. My eye watered.

"Identity verified. Access permitted."

The doors opened silently, releasing a draft of cool, tangerine-scented air. I felt like a million tiny fingers were tickling my body. The tickling ended abruptly once I was inside the antechamber. The doors closed automatically, shutting out the sunlight, and the soft glow of illuminated orbs, set in wall niches, provided a more comfortable light. I removed my suncloak and hung it on a rack with others. My footsteps echoed when I walked along a hall towards a distant archway. My destination was a large chamber deeper in the building, known as the Gate Room.

Gileanor was there, lying on a crystalline couch cushioned by blue velvet pillows. She was one of sixteen senior navigators resting on identical couches circling the monolithic Key Stone, the guild's interface with the alien machine operating the field generators. Like the other guild members, Gileanor was responsible for maintaining the hyperspace gateways to distant worlds. She was wearing a white ceremonial robe and a chrome skullcap over her long, silver-white hair. Trails of cables connected her skullcap to the Key Stone. Gileanor looked as though she was sleeping—until she opened her eyes and sat up. She smiled as she stood, carefully removing her skullcap. Gileanor was a senior member of the Guild, having joined centuries ago, when she wasn't much older than I was now. She looked good for someone in her fourth or fifth century.

"Veya, it's good to see you," my mentor said. "You seem a little distracted. If you aren't feeling well, we can postpone your lesson for another week."

"No, I'm fine," I said. "I'm ready."

Gileanor looked sceptical. "Are you sure?"

"There is a personal matter bothering me, but I won't affect my performance. I am focussed."

"Very well," she said. "Put on your skullcap."

I did so and laid down on the couch, which was more comfortable than it looked. Remembering my training, I closed my eyes and slipped into a dreamlike state. I sensed Gileanor standing behind me, a comforting presence, as I interfaced with the Key Stone, linking my mind into the vast machine running the gateway generators.

I was no longer aware of my body in the chamber.

Instead, I was in a dreamy place where the laws of physics were mutable. Like a god, I was seeing multiple locations on other worlds in remote galaxies. My mind had interfaced with the minds of a thousand navigators from alien civilisations. They were linked to other machines, maintaining a pseudo-telepathic union, expanding our collective consciousness. I was just a small cog in a great wheel keeping the hyperspace network functioning, but I felt like I had infinite power and wisdom. My mind was making subtle adjustments to space-time while thousands of living beings travelled world to world, blissfully unaware of our work. One lapse in concentration would put their lives at risk. It was a huge responsibility, but my training had prepared me well. Being part of the network felt as natural as breathing.

Gileanor's soft voice guided me, giving instructions I followed precisely. As a test, I opened a brief gateway to a desert planet, where I could taste the hot sand in the air. Then I opened another into deep space close to a colony ship.

"That's good," she said. "Now close it and open another one to a pulsar in the Andromeda Galaxy."

"Which one?"

"You choose."

I practised for hours, opening and closing small gateways. At the end of the session, Gileanor allowed me to experiment by choosing a few empty worlds. I found it easy to connect to them and create slightly larger, stable gateways. It would take years to make really large ones, like the official gateways, but Gileanor sounded pleased.

"That's excellent," she said. "We're done for today."

I sighed. I could have spent all day doing it. Idly, I wondered if I could use the network to look for my sister. Would I find her on another world, alive and happy? Would it be possible to search for her, using the interface? As an experiment, I tried to picture my sister. That thought made Marila appear in my mind as real as the last time I had seen her. I saw her smiling, her sun-reddened face basked in golden sunshine. She looked so full of joy that I ached to see her again. Distantly, like the real world was the dream, I felt tears running down my cheeks. My sister. I wanted my sister!

"Veya!" Gileanor shouted. "Concentrate on closing your gateway!"

"What?" I mumbled, realising I had been distracted. There was a feedback fluctuation in the hyperspace near Terminus. Eddies in the energy fields rippled and expanded. I reduced the energy input and stabilised the field strength, but my efforts were inadequate. I was creating more ripples. I didn't want to panic, but I was losing control. "I can't do it!"

I felt myself jerked back into the chamber as Gileanor disconnected my skullcap, ripping it off my head, breaking my connection to the Key Stone. My head throbbed. I felt sick. I was back in the chamber, disorientated by the sudden transition. Gileanor pulled me off the couch and took my place on it. Though her expression remained neutral, I could feel her scowling on the inside.

"Veya, you need to leave."

"I don't understand," I said. "What happened? Did I do something wrong?"

"You are not ready," she said. "I doubt you ever will be. You must leave the guild now. A sentinel will escort you from the building."

A sentinel was already in the room, striding towards me.

"You must come with me," it said.

As I was forced to leave, my mentor closed her eyes and interfaced with the Key Stone, while the other guild members twitched on their couches like they were having a terrible nightmare.

"I'm sorry," I said, but nobody heard.

The sentinel led me to the main exit. I collected my suncoat, then I was escorted outside and down the steps into the sunny street. The sunlight stung almost as much as the tears drying on my face.

I hurried home the quickest way, over the hanging bridges and up the cliff in a cable car. My home was among the suburbs on the western side of the canyon, shaded by spindly solar trees the colour of vintage wine. I called out when I entered, but my parents were not there. I was glad. I didn't want them to see me in my current state—hot and sweaty and red-eyed from crying.

Detecting my presence, Ava, the house's AI, welcomed me home. "Veya, you have one new text-only message from the Nova Guild Chancellor's Office. Shall I read it to you?"

"Yes."

"We are sorry to inform you that, due to a failure of your duties as a guild member, your apprenticeship with Guild Mistress Gileanor Marko has been temporarily suspended. Furthermore, your guild membership has also been revoked, pending the result of an internal inquiry into this serious matter. The guild will inform you within 90 days, in writing, if your membership will resume, or if it will be permanently revoked. During the inquiry, you must not

contact any guild members or attempt to enter the Guild, as this will result in immediate and permanent dismissal.'"

"They're throwing me out?"

"I'm sorry," Ava said. "Shall I draw you a relaxing bath?"

"No," I said. "I need ice cream. Lots of ice cream."

I stormed into the kitchen, wishing I had bought a Kranix plung so I could forget about my day. Ava's servitor prepared me a rich and creamy strawberry ice cream served in a large ceramic bowl. I ate it quickly until it gave me brain-freeze, then I ate it slowly. Afterwards, I slumped on my bed, staring at the ceiling, angry with myself. I'd let my feelings for my sister distract me at a crucial moment during my training. There was no chance of the Guild reinstating me, not after such a breach of the rules. If only my cousin had not dragged me into the market, making me think about her, I would have not messed up everything.

Paulo should not have bought the memory disk. Then I would not have been thinking about losing my sister.

I took out the disk and stomped over to the recycler, considering trashing it. But I didn't. What if the disk contained something useful? I went back to my bed and strapped an interface band onto my head, which was a less intrusive neural connector than the skullcap. While a skullcap could read my thoughts, the band could only send them into my brain, replaying whatever memories were recorded. When I was lying comfortably, I activated the device.

Immediately, I plunged into a stranger's mind, experiencing everything they had done as if it were happening now.

Blue sky and waterfalls. The scent of spices. Soft air on my silver-white skin. I'm spinning high above a huge, sprawling city, beating my wings to rise higher until I'm at the top of lush, green valley. I stop beating my wings and spread my arms to feel the suns on my almost-weightless body.

Gravity slows me down and I begin to fall. Looking down, I see my brothers and sisters dancing in the air in perfectly-coordinated, symmetrical patterns. I join them in a circle. We spin in a thermal, then spiral down, dancing. My wings beat once, twice, then I hurtle down and down towards a crowd of humans far below. The wind rushes. My heart quickens. The ground looms. Plunging down and down, faster and faster, I feel truly alive, knowing I'm only a few heartbeats away from death.

Only when I see individual faces staring up at me, only then, do I flick my wings and soar over the cheering crowd and...

I ripped off the band, jolting out of the trance like I had been electrocuted. I was stunned. I had just seen my sister in the crowd, watching as the airwalker swooped overhead. I'd seen only a glimpse of her in passing–the briefest, intangible flash of her among the sea of faces–but it had been enough to make me positive. My sister had definitely been watching at the beginning of the performance, but what had happened to her later?

It was my first clue to solving the mystery.

It took me a minute to recover from the shock, but then I returned to the memory, re-starting it seconds before I had seen my sister.

Once more, I was inside the airwalker's mind, soaring high over the crowd...

Three hours later, I knew what had happened to Marila that day. I needed to share my discovery with someone, but I didn't want it to be my parents, who had returned while I was experiencing the airwalker's memory. They had already suffered enough. They didn't need me dredging up the past. I acted like nothing was wrong when I left my room and encountered them in the kitchen. Ava was serving them dinner.

"Are you joining us?" my mother asked.

"I ate earlier," I said. "I've got some research to do at the Central Archives. Bye."

Outside, I contacted Paulo and asked him to meet me on the Bridge of Echoes, which hung over the Great Falls, connecting the upper city to the lower one. I arrived ten minutes before my cousin showed up in his parade uniform.

"I just sneaked out of a class," he said. "This had better be important."

I broke the news of my suspension, then, while Paulo absorbed that revelation, I told him something far more shocking. "I know what happened to Marila, thanks to reviewing the airwalker recording."

"You're serious?"

"Yeah."

"Tell me."

"My sister was in the crowd at the beginning of the show. Later on, about an hour into the recording, she left the market to get a better view from this bridge. In the recording you can clearly see her leaning over the rail, watching the dancing from up here. She did that for another hour. She was right here, where we're standing." I looked down over the rail. Far below, I could see the turbulent river under the Great Falls. "My sister was alone and looked like she was enjoying herself—until 127 minutes into the recording, when something creepy happened."

"What's that?"

"Someone else appeared on the bridge. A stranger in a black suncloak. You can see them walking towards my sister. Unfortunately, the airwalker turned its head in another direction at that point, so the actual encounter isn't recorded. The next time you see the bridge—at 132 minutes—my sister and the stranger are gone."

"We've got to tell the police. This is new evidence."

"No," I said. "We'll never find out the truth if we tell anyone. We have to investigate it ourselves."

"How?"

"We need to find more recorded memories from that day. One could provide evidence of what happened next on the bridge, like which direction the kidnapper took Marila. We'll have to go back to the market vendor to find the source of this recording."

"It's getting late. The gateway shuts down in another hour. The vendor's probably gone home already. It's probably too late."

"We'd better hurry."

The twin suns were low over the canyon when we returned to the market. Most traders had closed their stalls once they had sold out. Those that were still around were packing their goods. The Karrunian memory vendor had gone. We talked to the owner of the next stall, a local Screek who had seen the Karrunian leave only twenty minutes earlier in a transport bound for the subway train to the gateways.

"Maybe it hasn't left the planet yet," I said to Paulo. "We could beat the train if we hire a taxi."

Within a minute, an orange-and-black taxi dropped out of the sky, landing beside us. We boarded and paid for the flight as the craft lifted off in a cloud of vapour and dust. We flew over the city at breath-taking speed, then accelerated over the canyon to fly low across the Thork Desert.

There was nothing but sun-baked rock and red sand to the hazy horizon. We were flying at a speed that blurred the ground. We had departed ten minutes after the train, but we were still accelerating and expected to arrive ahead of it.

Nervously, I stared out of the windows, looking for the Gate Rings.

They became visible after twenty minutes.

They stood in a circle on a dry plain like an ancient Earth monument, towering over the desert floor, sixteen huge and imposing portals to other worlds. I could see transports flying in and out of the rings like a swarm of bees, racing to their destinations before the gateways shut down, stranding travellers on the wrong side.

About a kilometre from the Gate Rings, the railway emerged from underground into a dome where passengers and cargo transferred to transports waiting on the platform. Luckily, the last train had not yet appeared, so we landed and waited for it to come out of the subway tunnel.

We didn't wait long. The train emerged thirty seconds later. Servitors started unloading cargo as soon as it stopped. A large number of humans and aliens exited the carriages, making it far harder to spot a mirrored knight with four arms than you'd expect.

We located the transport heading for Karru and waited by it. I spotted a Karrunian in the crowd.

"Is that it?"

"No," Paulo said. "Different visor. Karrunians belong to clans with different face-plates. The one we are looking for it from the Ru Clan. It has a crescent engraving."

"How do you know that?"

"Navy graduates have to know all kinds of things. We are the peacekeepers of our galaxy, so we need to study every culture possible."

A Karrunian was approaching with a servitor carrying a black cargo box.

"Is that it?"

"Yes," Paulo said.

We approached the alien before it boarded.

"Hi," I said. "Do you remember me? I bought a disk from you this morning."

"No refunds," it said, its head-hands flapping in agitation.

"I don't want that," I said. "I want more recordings from the Traliad troupe on the same day. Do you have any?"

"I do not have time for business," it said, trying to pass.

Paulo blocked its way. "I'll pay you well."

The Karrunian ordered the servitor to stop. Then it opened the cargo box, containing thousands of disks in a compact barrel-shaped storage unit. Its large arms removed a segment and the smaller ones selected disks from it.

"Six recordings. Only copies."

It named an exorbitant price, way beyond my means.

Paulo didn't haggle. He paid the full amount. The Karrunian boarded the transport waving its head-hands like it was very happy.

"Well, I'm broke," Paulo said. "I hope these recordings are worth it."

"Thank you," I said, giving him a hug. "Don't worry about the money. I'll pay for the train back to Canyon Falls."

"Gee! How generous!"

It was after midnight when I got home. I was too old to have a curfew, but my parents were waiting up for me like I'd sneaked out to a hard-core narco club. Their faces were grim. My father glared.

"Veya, where have you been all night?"

I'd been at Paulo's apartment studying the airwalker disks, looking for clues to what had happened to my sister. But I didn't want my parents involved in my amateur detective work. Not yet. I didn't want to give them false hope. "I went to the archives. Then I hung out with Paulo, Dad."

"That's very interesting," he said. "Because you had a visitor. Your mentor from the guild. She came to discuss *your suspension*, but you weren't here. A suspension? You didn't tell *us*. What's going on, Veya? Are you into drugs or something?"

"No, Dad, it's nothing like that. I lost my concentration during a training session, that's all. The guild suspended me because they have stupid protocols. Did my mentor say much? Has the suspension been lifted?"

"No, it hasn't. She wants you to visit her in the morning if you need to talk. She sounded concerned, for what that's worth. I suggest you take her advice. Now, go to bed so you're fresh in the morning."

"We love you," my mother said. "We just want what's best for you."

"I know," I said.

I kissed them goodnight, then made a show of going to my bedroom. I switched off the lights so my parents would think I was going to sleep, and then waited for them to retire.

At Paulo's apartment, I'd tranced each of the airwalker memories and learnt all I could from them. The first three recordings hadn't helped much, because the airwalkers didn't look at the bridge. The fourth performer had been higher up, looking down as it twirled through the spray from the Great Falls. The bridge was far, far below, but even the sharp eyes of an airwalker couldn't see useful details at that distance. The fifth recording was better. The fifth airwalker had been flying lower and looking in the right direction. It captured the moment in its memory. My sister was there, leaning over the rail, when the stranger approached. The stranger said something and held out a pale hand. Amazingly, my sister took it and went with the stranger. The fifth airwalker lost sight of them moments later, but the final recording provided more clues. That airwalker had been circling over the city's rooftops. My sister was recorded leaving the bridge. Holding the stranger's hand, Marila boarded a taxi parked on the street. The craft was lifting off when the airwalker passed by. Its hawk-like vision captured the vehicle's ID.

"Ava, I need you to analyse something for me."

"Yes, Miss. How may I assist?"

"A taxi with the registration S724Q5 was parked on Ibis Road on the day my sister disappeared. Access the flight information and show me its route."

A map appeared on my tablet with the taxi's route marked in red, with stops marked in green circles. I studied it, my eyes widening, more questions forming in my mind than answers.

My sister had been kidnapped by Gileanor.

The next morning the streets were hot, as usual, but the air was cooler when Paulo and I reached Gileanor's home beneath the Great Falls. She lived in a white villa surrounded by a high security wall.

"So," Paulo said. "What's the plan?"

"I'll question her alone," I told him. "I'll record everything she says as evidence, with you listening in."

"You should take my weapon as protection." He offered me his Navy Peacekeeper. "Take this."

"No. I'm not going in armed. It'd just set off the home security. I want her confession. I don't want to kill her."

"Be careful," Paulo said. "I'll be listening. I'll come in shooting if I hear you're in danger."

Gileanor was expecting me, so I wasn't surprised when the security gates opened as I approached them, though it was a little creepy, given I knew she was a kidnapper. Her voice came out of a speaker.

"Come in!" she called out. "I'm making tea! Come down the hall to the kitchen!"

A spiral path led through her garden up to an entrance. I'd never been in Gileanor's home and didn't know what to expect inside. Filtered sunlight filled the atrium with soft pink light. It smelled of roses. The white walls were decorated with framed pictures of men, women, and children. I'd never known Gileanor had a family until I saw her with people I assumed were her children and grandchildren. They looked happy. I wondered why she would want to kidnap my sister when she already had a family. Why did she do it? Why?

Gileanor was in a light and airy kitchen with a panoramic view of the city, her back to me as she boiled a kettle on a marble counter. I was tempted to attack her before she turned around. It took strength staying calm and focussed.

"You wanted to discuss my suspension?"

"I think I can sort it out for you," she said. "But it might take months. The Guild moves very slowly in these matters. I'll explain everything, but first you should join me for tea. It's English Breakfast Tea imported from Earth."

"Sounds good," I said.

I didn't want tea, but I didn't want Gileanor anywhere near a source of boiling water when I confronted her. I followed her onto a balcony and acted like I appreciated her hospitality. She talked about how she was going to help me, making me want to throw my hot tea in her face. My right hand trembled. I had to put down my drink and hide my hand under the table.

Paulo's voice spoke into my ear, saying what I was already thinking. "Quit stalling. Confront her."

"Gileanor, I know you kidnapped my sister."

Her mouth became a tight line. "What makes you think that?"

"I've evidence: a memory recording of you kidnapping my sister. It shows you both getting into a taxi. That taxi came here. I've got all I need to have you arrested, but I don't care about that. I just want to know what you did to my sister. Tell me the truth. Where is she?"

"I'm right here," Gileanor said.

"What?"

"I'm your sister. I'm Marila."

"What are you talking about?"

"It's complicated. But I hope you'll believe me when I've explained. As you already know, your sister sneaked off to see the Tralian airwalkers. What you don't know is what happened *next*. Marila wasn't tall enough to see over the adults in the market, so she went onto a bridge to get a better look. During the show, she climbed on the rail to see better and fell to her death in the rapids below."

"What are you talking about? That never happened. I saw *you* kidnap her."

"Yes, you did. But I'm talking about what must have happened *originally*. The original Marila died. You were so grief-stricken that, years later, you tried to open a hyperspace gateway through time to save her. You succeeded, but not in the way you hoped. You probably intended to transport her somewhere nearby, but you made a miscalculation. The second Marila was transported to another planet in a different galaxy, five hundred years into the past. I'm that version of your sister, the one saved by you. A paradox-created version."

"I don't believe you."

"I have no reason to lie. One second I was falling off the bridge, then I was on another world with an orange sky and three moons. It was very confusing. I remember standing on a field of dark-blue grass that smelled like honey. In the distance, there was a farmhouse. I walked there and encountered an alien. It didn't speak my language and I couldn't understand it, but it took me in and gave me food and shelter. It was kind to me. When it became clear that I needed its help, it welcomed me to live with its family, adopting me like one of its brood. After being taught its language, I learnt I was on a planet called

Rashoo, roughly eighty million light-years from home. I grew up the only human on that world. I tried to forget my other life, but I never did. I always remembered you and Mom and Dad. I remembered how I'd ended up there, though at the time I didn't know how it had happened. I only worked that out when I eventually left Rashoo on a ship and returned home through a gateway. I arrived back here four hundred years ago. I've been living my life under a false identity ever since, being careful to not change the future too much. Five years ago, in the current time stream, I befriended my other self so that she would trust me when I came to save her on the bridge. I stopped her from dying that day, but I made another paradox."

"Where is she now?"

"I've kept that version of me here, safe, waiting for the right time to let her go back to her family. She's in stasis. Let me show you."

The woman claiming to be my sister showed me into a room with a coffin-shaped chamber containing my little sister. Marila looked asleep inside the stasis generator.

I believed her story then. "You've kept my sister frozen. Why?"

"I couldn't take her home."

"Why not?"

"I only exist if you continued on the same path, not knowing what happened. I became your mentor to train you. I was going to tell you the truth when you were fully trained. You were...are...supposed to attempt to save your sister's life using the Key Stone. I didn't know you'd find out the truth yourself before you are ready. This complicates everything. But it can still be fixed."

"How?"

"All you have to do is wait until the time is right to save your sister again. Once you do that, I can wake the other version of me and return her to your parents, alive and well. The paradox will no longer exist then. There will be two versions of me in the same time stream, but nobody else will know."

"I have a huge problem with that. My parents have been grieving for five years. You really want them to wait longer? How much longer? A month? A year? A decade?"

"I don't know," Gileanor said. "I can't predict the future. All I know is that the paradox must be resolved. I don't possess the natural skill to make a temporal adjustment, but you were born with that skill. Once the Guild reinstates you, we can continue your training. In a few years, you may be ready to manipulate time, resolving the paradox."

"No," I said. "It has to be sooner. The longer we leave things like this, the more my parents suffer and the harder it will be for my sister to come back. She's already lost five years. You know what I have to do. We need to do it now."

"You'd have to get back into the Guild. You can't do that when you're suspended."

"Yesterday I caused a ripple in space-time. The Guild might never reinstate me because of that. They could discover the paradox, unless we close the loop. Today."

"I suppose you could get in if I'm with you. I can open the doors and get us both inside, but the guards won't let two people in at once."

Paulo had been listening to everything. "Veya, I can help with the guards. I know where they eat breakfast. I have a plung left over. I can slip it to them in a drink."

Gileanor frowned. "Are you listening to someone?"

"Yes, my cousin. He's going to drug the guards."

An hour later, Gileanor and I climbed the steps of the Guildhall after the changing of the guards. Both men were drugged when we arrived, barely aware of our existence. Gileanor opened the door. I followed her inside. We reached the Gate Room without encountering a soul. It was deserted because the Key Stone was inactive.

"As soon as you connect, security will come to check because nobody is supposed to be here. You'll have under a minute to open the gateway. Are you confident you can do it?"

In truth, I was terrified of failing. But the risk was worth it. I attached the skullcap and lay on the couch. "Let's do it."

Slipping into the dreamlike state, I interfaced with the Key Stone. I was the only mind linked locally, which made it easier to focus on creating a single small gateway, if I could locate my sister on the bridge five years ago.

I targeted her physical location, then adjusted the temporal parameters, picturing my sister until I could feel her unique mass and energy signature in hyperspace. She appeared in my mind on the bridge. There she was, falling over the rail. Death was waiting below, but not if I acted. I reached out and opened a gateway under her and compensated for her acceleration. She passed through it into hyperspace.

At that moment I could have made the gateway exit anywhere in the universe. I could have transported her home on the same day as she disappeared, but if I did that Gileanor and her family would cease to exist in the altered future. Though it pained me, I had to repeat my error by opening the exit on Rashoo, condemning the original Marila to become Gileanor.

After I had done that, I closed the gateway and shut down my link.

I opened my eyes not knowing if I had done the right thing.

Gileanor was still there. I could hear a sentinel stomping down the hall. "You've done it?"

"Yes."

We hurried out of the Gate Room before anyone caught us.

The next day my sister was found wandering in the lower city. She had no memory of where she had been, but she was healthy and unharmed. My parents were overjoyed to have her home again.

Naturally, the police investigated her abduction, but they didn't find any clues. I had already destroyed the airwalker recordings as a precaution, so there was no evidence.

The Guild reinstated me after a six-month hiatus, concluding my mistake would never be repeated. They were more right than they would ever know.

Six months later, my apprenticeship ended with the Guild making me a full member. I'm a navigator now.

When I'm not working, I spend a lot of time with Marila, making up for the lost years with as much love as I can give her. I often take her into the market to show her the wonderful alien things, accompanied by Paulo and Min. I no longer hate Market Days, now I know I have nothing to fear.

It's strange knowing two versions of my sister, but I like it better than none. Nobody knows Gileanor is Marila from an alternative time-stream. Together, we decided it's best that way. I visit her regularly, now she's retired and moved to live on Oceania Prime, where she has many relatives. I'm looking forward to visiting her next summer. I hear it's much cooler there.

Someday, I will pay back Paulo for all of his help finding Marila, but that's in the unwritten future.

Just like everything is now.

John Moralee is the author of the crime novel Acting Dead, *the zombie apocalypse thriller* Journal of the Living, *and the first book in a dystopian science fiction/fantasy series* The House on Willow Lane. *He lives in England, where his short fiction has appeared in magazines and anthologies including* The Mammoth Book of Jack the Ripper Stories, Crimewave, *and the British Fantasy Society's magazine* Peeping Tom.

Several collections of his stories are available as ebooks and trade paperbacks. They include the horror titles The Bone Yard and Other Stories *and* Bloodways, *the crime omnibus* Edge of Crime, *and the science-fiction collection* The Tomorrow Tower.
More recently, his science-fiction stories have been published in Visions IIIı Beyond the Kuiper Belt, Visions IV: Space Between Stars, *and* Visions V: Milky Way. *He also has a story* "Ripplers" *in* Last Outpost, *an anthology of military SF released in October 2016.*
John Moralee's website is www.mybookspage.wordpress.com.

Can the communications officer of the GFSS *Empathy* convince his captain to endanger ship and crew, by answering a distress call to rescue the *life spark* of a supposed mythical, powerful species from the imminent demise of their galaxy?

THE GUARDIAN

S. M. Kraftchak

Auri trembled violently as he raised his head. Even his folded legs shuddered. Some shakiness after a connection was typical while his mind remembered his body was attached, but this was much more. This was fear; full-out, terrifying hopelessness.

Swiping at the perspiration on his forehead and then at the tears rolling down his cheeks with one hand, he reached for the glass of water he'd set on the floor next to him. The water sloshed onto his sleeve, the leg of his jumpsuit, and down his front before he could slurp from the glass. With two great gulps he finished the drink, let both hands and the glass fall into his lap, tipped his head back, and wailed.

"HOW? If *you* can't, then how can *we*?" He sobbed for several minutes with his eyes closed until he could take several deep cleansing breaths. He knew what he had to do, but had no idea how to accomplish it. That would take consideration, and time *they* didn't have.

The door com on the wall chirped with a lyrical woman's voice. "Lieutenant Loreq?"

Unfolding his legs, Auri crawled to the wall and activated the intercom, forcing his voice to sound normal. "What can I do for you, Lieutenant Epps?"

"Captain Chad sent me to check on you. May I come in?"

Auri glanced around his quarters to be sure he hadn't left any cognitive writing this time. "You may enter."

The door slid into the wall and a shapely woman with close-cropped auburn hair wearing a forest green jumpsuit took two steps in, clasped her hands behind her back, and examined him from beneath a creased brow. "You're late for duty again. This makes eight straight days you've been late and nearly two weeks that you've been lethargic, distracted, and quite frankly not your mischievous self. If you were female, I'd think you were pregnant. I've run out of excuses to give the Captain. He's demanding to know what's going on with you."

Auri stared at her with his mouth agape. He felt the heat in his face rise. "Uh . . ."

The woman's expression softened with a smile. In one smooth move, she retrieved the glass from the floor, placed it on the table, and offered Auri a hand to his feet.

Taking the offered hand, Auri stood. When the world spun, he grabbed his bunk and eased onto the edge, breathing deliberately.

Lieutenant Epps sat next to him and gently rubbed his back. "Don't worry. I told him the truth."

Auri looked into the woman's silver blue eyes and swallowed the lump in his throat. "But how—"

"Space sickness creeps up on everyone now and then. You don't need to be embarrassed. That's what this is, right?"

Auri exhaled loudly and nodded.

Crossing to the table, Lieutenant Epps ran her finger around the rim of the glass as she spoke. "I thought so, since all the tests I've surreptitiously run—"

"Kara, you had no right." Auri suddenly stood, a hand on the wall for steadiness as he took four steps to the tiny sink where he splashed water on his face; relieved she had no clue about the real reason he had been struggling to maintain his duty schedule.

"As the Medical Officer, when one of the crew appears unable to perform their duties effectively, it's my duty to find out why. Besides, I'm worried about you."

"You should have asked. I could have you reprimanded for invasion of privacy," he said into a small towel.

Kara laughed aloud. "Like the Captain would agree to that. Besides, you know full well there are very few secrets among a small crew. Our relationship," she made air quotes, "is no exception."

"An occasional night together hardly constitutes a relationship," Auri said as he turned his back on Kara and exchanged his wet uniform for a dry one. "Besides, what does Chief Runyon have to say about our *relationship*? I've heard he has a special place in engineering for your . . . together time."

Standing with her chin square, Epps said, "He understands it's natural for the men to seek companionship with the only—"

"So we don't have a relationship, I'm just a diversion." Auri zipped his jumpsuit and faced Kara while adjusting the pips on his collar, amused at her look of dismay.

"I didn't say that."

"Sadly, or not, we'll have to discuss this another time," he said and left Kara standing in his quarters.

"Thank you for joining us Lieutenant Loreq." The Captain watched Auri cross the ship's bridge to his duty station and glanced at Lieutenant Epps as she entered three steps later.

"Sorry Captain. It won't happen again," Loreq said.

"Has Lieutenant Epps cleared you for duty? You look like hell," the Captain looked to his Medical Officer for confirmation. Epps nodded as she slid into the science station.

"Yes, sir. Just a bit of space sickness. I think I'm past the worst of it," Loreq said.

"I'm glad to hear it. Lieutenant Epps, what's our last mapping excursion?"

"There's a small galaxy about two days beyond Beacon L10-7—"

"Excuse me, Captain Chad, Lieutenant Epps, but . . ." Auri's voice quavered. Terrified the Captain would decide not to respond, but also fearful of exposing his true nature, he paused to calm himself before he continued. "I was examining my long-distance scan logs last night and there's something important you should see."

Auri fought to control his trembling as the Captain and Epps gathered behind. How could he make them understand the criticality of this mission without exposing his symbiotic relationship with the Zazrachny? As a Connegant, he'd learned, the hard way, to not expose his symbiotic relationship. His fingers tip-toed over the communications touchscreen, running through the index of his scans, going to the exact reference his Other, Leas, had given him. Auri located the unusually dense wave pattern she told him about, and smiled when he saw her voice for the first time. "Here, listen."

"What's this? How is space noise important?" the Captain asked.

"I thought it was space noise as well because it's so dense, but the more I thought about it . . ."

"It looks like just one solid blast. It's got to be noise." Lieutenant Epps leaned closer to examine the display.

"Let me slow it way down." Auri adjusted the speed.

The Captain tipped his head toward the speaker. "Humming?"

"Here let me . . ." Auri made a few more adjustments, his heart beat fast when the computer gave voice to Leas's thoughts. A soft whispering voice, like a mother soothing her child, spoke. "We Zazrachny . . . beg assistance. We are in danger. Our galaxy is being consumed. We cannot resist—"

The Captain's hand shot in and tapped pause, and then laughed. "I'm glad your back to yourself, Loreq, and I'm amused by your ingenuity to come up with an inventive prank, but we're all ready to fill our quota and return to Station."

Auri turned to the captain. He felt his eyes burn with tears as his eyebrows rose and the corners of his mouth turned down. "Captain? This is no prank. Why would you—?"

"The Zazrachny are a myth." The Captain turned away. "I know it's been a long mission, Loreq."

Auri stood, nearly knocking over Epps. "Captain! I demand you not ignore this message. It's a distress call and we are bound by intergalactic law to respond."

The Captain turned slowly with his eyebrows raised and spoke deliberately. "I am *well* aware of intergalactic law and *nothing* requires me to respond to a prank."

"Captain, I guarantee the message is authentic and—"

Epps reached past Loreq, made a few more adjustments and the message continued. ". . . the pull of the black hole much longer. It is stripping our galaxy of planets. The planet we call Zazra holds the Zazrac Arc, which is the spark of the Zazrachny species. Without it, we will die . . . as will all those of other species who have accepted our symbiotic presence. I have imbedded the coordinates in this message. Please help."

Epps tapped the communications panel. "Captain, I don't believe this is one of Loreq's pranks."

"So now he's got you believing in an all-powerful, altruistic species with no desire to conquer the universe? As if any species like that could ever exist," Captain Chad said to Epps and then turned back to Loreq with a wide-eyed questioning expression. "If this was *real*, why didn't you mention it yesterday? Hmmm?" The Captain paused before sitting in his chair.

"Because I didn't know what to—"

Chad flopped back in his chair. "Because it took time to set your little rouse, probably half the night. I'm amused, now—"

Auri took a step forward. "Captain! You have the coordinates, verify them. Use long range scanners—"

"Oh yes, long range scanners, and what hilarious message will they show? Loreq, we're all tired and appreciate your attempt to lift our spirits, the tears are a nice touch by the way—"

Auri snapped to attention. "Captain, if you don't believe me, relieve me of my post."

With a shake of his head, Chad said, "Fine, I'll bite. Lieutenant Epps, get the coordinates and run them through the computer. Let's make Loreq feel better by going along with his little prank. In the meantime, Ensign Marcs, lay in a course for the L10-7 Atlas Beacon so we can fill our mapping quota and get Loreq back to his padded cell." Leaning back in his chair with his mouth twisted to one side, the Captain crossed his legs and drummed softly on the arm of his chair as he waited.

Epps gave Auri a worried look and whispered, "I hope you haven't gone too far," and then, "Aye, Captain. Lieutenant Loreq, please send the coordinates to Science."

A minute later the science panel chirped and Epps announced, "Captain, I've verified Lieutenant Loreq's coordinates and they take us approximately forty-eight hours past the last charted galaxy in the opposite direction of Prime."

The Captain leaned forward on his elbow, staring at Loreq who stood, with a pinched face. "No amusing message?"

"No, sir."

"So what do sensors say is there?"

"It appears to be a small terrestrial planet. Sensor readings may be distorted at this distance. However, if the computer extrapolation is correct, it appears the planet is being slowly dragged out of orbit, away from its sun."

"How is that possible? Widen the scan," the Captain said.

Epps studied her screen and then made several adjustments. "That's strange . . ."

"What?" the Captain said.

"Another minute, sir," she said without looking up. Two minutes later, Epps spoke over her shoulder to the Captain and then glanced at Loreq. "I've never seen anything like this. I'm not sure how it's even possible. Here's a computer generated model of the data, on the main screen, sir."

A model of a galaxy with five planets and a small sun appeared, but instead of a wide elliptical galaxy, the planet orbits were elongating away from the nearest sun in a corkscrew pattern along the z-axis.

The Captain stood, mouth agape, studying the screen. "How is that possible?"

Auri started to speak, but felt dizzy and dropped into his chair. His vision faded like it did when Leas connected with him; he heard her whispering voice coming from his own mouth. "Our combined efforts are failing. The black hole we have named Charybdis, from your Greek Mythos, is slowly consuming our galaxy. It has taken our collective consciousness to counterbalance its pull."

Watching through Leas's consciousness, Auri saw the Captain snap his fingers at Lieutenant Epps and point at him. The Captain listened to Leas and slowly approached his Communications Officer. "As our message said, when our strength fails, our Zazrac Arc, the spark of our species, will cease to exist. We regret our passing, but fear for our Connegants. They will perish when we do."

Leas turned to look at the Science Officer raising and lowering her scanner. "Yes, Kara, Aurealis Loreq is a Connegant. We do not lightly reveal our true nature, but there is no time for any other way."

The Captain pointed at the scanner.

Lieutenant Epps nodded. "The readings are consistent with Aur . . . Lieutenant Loreq's and a high-energy being co-existing. This isn't one of Loreq's pranks. From what little I know of them, he *appears* to be a Connegant."

"How could you not have known this?" Captain Chad asked Epps and then turned back to Loreq. "How do we know we can trust you?"

"The Zazrachny are an empathic race that serve only peaceful ends. We have never intentionally brought harm upon another. Our purpose for existing is to help others," Leas said.

"But yet you invade the body of my Communications Officer? That's unquestionably not peaceful."

"Aurealis is my matched form, my willing vehicle to fulfill our purpose, my symbiont. He assists me with those things that must be done. We were united in a ceremony over 150 of your Earth years ago."

"I demand to talk to Lieutenant Loreq." Captain Chad stepped close to Auri.

Auri felt Leas shift so he could regain his sight. "I'm still me, Captain Chad."

"Explain yourself. I've read your records and you're not 150 years old."

"That's a long story, I promise to tell you when there is more time. I assure you, I am the person you have counted on for the last five years, only a little more. The Zazrachny are responsible for many good things across the known and unknown Universe." He raised his hand, palm up, to the main view screen and a planet that could have been a miniature earth filled the screen. "You are looking at the planet Zazra and when it and the Zazrac Arc are pulled into the black hole, the Universe will be much poorer."

"Will you die?"

"Yes."

"So, if they are so all powerful, why can't they stop this? Why can't they just," the Captain flapped his arms and hands in the air, "blip this Arc to some other planet that's not in danger?"

"They do indeed have great power, enough to have kept their galaxy from sliding into oblivion for nearly two weeks now, but they are an incorporeal species without us, their Connegants. They can alter gravitational pull, but not directly affect solid matter."

"If they are so powerful then why didn't they stop the neutron star from collapsing?"

"They aren't clairvoyant."

Captain Chad huffed at the response and returned to his chair, turning it to face his Communications Officer.

"Does their plight have anything to do with your recent malaise?" Epps asked and stepped forward to scan Auri again.

Auri nodded once with an apologetic smile. "They diminished their connections with their Connegants to focus on saving their home world. They regret the discomfort they have caused."

"So, what do they want us to do? We're powerless humans . . . well most of us," the Captain said extending a hand to Loreq. "How are we supposed to stop a black hole?"

"I *am* mortal, sir, and I will die if we don't help. They are not asking us to stop the black hole, they are asking us to rescue their Arc," Auri said.

"Simple, right?" Captain Chad waved his hand to mimic flying. "We just fly right into a collapsing galaxy, grab this Arc thing that we've never seen before and fly away like we're floating down the Milky Way on a sight-seeing tour. And how long do we have to accomplish this, *if* I choose to endanger my ship and crew to help?"

Auri dipped his head and Leas said, "We are not prescient, Captain. By our estimation, there is no more than seventy-two hours until Zazra falls prey to the gravitational pull, and no rescue will be possible. The galaxy has already lost two planets."

Captain Chad looked at Ensign Marcs. "And it'll take us approximately forty-eight hours to accomplish this?"

"No, sir. It will take longer." Ensign Marcs said. "It will take forty-eight hours to arrive outside the galaxy where we must decelerate far enough out so that our own speed doesn't inadvertently slide us into the black hole's gravity well. I calculate the safest approach to be from the far side of their sun, where we'll encounter the least amount of pull. Our best chance to transfer onto Zazra to retrieve the Arc, lies in waiting until it's at its closest to their sun, which based on my liberal estimation of gravitational slippage and—"

"Just tell me how long, Ensign," the Captain said.

"Sixty-eight hours, sir, to arrive in position to begin the retrieval," Marcs said and then looked at Auri for confirmation.

"Your assessment is accurate, as we understand it," Leas said.

Captain Chad wiped his hand over his mouth as he looked between the main view screen and his Communications Officer, and then shook his head. "This is ludicrous. We've got a four-hour window to retrieve this Arc and leave the galaxy before we get sucked in along with everything else?"

"The Zazrac Arc is quite identifiable. Aurealis has already agreed to attempt the retrieval," Leas said.

"But he needs us to get him there and while he is apparently ready to die for you, I'm not."

Auri kept his head down as Leas spoke. "Does this mean you will not help us?"

"No Captain in his right mind would risk his ship and crew in a scenario that has so little chance of succeeding," he said, perched his fists on his hips, and turned toward Marcs and Epps.

"We understand your position, Captain Chad, and thank you for your consideration," Leas said.

Auri raised his head. "Captain, I respectfully request you accept my resignation and permit me use of the shuttle."

Epps stepped forward. "What do you think you're going to do, commit suicide? Captain, we can't let him."

"It is not suicide to meet one's inevitable death, in an honorable manner," Auri said.

The Captain slipped his hands behind his back. "Lieutenant Loreq, I will *not* accept your resignation and you will remain at your post. While there seems little chance for success, I'm not the kind of man to stand by and do nothing while others are in peril. We will attempt to retrieve this Zazrac Arc. But, I refuse to exceed reasonable operating parameters to do so. Is that clear?"

Loreq nodded to the Captain. "Thank you, sir. We can ask for nothing more."

Lieutenant Epps lowered her cup of chamomile and looked up from her e-reader when the door com chimed. "Kara? It's Auri. Can I come in? I need to speak with you."

Kara moved to meet him at the entry. They stood face to face when the door slid into the wall. "Now I understand why you never considered we had a relationship. You could have told me, you know."

"May I come in? I'd rather not have this discussion in the passageway."

"Afraid we'll be overheard? Oh, I guess we'll be overheard in here anyway with that . . . Other in you, huh?"

Auri smiled. "You're jealous!"

"I am not," Kara said as she walked back to the table and her tea.

Auri entered and pressed the lock on the door before sitting across from Kara.

"You couldn't even admit we had a relationship this morning, and now that you're going to die, you expect me to let you have one last parting romp?"

"No, I'm not asking that."

"Can she, make you feel like I do?"

"That's not a fair question. Being Connegant has little to do with sexuality. Our connections are more cerebral."

Kara smiled. "Exactly where all the pleasure centers are located, right?"

Auri returned her smile. "Well, at least that's where they're processed . . ."

"So, if we're not going to have one last romp in the sack, what are you here for?"

"I need to ask you a very big favor."

"I've already done almost everything for you. What's left?"

"Leas has told me more about the Zazrac Arc. I cannot retrieve the Arc by myself. It takes two corporeal beings to enter the . . . Tzakran . . . I guess Temple would be the closest translation."

Kara lifted her tea to her lips, paused and then sipped before asking, "Why me?"

"Leas told me to pick the person I trusted most," Auri said with a smile and then looked down at his folded hands to hide the flush he felt rising on his cheeks.

"So we do have a relationship," she said and smiled as she put her teacup down.

Auri nodded without looking up.

Kara lowered her head close to the table to be able to look up into Auri's face. "Am I talking with Auri or Leas?"

Auri raised his head, his mouth open and his eyebrows high. "Oh, no, the connection is not constant, I mean, it is, but . . . we give each other privacy. It's like having an unbreakable string connecting us. All we need do is tug to get the attention of the other. It takes getting used to, even though we share all the emotions eventually . . ."

"So, if they are non-corporeal, how do they . . .?"

"I . . . I don't think it's appropriate to discuss my symbiont this way."

"But you are asking me to risk my life for them."

"Yes, there is a risk, but hopefully, with the Captain's good judgement and Marcs's skill at the tiller, we'll be able to rescue the Zazrac Arc."

"Which will be like me saving you," Kara said.

Auri felt his cheeks warm again. "Yes, in a way you will be saving me. So are you willing to go?" he said and reached out to enclose her hands around her teacup as he looked into her blue eyes.

Kara licked and then bit her lower lip. "How can I say no to you?"

Twelve hours later, Lieutenants Loreq and Epps stood outside the shuttle craft, *Rover*, receiving instructions from Captain Chad. "You have two hours to retrieve the Zazrac Arc. After that, I'll move the *Empathy* to a higher orbit and if you can make it off, we'll be there to help, if we can. I can't risk my ship and the rest of her crew more than this. Epps, are you sure you want to do this? I know you two have a thing, but is it worth dying for?"

Epps nodded and smiled at Loreq. "We're not planning on dying, sir."

Loreq smiled and turned to enter the shuttle, but suddenly woofed like he'd been punched in the gut and grabbed for the doorway. As Epps and Chad reached for him, the ship shuddered violently.

Marcs' voice sounded on the ship's intercom. "Captain, we've slipped into *Charybdis'* gravity well; it appears larger than we thought.

"Move us to a higher orbit," Captain Chad called.

Loreq gasped and stood, tears running down his cheeks. "We have to go. The Zazrachny are losing control as they lose lives. The assembly protecting the fifth planet . . . went with it into the black hole."

"She's real sluggish, Sir," Marcs's voice vibrated with the ship.

"Ensign Runyon, we need more power," Captain Chad called.

"Working on it, Captain."

And then Chad turned to Loreq. "I can't let you go."

Auri lowered his head; and then Leas spoke as his head rose. "We apologize for this unexpected complication, Captain, but if the Arc is not retrieved, your ship will be overwhelmed by the gravitational pull much sooner than expected. As Zazrachny lives are consumed by Charybdis, those remaining assume more burden and are weakening. You are already feeling this."

"How will retrieving the Arc help us?"

"If we can rescue the Arc, those protecting the remaining planets will have a focus outside of the gravitational pull. They may be able anchor to it and transfer their focus away at the last minute, before the planet they are protecting is lost. Without that anchor, we will lose more. We estimate you have a little more than an hour before your ship will not be able to escape."

"Remind me to have words with you if we get out of this. Now go, and make it quick," Captain Chad said flinging his hands at the shuttle bay door before leaving the bay.

Auri looked over at Kara, his hand hovering over the launch button. "Ready?"

"It's a little late to ask," she said putting her head against the seat back.

When the shuttle catapulted into space, they suddenly felt weightless.

"What's going on?" Kara asked, her eyes wide.

"Leas and two others have refocused their energy on protecting us. We're smaller, so will get less pull, but we also have less power to escape. Let's get this done."

It took no more than five minutes for the shuttle to break through the cloud cover. Auri and Kara gazed out the windows. The surface of Zazra was not unlike the animated pictures of Earth Prime that spanned the walls of the exercise areas back on Station. Auri hadn't agreed with the psychobabble that said humans thrived better in Earth like surroundings; seeing a similar landscape below with his own eyes instantly changed his mind. Tufts of green trees dotted wide spans of low green plains and then changed places, leaving low green oases among miles of solid tree canopy. The shuttle gently turned and circled one of these oases, hung like a pendant at the base of an isolated rock outcropping that rose several hundred feet and was veiled with a wispy waterfall.

"Is this the their Tzakran?" Kara asked as she leaned forward to see where they were landing.

"These are the coordinates that Leas gave us. It must be nearby," Auri said. As the shuttle settled and the engine shut down, they felt the ground shudder.

Kara froze. "Tell me that was an earthquake and not a reaction from some giant living creature we landed on."

"Leas says it was an earthquake and we need to hurry. Things are deteriorating faster than expected."

Kara tapped the touchscreen in front of her several times and nodded when it chirped. "We don't have to worry about breathers. Atmosphere is breathable, in fact, much better than the environmentally controlled air we're used to."

Emerging from the shuttle, Auri said, "This would have made a nice vacation spot."

"Which way?" Kara peered out from behind him.

"Toward the falls." Auri pointed.

The two trotted for nearly ten minutes through waist high weeds that were dotted with brightly colored flowers bobbing in the gray light. They paused several times when the ground trembled, watching the small mountain for falling rocks. As they came alongside the falls, they stood transfixed by the crystal clear lake that appeared to be several meters deep.

Kara shouted over the roar of the falling water and pointed to the opposite side of the lake. "Shouldn't there be a river that carries the water away?"

Auri leaned toward her and shouted, "Leas says it drains from the bottom of the lake."

"So where's the Tzakran?"

"We're in it," Auri shouted. "This whole area is it."

"So then where is the Arc?" Kara shouted looking around.

"Behind the waterfall. Follow me."

"Are you sure she's not trying to drown us?"

Mist quickly soaked their clothes and coated their hair with diamond-like droplets of water as they held tight to each other and worked their way across moss covered boulders. They hesitated in front of a five-foot high by two-foot wide opening, and then inched their way into the darkness.

Kara's voice sounded loud away from the roar of the water, that muted as soon as they entered the cave. "How are we supposed to find anything in the dark?"

"There's a pale shaft of light ahead," Auri said more softly. Arriving at what appeared to be a dead-end, a shaft of light shone through a small hole in the rock.

"Great, how are we supposed to get through there?" Kara asked.

Auri sliced through the beam with his hand and a rumbling, like another quake, filled the cave. Kara cringed, like she was about to be crushed, until Auri tugged her hand and pointed into a small chamber where the wall had been. Hand in hand, the two stepped into the chamber, mouths agape in awe.

A pale green glow coated the walls and reflected off a mirror smooth floor. Kara released Auri's hand and went to examine the walls more closely. Auri watched from the middle of the chamber as she breathed gently on a section of the wall and it turned to a soft orange cream that slowly faded back to green as she pulled away. "I think it's a species of lichen. I wish we had more time. I've never seen anything like this. Do you think they'd mind if I took a sample?"

"Kara, we don't have time. The Zazrachny are losing their grip on the galaxy. Here, this is why we are here." Auri said, standing next to a cylindrical pedestal in the center of the chamber. An obsidian colored object, shaped like two square pyramids joined at their bases making a double pointed diamond. The same glowing lichen covering the walls illuminated the top of pedestal.

"This is the Zazrac Arc?" Kara leaned close to examine it and the lichen under the stone turned blue. "Hey, that's different. Maybe I can—"

"Please stand-up. There's no time for samples. We must lift the Arc together."

"Okay, maybe after this I can snag a few samples on our way out. Is it heavy? What do I do?"

Auri moved to the end of the Arc where the point laid on the lichen and directed Kara to the end where the opposite pyramid pointed toward her. "Let me position my hands first and then you do the same." Auri carefully placed his hands on the smooth sides of the pyramid. He smiled when his end of the pyramid grew clear and emitted a light from within. A moment later the chamber trembled and the lichen all turned a deep orange red.

"Whoa." Kara stepped back. "Is that supposed to happen?"

"Yes, the Arc is responding to my connection with Leas. The lichen is just responding to the quake. It's your turn. Just cup the sides with your hands. It won't hurt you."

"Are you sure?"

"You won't feel a thing."

Kara placed her hands wide around the stone and slowly drew them close. The moment her skin touched the cool obsidian, a shaft of blinding light shot from the tip of the pyramid toward her chest and her body flew backward, slamming into the lichen covered wall with a sickening thud, before slidding onto the smooth floor.

Auri left the empty pedestal and rushed to find Kara's pulse. He sighed with relief when he found it, scooped her into his arms, and left the cavern. He whispered to the unconscious woman as he walked. "I'm sorry I didn't tell you. Leas said it was better this way."

The GFSS Empathy rattled against the strain of the gravitational pull. Captain Chad held tightly to his chair, his voice shaking as he gave Ensign Marcs a command. "Set course for the L10-7 Atlas Beacon and once the shuttle is on board, get us out of here with everything Runyon can give you."

"Aye, Captain."

"Course laid in Captain, but we're losing ground."

"Boost power, Ensign." The Captain pressed the intercom on his chair panel. "Loreq, get that shuttle aboard or we're taking a short trip into oblivion!"

"Landing now, sir. Shuttle bay secure."

"Ensign, engage!"

The ship rattled violently as the engine whined.

"Captain, we're not making any progress," Ensign Marcs shouted.

"Runyon, we need more power."

"I've connected the last of the reserve and added impulse since if we don't make it out, we won't be needing it. You've got it all," Runyon said.

"Ensign, give it everything. Loreq, what happened to your friends shielding us from the gravitational pull of Charybdis?"

The ship suddenly lurched forward and the engine whine rose to a scream before it dropped to a steady low hum.

"Runyon, status?"

"She held together, sir. Pulling back reserves and impulse."

"Loreq, Epps report."

"We're in sick bay, Captain," Loreq said.

"On my way."

"What the hell happened?" the Captain said as he entered sick bay. "Did you get the Arc?"

Auri stood beside a diagnostic bed, holding Epps's hand. "She hit her head pretty hard, but I think she'll be fine."

"How did that happen?" the Captain said looking at the bed's diagnostic readout.

"Apparently the transfer was more powerful than anyone expected," Loreq said.

"What transfer?"

Loreq lifted their clasped hands to reveal a black pyramid tattooed into her palm and the same in his. "We got the arc."

"What the hell? No one said anything about Epps being possessed."

"She's not, sir."

"Then explain why she's unconscious and why the display shows two heartbeats?"

"She's pregnant," Auri said.

The Captain looked at Auri with his mouth agape. "Did you know this before . . .?"

He paused before nodding his head once. "Leas told me last night."

"You son of a bitch! And you let her put herself in danger anyway? Does she know? So she's now a slave to these . . . these . . .?"

"Symbionts, sir, and she's not a slave."

"A nice word for possession, if you ask me. Did she agree to this or did you and your *symbiont* use your mystical powers to persuade her?"

"She's not a symbiont, sir, and she did agree to help. And yes, she was aware of the danger, just not that she is pregnant."

"Captain, why are you shouting?" Epps asked. "I'm fine. My head hurts a little, but I'm fine," she said sitting up.

The Captain turned to Epps. "Are you sure? Do you remember what happened? Do you feel any different?"

"I remember lifting the Arc with Auri . . ." she looked over at him and squeezed his hand, "and then being engulfed in white light. An earthquake must have hit at the same time, because the next thing I remember is looking up from the floor at the beautiful lichen, it had turned from its mesmerizing green to a panicked deep orange-red. I remember feeling relieved when the ship broke free of the black hole."

"Do you hear yourself?" the Captain asked. "Loreq's aliens have possessed you!"

Auri lowered his head. "Captain, please allow me to explain before the weak vein in your frontal lobe bursts," Leas said calmly.

"Trying to scare me into going along with your plan isn't going to work."

"Have you had increasing headaches?" Leas asked. "If you don't believe me, allow Kara to scan you."

"No, I'll scan myself. Then I'll know you haven't influenced it," the Captain grabbed a scanner from its charger and scanned his head and then down his body. He leaned against the second bed as he read the results and slowly lowered the scanner. "Okay, talk."

"Kara is not a symbiont; she is the keeper of the Arc."

"How is that different?"

"She has not accepted one of the Zazrachny to meld with her. She simply holds the focus or the spark of our species."

"Okay, how does she get rid of this . . . this . . . spark thing?"

"Give birth," Leas said, as Auri turned to Kara.

"And how long is that?" the Captain asked.

"The usual human gestation period of nine months," Leas said looking into Kara's eyes.

Kara turned her head to the Captain. "I don't believe I'm in any danger, sir. Actually, I feel better than new and my head has even stopped hurting. I don't mind carrying the spark."

Leas continued. "You are safe and there will be plenty of time, once we escape our galaxy to have this discussion. However, we are compelled to make one more request."

"I think we've done our part for your species. You can let us know where you want to drop this Arc off and we'll be on our way."

Auri smiled. "Were it that simple, Captain," Leas said. "While we have rescued the Arc, we request you assist us with one more task. There is still a chance for this galaxy, but it will take our combined efforts."

The Captain threw his hands in the air and let them fall. "*We* don't have the ability to do anything about a black hole and if *you* did, we wouldn't be here, so what could we possibly do to rescue your galaxy?"

Leas' voice sounded crisp as she explained. "In all the centuries since the theory was first put forth, I don't believe any species has attempted to diminish a black hole. But it is theoretically possible. While it will not completely disappear in your lifetime, we may see the day when we can return to our planet. With your help."

The Captain tossed his head back and laughed. "*This* is Auri speaking and pulling one of his infamous pranks. I'm sure of it this time."

"Captain Chad, I *am* Leas of the Zazrachny, not your Communications Officer. Are you unaware of Hawking Radiation and how it can be used to measure the demise of a black hole?"

"I am an astral cartographer and leave the physics to greater minds than mine."

"Captain," Epps said, "I am familiar with these theories."

"Theories are just that, and we've already done everything we said we'd do. I'm not listening to any more nonsense."

"Captain, Ensign Marcs here. It appears we are not clear of the black hole gravity well. It is greatly diminished, but still keeping us from completely escaping this system. While we are behind the sun, it is acting like a shield. If we try to leave, we will be vulnerable again."

"As I was about to say, Captain," Leas continued in a calm voice. "We must further weaken *Charybdis* to escape completely."

"So what are we going to do, blow it up?"

Epps raised her finger and began speaking before Leas. "Any form of regular explosion would do nothing but provide the black hole massive energy, essentially food. However, if we could taint its food, by creating particle pairs on the apparent horizon, the negative particles would be sucked in, freeing the positive particles and essentially drowning Charybdis."

"You are correct," Leas said. "It would take several more centuries for it to completely evaporate, but the Zazrachny galaxy might have a chance to survive."

"All right, now I know both of you are in on this one."

"What more can we say to convince you, Captain Chad?" Leas's voice rose slightly from its sonorous timber.

The Captain ran his hands through his hair and paced the med bay until he finally stopped in front of Epps. "I'm not sure who to trust. Loreq isn't who we thought he was, and I'm sorry to say, now I'm not sure about you. Runyon and Marcs don't have the specialty we need to make informed decisions. So it comes back to—you're all I've got."

"I'm with you Captain. I'm still me and loyal to the ship and crew."

"Okay, I know Loreq is willing to die for the Zazrachny, but are you willing to die for them?"

Epps looked between Loreq and the Captain. "I'm willing do everything possible to protect a species who has given so much of themselves."

"But would you die to save them?"

Epps looked at Loreq. "Yes, I would die trying to save them."

Captain Chad crossed his arms. "Now would you let your child die to save them?"

Epps laughed. "Now who is being a prankster?" Her smile disappeared when the Captain didn't smile, only raised his eyebrows at her. "Are you saying I'm . . .?"

"Pregnant," Leas said and nodded once. "Your child now carries the spark of our species. You and Loreq are the Arc. You hold our lives in your bodies."

Epps pulled her hand away from Loreq's and examined her palm. She turned and looked at the diagnostic readout that confirmed she was approximately six weeks pregnant and then looked back at the Captain. "It appears it is the Zazrachny who are putting their lives in *our* hands. If they can trust us enough to do that, don't you think we can find it in ourselves to trust them?"

Captain Chad sighed noisily. "Okay, then tell me what we have to do, and this time don't leave out any of the details."

Two hours later, the crew gathered on the GFSS *Empathy's* bridge. "Ladies, gentlemen, and . . . symbionts. Our plan is set. The cost of failure is higher for some of us, but to do nothing, costs all of us. If things go wrong, I've set an explosive drone that will escape *Charybdis* with all the data we've collected to date, including information on the Zazrachny. It has been a pleasure serving with you and I hope to continue to do so after this. God speed. Stations, everyone."

"Lieutenant Loreq, have you rigged the gravitational stress detonator?"

"Aye, Captain."

"Ensign Runyon, make ready to eject the engine core on a trajectory that will take it toward *Charybdis*."

"Ready on your mark, Captain."

"Leas?" The Captain waited for Loreq to bow his head and then raise it.

"I am here, Captain Chad."

"Are your . . . Others prepared to convert the particle explosions to negative matter at the apparent horizon?"

"We have selected half our Others to perform the task needed to affect *Charybdis*."

"Half of your species?" Epps rose from the science station. "Are so many needed? And what about their symbionts?"

Leas turned to Epps. "It is better that half of us survive and ensure the spark lives. We are beings of energy. Those that are not taken by the black hole will return to the spark and find life again. We will mourn their symbionts when their bodies fail."

"Will you be joining them?" Epps asked and then pressed her lips together.

"The Others have chosen me to stay with Auri and you, Kara. I am dedicated to protecting you, who are the Arc, and finding our *spark*, that lives within your child, a new home."

Kara blushed as she smiled and took Auri's hand between hers. "I can live with that."

The Captain called, "Ensign Marcs, on my mark, 3 . . . 2 . . . 1 . . . launch."

S. M. Kraftchack
Whether voyaging the universe, or journeying in a fantasy world of my own making, I'm passionate about discovering all kinds of characters and relentlessly tracing their heartfelt stories so I can relate them to you. I love sunrise on the beach, sunset in the mountains and portraying Elizabeth Tudor. I have one dog who thinks she's a footrest, another who catches a Frisbee, and a cat who rents me my desk for open-window-time. I have three awesome daughters and a husband who is my best friend, my harshest critic, and my most fervent supporter. www.smkraftchak.com

A desperate group of people are attempting to escape an enemy that has already destroyed most of human civilization in the Milky Way. What they find along the way creates more questions —and moral dilemmas—than answers.

CLOUD MARATHON

Gustavo Bondoni

"I can't believe it. We made it."

Commander Mere gave him a hard look. "Cyran, you know as well as I do that this means nothing. It's just a way-station."

"Even so, I wasn't expecting to get this far."

Her silence was agreement enough. Images of the launch—desperate, uncoordinated, but most of all final—were fresh in his mind. He only hoped that they could eventually forgive themselves for leaving nearly everyone behind to cope as they could, or to kill themselves before being taken. There were three hundred thousand people on the *Kamina*, and countless billions who had been abandoned.

The only true comfort available was that the lucky ones had been dead for millions of years. The unlucky . . . well, it was better not to think of them.

Mere broke the silence. "Let's go see if any of the engineers survived the trip. We'll probably need them to see what this is—and to see if we can detect pursuit."

"Pursuit? Do you really think they'll follow us?"

"Why not? What makes you think they will be satisfied with just one galaxy? And what makes you think we won't find them waiting for us when we get there?"

"Impossible!"

"We've been asleep for three million years of non-relativistic time. The enemy has been awake, running their processors, doing research. For all we know, they can teleport between galaxies, or take shortcuts through the branes."

"But the Lorentz limit . . ." Cyran began, but knew it was a useless argument.

"Was valid when we left. Science can do a lot in three million years."

He struggled for a stronger argument. "If they could simply teleport around the universe, or bend it to whatever shape they wanted, we would never have woken up. Or if we did, we wouldn't have enjoyed it."

"Who says we're enjoying it? Come on. The engineering team is probably being reanimated already."

Slowdown, unlike freezing, did no harm to the body. It simply took everything to a near stop—making a few hundred years of ship time seem, to the body, like a few seconds. The engineering team would be ready for them, expecting questions, and wanting answers to their own.

"So, what does it look like?" Brannon inquired when they walked into the reanimation room.

"Whatever it is, it's cold." Mere had never gotten along all that well with the leader of the matter processing team.

"But it's there."

"Yes. We wouldn't have woken you up just to die of boredom in the middle of nowhere."

He nodded, acknowledging the fact that his question had been stupid. "Fair enough." Brannon switched his attention to Cyran. "Do we have any idea what it might be?"

"Nothing. We're not close enough for a visual, and its temperature is just a few tenths above absolute zero, all the way through We can barely make out the outline. Two kilometers across and irregular."

"How the hell did they manage to find it? I didn't even know we had instruments that could see that far."

"I don't know. And they're all dead now."

The engineer nodded curtly. "We'll try to make their sacrifice worth something. Lead the way."

The *Kamina* was, even by the colossal standards of interstellar ships, a behemoth, but it hadn't been designed to have mobile, active humans inside in any great numbers. It had been built to load as many people as possible into slowdown chambers—most of which, due to the sudden nature of the final enemy push, were empty—and keep them there. It also boasted the largest, most powerful propulsion system ever devised by humanity. It had been enough to get them out of the Milky Way, and to avoid capture.

So far.

The engineers lost no time in plugging themselves into the sensor array. Cyran knew that they would have preferred to travel as data in the mainframe, but that idea had been overruled from the outset: humanity was struggling for its survival, and that meant that only genetically original people had been accepted for the escape. Most of the engineers had needed to be assigned new, recently printed bodies.

Countless other escape missions, flying in every direction had consisted of memory storage devices and small nanofactories, but they wouldn't arrive anywhere for tens of millions of years. It was very likely that the only extant incorporated humans in the galaxy were aboard the *Kamina*. And whether they lived or died depended on what the engineers were able to dig out of the mass in front of them.

Brannon suddenly snapped back into the real world. "Crap," he said. "I certainly wasn't expecting that, to say the least."

"What? Don't tell me there's not enough mass to get us to the Cloud," Mere said. "It would be just our luck. The last of humanity, dead in the middle of nowhere."

"Relax," Brannon replied. "That isn't it." He certainly seemed to be in no hurry to ease her tension. He gave her a hard look that spoke volumes before continuing. "The mass in front of us isn't what we expected, but there's enough mass to get us to the Large Megellanic Cloud, or even to a couple of other galaxies, if you want to take the time to assimilate that much material into the holding fields." He grinned. "Hell, there's even enough mass to stop at the end."

"Funny," Mere replied, unsmiling. "Then what's wrong?"

"Nothing. Except that the mass over there is a starship. Ugly as hell, but definitely a ship."

Cyran sealed the suit, waiting impatiently as the display screen on the inside of his helmet cycled through system and redundancy checks. Everything was fine, as it always was. He'd been out hundreds of times, and never, not once, had the suit diagnostics found anything out of whack.

Brannon was already outside, setting up the tether cannon, and the three soldiers who'd been assigned to accompany him were standing alongside. He'd had to stop and argue with Mere, who'd wanted to come. In the end, she'd accepted the fact that she was the commander and had to stay aboard. But she hadn't accepted it gracefully.

The soldiers bantered, showing each other how tough they were, how unconcerned about having been unexpectedly reanimated and told to mount an exploratory raid into a starship of unknown origin, which was drifting in space between galaxies. They seemed equally nonchalant about everything being close enough to absolute zero that the difference barely showed up on their instruments.

Cyran wondered if they believed it, or if it really was all show. He was terrified, and knew everyone could tell. Not because of the mission, although it was a hell of a time to run into an unknown alien species. He was scared of what might be coming up behind them at any moment, and kept looking back in the direction they had come. It was ridiculous, of course. Long before anything would be visible to the naked eye, annihilation would have arrived. If they were lucky. If they were unlucky, the enemy would fire only enough ordnance to incapacitate the ship, and come collect them in their own sweet time. Cyran knew he'd open his suit and freeze before allowing them to get him. Or at least that was the plan—there were many, many horror stories about people who hadn't had the guts to end it when the time came.

The tether seemed taut and working to Brannon's satisfaction by the time they got out to him. One of the troops carefully checked his weapons and hooked himself to the line. Saving on booster fuel, one of his companions gave him a push, and he went, essentially frictionless, on his way.

A second troop followed as soon as the first had secured a handhold and a line on the alien starship. They would attempt to find a way in—or to blast an entry if they failed. It seemed like only a cursory attempt was made to try to find an opening before the soldiers began to unload their explosives. They molded directional charges on the hull in roughly the shape of a circle big enough to allow a single man to enter easily, and then moved off along the hull to safety. A small, bright light came from the charges, and the two troops went back to inspect their handiwork.

"We have an opening. Looks to be at least five meters deep. Do you want us to investigate, or do you want to come over?"

"What kind of risk do you calculate?" Brannon asked.

"Well, there's no movement, no atmosphere and the temperature is just barely above absolute zero. I'd say we'll be just as safe inside as outside—the conditions are just about the same."

Brannon looked over to Cyran, nodded once curtly, and replied: "All right, we're going over." He set off along the line.

Cyran followed as soon as the engineer reached the other ship. There was no danger in the procedure: as soon as the suit clamp's skin turned yellow, indicating that the material had sealed on the outer side, and that the wheels were engaged on the tether, he signaled to the soldier behind him to give him a shove. She complied without comment.

He was about halfway across when he made the mistake of looking around. There were stars in view, scattered here and there along the dark sky. The ship's floodlights dimmed them, but didn't quite shut them out.

And then it hit him. Those weren't stars he was looking at, but galaxies. He was infinitely far away from any meaningful habitable space, further than any other human had ever been. The tether was forgotten, the safety of the routine procedure ignored, and for those few seconds he floated alone in the vastness of forever, lost beyond any hope of recovery.

"Cyran, can you hear me?"

The voice in his ears brought him back to reality with a jerk. "Yes, I'm fine. Just looking at the stars for a bit. We've been out of commission for quite a while, you know." The rejoinder sounded weak, even to him, but it was all he could muster as he disengaged the suit's clamp from the tether and engaged it to the safety line the advance crew had rigged.

"Well, you sound like you were awake for the entire three million years."

Cyran attempted to ignore the sheer weight of that number and shrugged. "Don't worry about me."

The hole in the deck of the alien craft was wide enough for four people to enter abreast, but it was difficult to see what the lower reaches looked like, even with the light from one of the soldiers' suits illuminating it.

"There's a cross passage that got slightly blocked by the blast," the man said. "I'm going to open it up." The other four watched as he struggled with a dark sheet of what appeared to be metal. Finally, he came back on the line. "It's dark and a bit cramped, but other than that, it looks like a passageway on one of our ships. You can come down—the temperature is the same, nothing's moving, and there are no energy readings of any sort. This ship's about as dead as a ship can be."

They clambered down the gouge in the hull. Cyran found it interesting that, even though the soldiers insisted that it was safe, they also insisted on having two troops up front and one bringing up the rear in every movement.

They entered the passageway, which was precisely as described. Dark, cramped, and just slightly alien. In the extremely localized light from their suit beams, it was impossible to tell just what it was that gave things an alien tinge, but there was certainly something that would have made Cyran guess that is wasn't a human ship they were in.

It also didn't look like any of the alien ships he'd seen before their desperate escape, mainly museum pieces built by long-dead races that had had the misfortune to

116

encounter the enemy before humanity did. Those ships had always seemed truly alien, ripe with bulging organic shapes and gentle curves.

This one, on the other hand, was considerably more familiar. There were plenty of straight lines which seemed to him to denote a mind similar to that of humanity or at least a more utilitarian engineering process, perhaps the child of necessity as opposed to that of long years of development and refining. He knew that, in galactic history, many races had abandoned their aesthetic principles when necessity called. Anyone studying the *Kamina* would find the sheer utilitarianism completely at odds with the latter stages of human history, in which things such as comfort, color and even magnetic field alignment within ships to maximize passenger well-being were ubiquitous.

The *Kamina*, on the other hand, was uniformly gray, completely devoid of padding for the occupants, and no one really knew how the magnetic fields were aligned— probably randomly, whichever way the use of equipment dictated. In certain regards, a ship that stark and uncaring seemed the only possible tool to have brought humanity into the indifferent wastes of interstellar space.

Cyran walked on, bouncing lightly forward in the zero-gee passage, but missed a beat when he came to the intersection of two of the passages. He studied the corner for a second. "Brannon, have a look at this."

"What?"

"It's at a strange angle, slightly over square, do you see it?"

"Yeah, so?"

"It just hit me. That's why the ship looks alien to me."

"It looks alien because it's from another galaxy. No one has ever encountered anything like it."

"No. It looks pretty normal, except for one thing: there aren't any right angles. None. Look for yourself."

Brannon did. He checked a couple of panels, and even went back down the corridor they'd come in on. "Hmm. Interesting. If we didn't have to break this thing down to its component molecules just as soon as we're sure it's safe, I'd love to study this. How can you do any engineering at all without using right angles. It makes everything so much more complicated." He paused. "And most of all, why would you do it? What kind of mathematical system would make this more efficient than regular right-angle geometry—and unless I'm mistaken, they aren't basing their engineering on radial coordinates either."

Cyran didn't care. He just knew it didn't look right, didn't sit right with his mind, which seemed to be automatically correcting for right angles, so that he'd just miss a handhold, or miscalculate a step just enough to stumble slightly. He found himself wondering why they had even bothered to explore.

But there were some things that just had to be done. If they really didn't have a few hours to explore an artifact of the first extra-galactic civilization that humanity had encountered, they were dead anyway. And besides, they needed to make certain that the thing wouldn't blow up violently when they attempted to atomize it for fuel.

"This passage seems to lead towards the place where the sensors located higher concentrations of heavier metals," the soldier in the lead told them.

"All right," Brannon replied. "That's probably the propulsion system. It's located in the right place, at least, at one of the long ends of the ship. Let's move in that direction."

They did, encountering different passages as they advanced, some from the left, some from the right, a few intersecting above and below. Cyran wondered how it all worked under the gravity of acceleration. The thrust had to move along the centerline, which meant that all the unusual angles would make holding on for dear life an interesting challenge.

After a couple of wrong turns caused by the strange geometry of the interior, they came to a cavernous opening, whose depths were hidden well beyond the range of their suitlights. An exploratory expedition to either side and along the wall behind them—the lack of gravity made it easy to navigate in all three dimensions—established that the chamber was about three hundred meters wide and seventy tall.

"OK, let's go see what kind of engine we have in here," Brannon said.

They walked across the hangar-like expanse for twenty minutes before they came to a wall similar to the one they'd just left, but with no openings. Brannon checked the schematics. "Nothing but space on the other side of this one, judging by our position. We must have missed the engines in the dark. Let's split into two groups and walk along the walls. There must be some kind of exhaust ports or nozzles that open into space. On this side, we'd see some extremely large tubes."

They took an hour, but there were no tubes along the wall, and there was no evidence of anything that even remotely resembled machinery ranged along the floor of the chamber. By the time they finished checking the roof, their oxygen supply was getting close to critical, and they turned back.

Just as they were leaving the chamber, Cyran looked back and thought he saw a flash of light. It didn't surprise him in the least. He was certain there was something in there.

"What do you mean it has no engines?" Captain Mere, as always, seemed more curious than disturbed by the news. "How the hell did it get here, then?"

"I have no idea, but that's not the worst of it."

"Of course not. Tell me the rest."

"Well, it's hard to explain, but there's no way the mass of that ship can be as high as the original reading said it would be. We took samples of most of the surface materials and did some volume and density calculations, and with that big, empty space in there, we're still at about three percent of what the mass is supposed to be."

"Maybe the surface materials are just thin coverings?"

"We thought the same thing, and ran the simulations assuming depleted uranium structural materials. That would still only account for twenty-five percent of the mass that was detected when we launched. And I can guarantee that the ship isn't made of Uranium. Three percent is probably close to correct."

"Might they have jettisoned the star drive?"

"Not through that rear bulkhead they didn't. What we have here is what we get."

Mere thought for a few moments. She ran her hand through her dark hair and ignored Brannon's fidgeting until it grew too frantic. "I imagine there's more."

The engineer gave her a sour look. "Yeah, and the weirdest bit of all. Every single one of our gravitometers insists that all the mass is there, almost to the gram."

"Crap. Well, you're going to have to go back in. And you're going to take Timina with you."

"Timina? We'd have to use long-range transmissions to beam her in there. It's too risky at the kind of bandwidth she'd need to run."

"I'm going to download her into a body. Or rather Cyran is."

"Timina?" Cyran asked. "She'll go mental."

"I don't care. I need her, and I need her in that ship. If she goes nuts on us, I'll erase her backups until she agrees to play nice." She gave Cyran a steady look. "It might be a good idea to load her into a body we can handle easily. Try not to choose some kind of hulking Amazon."

"Whatever you say," Cyran replied. He wondered what could possibly be strange enough that the captain would risk alienating a scientist so important that she'd actually been allowed to come along in electronic form, while countless billions had been left behind to serve as food— or, shudder, much worse—for the enemy. More to the point, he also wondered how he was going to get her to cooperate.

"Are you completely stupid?" Timina shrieked at him. "Do you have any idea how hard it is to think in this meatbag?"

Cyran had printed her into a thin, pale woman's body, incapable of harming the much stronger physique he was wearing. There wasn't really any need for the finely proportioned features, the big brown eyes or the silky long hair, unless one counted the fact that, if he was going to get yelled at, at least it would be nice to have it done so by a woman who looked like the ones in his dreams. Plus, the only other woman he'd seen in three million years was the captain.

"Listen, we need your help."

"Well, you're not going to get it until you put me back inside, where I belong."

"You're still inside, we only copied you."

"Then scan these few minutes, put the memories in there and pulp this body."

Cyran didn't want to pulp the body, but he knew that even if he was successful, the thing would only be around for a couple of days.

Timina closed her eyes.

"Listen, I need you to think about this for a minute. We wouldn't have done it if we weren't desperate."

The physicist just ignored him, not moving a muscle, sitting perfectly still on the wheeled gurney where they'd woken her. Cyran talked and talked, but didn't manage to get a single reaction out of her.

Eventually he went to look for help, sealing the door behind him.

The Commander looked up with a smirk as he entered. "Gave up already? I thought you'd do a little better. At least you're in one piece—I was half expecting you to have gotten yourself clawed by now."

"Time is a bit tight, and she's locked herself into her shell."

"Typical. OK, tell her that we'll delete her backups if she won't cooperate."

His eyes widened. "You'd do that?"

Mere shrugged. "Probably not, but there's no need for her to know that. If she thinks she's the last version extant, and you tell her that she has the choice to cooperate and be restored to her cyberworld or be tossed out of an airlock, she'll play ball."

"There's probably a copy of her in every ship that made it out of the Milky Way. Sheer numbers mean that one of them has to survive."

"Probability isn't certainty, Cyran. She has to hedge."

He walked back, wondering how the hell he would tell her that. He also wondered how he'd been selected for this responsibility. There were millions more qualified than he was, but none had been near enough when the *Kamina* had launched. He'd been on duty, and others had simply been tossed into holds with no questions. Breeding stock—except in particular cases—had been deemed more important than qualifications. They'd figure it out, if they got to the Large Magellanic Cloud.

"I've been ordered to erase you from the ship's memory if you don't cooperate."

Not a twitch. The pretty girl in front of him—a somehow unfitting container for humanity's foremost physicist— didn't even twitch to show she'd heard him. Maybe she hadn't. "Did you hear me? We'll wipe you off the memory banks. You'll only exist in this body." Forgetting his orders, he took her by the shoulders and shook.

Nothing.

He sat heavily beside her, thinking furiously. But his thoughts betrayed him, turning inward, thinking of what his fate would be if the enemy caught them stranded out in the middle of the abyss. They sat, side by side, in silence, until Cyran really couldn't stand it any more.

"It's just that I'm so scared. We don't know where the Enemy is. For all we know, they might be right behind us, and we can't accelerate back up to speed, if they loaded more fuel." The mention of fuel reminded him of the even worse news. "And the item we were aiming for doesn't have all the mass we need to burn to get to the Magellanic Cloud—so we either need to find more matter with the limited ship scanners or go back."

"What? That's stupid."

Cyran jumped. He wasn't expecting a response from Timina, he was just letting his fears vent a bit. "Brannon has checked everything multiple times."

"Brannon couldn't find his ass with a 4-D locator. The mass readings were not only accurate to the milligram— they were also calculated with a healthy safety margin. "Tell him to check again."

"That's what he's doing. And that's also what I'm doing. We want to go into the ship to see if we can locate the missing mass, and we want you with us."

"And you couldn't just beam me in?"

"No. We're using line-of-sight comm only, for stealth reasons. No way we've got things set up for the kind of bandwidth you'd need."

She snorted, but said nothing. Timina might be difficult, but she certainly didn't want to fall into enemy hands.

"Fuck," she said, and Cyran knew he'd won.

"Well, that was a complete waste of time," Timina remarked, pulling the spacesuit off, standing naked in the suit locker while Cyran did his best not to stare at her. He knew that many people, who lived their entire lives uploaded, simply didn't care about bodies—to them, they were just bags of carbon, hydrogen, oxygen and nitrogen to be used and recycled when they were finished with them.

Cyran, on the other hand, wished he hadn't chosen such an attractive package for her, especially when she just hit the door button and walked, completely bare, towards the bridge.

Mere, Timina, Brannon and Cyran were seated around a table in the control center. Three of them listened, afraid to speak, as Timina expostulated.

"We know that the gravity sensors are working. Both the light curvature around the ship and the force the engines are exerting to keep us in position relative to it, prove that the mass is precisely what the instruments say it should be. Are we agreed?"

No one was brave enough to say no.

"Good. Then there are basically two options: the first is that the mass is concentrated in the structure of the ship, in some kind of heavy element which is either well shielded or stable enough that we're not seeing any decay effects. The second is that the mass is right there, but we simply can't see it. Which do you think is the case?"

"It would have to be the hyperdense element, I guess. But why would you build a starship that way? It's just more mass to accelerate, for no gain—unless the structural properties are amazing," Brannon said.

"Clearly, living in a flesh body has turned you into a hyperdense element. The structural theory is not only idiotic, but it doesn't begin to explain the evidence," Timina replied. "Please think before talking."

No one else responded.

"What I need you to think about is not so much what you've seen in the vessel, but what you haven't. The ship has no engines, no crew compartments, nothing that we can recognize as useful."

"Maybe it was just a cargo container, jettisoned after it stopped being useful," Mere interjected. "That would explain why it's moving so slowly—it hasn't accelerated to get here—it was just drifting for a few billion years."

Timina half-nodded. "I see you aren't all completely stupid here. That explains most of what we know, even if building a container ten times as heavy as it needs to be wouldn't be the most solid of economic decisions." She paused. "But there is one more thing. Look at this." She gestured, but nothing happened, and seemed to remember where she was. An irritated look crossed her features. "Brannon, can you bring up the map of the ship."

A 3-D schematic came onto the viewmaster, jagged images showing the passages that they'd explored or simply scanned from one side. The outside of the ship was semi-transparent, so they could see the interconnected lines.

"It's incomplete, but what does it look like?" Timina asked.

They stared at it for a few moments. Then Cyran saw it. "Latticework!"

Timina nodded. "Precisely. This isn't the actual ship. This is just a strong base on which the rest of the ship is built."

"But where is it?" Brannon asked, pointing at the external viewscreen, which showed the same ship it had always done. "What happened to it?"

"It's right there. And it's about ten times bigger than what we can actually see. If the interaction with regular matter were stronger, we'd have smacked right into it."

They stared at her, with expressions saying that they weren't happy about the direction the conversation seemed to be heading.

The light lab's computers took some minutes to come online, and it seemed to Cyran that Timina was barely keeping her impatience under control.

Once they had the systems up, however, it took Timina only 15 minutes to learn what she wanted—the space around the ship did not interact with anything in the electromagnetic spectrum.

"So there's nothing there, after all?" Brannon asked.

The physicist rolled her eyes, making Cyran wonder where, in her cyber-world, she'd picked up the mannerism. "No, it just confirms that we're not dealing with some exotic transparent form of Baryonic matter."

They stared blankly at her, so she went on. "Baryonic matter is the stuff we are used to calling matter. Regular matter which we can interact with, like the hull, the inner bulkheads and Brannon here, although most of it isn't as dense as Brannon. It's composed of particles which interact through the strong force, and can therefore be detected regularly." She checked their reactions, seemed satisfied with what she saw, and continued. "But to account for the gravity patterns of the universe without having to resort to gravity seepage from other branes, the only explanation is that most of the matter in the universe is composed of dark matter, which, according to the standard model, is composed of different particles that interact through the weak force."

"Standard model? Don't we know?" Brannon asked. As an engineer, he wasn't comfortable being reminded that after all the millennia of scientific research, there were still a few gaps in human knowledge.

"It's hard to study because we've never been close enough to a significant gravitational anomaly to study it. Until now. I just need a few minutes for the nanobots to build me an instrument on the hull. This will be much quicker if you plug me in."

"I can do better than that," Mere replied. "Your uploaded self has been listening to this whole conversation all the time. Let me just unmute her."

The commander did something on her compad, and another voice—Cyran assumed it was the other Timina—spoke to them through the sound system.

"So, a weak force interferometer?" it asked.

"Exactly," Timina replied, not at all surprised to be talking to herself.

"Good. I seem to be connected to the ship's central command unit, so this should only take a few moments."

They waited, and this time, the tension seemed to be on the crew's side. Cyran wanted to know what was going on, what the instruments would find.

"Online in a few seconds... there. I'm testing the instrument now."

Cyran watched the non-cybernetic Timina, trying to keep her from noticing his scrutiny. He was expecting her to fidget, to show her impatience at being locked in a meat body, but she didn't. She simply traced a continuous circle on the skin of her abdomen with one finger, watching the movement all the while. She didn't look up as her alter-ego listed the test results.

"All right, the systems seem to check out. Let's see what we can do with this."

Only then did the physical Timina look up at the screen where data was streaming. Lines of red and yellow numbers captured her attention, but she spoke. "Can't deal with the data streams at meat-mind processing speed. Could you set up a graphic visual?"

The image on the screen changed to a line graph, with various vibrating traces displayed. Seeing that no one else seemed to understand what they were seeing, Timina translated.

"The interferometer will read the interaction on the weak force of four known particle-wave streams which we reflect back through the supposedly empty area using a large mirror. Each stream is a different-colored line on the graph. The big difficulty has always been to get the reflector on the other side of a large mass of dark matter."

Suddenly, all four lines ceased being straight flat traces and began jumping all over the display. Timina smiled. "That was easier than I thought it would be, but then, there's a lot of mass in that ship."

"How much?" Mere asked her.

Timina held her gaze. "More than enough to get us to the Cloud. But only if we can figure out a way of getting access to it." She peered at the lines again. "And I think you need to ask my better self if she can understand what they're trying to say."

"Say?"

"Yes," the electronic version of Tinina replied. "There are rhythmic pulses coming through the interferometer—clearly attempts at communication of some sort."

"Tell me what they're saying."

"Easier said than done. This could take a while."

It took considerably more than a while. Modulation changes on the part of the human ship would immediately be followed by certain changes in the interferometer pattern—they were doing something right. After the two days had passed, virtual Timina spoke.

"These people are truly, truly frightened."

Everyone looked up from where they were pretending to be useful for the past two days, which Cyran couldn't help thinking was two days more that the Enemy had had to catch up. He glanced towards the rear of the ship—a useless gesture, as he couldn't see past the nearest bulkhead, but one he couldn't help.

Commander Mere glanced up sharply. "So are we. It's pretty obvious that no one would be out here by choice. It's not a huge surprise—they're probably running from someone, too, and judging by their speed relative to the nearest galaxies, it's likely that they've been out here quite a few million years longer than we have. I'd be desperate, in their shoes."

"Yes, desperate is an even better description, perhaps." Virtual Timina paused. "In fact, I think that was one of the reasons their communications were so hard to decipher: they were trying to go too fast, assuming we were like them. I had to explain that we are essentially baryonic in nature and interactions. And then they seemed to get even more desperate."

"Why?"

"I'm not certain, but I know what they want from us. They want the design for the propulsion unit of this ship."

"But why would they need that? They seem to have a sufficient grasp of physics that they can create starships out of a combination of dark matter and ordinary matter. What use could they have with something as simple as our mass/energy drive? If they needed it, they could have developed it ages ago."

Timina, the flesh and blood Timina, replied: "Perhaps they've never needed one before."

A hum of agreement came from the computer speakers. "Not bad for a meatbag," the virtual Timina said. "That's what I think, too. The universe is essentially composed of dark energy, with ordinary matter being an afterthought. So if you have that developed, you wouldn't bother with a drive like ours. Except that now they're caught in a pocket of ordinary matter. Not much dark matter in the neighborhood of the Milky Way. I didn't give them the drive, of course."

"What?" Brannon cried. "Why not? Do you have any idea how much they could help us? What kinds of tech they might have? Hell, we could go back and defeat the enemy, maybe, if they tell us how."

Flesh and blood Timina rolled her eyes, and Cyran wished she would put some clothes on, for the hundredth time over the past few days. He knew she saw herself as just a downloaded program, and also remained naked to protest their silly flesh and blood conventions... but when she acted human, or allowed little human expressions to cross her face, she became a major distraction.

"Well, considering that this starship is the biggest source of baryonic matter for light-years around, what, exactly, do you think they are planning to feed to their shiny new mass/energy drive?"

"Oh," Brannon said, blushing. Cyran was happy to note that he seemed distracted, too.

"So what do we do now?" Mere inquired. "I doubt that they'll start feeding us the secrets to their control of dark matter, especially if they only see us as a source of propulsion mass."

"Basically, we have two options," the computer-based Timina said. "We can either accelerate our research into using dark matter for propulsion—that way, we'll have enough energy to get us to the Magellanic Cloud—or use the baryonic part of their ship to get us to another mass cluster."

"Why can't we go all the way to the cloud on the mass we get from them? It will be slow, but we'd make it," Mere asked.

"For the same reason we couldn't go straight from the Milky Way to the Cloud," the flesh-and-blood Timina interjected. "The Slowdown field is only theoretically stable for five million years or so. After that, it would simply disintegrate, probably taking the ship with it. Not a great way to end humanity. We need to find enough mass that we can get there in less time than that—or, failing that, we'll need to take the trip in small jumps."

"The enemy will get us," Cyran said.

"Perhaps. Although they might have forgotten us by now."

"They never seemed like the type of creatures to forget something like that. If they haven't got us yet, it's probably because they haven't gotten around to it. Or they sent pursuit out later than we expected."

"Maybe they didn't detect us on the way out."

"Do you really believe that?" the uploaded Timina asked.

Cyran caught everyone—including Timina—glancing at the bulkhead to the rear, even as he did so himself.

"I didn't think so," the computer went on.

Mere broke the ensuing silence. "So what do you think our dark-matter friends are doing now?"

"If I had to guess, I'd say they're probably trying to design a mass-energy drive, and some way to grab our mass and feed it into the drive."

"Oh."

This time, the silence was much longer, and Cyran watched Mere surreptitiously. After all, she was the one who would have to make the decision to destroy the alien ship—or at least the parts of it they could interact with— or to try to find another solution.

She looked tired, seemingly feeling all the years of the trip so far on her shoulders, and the ones to come, as she asked, "Do we have another decent-sized fuel mass located somewhere we can reach in time?"

"All we really have are the gravity distortion analysis that the observatories ran before we left the Milky Way. There are two masses in range, on our path to the Cloud. I recommend we aim for the larger one."

There was a pause, as all eyes turned to their commander. Cyran found himself hoping that the woman who'd had all of humanity's future entrusted to her would come through at the crucial moment and suggest a solution that wouldn't imply the destruction of what might be all that remained of a highly advanced race.

Brannon seemed to be thinking along the same lines, his expression showing mixed hope and resignation. Even flesh-and-blood Timina watched the captain curiously.

Mere's face, however, showed no expression. He knew her well enough to know that that meant deep thought. He also knew her well enough that he thought he could guess what she was thinking. She was measuring the possibility of finding a solution that would allow her to look at herself in the mirror, against two ticking clocks: the dark-matter creatures' timeline for getting their science done and the arrival of the enemy itself, closing on them from behind.

Finally, she sighed, and her shoulders slumped. A single tear dropped from her eye. "All right. Activate the mass absorption sequence."

The *Kamina* lurched slightly, as powerful magnets and fields latched onto the alien craft. The tiny crew sat in silence, knowing they were killing a group of alien sentients, but not knowing just how many of them— hoping against hope that they weren't the last of their kind, but powerless to do anything about it.

The computer-based Timina startled them all by speaking. "The aliens have communicated again. They know what we're doing, and accept it, because they know how the universe works, and that, sometimes, survival depends on a technical advantage at the right moment. But they do have one final thing they wish to say."

"What is it?" Mere asked.

"They say we're going the wrong way. They tell us that no matter what we're running from, it isn't as bad as what we're running towards. They say we should turn back."

The commander nodded once, tersely. "I imagined as much. Anything that makes a species that is advanced enough to combine dark and baryonic matter run into the space between galaxies is probably best avoided. Please thank them for the warning."

Cyran thought about that for a second. Nothing could be worse than the enemy they were escaping, a species so foul that it thought nothing of violating the minds of those they vanquished, even as they fed on the flesh. And yet, he had no doubts whatsoever that their new friends were telling the truth. His dread deepened. "So what should we do?" he asked his captain.

She looked each of her crew in the eye.

"We go forward."

Gustavo Bondoni is an Argentine writer with over a hundred stories published in fourteen countries and seven languages. He is a winner in the National Space Society's "Return to Luna" Contest and the Marooned Award for Flash Fiction (2008). His fiction has appeared in the Texas STAAR English Test cycle, The Rose & Thorn, Albedo One, The Best of Every Day Fiction *and many others.*

His latest book, an ebook novella entitled Branch *was published in March 2014, while a new series of standalone ebook short stories has recently launched, starting with a tale entitled "Iced." He has also published two reprint collections,* Tenth Orbit and Other Faraway Places *(2010) and* Virtuoso and Other Stories *(2011, Dark Quest Books).* The Curse of El Bastardo *(2010) is a short fantasy novel.*
www.gustavobondoni.com.

As a gondolier in the biggest and only tourist trap in the Andromeda galaxy, Sonny Vellera was living the good life, ferrying tourists, smuggling cigarettes, and entertaining party girls. But when his daughter fell ill, the sole cure came from spirits of the ancients, who only helped the "pure of heart." Those with impure hearts failed the test and were sealed in a prison of stone for eternity. Sonny knew he would fail, but he had to risk it all for his little Angie.

MISS PATEL'S HOLIDAY

Mary P. Madigan

You must have heard the ad, broadcast up and down the Cosmic Superhighway: "Fly to Verona Moon, play among Andromeda's stars. Take an Intergalactic ship through the WormholeWeb, follow the volcanic tubes down Stromboli Mountain, to the magical city in Verona Moon's center. Stay in a beautiful, ancient villa, tiled with Byzantine mosaics, carved into the cliffs by everyone's favorite ancient star travelers, the Nabataeans. Marvel at the frosty clouds, the moon's surface-sky of ice. Glide through aqua-blue canals, where picturesque human gondoliers transport you back through the centuries, to the days when men were made of meat. A simpler time."

As one of those picturesque and meaty humans, I guarantee, simple isn't all it's cracked up to be.

Life used to be good. On a regular day, I'd get up around noon. Maggie was at work, Angie was in school, I could shower my meaty self and smoke in peace. Then, comb my thick black hair, pray the first novena, put on a pair of sunglasses to cover my bloodshot eyes and go to the cafe. Bang down some high-test espressos. Watch the skirts go by, shoot the shit with Uncle Stanz and the guys.

Before the tourists got in, I'd pack the underside of the seats with bootleg smokes and JoySticks, cover them with a cushion before the cops cruise by. Then wait for our marks, umm . . .chumps . . .umm . . .tourists to show.

On a scale from one to ten, farm girls from Tuscany in town for a bachelorette party were the best tourists, definite nines. Silicon Dendrites from one moon over were my least favorite. They were great trading partners—who else would buy tons of brine waste from our desalinization plants—but they talked in farts and ooze. Not great conversationalists.

Second from the worst were Deepwater Blavoks from two moons over. Educated and urbane, they saw us the way we saw the dendrites; lower creatures. With them it was a short exchange of sharp-toothed pleasantries, swipe the credit card and slither into the water, on their way to a methane spa.

The best, the absolute tens were our lost cousins, the Earthmen. Years ago Earthmen made first contact with us, in our language, via radio signal. We thought the signal was being broadcast from a lost probe on Kelt 3b, the gas planet our moon orbits. Imagine our surprise when we found the signal was from one of the least popular corners of the 'Verse, the Milky Way. Our lost cousins were advanced, warlike Surface Dwellers living 2.5 million light years away.

According to the Blavoks, this was a rare find. There aren't many Surface Dwellers in the 'Verse. Nine-tenths of all sentient beings live inside water or methane-bearing planets. Protected only by a wisp of atmosphere, Surface Dwellers rarely last long enough to evolve properly. Given the asteroid strikes, changes in magnetism, orbit, the tribalism and war that comes from living in such dangerous conditions, they're usually just a short blip on the evolutionary scale. When they do manage to survive, they evolve into something so powerful, so uncontrollable, they wind up killing themselves and their host planet.

The Earthlings said we were the descendants of astronauts manning an exploration vessel, the *SS Torres*, a space station traversing the Asteroid Belt between Jupiter and Mars. They'd built the station into the side of an asteroid, hoping that the rock would provide protection from radiation and meteoroids. This was before they realized that the asteroids on one side of the belt weren't the same as the ones on the other side. The Cosmic Superhighway, the network of wormholes that vacuums matter up from one galaxy and spits it out in another, cut right through the belt. As it had been doing for millions of years, it grabbed their ship and transported it millions of light years away.

Centuries later, a group of Astral Archeologists searching for a lost tribe of Aboriginals found us instead.

As Patriarch of House Vellera, I testified at the hearings to decide whether or not to welcome the Earthlings to our fair Verona Moon. Their story jibed with my great, great grandfather's records. Captain Mike Vellera was lauded for saving everyone's bacon when he decided to abandon all efforts to return to Earth. He chose our moon as the most promising site for a settlement, and, inspired by Jules Verne's *Journey to the Center of the Earth*, theorized that life was possible beneath the surface. They explored the mountain's underground volcano caves and found the canals. He named the mountain Stromboli as a nod to Verne.

If they hadn't come down here, they would have died when their supplies ran out. If he'd chosen another moon, they would also have been dead. The Blavoks now admit that they would have eaten our ancestors "if they hadn't been properly introduced."

While we debated about making first contact, the Earthlings sent us selfies. Gorgeous women, big white smiles. Don't run, we are your friends.

The Blavoks urged caution. "Surface Dwellers are quite keen on conquest. We recommend you cut off all contact." Our priests agreed, saying these were not men of God. But the Merchants disagreed. This was a gift from our Lord, for the tourist industry, for all of us.

Gotta admit, I sided with the money men. With extra coin coming in, I could replace the hundreds I'd been borrowing from petty cash. Profit and ass-covering, what we Veronans do best.

The Earthmen traveled the same way they sent their signal, following the Cosmic Superhighway that led to our door. They came in teams; research teams, diplomatic teams, archeological teams. But when we made contact in real life, we saw they weren't like us at all. We should have seen it in their selfies, their beautiful faces were only slight variations on a common theme. Like my daughter Angie's dolls—Black Ken, Doctor Barbie, Latino Barbie, Beachy Ken—the paint was different, but they all came from the same porcelain mold. The Earthlings were Cyborgs, mass-produced humanoids whose cells were constructed from carbon and silicon nanobots.

They told us they were the next step in evolution, and they might have been right about that. When we shook their hands, I could feel the tensile strength. Even the girls could kick my ass. They could easily have conquered us, but they'd been through so many wars, survived so many near-extinction events, they'd decided to give peace a chance. Thank the Lord for that.

Pacifists with a superiority complex are the best kinds of chumps. They think they're so clever, you can put anything over on them. When they finally figure out that they've been had, they're too embarrassed to speak up. So I took them for a ride. Fresh off the boat, downloads not activated yet, they had no idea what their money was worth. I'd dazzle them with my meaty songs and fast talk, walk away with pockets full of coin. Enough to pay the rent, and bail when necessary.

When the ships came in, we'd run for the dock, push past the kids with roses to sell, petals spinning onto the cobblestone streets. The ladies from the Station House were out the front door in a blast of perfume, wearing dresses so tight they made me dizzy. The guys would tease them, whistle, but Stanz would slap them down, saying "We're all whores, at least they're honest about it."

I'd gargle some fine Cabernet and get ready for a hard day of singing O Solo Mio to the Barbie dolls and the bachelorettes. After that hard work, it was grappa time. Then pray the nightly Novena for blessed Mother Mary to keep me safe from the Demon Malphas, and stagger home through the winding alleyways. By then Maggie was asleep, too tired to sniff out what I'd been up to. Good thing. All those things you hear about redheads and temper, they're all true.

Everybody down at the docks knew me. They'd say "Sonny, he's a dog, but he sings like an angel." I'm not proud of that, but they weren't lying.

It was a carefree life until the Devil took his due. There was a virus going around, a summertime thing, microbes that drip down when the surface ice melts. A few weeks ago, little Angie went swimming in the backwaters and caught the bug. Maggie called me from the hospital and I ran over right away. But there was nothing I could do. I wanted to stay with her every minute, wait for those few moments when she would open her eyes and whisper a few words. But there were bills to be paid.

Maggie and her mom were with her. They brought food, but Angie wasn't eating. Her friends brought toys but she didn't play. Doctors pumped medicines into her veins, but they didn't help.

One day I got off early, brought Angie a teddy bear to add to the pile. I opened the door to find the Demon Malphas crouched over my sick baby girl.

Every Garden of Eden has its serpent, and ours was Malphas. He could only appear outside of his estate if he was summoned, and no one in their right mind would do that, but people were sometimes so sick, so desperate, they would beg for his cures. He claimed to be able to bring the dying back to life, but his spells would only work if the subject was 'pure of heart.' If you weren't, his foul demon dust would turn you into a statue, trapped within a stony prison forever. The merchants, princes, and priests were powerless to do anything about him. None dared to take on a dark force who possessed magic, crack security forces, and a fleet of high-powered lawyers.

One side of his face was human, thin and craggy. The other half was a gargoyle's stony grimace. He turned his human eye to me and gave me a dry smile. "Sonny Vellera. I remember you."

When I was a kid, my buddies dared me to sneak into Malphas' estate. I used the sewers to get past security, crawled through the darkness and moldy mud, chattering glean bugs tickling my skin. I surfaced to find myself face-to-face with mosquitos and the stony dead. Some were crumbled so badly, I couldn't make out their features, but I could tell who they were; the way their shoulders sloped, the bowed legs, the cut of a ragged cloak. Scared shitless, I started humming. Malphas must have heard me. Quiet as death, he snuck up from behind, grabbed my arm. I tried to get away, tugged the veil from his face, saw the stony, grotesque half.

"I wasn't good enough for them. None of us are!" He shouted as I ran.

His veil was held in place with a safety pin now. "Vellera. Always showing up uninvited."

"You're the uninvited," I said, clenching a fist, taking a hard step towards him. "Now get the hell out."

Maggie jumped between us. "Stop it, Sonny. I called him."

"No way," I said.

"Way." He turned away and opened his stone jars, poured the foul dust, and began to chant.

Angie woke up, wide-eyed, damp brown curls stuck to her face. "Mommy, Daddy. Why'd you bring him here?"

I stood, frozen, with no idea what to do.

"It's okay, honey, he can't hurt you."

"But, I'm not a good person. Last year, I lied about doing my reading. Twice!"

"Get him out of here," I whispered.

"Don't worry," Maggie said. "There's a loophole. Even if she did sin, she hasn't had her Confirmation yet. So her sins don't count!"

"That's bullshit."

"Please, stop!" Angie cried. "I don't want to be a monster!"

"Memento, quia pulvis es, et in pulverem reverteris" Malphas chanted, stirring his potions into a smoky flame. Like any altar boy, I knew that one. "Remember, you are dust and to dust you will return."

138

"If you and all of the men in this city hadn't voted against letting the Cyborgs give us their medicine, I wouldn't have to do this," Maggie said.

"Their medicine is nanobots injected into your bloodstream. They'd turn her into a Cyborg. You want that?"

"No." Maggie covered her face with her hands, weeping. "I don't know what I want."

I went to put my arm around her but then Angie screamed. Malphas was pressing hot ash to her skin. Red blisters swelled under grey dust.

I couldn't take it anymore, didn't think, just pushed myself between her and him and shouted, "You want a damned soul, take mine!"

Maggie tried to pull me away. "Sonny! Are you, crazy?"

Malphas grinned. "I am not the angel of death. But since you offered . . ." He grabbed a handful of hot dust and blew it in my face. I gagged, blood pumped hot in my ears, pounding so loud I could barely hear myself screaming. He pressed his stony hand to my chest. This was it. I braced myself for the pain, the fall, endless imprisonment in stone.

Then, by some miracle, I was still breathing. And standing. Maggie and Angie were crying as Malphas dramatically wrapped his cloak around his shoulders. "You're not worth the trouble." He stormed out with so much hot air, the papers on the nurse's station blew like fall leaves.

After that, Maggie was still mad at me and Angie was still in the hospital. This flu was a bad one. The prognosis wasn't good.

Me, I felt so weak, I could barely make it through the day. I thought Malphas had messed with my heart, but Doc said it was stress and bad habits. If I didn't lay off booze, caffeine, and smokes, I wouldn't make it to my next birthday.

My sins brought this on Angie, so I did my penance, followed doctor's orders. The only addiction I could keep was food. The combination of sobriety and carbs made me feel like I had a grey blanket wrapped around my head.

That Monday morning, I was living the clean and sober life—get up at the break of dawn, eat too much, work too hard, and wallow in despair. Uncle Stanz sat watching me, sipping espresso with his pinky stuck out.

"Uncle Stanz."

He smoothed out his cassock, black eyes looking down his roman nose. "Hey. What'd I tell you?"

When we're outside, I'm supposed to call him Friar Stanz. "Yeah, Unc—Friar, ever think about what it's like after we die?"

"All the time. It depends on where you're going."

"Pretty sure I'm going to hell."

Another sip of espresso. "You may be right. But hell isn't so bad. We do try to make it sound bad, because, you know, it's good for business. But like everything, there are loopholes."

"Loopholes . . ."

"It's not just God making these decisions. Mother Mary has a say too. The deal she made is what any Mother would do. Hell is like a time out. You've got to stay in for a while but then they let you out, let you come back to life. But if you want to stay out, you have to be good. These tourists, these good and gullible Earthlings, must have been bad in a former life. When we take their money, we're giving them a chance to show God how good they can be."

"What about Malphas' judgement?"

"That Devil—he has no say."

"If you think he's the Devil, why'd you tell Maggie to call him?"

"I did not!"

"Some idiot told her Angie was protected, that sins committed before Confirmation don't count."

He sat back in his chair. "Oh. I was that idiot. But I didn't think she'd . . ."

"She's a mother, she'll do anything for her d. . ." Dying. I couldn't say it, hurt to even think it. "Her child."

Stanz fell silent.

I went back to scrubbing rot and bugs off my gondola. "I hear the House of Montague has been moving twice as much stash as us. Know why?" His eyes meet mine. "Everybody pitches in."

He put the cup down and jumped on board, patent leather shoes clacking against the painted edges of my boat. Still with the pinky out, he grabbed a bucket of bilge, dumped it, then wiped it dry with the skirt of his cassock. Apology accepted. I slid the velvet pillow down over our cargo. It was enough to pay this week's hospital bills, but it gave suspicious weight to my boat. Not good when the place was lousy with cops.

Stanz said, "If they had enough to pinch us, we'd be behind bars now."

"What's this 'we', kemo sabe. Friars don't go to jail."

"I'd be imprisoned by despair for you."

"Yeah, that means a lot."

"Get some skinny customers," Stanz said. "Or a loner."

"Earthlings travel in teams." You can tell which team they are by the color of their hats. Green for science, blue for diplomats, yellow for archeologists. Sometimes they wander away. Like—her."

He pointed to a wandering Cyborg, a tall Black Jogger Barbie. She had a yellow hat, but she'd wandered from her team. None of the other yellow hats seemed to miss her.

"Alone, but doesn't want to be," Stanz said. "Flex a little muscle." I raised my oar. "Look at those guns!"

My arms jiggled. "More like fat bombs." I said.

Other gondoliers were chasing the yellow hats, doing the hard sell, but I knew that would scare her off. I stood back, gave a little smile, didn't wink. She zeroed in on me, didn't ask how much it cost, didn't go through the "what language should we speak?" routine. Apparently she'd already set her language to 21st century, New York City. She shouted "Hey! Can I get a ride?"

Close up, I could see she wasn't all that young. Cyborgs aged slowly, but some had lived for more than a hundred years. Being exposed to gravity, wind, sun, showed in her posture, the way she walked. I gave her an old-style bow. "Sonny Vellera, at your service."

"Miss Patel 587." She said briskly.

I gave her my hand, tried to guide her gently to the middle, but she pushed past me, slammed a foot down on the edge and nearly upended the gondola. Of course, the cops took notice.

"I hate boats." she said as she sloshed onto the velvet cushion.

For two hours, that was all she said.

"If you dip your fingers in the water, you can feel how warm it is." I said as I rowed "The gas giant we orbit, Kelt 3b, makes the waves that keep the water warm. We have our own little ecology here—warm weather, dry sandy soil, just like Earth's Tuscan region. It's great for growing the crops and trees that keep our air clean. And it's perfect for wine. If you want to try some, there's a bottle beside your chair."

She didn't.

"We're at the foot of Stromboli mountain. If you look to your right, you'll see a three-story high mural. These are portraits of our founders, all 49 of them. After finding themselves millions of light-years off course, these men and women took shelter in this abandoned Nabatean city and built a civilization."

This was the point where they all took a picture, but she was still sitting, ramrod stiff. I told her to turn on her camera. She took her eyeball out, adjusted the lens and popped it back in. I hate when they do that.

"As you can tell by our matching shnozzolas, the Captain there was my ancestor. He came from New Jersey, USA, but his mother was from Venice, Italy. He modeled our city on his fond memories of the city of canals. That beautiful lady there, Chief Engineer Janice Cooper, changed her name to 'Capulet' and named the city after Romeo and Juliet's Verona.

I followed the curve around the mountain, twisted the paddle sideways to slow down. This was Verona's golden hour, when the sun's light shone straight through the frozen sky, generating bright crackles of gold and blue, an effect that was multiplied by the water's reflection, bathing the Villas in kaleidoscopic shocks of light. I've seen it a thousand times and it still gives me chills.

She raised her eye and gave an obligatory click of the camera. Unbelievable.

"You just got off the transport?"

"Yes."

"Never seen this before?"

"No."

Cyborgs aren't emotional, but most can pass the Turing Test. Not this one.

In the silence, I heard the buzz of a radio behind me. The cops, thinking they were being discreet, followed close by. They had to be wondering why she was being such a stiff. Time to start a conversation.

"You never told me your first name. "

"Is that required?"

"No, but it would be nice."

"I don't have one. I'm Patel 587."

"Patel—are you Hindu?"

"I forgot that humans classify according to ethnocultural identity. My bad. I should have chosen a coordinating skin color."

"What is your ethnoculture?"

"Black and Chinese. The Patel Corporation, LLC produced me and my co-workers. We're a Unified Clutch of Anthropologists."

"Oh."

I kept paddling, cops trailing me all the while. I tried singing. Another sigh, another sad click of the camera. As we slid under the last bridge, I said. "Help me out here. You don't seem to be having any fun at all. Why'd you take this tour?"

She pointed to the high, stony fence surrounding the Malphas Estate. "I want to meet that man."

A chill ran down my spine. "He's not a man. He's a Demon."

"He is not a Demon! There is no such thing. I can't believe how often I've had this idiotic argument. Even my colleagues say it!"

This wasn't the conversation I'd planned. "Summoning the Demon is forbidden by law."

"Obviously you're not afraid of breaking the rules, given the bootleg cigarettes under my chair." She shifted in her seat. "And marijuana."

So Cyborgs did, literally, have sensors up the wazoo. "Jeez, keep it down!" I whispered. Why do you want to see Malphas?"

"He destroyed Nabatean relics." She opened the palm of her hand and showed me her holographic badge. "It's an interstellar crime. I have the authority to bring him in."

If they were going to do something about Malphas, they'd have done it a long time ago. There was more to this. I looked past the badge. Her hands were yellowed, purple at the edges of her nails. Her big Barbie eyes were cloudy, her lashes, sparse. Like Angie's.

I shouldn't have said it out loud, but I did. "You're dying."

Her pretty, plump lips quivered, holding back tears. I didn't know Cyborgs could cry. I reached over to pat her shoulder, comfort her. She pulled away.

The cops slid up beside me. The chief, Tony Capulet said. "Is Sonny showing you the sights of our fair Verona Moon—or is he giving you trouble?"

Shit, this was it, locked away for life. I'd never see Angie again. Maggie would never forgive me.

Patel sniffed and turned to them, her ashy skin stretched into a smile. "Why, no, officer," she said. "I'm having a lovely time."

"But . . ."

"Thank you for asking."

"Ma'am." They said as they rowed away.

She gave me a knowing nod. She could have ratted me out, but she didn't. I owed her. For a Cyborg she was good at working the unspoken contract.

I rounded the last curve, and, with her still in the boat, stopped at the Montague estate. Their guys came out in track suits and started unloading the cargo. No sense hiding it now. I swiped a pack of cigarettes, lit one and took a deep drag.

"Oh, I forgot." she tossed me a fat wad of coin. "Your tip."

When I say fat, I mean huge. Enough to pay all Angie's bills.

"Now bring me to your Demon."

"Why me?"

"Because you're a good man"

"You know I'm not—"

"Then because I paid you. Do we have a deal?"

"Yeah."

We tied up the boat and headed to the sewers. She followed me through alleyways, her universal positioning system blinked behind her irises. "I'm from the first edition of Patels. We were only bred to live a few hundred years. The nano-cells can repair my organic elements, but they can't heal themselves." Her voice echoed off the ancient walls, "I have approximately two months to live."

I lit another cigarette. "I'm sorry."

"Why? It's not your fault. I heard about your Malphas, the man who uses ancient Nabatean medicine to ward off death. But his cure will only work under certain, morally proscribed conditions."

"Yeah, you have to be 'pure of heart.' Good luck fitting that bill. My wife summoned him, tried to get him to help our little girl. Angie's six years old, she's as good as good gets, but I saw how it was going, stopped him just in time. You and me, our souls wouldn't stand a chance."

She looked at me quizzically.

"Yeah, I know, Cyborgs don't like the religious talk."

"I can't complain about superstition when my last hope is a so-called Demon." We walked past the shops, closed now but still lit up. "I see those masks everywhere, with the long noses. What are they?"

"In the early days we wore them to keep disease away. We stuffed the long nose with ground herbs and disinfectant."

"Sometimes I wish I'd spent more time researching ancient medicines. With the nanobots, we've lost track of the old cures." We turned the corner to the fish market.

The vendors were packing up, washing the stony pavement. "Can those masks cure your little girl?"

"No."

"The nanobots could, but I suppose she doesn't want to become a cyborg."

"It's forbidden." I sighed and said, "All we can do is pray for her soul."

"You keep using that word. What is a soul?"

"Your consciousness, the thing that makes you yourself. Uncle . . . uh, Friar Stanz says, you can't see them because they're so small, but souls are like soda bubbles. Usually they float straight up, to heaven, but sometimes they sink down."

She gave a wry smile.

"You think that's silly."

"No I don't. I've seen souls."

"You're kidding me."

We stopped at a cafe. I ordered a double espresso, lit another cigarette. So much for the clean life. Between gulps of caffeine, Patel was talking a mile a minute. "My clutch and I studied Ancient Aboriginal Earth tribes, like the Anasazi, the Nabataeans. We used to think these tribes were human, but when we found the remains of their later colonies on other planets, we realized they were something else. Long ago, they had evolved to the point of being human, but then they evolved far beyond us."

"The guys who built our city settled other planets?"

"Yes, and they followed a certain pattern. They'd build increasingly more complex infrastructures until they reached a point when they no longer needed them."

"Why didn't they need them?"

"They entered their final stage of evolution, becoming cloud beings whose consciousness exists at a quantum level."

"Um . . . what? You lost me."

"You're right here."

"I mean . . ."

"Am I exceeding your ability to comprehend? Cyborgs process information thousands of times faster than humans. I'll slow my CPU."

"Just stop with the coffee." I paid the check.

"We based this theory on what we knew about Cyborg evolution. Let me demonstrate." She walked to a fish cleaning station, reached around her ear and yanked hard, pulling her ear and all the stuff that was attached to it out of her skull. Then she plopped the mass of skin, veins and squiggly things onto the chopping block. The diners around us also asked for the check. "My cells are half nanobots, half organic. If I injure my cochlea . . ." She made a fist.

"Jesus Christ, don't—"

She slammed her fist down, reduced her cochlea to a squish. "My cells are programmed by the nanobots to reconstruct. Look closely. You can see it reforming."

"I'll take your word for it," I said, trying not to vomit.

"This is what we can do now, simple computer-assisted cellular replication. But our current quantum chips can only hold so much data." She squished her ear back into her skull. I watched, openmouthed, as the flesh of her scalp precisely knitted into the pulpy mass around her ear. Blood streamed into the fabric of her jogging suit, flowing until the wound was closed. "The next stage in our evolution will be for us to be able to transmogrify ourselves."

"Trans-what?"

"Transmogrify, defined as 'to transmogrify, change or alter greatly.' Our spaceships are constructed with foglets that transmogrify. They're composed of nanobots mechanically linked to one another that share information and energy and unite to create a coherent form. They're self-replicating, but like our cells, their storage space is limited. If each atom of our organic cells had enough space to store a consciousness, we could take on any physical form."

"You could be anything you wanted to be."

"Yes. Aboriginals like Nabateans could make themselves into a lion, a cat, or a tree. If they were blasted by an ion accelerator and every cell in their body but one was destroyed, they could reconstruct themselves from

147

that one cell. They would keep their consciousness. Their soul."

"So, Malphas' magic dust wasn't left behind by the Nabataeans. It is the Nabataeans."

"In a way. I've seen their cells under a microscope. It's like the dust in human homes, which is composed of dead skin cells. But since it's from Aboriginals, their dust contains a data record of what they were. Their essence."

"And the Demon uses it in his ritual."

"He's not a Demon!"

"Ok, ok, what is he?"

"A man. I believe he was one of the astronauts on the *SS Torres*."

"No way. He'd be, like, four hundred years old. Humans don't live that long."

"He could if he hacked Aboriginal cell programming and reverse-engineered it. Or maybe their cells re-engineered him."

"Malphas hacked death?"

"Yes. I want to find out how he did it."

We walked by the edges of the canals, water sloshing against our feet. The sewers leading to Malphas' place were a few blocks away. Cold fear slid through me. It was crazy to do this without some sort of weapon, digital, liturgical, or old-fashioned steel. For all her supercomputing power, Patel didn't look like she'd be much help. She stood close behind me, as if I could protect her.

"How should we do this, exactly?" I said.

"I don't know. You've confronted Malphas twice, and you survived. You must have a plan."

"Yeah, the plan is, don't die on an empty stomach. Let's get some pizza."

When we got to Angie's room, she was sleeping. Her IV was full, her monitor humming. I'd ordered the pizza, Stanz was bringing it up. Maggie and her mom were already spooning out the ziti. A couple bottles of Prosecco cooled on the windowsill.

Patel said. "You're eating and talking around a sick child?"

"What's better for her, hearing us having a good time or sitting in silence?"

Maggie introduced herself to Patel, then brought me a plate of ziti, whispering. "Is she one of your bachelorettes?"

"Babe, she's a paying customer. Look." I showed her the money.

"What do you have to do for that?"

"Take her to Malphas."

She gasped, ran to Patel, handed her my ziti. "Honey, stay away from that Demon! If we'd gone through with it, Angie's soul would have been taken for all eternity."

Stanz leaned over and put down the pizzas. "You don't need the *all*." He said, opening a box and grabbing a slice "*Eternity* covers it."

Patel said "Sonny and I think we might have found a way to reprogram Malphas' potions, to hack them, as it were."

"Sonny, a hacker?" Maggie laughed. "He can't even get his phone to work."

I started with the Prosecco. When you lay off the sauce for a while, you lose all your tolerance, which can sometimes be a good thing. Kept me from losing it when Angie woke up and started talking to Patel.

"Patel 567 isn't a real name." Angie said. "I'll call you Tina."

Patel sat beside her, gingerly touched her burned arm. "What name would fit you better?"

"Little dead girl." Angie said.

I quietly wiped my eyes and downed the bubbly. Poured another.

She brushed the damp curls from Angie's forehead. "Are you afraid to die?"

"I remember what it used to be like, before I was born. It was like when you first fall asleep. You feel like you're floating, and you hear voices, all around."

"Whose voices?"

"Guardian angels."

"To family," Stanz said. I raised my glass.

149

Angie tried to eat, but it was hard with the tube in her nose. The effort tired her out. She went back to sleep. I finished the bottle.

When visiting hours were over, we gathered around the fountain. Stanz pulled a bottle of grappa from his cassock pocket. That's when things got fuzzy. I remember Stanz sitting at the edge of the fountain saying "If Aboriginals are souls, maybe we're all aboriginals."

Then I was in the fountain, water splashing my face.

I asked Stanz, "You understand what she's talking about, the foglets?"

"Yeah. Foglets are angels, little angel protons that shape themselves into different things. They follow basic angel rules. They mean well, but it's easy to piss them off. Once you do that, watch out! Angels never forget."

The bottle fell onto the cobbled street. I don't know who dropped it. We watched the broken glass merge with the canal water. "Transmogrifidation." We said in unison.

Then I was back at the house, and Maggie was saying "Sonny told Malphas to take his life instead of Angie's. The Demon said he *wouldn't* do it—but maybe he *couldn't*. I think the Aboriginals decided that Sonny was good man."

"Because he would sacrifice his soul for his daughter," Patel said.

Maggie's voice caught in her throat. "I always knew he was a sweetheart. That's why I fell in love with him." She burped. "Don't tell him I said that."

"Where is he?"

"On the floor, trying to get some sleep," Maggie said.

She was right. I was.

The next day, nursing pounding hangovers, Stanz, Patel, and I were suiting up to face Malphas. I helped Stanz wrap his flashlight up, tied it to his sunglasses.

Stanz crouched down beside the tunnel. "What's that smell?"

"You don't want to know."

He brushed his cassock. "I just got this thing dry cleaned."

"Look, if you don't want to come, stay here. The last thing we need is your princess routine."

"Screw you! You said there'd be danger to my eternal soul. You didn't mention bugs."

Patel strode by and pulled her dark hair back into a defiant ponytail. Her flashlight was embedded in her all-purpose irises. She blinked a few times to turn it on, then turned to Stanz and shone her blue light in his face. "If you're going to be a hindrance, you should stay here."

"No." Stanz said, pulling off his cassock, revealing the black pants and t-shirt beneath. He kept the sunglasses and the Padre hat. "I'm ready to roll."

The sewers hadn't changed much since I was a kid. Same bugs, more mold. We came up topside, in the garden. That had changed. Years ago, the lawn had been freshly mowed. Tracks carefully circled the stony dead. Now, they were nearly covered by weeds.

Stanz emerged cursing, slapping mosquitos. Patel brushed past him and banged on the back door. That was a crumbling wreck too. Paint from the neglected, formerly posh door crumbled onto the stone stairs.

No one answered.

I ducked into a shed to have a smoke, fight off the nausea. The place was like a cave, thick with mildew. I lit a match. Firelight reflected off a thickly woven spider web. With shaking hands, I kept the fire going. Hash marks, thousands of them, were scratched into the wall. I started counting them, 5, 10, 15, until the fire burned my hand. I blew it out.

Patel walked in, glanced at the wall and said. "One hundred thirty-three thousand, forty-two."

Stanz followed and said. "Those were made by a prisoner, counting the days until he's released."

"He's been counting for approximately three hundred sixty-four years," Patel said. "Allowing for time-space anomalies, the realization of their predicament and leap years, that's the time that has passed since the *SS Torres* was lost." She turned up her eye-lights and took a closer look.

Stanz took me aside and whispered, "Sonny, there's something I need to tell you. A little family secret. There was a Mission Specialist, Walker, who refused to follow Captain Vellera's orders. He demanded they go back to Earth. He tried to incite a rebellion, a, um . . . what do you sailors say . . .?"

"A mutiny?"

"Yes. He and the Captain had a terrible fight."

"Why wasn't that in the logbook?"

"The man died." Stanz shrugged. "Some things, you don't want to log."

Patel touched the wall. "These scratches—the same stroke, equal amount of pressure. All made by the same person." She turned to us "I don't think Walker died."

The shed door blew open, revealing a blast of hot air and a caped shadow, "No, he didn't," Malphas roared.

"Speak of the Devil," Stanz said.

"You!" Malphas strode towards me. I reached for the knife in my belt, but stopped. He was —smiling?

He pushed me aside and ran to Patel, hugged her like she was long-lost kin. "Take me with you, beautiful Earthling! Take me home!"

"I came here to make a deal," she said, trying to push him away.

From beneath his cape he produced a dusty earthenware jar, held it under her nose "Yes, a deal! I have relics worth millions!"

"I want to know how you reprogrammed—"

"Programming? I don't code, I'm a Demon! The all-powerful Malphas!" He grabbed her arm. "With you, I shall rule the Earth!"

"Let go of me!" She twisted his stony arm behind his back, dislocated it with a grinding snap. He groaned and slouched sideways, his misaligned shoulder hanging at a sickening angle. Dropping to his knees, he touched the lid and said, "Take me back—or we will all die, right here, right now."

"Don't open that!" Stanz cried.

"Ah, Stanz and Sonny, from the oh-so-noble House of Vellera." He turned his stony side to us. "Do you know how long I've been waiting to say this?"

"What?" Stanz said.

"See you in hell!" He upended the jar, dust flew thickly around us. Patel screamed, wide eyes glowing with frantic calculations. Stanz fell to the ground, crouched into a ball and prayed. Sharp, ashy circles swirled through the air. The knife was no good, I reached for something, anything, and found an oar. I swung it, turned it flat. The breeze blew some of the dust away.

"You can't kill them!" Malphas shouted. "It's like trying to kill a dustball." He stood up and screamed "That's all that remains of the great Aboriginals. Dustballs!"

Like a murmuration of starlings, the cloud of dust twisted and turned, changing direction as if they were choreographed. They swirled towards him, shrieking against his skin, a million tiny spinning shards. He screamed in agony as the air fogged with his blood. In the silence that followed, a stony skeleton fell to the floor.

Then they came for me.

"Remember what you did in the hospital room. Don't fight them." Patel cried.

Trembling, I closed my eyes. The noise was deafening, my blood went hot, my entire body was pain. I was falling into white. Then, there was nothing but my heartbeat, thump, thump, pounding in my ears.

I opened my eyes. For a second, I thought I'd fallen asleep in a museum. All around me were 3D photographs, stacked up, down, and sideways, as far as I could see. But I could still hear the heartbeat. I turned my body sideways and floated towards the noise, into one of the photographs, and found myself standing on Liberty Bridge. It was like a 3D photo I could walk through. Everything around me was still, frozen in place—bugs in midflight, a dog with its mouth open wide as if to bark. And there was that noise, thump thump, echoing off the ancient walls.

I followed until the thumping got louder, clearer, until I finally found the source. It was a basketball, bounced by a man with Dad's droopy eyes. That schnoz. Captain Mike Vellera, doctor of astrophysics, interstellar explorer, founder of our fair Verona.

He took a shot, straight into my recycling can. "Score!" I waved.

"Hey, Sonny."

"You know me?"

"I always dream this after a midnight snack. Cold pizza and beer, never a good idea." He tossed me the ball. "Up for a game?"

It was a real ball, pockmarked orange plastic, black lines running through it. It even smelled like a basketball—stale hand sweat, rubber and dirt. "Is this real?"

"Yeah. Take a shot."

"Am I dead?"

"Am I?" he asked.

"I don't know."

"Then let's play."

I started a slow dribble. "What is this place?"

"A moment in time."

"How come we can move, but nothing else does?"

He blocked me. "Stop half-assing it."

I whirled around him, twisted sideways, took my shot. Score.

"Nice."

"So talk to me. What is this place?"

"Ask her."

Patel floated onto the patio. "Things aren't moving because each moment is like a picture in a filmstrip. When we're living our usual three-dimensional lives, our brains make the film of time go. But now we're in another dimension. The Aboriginal dust helped us survive the trip, but our brains have trouble making sense of it."

"Where's Stanz?"

Patel turned around. "I thought he was behind me."

"Where's Angie?" I didn't wait for the answer, I was off, running through the frozen streets, ducking the oncoming birds and the rush hour traffic, which consisted of ten gondolas crammed under Liberty Point Bridge.

In Angie's room, a nurse was frozen in place, changing her IV. Angie's face was pale. Her eyes were closed.

The Captain was right behind me. "Poor kid."

"She went swimming in the backwaters. Caught a bug."

"When?"

"A few weeks ago."

"Follow me." He ran right for the wall, didn't slow down. I winced, expecting him to smack into the plaster. He didn't, he was running up the wall, past the window to the ceiling, where there was a stack of moments piled up to the sky. When I followed, I felt a light gravity pulling me to the wall.

"It takes hundreds of these to make a minute. You want to make time; you have to haul ass." he shouted.

As I gained momentum, birds started flying backwards. Gondolas reversed under the bridge, gondoliers went from shouting to confusion to happy faces. Fish flew out of gull's mouths and swam backwards to freedom.

My lungs felt like they'd burst. I cursed every cigarette I'd ever had. After miles, or maybe lightyears of this I saw Angie, with her bathing suit on, running towards the water.

"Stop!" I gasped.

She turned, but didn't seem to see me.

"You're in another dimension. Angie can't see you, but she can feel you. Knock her down!" The Captain grabbed my hand and Patel's. We ran together and plowed into my little girl. She fell, crying.

"Not what I'd call good parenting, but sometimes you gotta improvise," The Captain said. Then he started running again. I followed. Time passed. Angie sat in the grass, pulled her phone from her swim bag and nursed her skinned knee. She called Maggie. "Mommy, it's really windy and I fell down. Can you Uber me a water taxi?"

I collapsed on the grass, exhausted. Angie froze in mid-hang-up. The Captain crouched beside me.

"Is she all right?" I gasped.

"Go back and find out."

"I can go back?"

155

"Yeah. You have to retrace some steps."

Patel was off and running. I could barely pull myself up. "Can we walk this?"

"Sure." Captain said. We float-walked forward. The landscape moved in slow motion. People's voices were low and slow, like whales singing across the ocean. He slapped me on the back. "Sonny, that business you've got, playing *catch me if you can* with the cops. The bachelorettes. You're better than that."

I shrugged.

"You're an explorer, it's in your blood. Find something that gives you satisfaction, excitement. Something that doesn't piss your wife off."

"Like what?"

"There's forty-one uncharted moons orbiting Kelt 3b. Hop an ion ship and chart one."

I watched a pigeon poop in slow motion. "I'm kind of locked into this job."

"You just brought your consciousness into the fifth dimension and transcended the laws of time and space. You can do anything you want."

We were back at my patio. Patel was waiting.

"Come on." I said to her.

"No, I'm staying." She loosened her ponytail. Her long black hair curled in low-gravity tendrils. "This is what I've been looking for all along."

"But you can come back later. There's more life to be lived"

"Two hundred and five years is enough."

The Captain smiled and tossed her the ball. "Want to play some one-on-one?"

She caught it with one hand. "No, but I'd like to play some basketball."

I took a step back, fell into the white, onto a crumpled quilt back home. I tried to get up. It was like getting out of the water after swimming all day. Just moving took a huge effort.

A fly buzzed near my ear. Never thought I'd be happy to hear that.

Maggie was in the kitchen, watching morning shows. "Stanz called." she said between bites of cereal. "He wants to talk to you about a dry cleaning bill."

"Where's Angie?"

"In the bath. She should be out soon."

"She's okay." I laughed

"No she's not."

"What?"

"Remember yesterday? The teacher's conference? She's not doing her reading."

Angie opened the bathroom door. The steamy tub was covered with green goop. "Oh, would you look at that." Maggie cried. "No more Groovy Green bubble bath for you!"

"I'm sorry," Angie wailed.

"Groovy green bubble bath!" I laughed, giving Angie a hug. I grabbed Maggie too, danced them across the floor, singing "Baby, we got a Groovy Greeny love." Angie giggled, spun away, faster and faster, until she fell onto the couch.

"What is with you?" Maggie laughed. She twirled, like she used to do on the dance floor. Groovy Green splattered the counter and the TV news showing a photograph of Patel. I staggered to a stop and read the news ticker.

"The Earthling visitor checked into her hotel, went to sleep and never woke up," it scrolled. "Her Unified Clutch of Anthropologists has come here for her funeral."

"Daddy," Angie said. "Isn't that your friend Tina?"

"What friend?" Maggie said.

"I think so," I said.

"Goodbye, Tina." Angie waved greenly. "Goodbye."

Mary Madigan is a writer, artist, and photographer. She researched and photographed political uncertainty in the Middle East and somehow managed to stay left of boom. She likes to explore the civilized and the wild, to imagine places that don't exist yet. She's written and published short stories about life, death, and interplanetary travel. She's currently working on the **Murmuration** *series, about an apparently ordinary family's lives before and after the Singularity.*
www.marypmadigan.com.

First contact with an alien species will be difficult and dangerous. Final contact may impart even more danger to a species' psyche.

FINAL CONTACT

Al Onia

First contact.

"Ensign Pursang. Assessment. Tell me what the hell that object is?"

Jared Pursang, newly-minted officer in the exploration corps, studied his sensors. It's big, Commander. Mass, twenty-thousand metric tonnes. Metal shell, composition unknown."

Commander Korell ordered. "Stop the buggy. Camouflage mode. All systems, active and passive off. Visual only. Lieutenant. Weaponry evaluation of our visitor?"

The hum from the six-electric drivers wound down. The Greep came to a halt and settled into the surface of the planet. Hull photocells absorbed and mimicked the surrounding rocks and foliage.

"Substantial, if commensurate with its size, sir."

Korell slid open the viewing slit. Sunlight illuminated the now-quiescent cabin of the ground-exploration vehicle. The sun eclipsed as the leading edge of the intruder passed over.

Jared counted in his head until the shadow passed. Fifteen seconds. He was right. Huge.

Korell expelled his breath. "I guess we're not alone on this ball of dirt after all." He opened a second slit pointed in the direction of the unknown vessel's retreat. "We'll hightail it back to the shuttle once it's out of sight. If they registered us, apparently they're not hostile."

They waited in silence, each man, like Jared, evaluating how much earth's exploration agenda had just changed. A first contact. Or at least, a first encounter. No contact yet.

Korell closed the slit. "Let's make tracks."

"Commander."

"Ensign?"

"Speaking of tracks. Wouldn't they have seen our tracks?"

"If they did, they didn't care to acknowledge us. At this point, that's fine by me. Let the diplomats figure it out. Our job is to report the presence of another someone or something."

The Greep retraced her path and two hours later, they reached their camo'd ship. Commander Korell slid the hatch open. "Man your stations aboard."

The earth shivered under Jared's feet. He whirled in the direction they'd come. The vessel returned, a single blue beam emanated from the nose of the ship. Smoke and fire belched from the surface beneath the beam.

"Sweet mercy. It's melting the crust." Korell ordered, "Leave the Greep. More important to relay our news." His next command never came. A streak of molten rock arced over the tree tops and sliced their escape in two.

Jared was moving instinctively without orders, putting distance between himself and the larger targets of the ship and the Greep. The others, including Commander Korell did the same.

The vessel never changed course but continued its path past them by five or six kilometers.

The team regrouped. "All accounted for?"

"Missing two Commander. Evans and deGaulle were aboard the ship."

"Check inside the remains, Lieutenant. Ensign Pursang, send a warning signal to fleet. Use the radio in the Greep. The rest of you, salvage what you can from the ship. We'll be here a while."

Jared asked. "Distress call as well, Commander?"

"They'll come soon enough. I want them prepared for that crust-carver or whatever it is."

"I don't think they even knew we were here, Commander. It could be unmanned."

"It could be. But manned or not, benign or not, it's a hell of dangerous machine. Put your training to use while we wait it out, Ensign. Design us a counter-weapon."

It took Pursang twelve years and three ascensions in rank to complete and test his counter-weapon. Korell hadn't made it off the unnamed planet of first encounter with the Kym, as they became known.

"Lieutenant Commander Pursang reporting to the bridge, Captain Asario."

"Glad to have you and your armament aboard, Pursang. We've got the Kym cornered on that planet you discovered them on a dozen years ago."

"We named it Walburg, sir. After Commander Korell's home town. Why are they there, any idea?"

"Don't know, don't care. Scouting indicates at least three of those crust carvers are building an inland sea of substantial size."

"Colonization?"

"Good guess. Mine too. If your rig succeeds, the Kym'll have saved us a lot of work. We'll be there in fourteen hours. Make yourself at home and make sure your gun's working."

"Aye aye, sir."

One shift later, Jared was back on the bridge, watching the approach to the site of his first battle. He hadn't called it that, but the force's official spin concentrated on the one-sidedness of the encounter. Motivation for it not to repeat.

"Closing on orbit, Captain. No sign of any other orbital vessels."

"Located the carvers?"

"Yes sir. Bringing up the image now."

Jared inhaled with a whistle. Two of the discs circled in unison, flame belching from underneath them as they blasted a massive crater out of the planet's crust. A third carver straight-lined from the coastline of the major southern hemisphere's ocean. "The conduit."

"Tell us where we need to be, Lieutenant Commander."

Pursang took a seat at the navigation center. "Let's try for the lone carver first. We need to be in front of it at . . ." he fingered the screen at his fingertips, ". . . this angle. We refract their own beam directly under the carver. I saw what the molten crust did to Korell's ship. We're confident it can do the same to theirs."

The minutes passed as the ship settled into position. Captain Asario said, "No hostiles in orbit?"

"Clear sir. Outer system sensors indicate no activity. All right, weave your voodoo, Pursang."

Pursang linked to the technical team. "Tracking carver optimum reached, lock on. Commence."

The screen view highlighted the blue beam from the carver.

"I don't see any alteration," Asario said.

"Coming up in a few seconds, Captain."

The blue beam quivered and took on a pinkish hue. It didn't bend. The pink color changed to dark crimson and the magma plume soared straight for them.

Asario didn't bother to issue the command to retreat, he pounded his override and the ship lurched out of the path of the molten rock. Almost. The ship listed on edge before the automatic gyros took control. It righted but corkscrewed down into the atmosphere.

Jared brought up the ship's vitals. They were done. He was to be marooned on Walburg a second time.

"Abandon ship. I can hold it with full power to starboard for five minutes, no more. All hands to the lifeboats."

Asario's officers and crew were well-disciplined. As one, they ran from the bridge. Jared hesitated. "Captain?"

"Get the hell from my bridge, Lieutenant. Tell those idiots at home to give this one up. Our line in the sand just moved back a few lightyears." Asario gripped his command chair with one hand while he manipulated the ship's controls with the other. The deck lurched under Jared. He followed orders.

Admiral Jared Pursang scowled at his reflection once again. He turned the star on his collar slightly. Finally, it suited him. He stood away from the mirror and looked at his watch. The Kym would arrive in a few minutes.

"Admiral, will you stop primping. You're not being inspected by Fleet Admiral Vol. One would think *you* lost the battle for Walburg's planet, instead of the Kym."

Jared looked at the other man in the room. Ambassador Dreyfus. Here to fuss over the surrender. As if a man who just won a planet couldn't ensure the niceties of proper documentation. Jared said, "I am anticipating, not primping. I'm curious to meet the Kym commander we finally defeated."

"You want to gloat. I hope to establish a dialog between races which will avoid future military conflict. This could be third time luck. At least your fastidiousness shows respect. The Kym apparently like that."

Jared looked at his watch again, "I respect their apparent ruthlessness. I've been on the losing side twice, at the whims of overpowering machines. Unaware of our existence, if I didn't know better." He inhaled deeply, pushing his chest out. "I prefer victory. I savor absolute victory."

"Your reports had a hint of the Kym hardly noticing your forces until it was too late. They were distracted by another agenda?"

"We'll see. Walburg's a beach head. I was ordered to take it and I have. The fact that it is the scene of my previous clashes against the Kym is rewarding. Their defeat may not be an aberration. Maybe we've learned how to beat them. If so, you'll be negotiating for the next system and the one after that." Jared paused and went over to the window, looking down the mountain slope to the village below. "It's been too long since my counterpart was in an inferior position. This will give me satisfying closure."

"Has it stopped raining?"

Jared stared through the viewindow, ignoring the white-bearded reflection of himself in the glass. He wasn't looking directly outside, he knew that. The Kym headquarters was well fortified. This view was relayed by sensors. "Yes." He turned to see Dreyfus raising his feet in the chair. "You look comfortable. Are you going to sit there when he arrives?"

Dreyfus closed his eyes. "These chairs are marvelous. Considering the difference in human and Kym physiologies, I am amazed how successfully their furniture adapts to us. I shall ship one home with me." Dreyfus raised his head and looked around the room. "This post is unchanged from the moment the Kym commanders apparently fled under your barrage. I think you'll find it as comfortable to your command as I do this chair to my backside."

Jared clasped his hands behind his back and moved away from the window. He stopped next to a small sculpture. It was a figurine on top of a white pillar. The miniature depicted a Kym on one knee, its long arms flung forward in an arresting pose of both conquest and defiance. Jared said, "Yes, you are right, I fit well here. Three decades of service and I can finally put my demons to rest."

He caressed the statue. It looked like metal but it was not cool to the touch. "I see something new in this sculpture every hour."

"Interesting position, looks as if he is pleading and throwing a curse at the same time."

Jared spun it around on the pillar and shook his head. "No, I think the subject sees a new perspective and is revising his decisions." Jared looked at his watch again. "He should be here in five minutes. Are the Kym punctual?"

Dreyfus kept staring at the sculpture. "Their punctuality or lack of it is one of the many areas of knowledge we lack. You probably know as much about them as we do."

"Great. You're supposed to be my resource person. I only know how they fight and, up until now, it's been damn well."

Dreyfus said, "I'm here to observe the transition of power and to learn what I can about the Kym. I want to find out what we can do the next time we encounter them and avoid your job entirely."

"A diplomatic solution. Incomplete success." Jared shuddered.

"If we can. If not, it may turn out like Walburg's for them again."

Jared paced by the viewwindow. "The Kym did not flee under my attack. They left an opening in their defenses that was a onetime mistake. I did not expect it then and I doubt it will be repeated." Memories of that encounter returned.

Jared studied the holo of the Kym command center in his field camp. The enemy's stronghold provided an excellent view of the native village below. He addressed his team of officers. "Observations? Is it as impenetrable as it looks?"

His second-in-command, Captain Luyenbrock, took the lead as usual to get the others to start thinking out loud. "No obvious weakness. They're shielded above and they have full view of all inferior approaches."

"We draw them out."

"Or prepare for a long siege."

Suggestions began to flow freely from Jared's officers and he listened intently, waiting for the ideas to cease.

"Hold the village hostage."

"Infiltrate the keep with a traitorous local."

"Hold a villager hostage and send in a relative to sabotage."

"The Kym'll be expecting something like that."

"Frontal assault."

"Suicidal, but it might work with enough troops."

"What's the latest update on the storms?"

Jared said, "Good question. Eagle, you're the weather expert."

The officer replaced the holo of the Kym headquarters with a further view of the ocean beyond. Half a dozen circular cloud systems hid the view of the water surface. He said, "Each system is driven by the others. The first will hit land early tomorrow."

"Close to any of the villages?"

"Not within thirty kilometers. But the rains will precipitate flooding all along the coast and that'll threaten the villages. I've seen little evidence of evacuation planning, just minor flood preparations."

Another officer said, "We've seen evidence of the Kym personally observing in the field."

Jared said, "Well, they've a lot at stake." He moved the first picture back to main view. "Prepare to attack when the storms close on the keep. Ready your men at Luyenbrock's signal."

Fourteen hours later, Jared huddled with his own elite squad preparing for their assault. He watched the visual feed from orbit. Luyenbrock said, "The crest is coming faster than the locals predicted."

Jared said, "You're closer to the Kym base. Any sign they are distracted?"

"There's some activity now, Admiral."

Jared watched the new picture. "I see moving lights. Amplify." A yellow tinge provided more contrast at the higher magnification.

"Machinery. Large machinery. A crust-carver?"

"I've seen them before, Captain. We are prepared. They're coming out with two of them."

Luyenbrock directed his troops. "Get moving. If they catch us standing still with that, we'll be part of the rock."

Jared was on his feet, signaling his own men. He watched the picture on his face shield. Luyenbrock's group was heading for the gap in the trees where the crust-carvers would come through. Jared said, "Don't alert them to your presence. Hold fire unless they attack us." He watched the two large machines drift over his men. The noise of them came through his head gear and was amplified by the trembling of the ground. The carvers were heading down slope, away from his attack force. Jared yelled to his men, "They're going to help the natives divert the flooding rivers."

Luyenbrock radioed, "We're in."

"We're on your tail. Prisoners?"

"No one here. Watch your back, Admiral."

Twenty minutes later Jared was sitting in the command room of the Kym post. Luyenbrock was in contact with the rest of the squads. "The Kym have indicated the battle is over. The crust carvers have completed their task. The Kym were on the ground, directing the locals during the storm. They will not engage us. Their commander will formally surrender two days hence but not to expect to hear from him in the meantime. They're intermingled among the locals."

"Strange protocol," Jared observed. "Uncharacteristic of the Kym to *hide*. Remain on full alert until the surrender is executed. Ambassador Dreyfus is due tomorrow. God, what were the Kym doing, leaving these quarters so vulnerable?"

Luyenbrock said, "Diverting the flood waters from the villages. They're out there still, cutting new rivercourses."

Jared said, "All forces to remain on high alert. The carvers are a threat."

"Shall we demand them as reparation, sir?"

"Leave that to Dreyfus."

A rap returned Jared's attention to the door and away from the puzzling victory. It brought Dreyfus to his feet.

The door opened and Luyenbrock stepped in, "Kym representative Obiesse, Admiral Pursang."

The blue-skinned Kym looked tall even from across the room. Jared strode quickly to him, his right hand raised, palm outward. The Kym stepped back at his approach and glanced between Jared and Dreyfus.

"Commander Obiesse, I am Jared Pursang, this is Ambassador Arn Dreyfus."

The Kym stopped his retreat. "I was never a Commander; I was Observer Obiesse. I am now Citizen Obiesse."

"I am sorry to be the one responsible for your demotion, Citizen. The vagaries of battle."

"Citizen is not a demotion, Admiral Pursang. It is a Kym's highest rank."

Dreyfus said, "Will you be seated, Citizen Obiesse?" He offered the chair he had been seated in earlier.

"I will stand. These are your quarters now."

Dreyfus remained standing as well. "We thank you for agreeing to this amicable turnover."

The Kym did not reply but moved to the viewindow. Jared came beside him and looked at the village and lands below, water glistening in temporary lakes everywhere. "It is an excellent location, strategic and naturally secure."

"Strategic?" the Kym paused. "Ah, yes. A military reference. We found it a good place from which to observe. We spent many years preparing this world for its transplanted refugees. A vanity to continue our scrutiny after the major work was completed."

Dreyfus said, "Admiral Pursang refers to the advantageous location of Walburg's planet as well."

"This planet is called G'er L'iss by its inhabitants. It fulfills a need for your civilization? It was important to us, too. A world to harbor the L'issans when we discovered their home planet was doomed. A pre-space culture we wanted to preserve. I hope your race will see fit to honor their singularity. I have duties below with the L'issans before tomorrow's departure. Do you require my presence further?"

Jared said, "Only a short time longer. Ambassador Dreyfus wishes you to sign this." He placed the surrender on the Kym's own desk. "You keep referring to yourself as an observer, yet your influence on the locals is noticeable."

"We do not follow a policy of selective non-interference; we try to help. As we did in the floods." The Kym handed the executed document back to Jared. "When you took possession of this post."

Jared shrugged.

Dreyfus said, "The battle for Walburg, I mean G'er L'iss, is over. We are ready to negotiate now."

"There is no need. We will withdraw."

Dreyfus' role evaporated in three simple words, Jared thought. "At least grant us time for a request or two."

"Ask what you will."

Jared said, "For myself, I wanted to meet you in peaceful circumstances." A glance from Dreyfus kept him from expanding his point. "As one commander to another, good luck." He held out his palm again.

Obiesse hesitated a moment, then returned the gesture. "Goodbye."

"A further moment," Dreyfus said. "We would like to study your crust carvers."

The Kym lowered his head. "You would convert them to weaponry. They have been destroyed."

"I assure you, our curiosity is in the technology of those machines but I won't insult you by denying a military interest. A peace accord between earth and Kym would guarantee no military use could ever be employed against either side."

"Destruction is our guarantee. I must leave if you have nothing further to ask."

Dreyfus regained his diplomatic calm. "Are there any personal items you wish to recover?"

Obiesse stopped to survey the room. His gaze focused on the sculpture. He walked to it and picked it up gently with both hands.

"From your homeworld? Someone famous?"

"No, Ambassador Dreyfus, it was created by a resident of the village below. An artist named H'an L'ler."

Jared said, "Please, take it."

Obiesse held it. "As we learned from them, they learned from us. The figure is of no one individual of my race, yet it expresses our individual yearnings quite well. I've never had a visitor who wasn't moved by it. Thank you, I will carry it with me on our departure tomorrow." The Kym nodded his head and left.

Dreyfus sat back in his chair. "I'm glad he didn't ask for this. Well, did you get what you wanted?"

Jared stared at the vacant pedestal, trying to recreate the image of the sculpture but could not. "No. He didn't act like a loser. I am going to talk to him again tomorrow at the departure. Maybe Citizen Obiesse won't be so cocky when he realizes the Kym presence on Walburg is truly finished. The next sculpture made by this local craftsman will be of a human. I will pay a visit to H'an L'ler this afternoon."

Dreyfus put his hands behind his head and sighed. "I've got the formal surrender and a new chair. I'm happy. But I'll join you if you've no objection."

Jared's translator, Eagle, returned to the armored carrier containing Jared, Dreyfus, and two other guards.

"He says the studio of H'an L'ler is over one street and half-a-something that way."

Jared said, "Thank him and offer to pay him to lead us there."

Eagle nodded and called to the native who in return shouted a reply.

"He says our transport won't fit the lane."

Jared said, "The empty streets are making the ambassador nervous. Relax Dreyfus, the L'issans don't have the necessary attitude to set a trap. We can walk from here."

"Shouldn't we leave a guard?" Dreyfus asked.

Eagle said, "No need, it won't be touched."

Jared was already out of the vehicle. "Let's go."

The group followed the local around a corner and down a narrow lane shadowed by unbroken walls four meters high on each side. Jared said, "The silt mark from the flood is a full third the way up."

Dreyfus looked where he was pointing at the change in the shadow's tint. "Strong walls," he said.

The men reached the next street and the guide pointed to a yellow and blue banner above a small door less than thirty meters distant.

Jared said, "Pay him, Eagle."

"He accepts no payment for obligation."

Jared looked at Dreyfus for guidance. The ambassador merely shrugged.

Jared instructed the guards, "Remain outside, Ambassador Dreyfus and I will call you if H'an L'ler does not speak universal."

The two walked past shops spewing exotic smells and odd noises. Signs of quick recovery after the storm's damage. They entered the artist's workshop. There was no one in sight.

"It's dazzling," Jared said.

"The colors are surprising," Dreyfus said. "I haven't seen the natives wearing anything this vivid."

Decorating the walls of the atelier were fabric bolts of bright yellows, soft blues, rich purples and glowing reds. Jared said, "I thought H'an L'ler was a sculptor."

"I am that too, good sirs."

Jared turned to the owner of the voice. A large native had entered through a curtain in the back of the shop. "H'an L'ler, you speak our language well. I am Admiral Pursang and this is . . ."

H'an L'ler finished the introduction himself. "Ambassador Dreyfus. Welcome to my studio."

"You know who we are, do you know why we are here?"

The pale-skinned artist said, "I know who you are only because the Kym explained it to us and you have been in the streets asking for me. I am not a seer so I do not divine the reason for your presence. Come into my compound and we will share R'inge."

Jared said, "Your offer is kind, I would like to see your sculpting workshop but I . . ."

Dreyfus interrupted before Jared could refuse the R'inge, whatever that was. "We would be honored to share R'inge with such a multi-talented artist." Dreyfus nudged Jared's ribs as he spoke.

They passed through the curtained doorway and found themselves in a sunlit compound, shaded by a brightly striped awning.

Jared examined the sculptures in various stages of completion while H'an L'ler fussed with a pot suspended above a glowing fire. Jared said, "You were fortunate to keep your firewood dry in the floods."

H'an offered Jared a steaming cup of brew. "Alas, I could not, but the Kym were here after the crest and dried my fuel store for me." He sat on a bench and Jared and Dreyfus did the same.

Jared tasted the R'inge. It wasn't too hot, despite the steam, and reminded him of tomato and cinnamon. "A piece of yours is, or rather *was*, in the observation post."

"Citizen Obiesse," H'an said.

"It's a beautiful work of art. Could you sculpt one for me?"

The native put his cup aside and walked around Jared. "I haven't the right piece of freestone at the moment. But I will let you know if I find a suitable one."

Jared put his cup down firmly.

Dreyfus placed a hand on Jared's arm and spoke first, "How long did it take to find the right piece for Citizen Obiesse?"

Jared realized what Dreyfus had done and relaxed, grateful for the diplomat's intervention.

H'an replied, "Nearly a year."

"There. You see, Admiral? It could be a year before you get your sculpture started. Now that H'an appreciates your keen interest, I'm certain a retainer will keep him looking."

Jared felt controlled enough to speak. "Your fabrics are very vivid; why do we not see them worn?"

H'an glanced inside his shop and then back at them. "It's the wrong time of year. We publicly display ourselves in the colors of rejoice only during planting month and final harvest. You might see them at other times, if you were invited into one of our homes. Some L'issans wear them privately." H'an paused and then added, "Though many are currently still in mourning."

"The floods?" said Dreyfus.

"The departure of the Kym."

Jared finished his drink and stood. "It was an honor to meet you, H'an L'ler. I look forward to our next meeting when you have the freestone." He passed a folded piece of Command Currency to him.

The L'issan didn't accept the retainer. "The honor is mine, Admiral, Ambassador. Good day to you both."

Outside, in the street, Jared said, "A year? Why couldn't he use one of the pieces he had lying around?"

Dreyfus said, "Artists. You get the same attitude everywhere. No deadlines. Why don't you ask Obiesse if he has changed his mind about taking the figure with him? I'll go with you tomorrow."

Jared shook his head, "No, I want to see him alone." He tried to picture a statue of himself on the pedestal but the image would not come.

Jared and Eagle forged a path through the multitude of L'issans crowding the Kym departure pad. He could see a few scattered Kym towering above clusters of villagers. He looked at his watch. A quarter hour to lift-off. They should be boarding.

Obiesse was surrounded too when Jared spotted his back moving toward the departure ship.

"Stay here," Jared ordered his men. He headed for the Kym ship.

He and Obiesse arrived at the same time. "Good day, Citizen." Jared remembered the proper address. "There are more of your fellows than we knew were left on Walburg." Jared pointed to the forty or so Kym now converging on the ship.

"Many of my fellow Observers were scattered across the planet."

"I will soon be sending out scouting missions myself. With the cooperation of the L'issans to spread the news of the transfer of power."

"Do not approach from the air. The L'aquoy in particular distrust aerial travelers, though they've had the technology for glide flight for five generations."

"Thank you, I will consider your advice. We'll set up a planet-wide communication network to eliminate the need for much personal travel. Come back in two years and you won't recognize the progress we will have made."

The noon chime sounded and the Kym began entering the ship. Jared watched each one touch the ground with their hand before disappearing inside.

Obiesse waited until the last one had gone. "We won't return to G'er L'iss in two years, Admiral. Or two thousand. The Kym will not remain in any system in contact with your race. There will be no further encounters."

Jared said, "Our purpose is not to drive you away. With your technology, there are worlds uninhabitable to us that you could make suitable."

"The Kym purpose is far removed from yours. We do not seek to tame and change places to suit *us*. We are quarantining ourselves from you. Permanently. Excuse me, Admiral Pursang, it is my turn."

Obiesse turned and walked to the ramp base. He touched the ground with one hand, then the other. With one knee touching G'er L'iss' surface he held out his arms in imitation of the sculpture he had retained. He bowed his head to the natives then ascended inside the ship.

Jared stood back to watch the ship depart. Dreyfus appeared beside him.

"I couldn't resist seeing them leave. Did you find your answer?"

Jared said, "No. An ephemeral victory. I've a feeling we lost more than we'll ever know." His words were drowned out by the noise of lift-off.

Al Onia is a retired geophysicist, now fulltime writer, living in Calgary, Canada. His novels Javenny *and* Transient City *are published by Bundoran Press. A sequel to* Transient City *will be released in Spring, 2017. His short fiction has appeared in* Ares, AB Negative, Perihelion SF, On Spec, The Speculative Edge, Heroic Fantasy Quarterly, Spinetingler, *Marion Zimmer Bradley's* Fantasy Magazine, *and the anthologies* Casserole Diplomacy, Body-Smith 401, North of Infinity, *and* Warrior Wisewoman 3.
Al is a two-time Aurora Award finalist in the short story category.
www.ajonia.com

The United Milky Way Galaxy is linked with two other united galaxies through a transdimensional space portal. When militant secessionists destroy the Universe Gate, loyalists in the Milky Way are cut off from the rest of the Intergalactic Confederation. Loyalties, both political and familial, are strained to the limit as interstellar war rages across the galaxy. The fate of humanity, and many other races, hangs in the balance.

UNITY

Tom Olbert

Cassandra DeVries was hurled from the gunnery control station, the deafening explosion of plasma conduction lines suddenly silenced in dead vacuum. Her head swam, the bulkhead splitting wide open as she was blasted into the black void of space.

She spun end-over-end, her breathing raspy and labored in her oxygen helmet. She struggled with the controls of her suit's propulsion jets, finally righting herself. The blazing panorama of the galactic spiral was breathtaking. She looked down and saw the wreckage of gunnery port 3 splintering off through space. Enemy defense fighters were closing on the particle beam cannon ship, its photon turrets blasting wildly. And ahead, in orbit about the outlying neutron star at the edge of the Milky Way core sectors, was their target: The Universe Gate. The vast, alien, ring-like mechanism was even now activating, silver-blue energy streams intersecting at its center as space seemed to ripple and implode in the gigantic ring. The trans-dimensional gateway to two alien galaxies. She grit her teeth in anger as the wreckage of escort fighters spun across her field of vision, thoughts of slain comrades and friends filling her mind. *Alien scum.*

An enemy fighter swept towards the cannon ship, its particle tubes blazing. Calculating course and trajectory, she fired her jets and paralleled the IGC fighter as it passed her. She launched a rocket line, its magnetic grapple snagging the fighter's hull. Straining against the pressure of acceleration, she reeled in the line and struggled to reach the prow. She held onto the rocket line with one hand and pulled a grenade from her suit pack with the other. She attached the grenade and jetted away. As the fighter exploded in a white-hot flash, she felt a surge of satisfaction, like fire in her blood.

A secessionist escort fighter turned and slowed. Firing another line and securing herself to the hull, she held on as the fighter docked with the cannon ship. The landing bay pressurizing, she blew the seals on her suit and pulled off her helmet as the pilot opened the fighter's hatch. She smiled as the pilot removed his helmet, Victor Marsden's strong, smiling face emerging. The cannon ship's focused energy seemed to pass like an electrical vibrancy through Cassandra's body. Through the observation dome, she saw a blue-white stream of energy pulse down the length of the cannon ship, a brilliant white beam lancing out from the lens at its prow and striking the alien ring ahead.

As the ring shattered and dissolved in an explosion of searing white light, her heart soared. Victor and others in the bay around them cheered wildly, holding their fists aloft in the rebel salute. They had won. The galaxy was now independent and free of the Inter-Galactic Confederation. Victor took her in his strong arms. Her blood raced hot. They kissed, the light of the exploding Universe Gate washing over them.

The capitol city of the United Milky Way Galaxy floated on the pitching ocean waves of the planet Andaar in the Altair system.

In the city's heart, Landra Ventari, Prime Counselor of the United Milky Way Galaxy stood in the audience chamber. Her fellow galactic counselors and representatives of the other two member galaxies of the Inter-Galactic Confederation gathered around the old woman.

"The situation is grave," Moon Song, the Orca whale, Governing Counselor of the Milky Way rim sectors said from her tank, her eye fixed on Landra through the glass wall. "The secessionists are attacking ruthlessly in all core sectors, targeting all non-human populations, both organic and A.I., without mercy or discretion. Refugees are flooding out of the core sectors towards the galactic rim. With the Universe Gate gone, the limited resources at the rim are being stretched to the limit. How are you responding?"

Landra drew a deep breath, gathering her strength. "We are withdrawing our military forces from the core sectors and re-grouping them at the rim for a counter-strike."

"And, what of our responsibility to safeguard civilian populations in the core sectors?" Asked Zaal-4 the fluidic A.I., Governing Counselor of the globular star clusters beyond the galactic rim. Its shapeless, silvery liquid form took the shape of a shimmering globe.

Landra clenched a fist. "Intelligence is doing what it can to supply the resistance cadres and set up escape routes for the refugees, but we cannot afford to scatter our space fleets." She fought to keep steady, her own emotions of grief, rage, and fear welling up. She tried to focus on the larger objectives, but thoughts of her own children and grand-children in the core sectors intruded. She cleared her throat. "All collective logic centers concur, we must wait for the secessionists to over-extend and turn on each other. When they are at their weakest, we will have our forces in position to strike." She blinked back her tears.

"How did this happen?" Traal-na-Raath, the representative of the Magellanic Clouds said from a vat of chlorine gas, its three bristly semi-triangular sections separating as its fin-like sensory organs rose through the greenish mists.

Landra sighed. "The answer to that question goes back centuries," she said. The central A.I. accessed the telepathic link to the historical archives and holographic three-dimensional starfields formed in the chamber around Landra. "For nearly a thousand years since the galactic unification wars, human star colonies throughout the galaxy lived in peace within the Inter-Galactic

Confederation." Fleets of space ships swept through the hologram. "The disruption began nearly four hundred standard years ago, when automated sleeper ships from Old Earth, their passengers in cryogenic cold sleep for thousands of years, finally arrived in inhabited systems and began to mix with the more civilized human populations who had preceded them there during the FTL (faster than light) era. These Old Earth humans were of a different era, unaccustomed to alien contact, human-A.I. interface, or sentient non-human terrestrials. The cultural shock of their integration into our societies was a disruption that spread for generations, manifesting in a growing sense of resentment among the predominantly human-occupied galactic sectors against the IGC. This was exacerbated by the arrival of multi-generational Earth ships." Ships the size of small planets entered the hologram, their shadows falling over IGC colony planets. "The generation ships' closed human societies had lived for millennia under dictatorial regimes that rejected all external ideas and concepts. Their arrival in the human sectors provided focus and leadership for the growing anti-alien fervor. That was the beginning of the secessionist movement."

"What efforts are underway to re-build the Universe Gate?" Tessryn Gur, the representative of Andromeda asked, its form like a gigantic, steaming spider-web clustering into a series of gummy knots, the spheres near its center glowing slightly.

Landra wiped perspiration from her upper lip. "With the flow of resources cut off from the core sectors, we can do little toward restoring physical contact between the three galaxies, and therefore can obviously expect no military support from outside the Milky Way. We're on our own and must concentrate all available resources into the military counter-strike. We are, however, making every effort to set up sub-space communications relays, so we can at least keep Andromeda and the Magellanic Clouds apprised of our situation, and try to coordinate strategy in dealing with the economic instability which will obviously occur between Andromeda and the M.C. during the crisis."

She looked to the stars surrounding her. "My brothers and sisters, we must stand now as one, more so than ever before." She forced down her fear and despair, steeling her resolve to inspire those depending upon her. "We have survived far greater trials. Super novae, inter-galactic wars. We will survive this." She closed her eyes. *If there is a Cosmic One . . . Please, don't let the dream die.*

The worldships advanced like dark harbingers through the core sectors, destroying at will.

On the command bridge of Worldship Omega, Jason DeVries smiled amid celebration and revelry. His wife Corrinne laughed beside him, resting her head on his shoulder.

The holographic images of several other men, Garver, Marcus, Desjardine, Halvorson—the commanders of the other four worldships—appeared, surrounding DeVries. "How goes the attack, my friends?" DeVries asked.

Each of the other men gave favorable reports. Even as he raised his wine glass and toasted victories on all galactic fronts, DeVries quietly studied each man, taking in the crouching envy peeking out from behind the genial smiles. Garver and Marcus could be handled easily enough, he thought. Too busy watching each other . . . and one day, fighting each other, he was certain . . . to unite against him. Halvorson was the most devious of the lot, but slow and cautious. He'd angle a position of power for himself, of course, but he'd make no outright move against DeVries. Not alone. That left Desjardine. DeVries sipped his wine and studied the other man's strong features and cold eyes, his own eyes narrowing. That swine had a knife pointed at his throat. But, he was sure Desjardine would make no move until the New Galactic Empire was officially declared. By then, DeVries would have gathered enough allies to secure his position and destroy Desjardine. Of that he was certain. "Until next time, my friends." The images all faded.

"Well, Desmond, my friend," DeVries said, stepping away from Corrinne and turning to Fleet Admiral Desmond Marsden, his closest and most valued ally. "I believe congratulations are in order," he said, heartily clasping the other man's hand. "Now that my daughter Cassandra and your son Victor have declared their engagement. A finer pairing one couldn't hope for."

"I wholeheartedly agree, Jason," Marsden said with a hungry smile. "And, as always . . . you have my absolute support."

Of course I do, DeVries thought. *As a member of my family, you expect a rich share of my power in the coming government. You'll have it. Until I've eliminated you and your lusty son, and all your holdings are mine.* They clinked glasses.

IGC Space Commander Marla Ventari was startled by the interstellar communication signal cutting across her usual comm sweeps. She froze, her blood running cold as ice water as she realized the signal was Security One, and on her grandmother's personal code. The Prime Counselor of the Milky Way would not be contacting her directly unless . . . She closed her eyes. *No. Please, by the Cosmic One, no.*

"Marla . . . " her second-in-command, Skyheart signaled her from the adjoining control compartment, her voice translated by the intercom A.I. "Would you like me to take it?"

Marla shook off the numbing fear. "No, old friend," she said quietly, looking over at her first officer and best friend and managing a grim smile. "This is one time you can't protect me." She put her hand against the glass wall separating them. The face of the dolphin on the other side looked at her through the water with a cast in her dark eyes Marla had come to recognize as loving concern. She answered the transmission, her voice dry. "Commander Ventari acknowledging."

Her grandmother Landra's lined, distinguished face appeared before her in hologram. The quiet strength Marla had come to admire in those aging eyes, now rimmed with redness told her what she'd already dreaded. "Marla . . . my beloved, brave Marla . . . "

"David," she said, not making it a question.

"I am so sorry. He died with honor and bravery, defending the Universe Gate. He didn't suffer."

Marla drew a deep breath, her memories of the man she'd loved slipping through her mind like fleeting ghosts, one parting warm smile on his handsome face, one last loving embrace in his strong arms . . . one life slipping away like a dream as another began. "Thank you for telling me, Grandmother. The fear was becoming a burden."

"Marla . . . you have my clearance to proceed immediately to the rim, if you so choose. You needn't confer with Intelligence if . . . "

"I've already sent the rest of my squadron home, as ordered. Only this command ship and a few escort strikers remain. My duty is here, helping with the civilian evacuation, and the resistance," she said, marshalling her strength and focusing on the task ahead. "I ask only one thing. Is there visual data from the Universe Gate?"

Her grandmother seemed to hesitate. Then, she complied. The telepathic link activated, visual images from the battle of the Universe Gate flooding into Marla's mind. She saw David's fighter circling the secessionist particle beam cannon ship, firing, angling for a shot at the bridge section. A secessionist soldier in an atmosphere suit jetted in and fired a rocket line into the fighter. Marla gritted her teeth as the secessionist reeled in the line and planted a grenade near the cockpit. She winced as the enemy soldier jetted away, David's fighter exploding in a white flash.

Marla looked at the rebel soldier who had destroyed her life. So brave and daring a soldier. She watched as the rebel fired a second rocket line into a secessionist fighter and escaped. As the fighter turned in for a landing on the attacking cannon ship, a view from one of the IGC defense fighters zoomed in on the soldier's helmet, and in the light of an explosion caught a clear image of the face behind the view plate. The face of a beautiful young woman, the bright explosion reflected in her large, dark eyes. Marla froze the image, burning every line, every detail of that face into her mind. So lovely. So very brave.

She would savor every moment of killing her.

Three months later.

Cassandra DeVries-Marsden grit her teeth and gagged at the sight of mass slaughter.

Nazaar Minor was a bloody battlefield. Secessionist troop carriers lay in smoking ruin as Graaz resistance fighters pressed their attack, the air thick with photon fire. Nazaar Major filled a third of the pale blue sky, the planet's two moons hanging against its cloudy crescent, like silent witnesses to the butchery below.

Cassandra ran to a fallen secessionist soldier lying near the flaming wreckage of a gun turret, only to find his charred body lifeless. She took the remaining power packs from his blaster and stuffed them in her belt pack. She choked in the black smoke, her eyes straining vainly, searching the morning sky for relief transports that should have been here by now. *What the hell is Space Command doing,* she wondered in disgust. The ground shook as a second wave of Graaz ground troops attacked from the north, cutting away at the secessionist emplacements with the weapons the IGC loyalists had been smuggling in. A photon blast flashed over her head, a downed transport exploding behind her.

She came up firing. The Graaz native insurgents were a fearsome sight. Nearly nine feet in height. They moved on four powerful, clawed limbs, their upper sections consisting of a thick, spiny trunk and two forward clawed appendages. Skin like scaly armor plating. Fierce fighters. And, evolved from herd animals, blindly cohesive and united in battle. She almost admired them. She fired at the forward leg of a Graaz group leader. The monster roared and toppled, still firing at secessionist turrets in the rock outcroppings nearby. They fought to their last breath, she thought as she fired at the native's brain case, finishing her off. She felt no surge of fire as she had that day at the Universe Gate. She felt nothing. It seemed every battle cut away a piece of her, killing her by inches.

The Graaz swarm charged in, blasting down what was left of the secessionist photon batteries. Cassandra looked up and prayed, wondering if she'd ever see Victor again. Photon bolts rained from the sky, explosions ripping up the dusty ground, the Graaz roaring as they fell.

Cassandra looked up and shouted the rebel cheer as secessionist hover fighters swooped in, guns blazing. She sheltered behind the bulk of a dead Graaz as one of the fighters swept in low for a strafing run. She leapt up on top of the Graaz corpse, and from there leapt for the fighter as it turned, its magna thrusters pulsing and shimmering on the hot air.

"Welcome aboard, Lieutenant," the gunner said with a smile crossing his sweaty face as he clasped her hand and hoisted her aboard. "Here to help us clean house?" He smiled broadly, his face burned bloody red in the blazing sunlight of Arcturas. Cassandra fired, sweeping one flank with her blaster as the gunner swept the other. They cheered as the Graaz retreated, crawling back into their network of holes like ants. "Look at 'em scatter!" the gunner yelled. "Eat it, you sand-crawlin' scum!" he shouted through his cupped hands. "Man rules!"

"They'll be back," Cassandra reminded him, wiping sweat from her brow, her hair blowing in the hot wind.

"Don't be too sure, Lieutenant. You just come down with the I.S. forces?" the gunner asked.

"Yeah," she said, pulling her canteen and taking a swallow. "I've been planetside one day. Hell of a welcome." She offered him the canteen. He accepted and eagerly took a swallow.

"Thanks, Lieutenant," he said, handing her back the canteen. "Seen much action out-system?"

She sighed, remembering a dozen battles. "Deneb. Rigel."

"Killed plenty of Confederation scum, I hope?" He smiled, running his thumb across the notches carved on the casing of his photon turret.

"I haven't kept track," she said quietly. She felt so damned tired. The wind stung her eyes. A day, an hour in Victor's arms, away from the damned blood and killing. That was all she wanted. "Where are we headed?" she asked as the hover fighter swept on westward over the rocky desert landscape.

"We've got some clean-up work west of Dover's Ridge, Lieutenant"

As they passed over the floor of a valley rung with spiny mountains, she saw a squad of secessionist soldiers forming a firing line. She looked down and choked as they blasted down a line of prisoners. Human prisoners. "My God," she whispered. "Who . . . "

"Traitors," the gunner said. "Collaborators who helped the loyalists ship in guns for the Graaz." She felt numb and empty. Clearing the valley, they came upon a wide, sandy plain. Here and there were oases of soft, lavender-blossomed plants. Clustered around them were lumpy mounds. Something crawled there. As the fighter swooped in lower, she could discern the exo-skeletal insect-like forms, multi-legged things the size of dogs crawling over the mounds which, she could now see were clusters of eggs. She remembered reading that the Graaz were egg-layers. These bug-like things were their evolutionary equivalent of males; parasites that carried and combined genetic bits from the Graaz femes in fertilizing their eggs in the sand.

The descending fighters stirred up a swirl of dust around the mounds. Graaz working in the oases cultivating the moss-like growths that served as their food stopped working and swarmed into the open. They encircled the mounds, raising their upper limbs. It almost looked like surrender. "Die, scum!" the gunner shouted as he opened fire, blasting down the defenseless, unarmed natives.

Cassandra's jaw dropped. "What the hell are you doing?" she demanded, grabbing the gunner's arm and roughly pulling the man away from the gun. "Those are civilians!"

"No civilians in this war, Lieutenant" the gunner said, glancing to the west. "We need the strontium on this planet for the war effort, and the Graaz won't let us mine it. So, our orders are to clear 'em out." Cassandra gasped at the hideous sight of hover sleds moving in from the west, hovering about a meter off the ground. Their huge, ugly gray shapes were grinding up the desert, stirring up a whirlwind as their concentrated ion fields irradiated the soil, killing a generation of unborn Graaz in their nests.

"This is murder! It's illegal."

"Inter-galactic law's dead and buried. We answer only to Imperial law now."

"I am ordering you to stand down, soldier!"

"We have orders, Lieutenant. From Space Central. No Graaz left alive. That comes down from the top."

Her blood ran cold. "No. My father would never allow . . ."

"The order comes from your father, ma'am. And, from your father-in-law Fleet Admiral Marsden. Your husband General Marsden can confirm that quite easily when he arrives planetside. And, the general expects every last sand crawler dead by the time he leaves this system." She shook her head, nauseated. The atrocities she had assumed to be IGC propaganda were actually happening? By her father's order? By Victor's? "Now, if the Lt. will excuse me . . ." He reached for the gun.

She acted on reflex, knocking him aside with the butt of her blaster. The man reached for his side-arm. She landed a kick to his gut, sending him sprawling backwards. As he fell, screaming from the fighter, she swung the photon turret, blasting out the magna thrusters of other hover fighters even now firing on other clusters of Graaz civies. Secessionist soldiers jumped to the ground as their fighters exploded, crashing into the sand in flames. The pilot locked the fighter on auto control and turned, drawing his blaster. She swung her blaster up and fired. Her heart stopped beating. Time seemed to slow to treacle pace as what was left of the man toppled backwards from the fighter. She could only stare, frozen in shock.

Her head cleared quickly as photon bursts swept by, surges of heat boiling the air around her. Shaking off the numbness, she switched the controls back to manual and steered the fighter straight towards the nearest hover sled. The grey metal monstrosity was closing fast on a mound of Graaz eggs. Graaz civilians gathered in its path trying to ward it off, but it stayed its course. She steered in low, aiming for the hover sled's flank. Locking the controls, she jumped. Her last thought before the explosion was of Victor.

Water splashed against her face. Her head swam, hot sunlight on her face. Her head throbbed, explosions all around her. She blinked her eyes. A dark blur clarified into the hideous gaping maw and slithering tendrils of a Graaz face. Or, the closest thing these creatures had to a face. She started, instinctively reaching for her side arm, finding it missing.

"Do not fear," the Graaz said, her thoughts translated into a scratchy, mechanical approximation of a human voice. It was then Cassandra noticed the translator device the hulking Graaz wore on her battle harness, beside the gold tri-galaxy emblem of the Inter-Galactic Confederation. Cassandra recalled wearing one of those once. What now seemed a lifetime ago. She glanced around. Graaz resistance soldiers were moving in, finishing off the last of the secessionist death squad. Cassandra looked at the charred human corpses littering the ground and vomited.

Graaz civilians poured water over the smoldering craters that were once their unborn children. "What are they doing?" Cassandra asked.

"Water for the dead. A prayer for the living," The large Graaz said, offering Cassandra a cup of water.

Cassandra's hand trembled as she hesitantly reached for the cup held in the massive claw-like appendage of the monstrous creature crouching over her. She took a mouthful of water, swished it and spat. "Why are you being kind to me?" she asked, noticing the ugly battle scar on the alien's side.

"We are indebted to you for fighting to save our progeny. But, you are a curiosity. This is the second time you have betrayed your comrades," the Graaz said, passing a claw across her IGC emblem. "You seem lost. You search in many directions. What do you search for?"

Cassandra looked over the smoking battle field and sighed. "Peace."

"Peace comes from within. Your battle is there." One of the other Graaz squealed shrilly, waving her blaster and rearing up on her hind limbs. "Your reinforcements are moving in. We must go. Will you accompany us? Perhaps we can offer you a path to what you seek."

Cassandra slowly got to her feet. She stared at the wedding band on her finger and thought of Victor one last time. She pried the ring off her finger and tossed it to the edge of one of those smoldering graves. "Let's go."

"I'm glad," the alien said, gently laying a huge claw on Cassandra's shoulder. "I am Saav."

"Cassandra," she said, laying her hand on Saav's.

The officer placed the gold wedding band in the palm of Victor Marsden's hand. "Where is she?" Victor asked, staring at the ring.

"All indications are she's gone offworld with a group of Graaz refugees, sir. Orders?"

He sighed. "Find her and kill her." The officer saluted and left. As the door slid shut behind the man, Victor clenched the ring in his hand and winced, blinking back tears.

Marla Ventari turned her space fighter in a downward spiral run, pressing the firing button and blasting apart the forward weapons array of a secessionist star striker as it closed on the escaping Graaz spacecraft. Her heart raced, her blood burning. She knew from bitter experience that vengeance could be a dangerously potent addiction, but she couldn't deny it. Another IGC fighter swept up and fired on the enemy ship's tail section, spinning off as the striker's engine pod ignited. Marla turned her fighter aside and went to mega thrust as the enemy ship disintegrated in a blinding shower of light.

"Well done, Skyheart," she said through her comm link, a smile crossing her face. She'd recognize Skyheart's flying technique anywhere.

"Thank you, Commander," Skyheart transmitted from the cybernetic aqua-pod at the control center of her fighter. "But, if the Commander will forgive my saying so . . . you should not be putting yourself at risk this way. You should be on the command bridge."

Marla sighed. She had learned to detect worry in Skyheart's voice, even filtered through the translator. She brushed off her friend's touching though intrusive concern. "To quote a commander of Old Earth: You can't lead from behind."

"General Longstreet. Yes, I've studied Old Earth history as well."

Marla smiled grimly, knowing full well Skyheart feared she'd been putting herself too close to danger since David's death, and had been putting herself there as well to watch over her. Pushing aside her guilt, Marla focused on the matter at hand. "Shall we greet our guests?"

Marla and Skyheart docked with the command ship. Climbing out of her atmosphere suit, Marla walked across the landing bay to the recently arrived ship. Skyheart floated beside her, the dolphin's aquapod suspended on a magnetic forcefield. Noticing the blast marks on the Graaz ship's hull, Marla could see they'd had a rough trip. A wonder they'd made it all the way from the Arcturan system through the secessionist star blockades. *Whoever steered that ship here must be a damn good space pilot,* Marla thought.

"Commander on deck," one of her officers announced, the launch bay crew saluting and snapping to attention.

"At ease," Marla ordered. The boarding hatch lowered and a very ragged-looking group of Graaz refugees piled out. "Get these people rations and a change of clothes," she ordered. "Med bay for those that need it." A large Graaz wearing IGC insignia climbed down the boarding ramp. The strength in stature and the battle scar left no doubt as to the alien's identity. "Saav," Marla called out with a smile, running over to greet a comrade she'd come to greatly admire. Marla had been through two space battles helping Saav's ship to clear the blockade before, running refugees off Nazaar Minor. "I might have known it was you," she said, raising her hand in the traditional IGC gesture of friendship. "No rebel blockade could ever stop you."

"It's good to see you again, Marla my friend," Saav said, returning the gesture and laying a claw gently on Marla's shoulder. "But, the credit for our escape goes to my new friend here. She saved all our lives at great risk to herself."

"Then, I very much want to meet her." The smile dropped from Marla's face as a young woman whose face had haunted her dreams for the past three months stepped into view.

Saav raised a claw. "Commander Marla Ventari, allow me to introduce . . . "

"Cassandra DeVries-Marsden?" Marla asked coldly.

"It's just Cassandra DeVries now, Commander," the woman said quietly.

"Oh? Is your husband dead?"

"No, Ma'am," she said quieter still, lowering her eyes slightly.

"I see. I can't say the same for mine." Her teeth clenched, her body trembling in anger. The other woman looked up just as Marla lashed out, smashing her across the jaw with a solid right cross, knocking her to the floor.

"Marla!" Skyheart called out.

"My husband was the pilot you killed at the Universe Gate," she said in a strangled throat, barely able to speak through the hate. Marla reached for her sidearm. She felt a tingling wave of numbness in that arm. She recognized it as Skyheart restraining that hand with her forcefield.

Saav stepped in front of DeVries, shielding the woman with one of her massive arms. "Marla, don't. I share your grief, my friend, but Cassandra and I are bonded. Where she goes, I go."

"It's all right, Saav," DeVries said, laying a hand on Saav's arm and pulling herself to her feet. "The woman who killed your husband died on Nazaar Minor," she said, wiping blood from her mouth on the back of her hand. "If you want to finish the job, go ahead." She stepped clear of Saav. "But, if you want to make use of the intel in my head, you'd be well advised to let me live. For a time, at least."

"The word of a traitor?" Marla asked, her hand clenching on the butt of her gun. "I'm to trust that?"

"I trust her," Saav said, laying her claw on Cassandra's shoulder.

Marla slowly moved her hand away from her gun. "Saav is the only reason you're still breathing," she said, slowly and quietly, her heart pounding. "You'll have to go a lot farther to earn my trust."

Cassandra met her eyes, steadily. "Bring it on."

2 months later.

Taan Li Trans galactic University and Military Academy was a vast conglomerate of biospheric space habitats in orbit around a proto-star at the heart of a stellar nebula at the outer edge of the galactic core sectors.

Teiko Wekesa was still a bit light-headed as she passed weightless through the connecting tube linking the recreation sphere with the observation deck. She realized she'd had a few too many, celebrating the end of finals. She laughed as she twirled acrobatically in zero-gee, recalling the moves she'd used in her last dance class. Her head swam a bit as she made the transition to normal gravity. She found her friend Kevin Desjardine seated alone in a corner of a little-used observation node, staring off into the bright, swirling gaseous interior of the nebula. "We missed you at the celebration," she said as she walked over to him. "You okay?"

"Yeah, just not in a very celebratory mood," he muttered.

She studied his face as she sat down beside him. Teiko could see Kevin was in pretty bad shape. A lot worse than his usual bouts of dark introspection. She gently massaged his shoulder. "Want to talk about it?"

He sighed. "One bit of news from my home sector finally trickled through the Imperial sensors. My little brother Pete is now a soldier of the Imperial Space Service."

Teiko silently cursed in disgust, knowing full well the rebel pigs let that kind of news leak out for the sake of demoralizing the loyalists. She stroked his hair. "I'm sorry."

He stared off into space. "I can still see the look of hurt in his eyes the day I announced I was working my way through Taan Li, instead of going to New Earth Military Academy like Dad wanted. Pete just stood there, looking at me like I'd abandoned him. We haven't spoken since. Every sleep cycle, I have nightmares about killing him. Or, him killing me. I'm honestly not sure which I fear more."

"It's not going to come to that," she whispered, trying to comfort him. "This stupid war will be over before we know it. They'll get the Universe Gate back up, the IGC will pull back together..." She rested her head on his strong shoulder. "Hey . . . we're family, right? The four of us made it this far together, and we'll stay together after graduation like we promised, right?"

"If we all get shipped out together, that is. You, me, Traeve, and Proteus."

"Of course, we will. Who else could stand us?"

They both laughed as he put his arm around her shoulders. "What would I do without you, pal?"

She felt a cool, electrical tingling which told her that her best friend, Proteus was drawing near. The strong telepathic connection they shared through Teiko's brain implant told her Proteus was greatly distressed, and knowing what it took to frighten Proteus, that bothered her. She turned to the connector hatch. There Proteus entered. Currently in its undisguised form of a slithering tide of magnetized, sharp-edged, silver-metallic fragments, the sentient A.I. swirled in a shimmer of blue electrical energy, its countless segments assembling into one of the forms Teiko knew Proteus liked. A beautiful white wolf with keenly shining blue eyes. An image Proteus had taken from deep within Teiko's mind, knowing it pleased her. "Proteus, what's wrong?"

"We have to get off Taan Li at once," Proteus answered, a simulated human voice emanating from its pseudo-lupine mouth. "All of us. Secessionist troops have occupied the university, seizing it in the name of the New Galactic Empire."

Teiko's blood ran cold. "That's crazy," Kevin said, his face going pale. "They wouldn't dare. Too many prominent families from both sides send their kids here."

"It's being done, Kevin," Proteus said. "I've tapped into every telepathy node in the university. Imperial troops are sweeping every sphere. A.I.'s and non-human organic sentients are being killed on site. Humans are being forcibly conscripted and taken off-station. Based on what little I could gather through secessionist jamming, the IGC is sending evacuation shuttles. One is docking at Bay-7 now. We have to leave!"

Shaking her head clear, Teiko got to her feet, her battle training coming back to her on reflex. "Okay, let's go."

"You two go ahead," Kevin said as they reached the other end of the connector tube. "I'm going back to my sleep sphere to find Traeve."

"We'll all go," Teiko said.

"No sense risking all of us," Kevin insisted. "Proteus, back me up here. You two get to Bay-7. Traeve and I'll join you there. Go!"

"Kevin makes a valid point, Teiko," Proteus said. "Splitting our number increases our chances of escape by fifty percent." Something Teiko had come to interpret as the vaguest hint of almost human-like hesitation slipped into Proteus's thoughts through their mind link.

She sighed, realizing they were both right. "All right, but be careful, will you?" she said, giving Kevin's strong hand a parting squeeze as he propelled himself down the branching passageway. Forcing herself to turn away, Teiko started towards Bay-7. Proteus followed beside her, shifting its form into that of a lovely young woman. Another image taken from Teiko's subconscious. They'd reached the interstation juncture at Delta Section and transitioned to normal gee when a squad of Imperial troopers blocked the passageway. Teiko froze, her fists clenched, her heart racing. She instinctively stepped protectively in front of Proteus.

One of the troopers stepped forward, reading a scanner pad. He looked up. "A.I." he declared. "Move aside, girl." The men drew their weapons even as Proteus abandoned its human shape, dissolving into its true state.

Proteus projected its intentions into Teiko's mind telepathically. Her fear drowning in adrenalin rush, her reflexes kicked in even as the A.I.'s light-speed calculations guided her. Her dance moves and martial arts techniques flowed together as she leapt and twirled in mid-air, suspended in Proteus' cohesive magnetic force field. She could feel its energy flowing through her, the A.I.'s many fragments swirling around her in a widely circling double ring. Blaster bolts scorched by her as she twisted again, evading them. Proteus became like a living extension of her mind and body, like twin whip-saws of razor-sharp metal fragments extending from Teiko's arms. She turned gracefully in mid-air, Proteus a blur of silver that sliced through the Imperial soldiers.

Teiko looked away as Proteus detached from her. Horror and excitement raced through her blood as she landed on her feet and snatched up two of the dead men's blasters. She dropped to one knee and opened fire as more Imperial troopers charged down the passageway.

Kevin's heart throbbed in anger as he entered his sleep sphere, finding two Imperial soldiers tearing the place apart. "What the hell are you doing?!" he roared.

"Shut your mouth, kid," one of the soldiers snapped. "You're coming with us. Right after you tell us where your roommate is."

The hair on the back of Kevin's neck bristled. "Do you know who I am?" he demanded.

One of the troopers sneered. "Sure we know, kid. You're Otto Desjardine's son. DeVries will probably commission us when we deliver you. Now, talk. Where's that damn Scryvv you room with?"

He struggled to keep his eyes level with the other man's. "How should I know? He probably headed for the nearest outgoing shuttle when you goons broke into the university."

"Watch your mouth, boy!" one of them shouted.

The other one looked around, noticing Traev's artwork. Wire filaments thin as human hair, spun like silk, arranged in a delicate cascade of shimmering rainbow shades that seemed to vibrate with ethereal song. "Scryvv art. I saw it once on Bellatrix II before we burned out those stinking IGC cities. You actually live with that inhuman thing?" Kevin's teeth clenched, his fists trembling with rage. "Trash," the trooper said as he drew a laser blade and sliced through the delicate curtain of light and vibrancy, destroying weeks of Traeve's work.

Kevin roared as he pounced, his rage blasting through him like a storm. He knocked the laser knife out of the trooper's hand with a kick and then smashed in the swine's face. His blood turned to fire as he pounded and pounded. He glanced up to see the second trooper pointing his blaster at him, his finger tightening on the trigger. The man's face twisted in pain as Traeve shifted out of hiding, his stinger-tipped feeding tube lancing out and skewering the trooper through his side. The man fell senseless to the floor, doubtlessly near death, given the amount of venom Traeve had just pumped into him.

"Thanks," Kevin said, breathless as he picked up the other guard's blaster. Traeve's shaggy, multi-legged form unfurled from the corner where he'd hidden himself, the feeding tube withdrawing from the dead man's body and retracting into Traeve's forward orifice. The Scryvv's natural chameleon-like ability to hide from predators through a kind of hypno-visual masking trick hadn't fooled Kevin, acquainted as he was with Traeve's pungently sweet bodily secretions.

"I can't believe you risked your life over defaced art," Traeve remarked, the translator conveying the Scryvv's characteristic intellectual hauteur. "You really should learn to control your emotions, my friend," Traeve said as he picked up the other blaster in one of his many claws.

"You're welcome," Kevin said, pulling off the unconscious guard's uniform. "Camouflage yourself as best you can. Teiko and Proteus are meeting us in Bay-7."

"Thank you for coming back for me, Kevin," Traeve said, his change in scent betraying embarrassment at a display of gratitude that Kevin knew was hard for him. A beautiful mind, Traeve, but art came a lot easier to him than words.

"Don't mention it, pal. You'd have done the same for me." He knew that was true.

3 years later.

Space Admiral Marla Ventari gathered her strike team commanders on the bridge of her command ship, her fleets now on the outskirts of IGC loyalist space.

Saav, Kevin Desjardine, Traeve, Teiko, Proteus, now in wolf-form . . . and Cassandra DeVries . . . stood before her. "Well," Marla remarked. "You six have built up quite a reputation for daring and unorthodox methods. That raid you led on Epsilon II is practically legendary. The enemy refers to you as the death squad. You'll soon have a chance to live up to that." She tied in the bridge A.I., a three-dimensional hologram of a planetary system filling the room around her.

"The enemy is making its move in the Antares system. A center for supplies and communications vital to our cause. Omega Worldship, under Jason DeVries . . . " She glanced over at Cassandra. Their eyes met. Memories of a time when she would have gratefully killed that young woman lingered, but the wounds had healed. Now, she saw a commander she respected. " . . . is attacking from this vector, deploying a particle-beam cannon ship against the Antares III outpost, the heart of the system. His rival, Otto Desjardine of Delta Worldship . . . " she glanced at Kevin. " . . . will be attacking from the opposing direction, his cannon ship targeting our base on the planet's third moon. They're both obviously vying for strategic advantage, over each other as well as us."

"I will command the fleet intercepting the Omega escort squadron here. Commander Skyheart will command the fleet intercepting the Delta escort squadron here. You've all been briefed. I don't have to tell you what's at stake. Any questions?" They all stood silent. "Have your teams ready at 0:900. Dismissed." As they began to file out, Marla cleared her throat. "Oh, uh . . . Lieutenant

Wekesa . . . stay for a moment. I'd like to go over a few of the technical specs with you." Teiko nodded to Proteus as it and the others left.

When they were alone, Marla approached Teiko, taking in every curve of her lovely face . . . perhaps for the final time. They fell into each other's arms and kissed. Marla sighed. She gently ran her fingers though Teiko's hair. "It's been so long," she whispered, kissing her again. "It tears my heart out every time I have to send you into danger. My love." She held her close, savoring what might be their last moment together.

"Don't let the fear in," Teiko whispered in her ear. "Just be with me." As they disrobed, Teiko's fingers caressed the back of Marla's neck, touching the spot where Marla had undergone the cybernetic implant two years before, reconfiguring her brain stem. And, with it, her sexuality. She had loved Teiko from the moment they'd met. Her courage, her grace, her love of life. Teiko's love for her had been equally strong, though different. Marla's love had simply needed to take on a slightly different form in order for them to be together in every way. It had been a choice Marla had never regretted.

"Teiko may be occupied for a time," Proteus remarked. Cassandra repressed a smile, having learned to discern something akin to jealousy in the tone of the A.I.'s thoughts where Teiko and Marla were concerned. "Any of you care to join me for a spacewalk? This may be our last night together."

"I would like that, my friend," Saav said.

"Delighted," Traeve said, scuttling along the wall. "Coming, Kevin?"

"Uh . . . I'll catch up. Cass . . . ?"

"Go on, Saav," she said. "I'll be along."

"Will you, my friend?" Saav remarked as she left with the others.

"Cass . . . " Kevin approached her. She felt her heart quicken as he drew close. His presence had a way of arousing her. Remembering the last time she'd fallen in love on the eve of battle, she had tried to suppress the feeling. But, it had grown hard. Very hard. And now . . . "Cassie, I know we've had our fights and all. And, I know the timing couldn't be worse, but . . . If this is the last time we're together, I just . . . "

She put her arms around his neck and kissed him on the lips, long and hard. "I know," she whispered, stroking his rugged face and kissing him again. "Let's not waste it. Come to my quarters." He smiled as he embraced her.

"Tactical report!" Marla ordered from her command chair, the black void beyond the viewport of her bridge alight with exploding spaceships.

"All squadron commanders report successful operations, Admiral," her tactical officer, Gelbh reported through its translator device, the Denebian's immense, hydra-like form reaching up from its control station, its many spiny serpentine extensions operating controls that fed data to Marla's monitor console.

Marla looked over the tactical analysis and nodded. All was going as planned. "Comm officer," she said, stepping over to the communications station. "Status of second fleet?"

The communications officer sat upright at his station, his three tentacle-like extensions operating the controls, his horseshoe-shaped head turning in Marla's direction. "Commander Skyheart reports Phase One successfully completed, Admiral."

She sighed, studying the planetary curve of Antares III dead ahead. *All the pieces are in place,* she thought. *It's up to the teams now.*

"Forward!" Cassandra shouted, opening fire as her boarding party stormed the command bridge of her father's particle beam cannon ship. Her telepathic implant informed her Teiko's team had secured the engineering section and Proteus's team the navigation section. The ship was theirs. "Secure weapons control," she ordered. "Navigation, come about. And, prepare to fire on Delta Worldship." Her thoughts turned to Kevin.

"Advance!" Kevin ordered, his squads taking the bridge of his father's cannon ship. Saav's teams had secured the landing bay and Traeve reported the computer control had been over-ridden. They'd won. "Over-ride targeting system, and prepare to fire on Omega Worldship." *This one's for you, Cassie,* he thought.

Jason DeVries and Otto Desjardine perished almost simultaneously, their respective worldships destroyed by each other's cannon ships. Their allies, blaming each other for the apparent betrayal, turned their fleets on each other. The three remaining worldships were drawn into the conflict on opposing sides and were soon so weakened by each other's forces as to be easy prey for the IGC space fleets. Scattered and without leadership, the surviving rebel fleets soon retreated to their home sectors and quickly surrendered in the face of the IGC invasion.

Marla knelt at the tomb of her grandmother, the late Landra Ventari. "I'm sorry you didn't live to see it, Grandmother," she whispered. "But, the dream lives."

Commander Skyheart hovered above the marital altar on the planet Andaar, her translated voice completing the ceremony. "By the power vested in me by the Inter-Galactic Confederation, I pronounce you married."
Marla smiled as she and Teiko joined hands at the altar. As they kissed, Proteus formed a shimmering arc of light over them. Saav cheered along with the other guests. Traeve watched and composed an artistic record. Cassandra and Kevin smiled and joined hands.

1 year later.
The newly completed Universe Gate pulsed and shimmered, silver-blue energy streams intersecting at its center as space seemed to ripple and implode in the gigantic ring. The trans-dimensional gateway to Andromeda and the Magellanic Clouds was re-opened. As ships passed through the gate from the other side, Cassandra's heart soared.

Kevin took her in his strong arms. Her blood raced hot. They kissed, the light of the Universe Gate washing over them.

Tom Olbert lives in Cambridge, Massachusetts, home of Harvard, M.I.T., wacky street performers, and dedicated progressive social activists. Tom has had the privilege of interacting with some great people in volunteering for environmentally friendly causes and progressive candidates. Tom's father, Stan Olbert, is a retired professor of physics and a veteran of the Polish resistance of WWII. Tom's mother, Norma Olbert, has written and self-published Stan's biography A Boy From Lwow, *now available in paperback. Tom's sister, Elizabeth Olbert, is an accomplished modern artist and art teacher.*

Tom's fiction has appeared in Lillicat Publishers' Visions II: Milky Way, Visions III: Inside the Kuiper Belt, Visions IV: Space Between Stars, *and* Visions V: Milky Way, *as well as the anthology* An Improbable Truth: The Paranormal Adventures of Sherlock Holmes, *now available from Mocha Memoirs Press. Also available from Mocha is Tom's dark science fiction novella* Black Goddess. *Tom's full-length science fiction novel* Dissent: Book I of the Nexus *is available from Phase5 Publishing.*

What if your planet was destroyed by a Hypernova and remnants of your civilization were housed in a fleet just barely able to stay ahead of the ever advancing storm of light? Would you simply give up and wait for the end or would you fight on, against all odds?

WARLIGHT

Sidney Blaylock, Jr.

Honour the charge they made!
Honour the Light Brigade, . . .
~ Charge of the Light Brigade, *Alfred, Lord Tennyson*

I. Shattered and Sundered

The scorching whine of plasma ejectors thundered around him, but Tyrenell knelt before the broken bodies and shattered armor like a penitent knight in prayer. They were his family—his sisters and brothers. He had long lost his mother and his father on planets far distant from this one. Unshed tears pooled in his eyes. But they would not fall. He would not give this planet the satisfaction. It would die of draught if it needed his tears. He was resolved in that, but apparently the planet cared not. Its vermillion sand was the color of drying blood. The sky above should have been a deep black with the pinpoint white of stars, but was instead crisscrossed with florid red crescent lines of an energy web that flashed intermittently, as the Fleets above tried desperately, and in vain, to pierce them.

Why? he thought. *What's the point?*

He looked at the twisted, torn, and broken bodies of his Cohort. Siblings all of them, but there were more. Uncles and aunts. Grandmothers and grandfathers. Friends from birth. And more. His gaze fell upon his

203

Promised. He stroked her face, ignoring the blood pooling at the base of her upturned eyes.

Tyrenell heard the tread of the steel encased bones slowly closing behind him. So they had finally noticed that he was not dead. The self-loathing gave way to something new and different.

Something terrible.

He reached over and closed Myris' unseeing eyes. She would see him again soon enough.

The Tip of the Spear. The Light that Shines Forever. The Cleansing Wind. The Searing Light that Scourges. The Bringer of the Light. All those names he was and more. He was a Phaeton, a Lightbringer. And he was forbidden to die but through combat or old age.

The crunching of metallic bone was closer now and there were more footfalls. Several more had joined. So death by combat it would be for him. He nodded. It was enough.

The weapon pods on his arms slid forward and locked into place with a *snap-click*. He tapped his breastplate with his now weapon-encased hand. A salute to those to whom a salute no longer mattered.

Death. He needed it. He wanted it. Now. His or that of something else. It no longer mattered.

He shook, he trembled, and a white-hot mist rose behind his eyes, like that of a man dying of fever. He was a *Lightbringer*. Tyrenell turned and leapt into the air. The suit augmented his jump and carried him high over the Revenants lurking behind him. He brought his plasma ejector online as he arced over their forms.

"Who brings the Light?" he screamed at their undead forms as they ponderously brought their weapons to bear. "I bring the Light!" His plasma ejectors erupted again and again.

II. Into the Valley of Death

Death comes for us all. Embrace therefore the Light. See how it burns. See how it cleanses. Turn your face to the Light. Let the ever-flowing wave not envelop you. Fight therefore. Fight for yourself. Fight for your brethren. Fight for the Light lest it consume us all.

The Great Catechism ran through Tyrenell's mind as he downed another Revenant. He snarled. The Revenant had not been good enough. None of them had been so far. Was his death so hard? No matter how many of them he seemed to throw himself into, he always came out alive.

Well, it will be over soon enough, he thought. Lightfall would consume them all—the Brigades, the Fleet, the energy shield that held them trapped, the planet, himself—soon enough. The energy wave of the Hypernova would not be denied. Its light and energy would obliterate everything in its path.

He looked at the Revenant he had just felled. This skeleton was humanoid: two eye sockets, two arm-like limbs, bipedal legs. One of the indigenous population? The original creators of this nightmare? He had no way of knowing, but judging by the numbers he had encountered so far, he thought so. The dead as unliving weapons. Madness. Except that it made a perverse sense. What type of soldier gave you nearly unlimited numbers? What type of soldier could be replenished and repurposed after falling in battle? What type of soldier could you field that would render the other army's tactical advantage of increasing numbers useless?

The dead cared not for losses. They did not need to eat or sleep. There was no fatigue. All they did was follow the programing of the AI slaved to their body by cybernetic augmentation. Meaning: they could run, jump, and hit harder. And worse yet, the fallen of Tyrenell's race were being ruthlessly and efficiently converted, the same as countless other alien species. The worst Revenant he'd faced so far was a lithe snake-man hybrid with a bone-spike at the end its tail.

Tyrenell's arm still felt stiff from nearly having it severed from his body. Only the advanced nanotechs in his suit had kept him from bleeding out as the nanites coursing through his blood knitted the tendons, muscles, and skin back together. The powered armor that the Brigades wore was all that kept them from being decimated immediately, but even with that, they were still losing.

Badly.

The desolate field was clear except for a few pockets of shambling Revenants. They would be no match for him. He needed more dangerous foes. His eyes, augmented by his suit and tactical overlay, scanned the battlefield. Most, if not all of his Brigade were already dead or dying, as they were the first on the planet's surface. They were Lightbringers, after all, the very tip of the spear. Soon the planet would begin converting even them.

It seemed it was his fate to die in the Lightfall, the shockwave of the hypernova that had destroyed his homeworld and countless worlds and stars in its path. Like a great rushing wind of energy and light, the shockwave traveled outward at the speed of light. The Fleet, all that was left of his planet and its great civilizations, fled from it. The ships of the Fleet had discovered Jumpspace technology—stolen from a world it had stumbled upon early in the final days after the great Generation Ships had left the planet. Integration with the ships, however, had been problematic and Jumping only allowed them to stay ahead of the on-rushing wave, from a few days to a few weeks, while the engines recycled their energy, but never more than that.

Even now the holographic display showed the countdown rushing closer to little more than ten standard hours.

He spied a large contingent of Revenants decimating a squad of Apeirons. He started to turn away. The Indefinites weren't a part of his Brigade, but two things caught his eye almost simultaneously. First, he noticed one of the Revenants was another one of those snake-man things and secondly, he saw an Indefinite weeping and cradling the broken figure of her Promised even as the members of her Cohort died around her.

The image was too striking to ignore. The pain of his own loss flooded into his heart and tears stung his eyes.

With a cry torn from him, he dove into the midst of the battle. "Who brings the Light?" he thundered to Revenants, to the planet, to the uncaring void of space. "I bring the Light!"

The remaining Apeirons looked up, too stunned to do anything, and if it weren't for Tyrenell, they would have died right there. He hit the ground, rolled, and came up firing. Plasma ejectors hissed and whined as they threw super-heated balls of energy. Revenant after Revenant fell, all except the snake-man corpse that deftly avoided every blast that Tyrenell sent his way.

With a speed that almost defied description, the alien Revenant closed on him and Tyrenell found himself looking at the bone-spike as it hovered just above his skull. His heart raced. Not even the helmet of the power armor would be able to completely stop the strike.

Suddenly, he felt a wrenching dislocation as if his body were torn from space and poured into another. This doesn't feel like death, this feels like . . . Jumpspace.

His elation turned to dust and ashes as his consciousness fully returned and he realized that the Indefinite who had lost her Promised held him and that he was several feet away *and behind* the Revenant.

He snarled. Just as his Brigade was called a Phaetons because their suit's energy weapons brought light to the battlefield, so too were the Apeirons called Indefinites because their suits allowed them to "jump" across the battlefield, wreaking havoc.

He roared and channeled all of his rage into his suit. The blast that leapt from his plasma ejector screamed as it all but disintegrated the Revenant just as it was turning towards them.

Tyrenell glared down at the Indefinite, but his helmet visor was darkened and he knew she couldn't see his face. She, however, was staring at the darkened circle of his Promised badge on his suit's chest, darkened as was hers.

Suppressing another snarl, he turned away and tore from her grip. He stalked away to find other prey, and hopefully, other predators.

III. Into the Mouth of Hell

Into fight after fight he waded and with each fight his disillusionment grew. The Indefinites that he had saved fought with him. He did not want them. They were a burden, but with each battle his burden seemingly grew.

Tyrenell ranged further and further afield, closer to the desiccated and crumbling towers of the dead world. He sought ever more Revenants. Yet, all he found were more and more stragglers and survivors of Cohorts from other Brigades. The Hyperions, or Starkillers, imploded Revenants with their Void-lances. The Aeons, or Eternals, killed and died and killed again until all their possible lives were extinguished like dying embers in a fire. And still they came, until all ten Brigades were represented.

The more he killed, the more he unintentionally saved. At his side was the almost constant presence of the Apeiron that he had saved. She seemed to have made it her mission to keep him from harm, flashing him out of harm's way whenever it seemed that a Revenant might actually be capable of killing him. With grim determination, Tyrenell would scour the battlefield until he saw the next impossible battle and then he'd throw himself into the fray.

His chronometer countdown had reached five hours until the Great Light caught up to them and obliterated everything in its path. He wanted to tell the unknown Indefinite that her actions would make no difference, but the Brigades did not work together. Their comms didn't interface. There was no way he could talk to her, or any of the other hundreds of stragglers that had joined him, except the few Lightbringers that clustered around him like snarling wolves, seemingly determined to give their very lives for him.

Then why was his comm system pinging?

He activated it and was immediately assaulted with screams, shouts, yells, klaxons, sirens, and a general cacophony of noise. The dampeners kicked in, moderating the level, but it was still hard to hear. He was just about to shut it off again when he made out a voice above the tulmut.

"This is Light Commander Kachellon of the Lightship *Starfall* to the Lightbringer at coordinates five sigma, zero tau, eight delta. Reply Priority One tight-beam."

Tyrenell's suit alerted him that he was the Lightbringer listed at those coordinates and he slammed his suit into tight-beam mode, locking him in direct communication with the Lightship.

"What do you want?" he snarled into the comms.

One did not talk to a Light Commander in that manner, but he was beyond caring.

"Do you see three spires off to your left?" came the reply in a tight voice.

Tyrenell glanced to his left. "Yeah, I see them, so what?"

An intake of breath as if someone were preparing to call Tyrenell down. He put his hand on the comms unit, ready to shut it off the moment the rebuke came.

"Your Cohort needs to take it out. Analysis indicates that it is part of the shield generator. If your Cohort can find a way to destroy it, then our Techs say that the shield in this quadrant will fail. We only need a gap, any gap, and the Fleet can jump out safely."

"Sorry, but I'm not your man. My Cohort's dead. All of them."

Light Commander Kachellon's voice hissed. "I'm showing nearly a full complement. You're the only Cohort of Lightbringers that's still combat-effective. If we die here, then we're extinct!"

"Do you think I don't know that," he growled, "but you're not down here! Let me spell it out for you: My. Cohort. Is. Dead. What you're picking up on your sensors are others from other Brigades who have latched on to me. Only the Light knows why."

Silence. It was long and deafening. "There are too many Revenants around for anything less than a full Cohort to take out. Even then it might not be possible. There are so many."

Tyrenell's head jerked up. "How many?"

"More than I've ever seen in any one place. It almost looks like they're assaulting the towers themselves, but that can't be right. Why in the Light would they want to take down one of their own generators?"

So many Revenants in one place. The answer seemed simple: to escape the planet. He wondered why the Light Commander didn't see it, but then Tyrenell had experienced personally the Revenant's single minded drive. The Revenants were trapped, just as the Fleet was. They were like a disease, however, and were built to spread. If they escaped and managed to make it to Jumpspace, they would scourge the galaxy.

"I'll do it," he said as he began to trudge toward the spires. "Warn the ships of the other Brigades and tell them to let their people know what I'm going to do."

"But you just said your Cohort is dead. The other Brigades will never—"

"Just do it!" he snapped. "I don't want their deaths on my hands. They need to know what I'm going to do, so they can decide for themselves and I can't tell them."

"And if they don't back you?" Kachellon challenged. "You can't do it alone."

"Then I'll see you in the Light. Tyrenell out." He cut the comms, not really caring that he could be imprisoned for his disrespect.

The others were following him toward the Towers as always, oblivious to the danger. *Well, that would change soon enough.*

They began to fall behind singularly, in pairs, or in groups of three's and four's as they were given the details of the plan by their respective Brigades. *Good enough.* None of them were going to survive this. Even if by some miracle, he managed to disable whatever lay at the top of the tower, that would only free the Fleet in orbit around the planet. They would not have enough time to send shuttles down to the planet. This would be their graveyard as well.

It was only how one chose to go.

Tyrenell lifted his head high and began to run toward the spires with a long loping run. He was a Lightbringer. He would go out in battle. Without stopping or looking back, he came to the doorway of the innermost spire. It looked like a gateway to the very depths of hell itself.

Charging his plasma ejectors, he trudged inside.

IV. *"Forward, the Light Brigade!"*

He met the Revenants almost immediately, almost as if they were waiting for him.

Tyrenell stood face to face with his old Brigade with Myris at the forefront. Why now? Why did the planet decide to spit them up at him now? Other Revenants stood behind them. A few seemed to be of the indigenous population with several different alien races mixed in, but most were the decomposing bodies of the other Brigades. He thought he even recognized the fallen Apeiron that had been the Promised of the Indefinite who had first joined him. A part of him was glad that she and the others had fallen to the wayside. Dead eyes stared at him, the pupils fixed straight ahead, her gaze locked, as the nanites manipulating the body had no need of the optic nerves to steer the body.

As one, they began to advance.

Death by Myris' hand or by being swarmed under as he fought toward the stairs to the top of the Tower?

He was still contemplating when he felt a presence at his side. The Apeiron stood beside him, her gaze fixed on her former Promised, just as his had been on Myris. He knew exactly what she was feeling. Instinctively, he took her hand and squeezed. She looked at him for a long moment, and then nodded once.

Tyrenell let her hand fall.

He felt her pain and she understood. In a strange way, helping her helped him as well. The pain faded to the background. He took a long deep breath and stood a little taller. For the first time since entering the chamber, he looked past the Revenants to the winding stairs. That was his objective. If he died getting there, then so be it.

He was a Lightbringer.

Movement behind him caused Tyrenell to quickly glance around. Swelling behind him were the remnants of all ten Brigades, far more than had joined him before. At least two or three Cohorts worth filled the corridor, with more streaming in even as he looked. The Commands of all the Fleetships must have alerted every Cohort to this mission.

The Revenants still moved toward him even though they were now woefully outnumbered, although reinforcements were coming down the staircase.

With a deliberate motion born of a need to show this planet that it hadn't broken him, Tyrenell brought up his right arm, aimed his plasma ejector directly at Myris' shambling form and fired.

Her lifeless body fell and was still—the nanites inside burned away by his cleansing fire. She was at peace now. It was the least he could do for her.

Tyrenell pushed forward with all the warriors surging forward behind him.

They quickly overwhelmed the Revenants in front of them and made their way up the stairs. Floor after floor they found Revenants and they crushed them. Tyrenell's force took loses as well, but nothing like the decimation they had experienced. They fought as one—Phaeton and Apeiron, Hyperion and Aeon, and the other six Brigades as well. All fighting for one purpose. Their skills sets complementing one another. The Revenants, who had been such a fearsome foe when they had fought them alone as individual Brigades, now fell again and again to Tyrenell and his newfound "Cohort."

Finally, they came to a door at the top of the staircase. Tyrenell searched for some way to open it, but it was sealed shut.

He felt arms about his waist. The female Apeiron had grabbed him. He was just about to protest when the world fuzzed and blurred and then became stable again.

She had jumped them both inside the room. He scanned the door. There was a console.

Ah, he thought, *a blast door of some kind, reinforced, and only allowing entry from this side. So that's why the Revenants couldn't get inside.*

But why would they want to?

He shook himself. He loped to the end of the cavernous room. There were control nodes scattered throughout the room, but he had no idea of the function of any of them. He turned to the Apeiron, but she shook her head.

He stabbed at his comms. "I'm here! But I don't know how to work this machinery."

The Light Commander came on. "You're inside the Spire?"

"How do I shut this down?"

"You don't. We do."

Tyrenell heard the Light Commander give his command staff orders to bring the Lightcannon online. "Just set a beacon and get out of there. We'll take care of the rest."

"Don't have one," he said. "Use me. Lock on to me and fire."

"You won't have enough time," Kachellon objected.

"I'll be fine," he lied. "Tell the others, they're going to need to get clear."

A short silence. "I'll pass along the word. And Tyrenell...thank you."

"Thank me after you've jumped away," he said, then he cut the comms.

He moved to the center of the room and waited for the "Cohort" to start down. He was doubtful they would make it out in time, but it was better than surely burning to death.

Strangely, however, no one made a move to the staircase. Even more strangely, the Apeiron, once the news had obviously been relayed to her, stalked to him shaking her head vehemently. Several others came with her, apparently to try to change his mind.

A red mist rose in his vision, his fist balled, and he began to tremble. What more did they want from him? What more did they want him to endure?

Then a plan came to him. It was at once brilliant and simple. As soon as they closed with him, he grabbed one and slung him forward, the momentum sending the unfortunate Hyperion hurling out of the Spire. There was a moment of stunned silence and then weapons snapped up and trained on him.

He ignored them. He speared an Apeiron with his finger in the chest then pointed to the still falling form of the Hyperion. It took a moment for the Apeiron to understand, then he blinked away. He appeared in midair halfway between the falling Hyperion and then blinked again. This time when he reappeared, he was beside the Hyperion and grabbed him. He blinked several more times, apparently bleeding off as much of their momentum as possible.

They landed hard, rolled for a short distance, but both got up and waved.

Turning back to his assembled "Cohort," Tyrenell pointed at the assemblage and then pointed out of the broken window. They lowered their weapons and began fleeing the doomed spire with Aperions blinking like miniature starlights to Jump them all safely to the ground.

In minutes, it was just Tyrenell and the female Aperion. He had motioned her to go, to leave him, but she had simply ignored him.

"Light Cannons online. We're running the final firing solution now. You need to get clear now!"

The Light Commander had no jurisdiction over ground troops just as Tyrenell would have no authority on a Lightship. Tyrenell appreciated the sentiment, however.

He felt a gentle touch around his waist. How could he tell her? He had to, however. She deserved to know.

But when he turned and looked into her eyes, he saw. She understood. She would not Jump him away this time. He would burn and she would burn with him.

Tyrenell heard a terrible roar in his comms. "Light Cannon is spinning up. Get clear!"

To burn or to fall. To die or live. It was his decision. It had always been his decision. But now it wasn't just his life at stake. And then he understood. Life hurt. It was filled with burdens, contradictions, problems. It was how you carried those burdens, how you dealt with those contradictions, how you overcame those problems, that made you alive.

He leapt out of the broken window.

He felt her arms tighten around him and world fuzzed as she blinked them away. When they reappeared, they were falling and a shaft of light, broader than a mountain engulfed the Spire. The world fuzzed out again and again. They hit the ground and rolled.

When he and the Apeiron arose, the Spire was gone and the column of energy surging up to the shield was no more. A small hole of inky blackness opened in the crimson shield. They had done it! The Fleet was saved. But he and the Apeiron looked at each other. They were all still going to burn.

V. Honour the Light Brigade

"We are leaving! Get your Cohort back to the space elevator!"

He shook his head without replying. Not enough time. The trip up was too slow. The Lightfall would be on them before they could ever reach the *Starfall*.

Points of light were flashing in the sky as ships were Jumping out. His Cohort looked to him, but for once he was out of answers—then he looked around. All the Revenants were surging toward the long dead colony ships.

Tyrenell stood gaping, but then it hit him. Of course, the nanites were like a plague, infecting every dead being they touched. The original inhabitants of the planet must have understood that they were doomed and tried to escape. But, like a plague, the nanites also wanted to escape, wanted to infect, wanted to thrive. They seemingly could infect any kind of organic life once it perished.

Looking at the dead colony ships, he understood. The inhabitants had abandoned their original plan to flee and built an energy shield, not to entrap the unwary, but to keep the Revenants from escaping.

It must be automated and it must only activate in case the Revenants were awakened by curious alien species.

Now that the shield was breached, the Revenants sought to escape and infect. The machine intelligence couldn't know about the imminent shockwave from the

215

Hypernova. The colony ships had no Jump Drives. Any Revenants making it into space would be obliterated before they even made it past the planet's three chrysalis-like moons.

However, those colony ships gave Tyrenell an idea.

"Hold orbit—we've got a different way up!"

He raised his arm and pointed to a colony ship still on its launch pad. He took off at a dead run followed closely by the Aperion. His displays showed that the others of his "Cohort" were following closely behind him.

The fight for the ship was short and brutal. Several of the Cohort were felled by the swarming dead, but they finally made it aboard. It took long minutes to launch the ship into space, but even as their chronometers began screaming in warning of the imminent incoming shockwave, they saw the *Starfall* moving toward them.

Tyrenell blew open the colony ship's outer hatch and launched one of the Cohort into space. This time, however, the Cohort understood. They hurled themselves into space and the Aperions Jumped them into the waiting hold of the *Starfall.*

He and the female Aperion were the last to make the Jump. It seemed as if Tyrenell's feet had just touched the floor of the ship's hold that everything wrenched under him again. The *Starfall* Jumped away.

Tyrenell looked out of the holoport that showed the Fleet as it cruised against the inky background of space. Ships of every size, large and small, moved slowly through space, their Jump Engines slowly cycling as they began to recharge from recent use while the relativistic drives pushed the great Fleet ever forward. They were safe, for another few weeks at least. Maybe this time they could find a world with the resources they needed without setting off an ancient trap.

He felt Adira's hand in his. He looked at her and was grateful for her strength and presence beside him. The Aperion had not renounced her Brigade—neither had any of the others that had been saved, as a matter of fact, but they also had not gone back to their respective Brigades.

There was talk that this might be the formation of an Eleventh Brigade—one made up from volunteers of the other Brigades. A strike force like no other. With him as its Commander. He shook his head. Madness.

Still, with Adira by his side, he felt ready to take on any challenge.

They stood looking at the stars.

She squeezed his hand. "Who brings the Light?"

So, she had read the Catechism of Phaetons that he had given her, just as he had read her Brigade's Catechism.

He returned the gesture. "We bring the Light."

Sidney Blaylock is a beginning PhD student in English at Middle Tennessee State University (starting August 2016). He has previously worked as a Bookseller, Library Assistant, Adjunct Instructor, and 6th Grade Language Arts Teacher. He is an avid reader of science fiction and fantasy, and he writes creatively in those genres as well.

His most recent publication is a sci-fi story, "Ship of Shadows," in the anthology Visions IV: Space Between Stars, *edited by Carrol Fix (April 2016). Previous publications (in print via Amazon.com) include the fantasy story "Faerie Knight," which appeared in the anthology* Fae, *edited by Rhonda Parrish (July 2014), and selected for inclusion on* Tangent Online's *2014 Recommended Reading List, and a fantasy short-story entitled, "Dragonhawk," in the magazine* Tales of the Talisman *(Winter 2013 issue), edited by David Lee Summers. You can find Sidney's blog at sidneyblaylockjr.wordpress.com.*

When five billion people unexpectedly die in an instant, who could ever predict what they'd leave behind in the universe? The Event triggered bizarre storms of random passions that repeatedly scorch a desolate research outpost, an unexpected lifeboat for survivors stranded without a home planet.

FORECASTS

Bridges DelPonte

Nobody was going home tonight. Not after that forecast: *homicidal rage* and *suicidal depression.* No crashing in her home cube and clicking through her vids tonight, Serena thought. She reluctantly yanked a new chem jacket out of a sterilizer and pulled her silky black hair into a ponytail. Returning to her squad room, she scanned the long narrow room with low ceilings and dozens of flat black benches. Its beige walls remained bare, except for a tattered, yellowed map of their exoplanet colony tacked to a front wall. A couple of new platoon cadets replayed the shrink's hologram, laughing as they disrupted his transmission with quick laser bursts from their detainers. Serena shook her head. Those rookies wouldn't be goofing on any daily forecast after a year of chasing Naturals, if they survived another night beating back the emotional remnants of the dead.

She unlocked a pharm lab, as details of this evening's prescription burbled in her earpiece from Central Services. Punching in her pharm code to mix the chemicals, she adjusted several enviromisters for this building, which immediately puffed out a fine chemical spray, a soft lavender scent masking the mixture's musky odor. Might as well remotely adjust her own enviromister, while she was at it. Better not to risk returning home to untreated air. She tried to access Ronny's enviromister but he kept blocking her transmissions. That little brat must still be pissed at his big sis, prolonging their two-week war of silence. She

219

forwarded tonight's bleak forecast to the info screen at his home cube and at his tutoring job at the education center, hoping he'd adjust his misters and take these prescribed orals on his own. Brushing an alcohol wipe across her stomach, Serena squeezed a syringe's plunger, feeling a cool rush of tonight's pharm mix in her veins. She liked to stay even. No steep highs, no deep lows, just a predictable middle range of emotions.

"We're going to get our asses kicked pretty hard," said Azer, a sturdy fireplug of a man with a chocolate brown buzz cut and intense hazel eyes.

Serena was the only person shorter than him in his entire unit, but nobody messed with the feisty Moroccan. At times, he stood closer to her than a commander should. Sometimes she didn't mind, sometimes she did. Tonight she didn't.

"Do you want me to dose you?" she asked, watching liquids flow into a long row of syringes.

"No orals tonight?" He leaned against a lab doorway, his massive mocha biceps folded across his solid chest. "No. We'll need something stronger for these storms. Do you want me to dose you?"

"Yeah, but be gentle," said Azer. He smiled as he rolled up his uniform shirt.

Like most long-term security forces, needle tracks scarred much of his stomach. She pinched a small square of smooth skin on his side and quickly stuck a needle in, discharging tonight's medicine.

"Think we'll ever be done with this crap?"

She shrugged. The Event set into motion these bizarre storms of random passions that sporadically surfed blistering solar winds. No one could predict when or if these fronts would ever end. But when five billion people unexpectedly die in an instant, who could really ever predict what they'd leave behind in the universe? Impassioned shreds of their last moments of existence howled across this somber outpost as plaintive echoes of lives torn away without warning.

"You're gonna have to find some new spots for your doses. Your stomach's pretty much had it."

"How about my ass?" He waggled his butt in his khakis.

"Pretty nice. Sure you want me sticking you there?" She pretended to kick his ass with her black boot.

"Yeah, as long as I get to stick you back." Azer playfully aimed a fresh syringe at her butt.

"It's a big enough target."

"Seems mighty fine to me," he said, grinning.

Serena glanced at him a second longer than she intended.

"What?"

"Nothing," she replied.

"Don't worry, Doc." Azer stared intently into her almond-shaped green eyes. "I've got your back. Good psych pharms are hard to come by."

Lishman, their unit's blaster sharpshooter, popped into her lab. "Hey, Doc, wanna join our pool?"

"Dare I ask what I'm betting on?"

"We're taking bets on how many jumpers you talk down from a ledge, and how many still jump anyway," he said, with a smirk.

"Lish, stop screwing around and get those boys and girls up here for their shots," growled Azer.

"Did you bet on me or jumpers, Azer?"

"I split it 50-50, Doc."

"Thanks for your vote of confidence."

The chem loader beeped as it filled its final syringe. After Azer left for his squad room, Serena tried to reach Ronny one more time. No luck. She followed Azer and stood in the back of the room to listen to his pep talk.

"Okay, folks. Settle down," said Azer, silencing a buzz of anxious troops. "You've seen tonight's forecast. Two big-ass fronts blowing across our crappy little rock. Worst storms in our colony's history. Each packs a lethal wallop. All we need now are some goddamn locusts."

A couple of young recruits laughed, but more seasoned troops knew that Azer wasn't trying to be funny.

"You'll be working in teams of six. We've got an all-colony curfew starting in a half-hour, so nobody should be roaming outside their home cubes."

"Think we'll get a chance to blast some Naturals tonight?" asked a toothy cadet. With his bright red freckles, he looked too young for this squad.

"You won't be doing any blasting tonight, Tarasoff," replied Azer. "Cadets only get detainers and tranq guns to subdue locals in our MetroCore."

"We don't get blasters?" Tarasoff sputtered.

Azer groaned. "Only people smart enough not to interrupt me get blasters." He inspected Tarasoff up and down. "In your case, probably never."

A couple of platoon leaders sniggered while smarter cadets kept their mouths shut. Only senior troops were allowed to have lethal blasters, for use mostly against Naturals. These renegades refused any medical care, preferring to squat in primitive tents in unprotected outskirts in Sector Q, known as Omega Gardens. There were no enviromisters in Sector Q's aeroponic farms and Omega Gardens to avoid potential contamination of vital food supplies and fragile plant life. If two bioweapons experts hadn't been ringleaders of these Naturals, security forces would've rooted them out years ago.

"If you get sent out to Omega Gardens, watch out for Naturals. They'll be on their home turf. If they want to kill each other, no problem. But don't let them take you down with 'em."

Serena winced as she thought of Ronny's latest infatuation, Evie, a would-be Natural who kept persuading him to stop dosing. She'd met Evie briefly once before, being hauled off with Ronny and a handful of others at an anti-dosing protest march. Serena knew that, like all Naturals, Evie was trouble.

"Dr. Watanabe is going to be dosing you pretty heavy tonight to make sure you don't kill your team members or yourselves while on duty. Keep an eye on each other, in case your partner's dosing isn't doing the trick. Stay sharp and stick with your team. Now line up for your dosing."

Serena tried hard not to think about how many might not return tomorrow morning, while Patel, a junior chem tech, helped her inoculate troops. In a *jealous wrath* front over two years ago, 30 colonists died and that storm was nowhere near as serious as tonight's forecast. She decided to bring five more syringes in her emergency kit, just in case her initial dosings weren't strong enough.

At Central Services, an enormous electronic map of their colony was displayed on a huge wall screen in the main monitoring station. A large digital storm timer clicked off the remaining 51 minutes until the two masses were predicted to collide over a remote section of their exoplanet. A dozen data techs stared at glowing computer screens as orbiting drones continually transmitted back data and digital pics about the progress of looming emotional masses of the departed. On the map, these fronts were estimated to sweep over MetroCore in two hours and then penetrate the outer rings, including Omega Gardens an hour after that. But forecasts weren't very precise, despite the use of sophisticated tracking drones. A cluster of shrinks spoke in hushed tones at the front of the room as more data flashed across the map.

When the group broke up, she noticed Dr. Bellevue, his familiar steel half-glasses resting on the tip of his nose, his round belly sticking out from the folds of his casual blue sweater. Dr. Bellevue had been a close family friend since her childhood, a little too close to her mother some hinted. He had recruited her to this research station four years ago as a psychiatric pharmaceutical researcher for a one-year stint after she completed her PhD program. From the relative safety of this remote base, the research colony initially undertook cutting edge scientific research, including advanced bioweapons and antidotes to existing weaponized diseases. Now it served as an unexpected lifeboat, without a home planet for them to return to someday. "Call me Walt," he always told people. But out of respect, most colonists still called him Dr. Bellevue, whose daily forecasts were essential to their continuing survival. It must be very grave for him to be walking among data techs, giving them reassuring smiles tonight. He stopped by one data tech's desk to congratulate him on his newborn daughter. A true optimist, she thought. When he glanced up, Dr. Bellevue smiled broadly.

"Despite these circumstances, I'm happy to see you, Serena." They briefly embraced. "You look more like your mother every day." He seemed momentarily lost in that thought.

"That's high praise, Dr. Bellevue."

"And brother Ronny?"

Serena rolled her eyes.

"Let me guess." He pushed his glasses up the bridge of his nose. "Keeps fighting his dosings?"

"Unfortunately, yes."

"Still has that crush on a Natural who reminds him of Nina?"

She nodded. Ronny's fiancée, Nina, perished in the Event. Theirs was a tempestuous relationship that swung between alternating bouts of dynamic passion and fierce discord. After a particularly nasty fight, Ronny impulsively caught one of the station's wormhole transports to crash on Serena's couch for a few days. He never forgave himself for not dying with her, living a half-life on this lonely exoplanet.

"Be patient, Serena. He'll come around."

"It's been three years. It's time he pulled himself together."

"He's always been a dreamer. Like your father. And dreamers find it hard to let go of their illusions."

"Yes, but our dad dreamed wonderful things, incredible visions he painted on canvas. Ronny dreams of destroying his life. If he misses one more dosing, he'll have plenty of time to dream when they lock him up and put him on mandatory meds for six weeks."

"Maybe not such a bad thing. Getting him on a regular dosing schedule may help to even him out. Give him a chance to see things more clearly," said Dr. Bellevue. "But never stop being his sister. Ronny needs you to steady him."

And she needed Ronny to keep some semblance of an ever-fading link to their shared past, their parents, their normal life back home.

"We've got a distressor," called out a data tech. His computer screen blinked red.

"Where?" asked Dr. Bellevue, sedately, as if requesting the time of day.

"MetroCore. Sector C. Level 4. Cube 16. MacLean, Cheryl and Dan, ages 32 and 33. Computer Programmers. Minor son, Joshua, age 6."

"Any past incidents?"

"Info feed notes family counseling, Dr. Bellevue," answered another data tech. "Husband's under treatment for PTSD."

PTSD colonists regularly flipped out before a bad forecast. Pressure from years of being trapped on this settlement, with its grinding routine and unpredictable storm paths, wore some people down to a cracking point.

"I'll take it," Serena said. She wanted to stay busy rather than wait out these coming fronts.

"I've got a team ready to go," said Azer, stepping up to her side. "Good psych pharms are hard to come by," he muttered.

Azer brought a six-person team with detainers and tranq guns to handle this call. Serena would apply her counseling skills to talk the distressor down while team members positioned themselves to knock him out. When they arrived, local safety techs were stretching a bounce pad along Level 1 in case the distressor decided to become a jumper.

"He's out on a balcony," a safety tech said.

"Lish, Cerletti, Beck, fan out to adjacent cubes. Set up for a clean tranq shot into their balcony. The rest of you come with Doc and me."

Serena's psych pharm access card allowed her entry into nearly every section of this colony. She swiped it across a card reader and strode toward an elevator with Azer and other troops. Stepping out on Level 4, she couldn't smell any lavender scent in the empty hallway. She tapped her nose, a signal to Azer's team of a malfunctioning enviromister. A woman's high-pitched scream echoed in her ears as the team trailed closely behind. A home cube's door lay open and a sobbing Cheryl sat collapsed on the floor of her cramped living area. Serena bent down, touching Cheryl's shoulder. She hadn't seen anyone shed real tears in a long time.

"My boy, Josh, my boy," she cried. Her trembling finger pointed toward an open glass door to a small terrace.

Azer silently gestured for his team to go to a bedroom to set up a tranq shot. Serena edged past an undersized table, untouched meals of vegetables and standard protein supplements sitting on plastic plates. Two metal chairs were knocked over and shards of broken glass littered a tile floor. She could hear a male voice mumbling over and over again, "Nothing to fear, but fear itself. Nothing to fear, but fear itself."

She peered out a sliding door. A slender, pale man, with dark circles under angry, twitching eyes, stood at one edge of a tiny balcony. He clutched a kitchen knife in his hand, his shirt drenched in sweat. A mop-haired boy peered out from behind his father's shaking pant leg, appearing more confused than afraid.

"Nothing to fear. Nothing to fear. Nothing to fear, but fear itself."

She had seen this many times before, rational people melting down after trying to sort out an existence that defied all logical analysis. And thinking too much about it didn't help these situations. Azer hung back, keeping out of the man's line of sight, while Serena picked up a dinner plate.

"Stay back," he yelled, as she stepped slowly on to his balcony.

"How are you, Dan?" Serena asked, in her most soothing psych pharm voice.

"Nothing but fear. Fear. Fear itself."

"Do you want to tell me what's happening, Dan?"

"Happening? Happening? Nothing but fear. Fear itself."

"Feelings can be difficult to understand. Let's talk about yours."

He paused and groaned, "Feeling."

"Let's finish dinner and talk about how things are going, Dan." Serena held a plate out in front of her and took another step forward. "I think you'll feel better after you eat something."

"I don't want to *feel* better. I want to *be* better." His voice and eyes were filled with ferocious pain. "Nothing to fear, but fear itself. Nothing to fear, but fear itself. Nothing to fear, but fear itself."

"Are you hungry, Josh?" she asked.

Dan suddenly yanked Josh from behind him, gripping his knife's handle more tightly.

"I won't let him drown. Drown in this fear, this nothingness."

"Why not let Josh finish his dinner first? He must be hungry."

She stuck the dish a bit closer. As Josh innocently reached out for it, Dan raised his knife high above his son. Serena instantly tossed the plate of food into Dan's face. A hail of tranqs shot through the air hitting Dan in his arm, neck, and chest as she grabbed Josh and shielded him with her body. Falling on to the hard green turf of his terrace floor, Dan slashed wildly in the air with his knife, ripping a minor gash into her right shoulder. Dan shuddered and moaned, then fell silent as several tranqs finally took a firm hold. His knife clanked as it hit floor tiles, falling from his faltering grip.

"Daddy, Daddy," cried Josh. He squirmed away from her and shook his father. "Wake up, Daddy. Wake up."

"It's okay, Josh," she said. "He'll be fine. He's just sleeping."

The boy rushed past her to the arms of his sobbing mother.

Serena felt a sharp pain in her right arm, and then warm blood gushed out of her wound. Azer grabbed a kitchen towel and pressed it against her slashed shoulder.

"I thought you were watching my back," she said to Azer.

"I did. Bought you a ticket to med ops, rather than the morgue," he said. "You can thank me later."

After getting her stitches, Serena checked an updated forecast feed on her comm. These fronts weren't expected in MetroCore for about 45 minutes. Serena knew she should return directly to Central Services but decided to jump a Sector N shuttle to Ronny's home cube before returning to her unit. An above ground shuttle zipped through the deserted MetroCore, screeching into a station under Ronny's building, a simple five-story concrete structure. She buzzed his unit, but he didn't respond. She swiped her access card to get into the building and then up an elevator to Level 3. Its hallways were silent, except for soft intermittent puffing sounds of the building's central enviromisters. At his home cube's entrance, she buzzed several times but got no answer. After running her access card through his reader, Ronny's front door glided open.

Except for an unmade mattress on his floor and a tiny kitchen table with two stools, Ronny's home cube remained largely bare. She sensed a stillness that suggested he hadn't been home tonight or maybe even in several days. Opening his chiller, a stench from a clump of black moldy veggies nearly knocked her over. His cube enviromister had been turned off. She beeped Azer on his comm.

"It's me. I gotta favor to ask."

"Shouldn't you still be in med ops?"

"I'm at Ronny's."

"Let me guess. He's not there."

"Yeah. Can you do a quick check to see if he's used his access card tonight?"

"It's against policy."

"Since when has that stopped you?"

"Since I know you'd be crazy enough to try to save his sorry ass if he's in Omega Gardens."

"But I gotta know if he's okay."

"He's a big boy. We need your help here with people who aren't intentionally being assholes. See you in twenty minutes or I'm sending out a search party."

Serena heard a quiet click of her comm as Azer closed his channel. She walked over to his cube's access panel and began to punch in a master code to restart Ronny's enviromisters.

"What the hell are you doing here?" Ronny said.

Serena turned around, relieved to see him standing there. He clutched a bagful of vegetables from Sector Q's aeroponic farm, his backpack flung over his shoulder. His hazel eyes and disheveled dark brown hair peeked out from under their dad's beat up fisherman's cap. Ronny always wore it, stained with flecks of paint from their father's long hours painting in his studio barn. She noticed his boots were muddy and hoped it came from a farm visit, and not from rambling around Omega Gardens with Evie.

"I've been trying to reach you," she said calmly, wanting to avoid a big battle with him. "It's past curfew."

"I'm not a psych pharm, so I'm not on call for you or anybody. I only report to me." He dropped his rucksack onto his floor mattress.

"I was worried about you. Wanted to make sure you're ready for tonight."

"Ready for what?" He put his grocery bag down on his galley counter.

"Tonight's forecast."

"Hardly anything to get worked up about. At least for those of us who still know how to get worked up about things."

"They're going to be two severe geomagnetic storms coming in. *Homicidal rage* and *suicidal depression.*"

"Oh, you mean, like somebody might lose their temper and say a bad word tonight. Or feel really bad about being stuck on this shitty rock. Expressing a little raw emotion might do people good around here."

"Ronny, you can't mean that. There might be a lot of horrific violence, maybe even senseless murders tonight."

"I don't have a PhD in psychiatry or pharmacology. But I'm pretty sure that people have been killing each other for no apparent reason, for a really long time. Actually, since the beginning of time. Way before these claimed fronts got everybody hooked on mandatory joy juice."

"It's not joy juice."

"Oh, that's right. Joy's on a list of banned emotions, too. Forgot about that." He opened his chiller and dumped his rotting veggies into a trash chute.

"Joy proved deadly for Sam. If he'd dosed properly, he'd still be alive."

Serena's former neighbor, Sam, an astronomer, liked to bake bread on Saturday mornings and spent his nights glued to his telescopes in an observatory. One time, a front of *giddy euphoria* was forecast and Sam, like some other colonists, thought he could dose down and get high on passing currents of joy. Sam got so damn happy that he flew right out an airlock into space to touch his beloved stars. Serena knew that feeling too much could kill.

"At least he died happy. Besides I want to manage my emotions on my own, without drugs. Like people did in the olden days. A whole four years ago, before the Event."

"Things have changed since then."

"Or have *we* changed because we're afraid of another Event. Even if we control every last person, it doesn't make us any safer or guarantee it won't happen here, too."

"Don't turn this into a control issue. It's rational common sense to take precautions."

"Rationality sucks. It's incredibly overrated. Maybe I don't like things all buttoned down, like you do. Like Mom did."

She hated to be compared to their mother, but she knew his claim was accurate.

"I don't want to debate this with you again."

"So don't. How about we arm-wrestle to settle this one?" He flexed his broad right bicep.

"That's ridiculous."

"Because you know that I'd win."

"What are we—in third grade or something? Wake up. This is a perilous situation."

"How about a coin toss?"

"You're hopeless."

"Then leave it at that. I'm hopeless and you got to get outta here. I've got plans tonight."

"What kind of plans?"

"Seems like a great night for a walk, or a picnic in the park with a friend."

"With that Natural?"

"She has a name. It's Evie."

"Yeah, Evie. Hopefully, you'll be sensible and stay in, adjust your enviromisters, and take your orals. And not do anything irrational like hanging out in Omega Gardens waiting for some crazed Natural to kill you."

"I gotta better idea. How about I run down this hallway buck naked, singing at the top of my lungs, drunk off my ass?"

"Not exactly a pretty sight."

"No, but it would be a lot more fun. And you know that if Dad was here, he'd be bolting down this hall right by my side, naked and yelling his heart out, too," he said, dancing around her.

Serena found herself grinning in spite of herself as she imagined them bopping along this corridor like a couple of smashed frat boys.

"Aha! Made you smile. Guess I'll have to report you to the authorities. Quick get out an electroshock machine." He started to shake his entire body, pretending to fight off powerful jolts.

"Shut up." She playfully swatted his arm.

"Hey, sis, I do appreciate your concern. But it's totally misplaced. So get outta here before that mad Moroccan kicks down my door looking for you and squishes my veggies with his big black boots."

"Can't you do this for me? Just this one time?"

"Good-bye, Serena," he said, hustling her out the door.

As she hurried toward an elevator, Ronny called out to her, "Hey, Serena."

She turned around to see him mooning her outside his home cube door.

"Nice. Go shave your ugly butt."

Before Serena pressed the elevator button, a floor arrow pinged and its doors flung open. There stood Evie, her short, jet-black hair framing her pale heart-shaped face, a yoga mat sticking out of her green cloth sack. They glared at each other for a moment without speaking.

"Making a house call?" Evie asked.

"I only want what's best for my brother."

"You commandos think you know what's best for everyone. Did you ever think you might be wrong?"

"I've seen enough to know we're doing the right thing."

"Right thing?" Evie snorted. "More like scaring good people into medicated submission."

"You don't know what you're talking about. Come out some time on one of our patrols during a bad storm. I'll show you people overwhelmed from these surges of emotion. Hurting themselves, their loved ones. Then you'd be begging us for meds."

"Yeah, whatever." Evie tried to exit, but Serena stood in the way.

"If you want to screw up your life with these silly ideas, go right ahead," she said calmly. "But leave my brother out of it. I don't want to see him flush his life down the drain for nothing."

Evie frowned. "Lecture over, Doc?"

"Yeah. You'd better get going. It's already past curfew. And I'd really hate to have to arrest you."

Serena stepped to one side and Evie rushed out. She waited until she heard Ronny's cube door whoosh open and then closed. She sighed with relief, hoping that they might stay put indoors tonight.

As she rode a shuttle back to Central Services, a recorded announcement began to echo through MetroCore. An automated voice in a composed tone repeatedly stated, "Geomagnetic storm approaching. Please move immediately inside your home cubes and check your vid screen for further safety instructions." She checked her watch. The storms were arriving about 25 minutes early. "Geomagnetic storm approaching. Please move immediately inside your home cubes and check your vid screen for further safety instructions." Her shuttle jerked into Central Services just as final warning sirens began blasting.

When she arrived back at the monitoring station, beautiful, frightening images of advancing gaseous clouds were transposed over a colony map. Enormous orange and blue billowing plumes heaved in solar winds, expanding then collapsing in a series of undulating dances across the outskirts of the barren exoplanet.

"They're gorgeous fuckers," murmured Azer, who now stood by her side.

"Stunning," she replied.

"Wanna give you a head's up. We pulled Sector Q duty for the rest of tonight."

"Lovely," she replied drily.

"So we'll be taking a hovercraft and blasters on any calls out there. You, too." Azer handed her a blaster.

For the next half-hour, everyone watched a running ticker of solar wind and magnetic field density, storm speed, acceleration rates, and temperatures scrolling alongside the electronic map. Solar winds were now moving much more slowly than the space storms, so the clouds began to rapidly decelerate.

"Oh shit, they're gonna stall," said one data tech.

A bunch of whistles and groans filled the air as the storms slowed to a snail's pace above the settlement.

"We got multiple distressors in Sectors A, G, L, and Q," called out another data tech. His computer screen blinked with several incoming emergencies.

"Let's go," said Azer, leading his team to a security hovercraft.

Serena had barely strapped in when Azer powered it full throttle for Sector Q, Barrack 7. A profile on her palm comp indicated that this distressor was Rafaela Carbarcas, female, age 51, an aeroponics botanist. No history of prior incidents or counseling. When Azer set down his hovercraft, warning sirens were already blasting across the sprawling acres of residential barracks, aeroponic greenhouses, and food storage huts. A group of three crop specialists, dressed in white coveralls, nylon mesh hairnets, and safety boots, waited for them.

"Who called it in?" asked Azer.

"I did. Adler, Senior Crop Specialist. Rafaela was doing fine one moment, then she seemed agitated and incoherent the next. She took a mini-rover. I think she drove toward Greenhouse 16, but I can't be sure." He pointed to a circular tri-level glass tower at one end of a line of vertical greenhouses.

"Okay. You folks get back inside your homes and we'll take it from here. Erickson, Schou, and Jaspers, grab mini-rovers and patrol those residential barracks and storage huts in case she's still roaming around there. Lish, Doc, you come with me to that greenhouse."

Azer, Serena, and Lishman jumped on separate mini-rovers and set off to Greenhouse 16. Two mini-rovers already sat outside, one was still running.

"Better grab some safety goggles. Sulfur microwave lamps are pretty harsh."

Each of them snatched a pair of tinted goggles hanging from an entryway metal rack. They rushed along narrow moving walkways, past dozens of narrow rows of leafy tomato plants suspended upside down on vertical cables, their bare roots exposed to artificially circulating oxygen. Azer swiped his access card for the facility's main security booth. Inside, six vid screens showed live feeds from surveillance cameras on each floor, while a seventh monitored aeroponic systems and access points.

"How come no one's monitoring this greenhouse?"

"Every unit got called into Central Services, Doc. Nobody worried about these plants going homicidal."

They scanned every security screen in silence for several minutes, squinting for any signs of Rafaela amid these dense plantings.

"Needle in a haystack," Lishman muttered.

"Any chance she kept going—right into Omega Gardens?" asked Lishman.

"Hope not," said Azer.

"Isn't it locked down?" asked Serena.

"It's gotta stay open. It's the nearest evac route for Sectors M through Q in case of system failures. But she'd have to use her access card to get in after curfew." He punched in his security code, pulling up this evening's access log for Sector Q. "What's her access card number, Lish?"

Lishman checked Carbarcas' profile on his palm comp. "DL0528-05."

Azer ran his finger down a list of access codes. "She's not on this list. Dammit. We're gonna have to do this the old-fashioned way. Grid-by-grid. Level-by-level."

Azer took the first two rows, Serena the second two, and Lishman, the third two in an initial grid of bulky tomato plants lashed to cables rising nine or ten feet high. In these narrow corridors, plant cables swayed and creaked as Serena gingerly pushed aside thick foliage of mature tomato plants. Parsing heavy vines, a random memory of divers swimming through kelp forests off San Diego's coast popped into Serena's thoughts. A film shown during a family trip to an aquarium when she and Ronny were kids.

"Rafaela, Rafaela," she called out softly. "It's okay to come out. We only want to help."

A plump red tomato dropped to the greenhouse floor and rolled about three feet in front of her. Reaching down to pick it up, she noticed what appeared to be a wispy spider web clinging to a tomato bush's ends near the middle of this row. As she got closer, she realized it was a white mesh hairnet, tangled in the vines. She looked up and examined a length of plantings cable, but saw only more leafy vines. Continuing to creep among the vertical plantings, she jostled them to one side and then to the other. She suddenly felt some resistance and tore the plantings back. Three or four more tomatoes thumped to the floor, but still nothing. Serena made out a small scattering of smashed tomatoes and torn leaves at the row's end. She hurried to that spot and gazed up. A limp figure in white coveralls dangled from a set of lashings on a plantings cable.

"Rafaela, Rafaela!" she called out, but received no response. "I've got her," she said into her comm.

Lishman arrived first and looked up. "How did she get up there?"

"Probably climbed down from that catwalk."

Serena pointed at a second-story metal footbridge above the cables intended for maintenance workers. Azer emerged out of some packed foliage and stared up the cable.

"You're one-for-one, Doc."

"Doesn't count. Dead before Doc even found her," said Lishman, laughing.

Serena shook her head in disgust.

"What, Schou?" barked Azer into his comm. "Okay. Roger that. I read you."

"Doc, can you punch it in and wait for a recovery team? Schou's reporting some Naturals trying to loot grain huts. Let's go, Lish."

Serena walked back to the central security booth to hail a recovery group over its main computer. She realized Azer had forgotten to log out of the computer's access card program. She quickly ran her fingers down the list and spotted Ronny's access card number. He entered a south entrance of Omega Gardens at 21:05 hours. Serena's hands clenched instinctively, but her dosing kept her heart from racing, her mind from flooding with anxiety.

When a recovery team arrived and started to haggle over how to free Rafaela, Serena slipped out. She tossed her visor into a recycling bin and grabbed a mini-rover, journeying into the cool darkness of the botanical gardens. She ran her access card and a wrought iron gate swung open. A clear starry sky, mimicking a beautiful night on their home planet, twinkled above Omega Gardens. She tucked her psych pharm badge into her pocket and put her blaster into the back of her waist band, to avoid provoking any confrontations. She drove slowly through the isolated park, watching carefully for Naturals.

She knew Ronny's favorite hangout, a thicket of bamboo encircling a walled sunken garden with an oval koi pond and bubbling fountain. It reminded him of their grandfather's Zen garden in Kyoto. Serena parked her mini-rover and pulled out two syringes from her kit. As she proceeded on foot over a narrow stone trail, she heard voices echoing in the meditation garden. Ducking behind an azalea bush, she spied Ronny and Evie practicing yoga poses near a neat pile of bamboo stalks from a pruning project. Serena crawled forward and then stood on top of a wall.

"Uttanasana," said Ronny. He and Evie bent forward in a swan dive, placing their palms on the ground.

"Ronny, what are you two doing here?" asked Serena, in her best psych pharm voice.

"Deep breath, in and out." Ronny ignored Serena as he and Evie audibly breathed in and out three times.

"The fronts are going to hit this sector in about ten minutes. We need to evacuate."

"Okay now, low lunge," Evie said. They both stuck their right leg out to the back of their mats for several breaths.

"It's time to go home."

Ronny and Evie continued to leisurely move through their next yoga pose, gazing at each other and never making eye contact with Serena.

"Did you hear me?"

"Yes, we did. But right now it's time for our favorite pose. Downward facing dog," Ronny said. "Oops, almost dropped it." He caught their father's cap and twisted it backwards before making this pose.

"I've got a mini-rover. You two can hop on back of it. It'll be tight, but we can make it to safety."

"We're perfectly safe where we are," said Evie, flexing her back.

A recorded announcement began to boom through the park. "Geomagnetic storm approaching. Please move immediately inside your home cubes and check your vid screen for further safety instructions."

"That's pretty annoying," said Ronny.

"How about Cobra?" called out Evie, as she and Ronny progressed through their next pose.

"You need to come back with me now, if you want to stay alive. Plenty of orals and enviromisters in MetroCore to blunt the force of these storms."

"Right now, I'm trying to open up my body, my mind. Not dull it with drugs."

"Why not learn to relax and hang with us?" added Evie.

She ignored Evie and tried to reason with her brother. "You remember last time, we lost 25 people. Trust me, these fronts are much worse."

Suddenly, the park's warning sirens blared as the storms penetrated Omega Gardens.

"I trust my own body wisdom. And I feel fine."

"Ronny, stop it. I just found a woman who hung herself in a greenhouse. These fronts are already proving lethal."

"I feel sorry for that woman. Only goes to show that your dosing doesn't really work."

"They work for most people. They are our best defense for now."

"Between our sun salutations and chamomile tea in our mug warmers, we'll do just fine, thank you."

"Poses and tea won't do much good against these storms. Come with me and you'll be safe."

"Safe? Or controlled? When will you ever get it? I'm not like you or most people on this station. I want to feel. I want to feel everything." His voice reverberated through the empty park.

"I'm done asking you. I'm ordering you to get in this mini-rover and back to MetroCore, or else."

"Or else what?" he asked laughing. "Going to tell Mommy on me? A little late for that."

Serena ripped a dosing syringe out of her cargo pants pocket and jumped down from the wall, springing at Ronny. But Evie grabbed a loose bamboo stalk and swung it, just missing Serena's jaw. Evie momentarily lost her balance and Serena shoved her hard to the ground. Serena charged at Ronny and they began to wrestle over her syringe. Ronny's eyes grew wild and he clamped one hand over Serena's throat, pushing her syringe away with his other hand. Serena gasped for air as Ronny tightened his grip. Choking, she fought passing out. Why was he doing this? Had those storms already begun to infect him? As she fell to her knees on a gravel path, Serena felt Evie pull her blaster out of her back waistband.

"Drop that needle or I'll kill you!" Evie screamed, pointing it at Serena.

A whistling sound of a discharged blaster pierced the evening air, striking Evie so hard that she spun around and then collapsed dead onto stone coping encircling the koi pond. Ronny let go of Serena and rushed to Evie, gathering her up in his arms. He kissed her pale face and stroked her dark hair with his hand. He picked up Serena's blaster and pointed it at her.

"Why couldn't you leave us alone? Why?" he howled.

Serena locked her eyes on Ronny and wanted to believe that he wouldn't kill her. Suddenly, he pointed her blaster at his own heart and squeezed its trigger, burning a hole through his chest. Ronny collapsed by Evie's side.

In her dazed state, Serena gaped at her brother's scorched body, smoldering from the deadly shot. His eyes lingered open and no longer flashed with anger or sorrow, only a fixed vacant stare of death. Their father's cap rested on a nearby gravel path. A fine spray of Ronny's blood mixed with their father's old paint spatters. She tried to reach for it with her outstretched hand.

"Doc, are you okay?" called out Lishman. He ran along a rocky trail to the enclave.

Instantly, she felt an overpowering, foreign sensation churning up inside herself. Her body started to convulse as a tide of crushing grief and devastating guilt gradually roused within her. Raw agony flooded her brain, as unshackled emotions coursed through her veins for the first time since the Event. A tormented wail nearly escaped her lips. But a swift prick of a tranq smothered any mournful cry, stomping out any fleeting spark of anguish.

She heard Azer's voice whispering into her ear. "Easy, Doc. Easy. Good psych pharms are hard to come by."

As the tranq quickly took effect, she couldn't feel anything. Not sorrow or loss. Neither remorse nor agony. Only . . . even.

Bridges DelPonte has published two novels, **Deadly Sacrifices** *and* **Bridles of Poseidon,** *three non-fiction books, several science fiction, fantasy, and mystery short stories, and numerous legal, travel, and business articles. Her mystery,* **Deadly Sacrifices,** *received a Royal Palm Literary Award (2nd place – unpublished mystery) from the Florida Writers Association (FWA) and her underwater fantasy,* **Bridles of Poseidon,** *was a finalist for a Royal Palm Literary Award (unpublished fantasy). She is a member of FWA, Sisters in Crime, Inc., and Citrus Crime Writers. When she is not tapping away on her laptop, she teaches law courses, creates educational game apps, and lives happily in sunny Central Florida. You can find out more about Bridges and her writing at www.bridgesdelponte.com.*

Billy Thain decides to spend his summer break with his grandmother transporting cougars on an interstellar vessel. First, they must gather the elusive animals, keep them safe during the trip, and then place them on a "preservation planet." Billy knows something's not right, and it'll take some quick thinking on his part to make sure his grandmother's dream doesn't end in disaster.

MOUNTAIN SCREAMERS

Doug C. Souza

The tawny cougar crept toward Grandma and let out a hiss. I lined the site atop the barrel to its shoulder. Thick fur rose in a prickly streak down its back. Its snarl quivered with each breath.

"Anytime you're ready, William," Grandma whispered, keeping her eyes locked on the approaching mountain lion.

Pfft! The dart shot out too high. The needle clinked off the sandstone.

Useless.

The cougar's black-tip tail puffed up, nearly doubling in width. Its attention shifted between Grandma and the spent tranq-dart. A soft squeal escaped my throat.

Now, I had its full attention. Sandy eyes locked with mine.

"Reload," Grandma said calmly and then gave several sharp clicks with her tongue. The mountain lion's gaze returned to her. For a moment, the large cat appeared to consider retreating. A high pitched whistle mixed with a guttural groan came from somewhere deep inside the animal. It gingerly stepped forward.

I grabbed a second dart—the movement didn't go unnoticed.

Grandma clicked her tongue louder.

I pulled back the bolt handle, set the dart, and lined up my second shot.

Deep breath, hold it, and fire.

Pfft.

It struck true.

The cougar let out a piercing cry. It curled, biting at the dart in its shoulder. When that didn't work it pawed with its hind legs.

"No, no, no." Grandma launched onto the large cat's back, her cowboy hat falling off behind her. "Don't go chokin' yourself." She slapped a poly-mesh net across its mouth. The wiry material cinched automatically around the snout.

I stepped forward to help.

"Back!" Grandma ordered as she jumped up and waved me away. "Reload and keep an eye for stragglers. Throw the Piezo-ball."

The cougar reached for the poly-mesh muzzle with claws extended. Its movements growing more sluggish with each attempt.

I wasn't worried about "stragglers." Grandma had taught me long ago that mountain lions were solitary animals. No cubs were around, so this wasn't a mother. I clicked the Piezo-ball on and rolled it away. Its whine pierced my eardrums before reaching a frequency I no longer heard. The ultrasonic pitch would deter any curious wildlife.

Finally, the beast let out a heavy sigh and crumpled to the ground. Grandma yanked the tranq-dart and tossed it away. The giant chest heaved much slower. Glassy eyes stared blankly ahead for a moment and then shut as the cougar stilled.

"Sorry, honey," Grandma said as she stood and loosened the poly-mesh. She wouldn't remove it completely until we had the magnificent beast tucked safely in its cage. "Didn't mean to yell atcha. Didn't want some flailing claw to snag you, that's all."

"It's okay." Again, my voice chirped like a second-grader. I coughed and cleared my throat. I handed her hat back to her. She bunched up loose gray strands, and retied her ponytail before pulling her hat taut. She had bought me a similar hat when I first arrived.

"Take care of that hat and you'll have it for life," she had said. I liked the stiff leather feel and the wide brim, but the tight fit took some getting used to.

"Your mother would have my neck if she knew I'd let you get this close." She shook her head and then waved me closer.

She pet the mountain lion's burly side. "Go ahead."

I did so. The fur went much deeper than I'd imagined. "Warm," I commented.

"Yeah, he was extra fired up."

"'Cause of us?"

"Not just that," Grandma laughed. "Nature." She pointed to the silver pole that stuck out of the ground a few feet away.

"What's that?"

"We use a blend of potent pheromones to draw males out. Imagine his disappointment when he goes looking for a girlfriend and finds us Relocators instead."

Relocators. Grandma had said the plural; meaning I was considered a Relocator. Mostly, I pictured myself as an assistant. A wave of pride ran through me as I knelt and pet the large cat. A capture I had helped with. *Best Summer Hiatus ever.*

We'd captured nearly ten mountain lions in the past three days, but this was the first that had me out of our Drifter, aiming a rifle. Somehow the creature had evaded our trackers while Grandma was checking on the whereabouts of a different mountain lion. The afternoon sun continued to bake the barren land. The Mexican border was just twenty miles to the south. How anything thrived out here was beyond me.

"Feel the ears," she whispered.

I pinched the velvet material, marveling at how delicate they felt. Grandma pulled her sIdekIck from its holster and ran it under the animal's chest. The datapad brought up various specs across the main screen.

"Interesting," she said. "There's a tracker-tag after all. Malfunctioning though, probably old. That explains how he snuck up on us."

Much like human Life-Chips, tracker-tags can be programmed to release a tranquilizing agent if needed. Grandma had sent the command from her sIdekIck when the mountain lion first snuck up on us, but nothing had happened.

"So, what do we do now?" I asked.

"Gotta pull it." She typed in a new command into her sIdekIck. Holding it near the chest, she waited for the information to come up.

"It's an old one?" I asked.

"Old as you," she nodded.

Sixteen years. No wonder it had malfunctioned. Tracker-tags were supposed to expel themselves after a decade. After sending a signal for reissuing, of course.

"Far from home too," she commented. "Kitlope, a small range in Canada."

"They travel that far?"

"Canada to lower Arizona is nothing for a mountain cat. Back in the mid-twenty-first century, game wardens tracked some from California to Maine. Crossing dangerous elevations as well as heavily industrialized cities." Grandma fastened the bio-strip across the cougar's chest. After checking to make sure her patient was completely out, she programmed the tendrils to inject and retrieve the faulty tracker-tag. The hair-thin tendrils were designed to snake into the animal's hide, avoid major organs, and pull the tag.

"That's crazy. The way they go so far. The cats, I mean, not the tendrils." I clarified.

"It's one of the reasons I pushed for them to be the major terrain predator introduced to LePhan," she said as the bio-strip beeped. A pebble-sized tracker-tag appeared at the end of a tendril. She pulled it away, detaching it completely. "Mountain cats, alligators, crows, and octopi are the most resourceful creatures to walk the Earth. Or swim, whatever. Prime candidates for the planetary wildlife preserve."

Preservation planet; the idea still tripped me out. A whole planet allotted for wildlife—plants and animals—no human settlements allowed. Grandma had showed me pics and vids of LePhan; the environment was far less harsh than the territories most wildlife roamed nowadays.

Grandma grabbed the tarp from the Drifter and slid it under the cougar as I attempted to roll the cat on top—the thing was heavy. She flipped the switch and the tow-cable dragged the sleeping giant into the crate. A separate line automatically pulled the crate onto the flatbed trailer.

I climbed the small step-ladder and hoisted myself into the passenger's seat asking, "How many mountain lions—"

"Excuse me?" Grandma turned, shifted into first, and jolted us down the dirt road.

"Erm, sorry," I sighed. "How many mountain *cats* are left?"

"That's better, but don't know what you mean. Mountain cats are spread all over." The Drifter had reinforced shocks and tires to keep the jostling minimal.

"No, I mean how many are left for today?"

"Oh," she checked the GPS, "got two more showing within a couple klicks. Don't know if we'll get to them in time."

The Relocation Project had plenty of cougars for LePhan, but this was the final wave of predator introduction and Grandma wanted to take as many as possible. She disapproved of the term "Mountain Lion" because it wasn't only inaccurate, but insulting. "Lions are lazy scavengers that lay around all day," she had said once. "They're called 'king of the jungle' because they have a pretty mane. They roar obnoxiously to show off. Mountain cats are precise. They can survive in a multitude of environments. Their shriek will chill you to the bone. It's rare to hear one cry out, but it's an unforgettable experience."

"By the way," she added. "Don't go mentioning his age to anyone." She thumbed towards the cougar crated in the back.

"Because he's sixteen?"

"Yeah, don't want some pencil-necked suit cancelling the poor cat's trip just 'cause he's only got four to five years left in him."

"You mean Dr. Quintos." I grinned.

"Him, couple others. They got different priorities than the rest of us."

We continued to drive on, but each time we neared a cougar's location they'd run off. Grandma would stop the Drifter intermittently to see if one would return to its territory. She'd tap in commands to set off the luring poles.

Late afternoon passed and the sIdekIck's alarm chimed, indicating it was time to head back.

But she was adamant about trying for at least one more. LePhan was a sanctuary she'd spent most her life working on. An idea started by a professor Grandma had known over fifty years ago. The professor was gone, but LePhan was near completion.

The plant life, herbivores, omnivores, and decomposers had all been sent in stages over the last four decades. Grandma was part of a team of ten superluminal transports in charge of predators.

Grandma slowed the Drifter and rounded a shallow bend, the tires crunching over a row of dried brush. She checked her sIdekIck one last time and nodded toward the distance past the hood. She didn't mention us being out after curfew, and I knew better than to bring it up.

"Sorry 'bout missing that first shot," I said.

For several heartbeats, she gazed quietly into the distance. "Missing the shot," she shook her head. "Hell, I'm sorry I didn't see the thing comin'." She kicked the e-brake and turned to face me straight on. "I was too busy looking at the tracker-feed to notice I had a mountain screamer closing in. Scared the dickens out of me."

Grandma rarely called them "mountain screamers." Said it was not *as* insulting as "lion," but unfortunately, fit well. Mountain cats don't roar; they hiss, spit, and scream.

"Scared me too."

She sighed. "Don't focus on the *miss*, but the hit. Only a certain caliber of person could pull off that shot when facing a pissed off cougar."

Caliber. Grandma loved that word. She didn't use it often, only when she was making a point. When I was eight, I had embarrassed myself at a piano recital. I couldn't complete one of Chopin's stupid runs; had to keep starting over and over. Same set of notes played nearly twenty times in a row.

My family had come to greet me in the reception area after. Every one stared at me. Kids whispered and pointed. Parents hushed them.

Grandma approached me first, and somehow I knew she'd know exactly what to say.

"Well, you didn't give up, did you?" she smiled softly. The comment dropped over me like one of those blankets you see rescuers give people after pulling them out of freezing water.

"Yeah." I shrugged.

"Takes a certain caliber of person to say hell with it, and keep on tryin' the way you did. Most would've ran off the stage bawling like a baby."

I looked the word up later that night. *Caliber: degree of capacity or competence; ability.* I didn't quite understand how it applied; only that Grandma had made me feel like I was something special.

"But don't you fret about how close that screamer got to me. I had my shocker charged." She patted the pulse-shot strapped to her thigh. The pistol-shaped weapon was set at 2,000 kV.

"Why didn't you just fry 'em?" I fingered my own pulse-shot, wondering what it would've been like to use it at close range. Only Relocators were allowed to carry pulse-shots.

"'Cause that's exactly what it would've done." She glanced back at the mountain cat in the cage. "Would've neutralized him, but also would have really hurt 'em. Might even caused internal injuries."

Internal injuries from a pulse-shot? Even I knew that wasn't true. Pulse-shots were used by police because they could stop criminals without long term side-effects. Grandma was a softy.

"Now be quiet for a bit," she said leaning on the steering wheel. She read something on her sIdekIck. "We got one just past the lip over there. A girl, no cubs." She pointed about half-a-mile (or a klick, I think) from our perch. I readied the tranq-rifle as we left the Drifter.

The mountain screamer was nowhere in sight as we hunched down behind the lip in the ground. "She probably saw or heard us." Grandma checked the tracker. "Looks like she's taking the long way around. She may still cross our path somewhere north."

The sun started its downward trek at our back. Probably two hours away from setting. If Grandma didn't care about coming in late, neither did I.

I unfurled my sleeves so the sun wouldn't bake my arms. It wasn't a blistering hot sun, but the breeze had stopped some time ago. Like Grandma, I kept checking our surroundings—having the surprise visit earlier had left us on guard. She had told me early on that patience and remaining still were key to catching any type of cougar. If my constant head turning bothered her, she didn't say so. I kept one hand ready to grab my pulse-shot; no mountain cat was gonna get the drop on me.

Nearly an hour later the cougar's stalking form appeared in the distance. Blending in with the vanilla land made determining her size tricky. Several times she seemed to disappear into the landscape.

Though she was too far, I knew her nostrils were flaring as she caught our scents. Her lips rippling, haunches tense, ready to attack.

I pictured this mountain screamer roaming the giant eucalyptus of LePhan, stalking prey. For some reason, pine trees didn't grow much larger than twenty feet on LePhan.

"Here we go," Grandma whispered. She deftly slid the menu option on her sIdekIck and brought up the tracker-tag's controls.

The mountain screamer's back leg twitched. Seconds later she sat placidly on the ground and then lay down altogether. She was sound asleep by the time we reached her in the Drifter.

"Seems too easy after the last one, eh?" Grandma smiled.

We loaded the cat and I checked the time: 6:45. Only an hour and forty-five minutes past curfew. Maybe it wouldn't be a problem. Normally, we pulled the Drifter over and spent some time basking in the Sadabe sun with the A/C cranked up. Grandma liked to stop and watch the landscape before returning to base-camp.

We were on the road for about twenty minutes when she hit the brakes and threw the Drifter into park. She motioned for me to grab the roll of paper-towels from the console. Her hand reached her mouth just as the coughing fit began. I tore one loose and placed it in her free hand.

She gurgled deeply as her breath came out in high wheezes. I couldn't look away; I had to hand her fresh paper-towels after she threw the spent ones aside.

Like the others, the fit lasted about five minutes. The Drifter idled loudly. Grandma leaned back and wiped her eyes with the back of her hand. The same strong hand that had ripped a tranq-dart from the mountain screamer's shoulder now looked old and frail.

I didn't choke up *during* the fits; only when I thought about them at night. She didn't explain what was going on. She just coached me on what to do and thanked me for helping.

She was adamant about not letting others witness a fit. Around camp, I was sure others had to have heard, but no one said anything.

There was a line outside the shower stalls as we returned to base-camp. Grandma had warned me early on about this. "Let the dirt settle behind your ears. You'll get used to it by the end of the day," she had said when we first arrived a few days ago.

She was right, of course. Black grit lined my fingernails. Blotches of dust caked my arms. I didn't care.

Several of the grad-students had dropped out by the second day, opting for an "incomplete" in the assignment.

Of those that remained, most looked miserable. Each always gave a pleasant wave to Grandma. Somehow, they all seemed to know her. I asked her how she knew so many people, but she just said, "Seen them around."

After a welcome dinner of hotdogs fresh off the grill, Grandma got called to the main office. She brought me along.

"This fella's rude as all-get-out, but don't worry none. He's just got a stern tone, that's all." Grandma was hinting that we were about to eat trouble with this guy. Not a good sign.

Once inside the cramped, yet immaculate office, Director Lawrence Quintos had us stand there while he finished some task at his desk. He acknowledged us with a wince, as if the dirt that covered us might infect his prissy aura. His clothes were made for outdoor use, but he kept them immaculate. The thin layer of red hair atop his head was slicked back. A tornado couldn't muss that do.

"You're over two hours late," Quintos commented dryly.

"Yes," Grandma answered.

"Make sure it doesn't happen again. The loaders have a tight schedule for the overnight haul to the space-dock."

"Yes." Grandma said, even though this was our last day retrieving. Returning late was an impossibility. As Quintos said himself, the loaders were heading to Texas with the mountain cats *tonight*; no one was retrieving mountain cats after today.

"I notice we retrieved a male absent a tag."

"Yep."

"You prepped the new tag?"

"Yep."

"I took a look at the specimen." Only Quintos would refer to the beautiful animal as a "specimen." He waited for Grandma to say something.

She simply waited quietly.

"You recorded age estimation at three years," Quintos scrolled through the data. "He's clearly much older than that. You've wasted resources bringing him here."

"Made a mistake I guess."

Quintos was doubtful. "A mistake?"

"Guess those of us out in the heat of the day are bound to err every once in a while." Grandma removed her hat and fanned herself.

"I've reported the error. Make sure it doesn't happen again. Also, I checked your whereabouts via your Life-Chip. Make sure you remain within the designated plots from now on."

None of this made sense. Everyone was leaving for the space-dock as soon as the mountain cats were delivered tomorrow. Quintos' orders were empty.

"That it?" Grandma asked, but it came out more like a statement. She was already leading me out of the office.

"Yes, you're excused," Quintos said to our backs. I absent-mindedly held my side as we climbed down the steel staircase. Somewhere inside me, my own Life-Chip rested. I'd never heard of a regular person using someone's Life-Chip to track them. Human Life-Chips were only used to solve kidnappings or murders. Schools weren't even allowed to use them to watch over students. Quintos didn't seem fazed at all when he mentioned the breach in etiquette.

No wonder Grandma didn't like the guy.

"Don't let his little posturing episode get to you," Grandma said, noticing my discomfort. "I figure he's had a frustratin' life, probably was expecting this not-for-profit life to be a bit more profitable at the admin level."

"He's an odd duck," I said. It was one of Grandma's favorite phrases.

"Yep," she laughed. "But forget about him. Tomorrow, we board the transport. Get ready to have your breath taken away."

"What do you mean?"

"Well, I could tell you about the massive ship and all. How it towers over you. A marvelous . . . uh, *marvel* of human achievement, but nothing compares to standing in the presence of a superluminal freight-transport." She grinned and patted my cheek. "You'll see."

Grandma wasn't kidding. The transport resembled a stadium. Over two hundred yards long and six stories high. Smaller tug-ships fastened onto brackets at the freighter's sides; the tug-ship propulsion jets made up the bulk of their hulls. Grandma had said the tug-ships were the most under-appreciated vessels of the lot.

"Twenty pilots have to stay in-tune within a tenth of each other's debarking speed to lift this behemoth. Then they send it off toward the slingshot, only to pop off and repeat again with some other giant transport. No credit, no glory. And they get paid midrange of all superluminal crews."

A small crowd had gathered near the conveyer belt to watch the caged animals being loaded. This transport only carried mountain cats and hunter hawks. Not surprisingly, the hawks' screeches drowned out the mountain screamers' hisses and barks. The other transports would carry hyenas, wolves, Tasmanian devils, grizzly bears, Komodo dragons, and crocodiles.

Most of the crowd were college students. They gawked, pointed, and recorded. Some noticed me standing on the "authorized personnel" platform, beyond the barricade. Only Relocators were allowed to disperse the predators onto LePhan. I stood proud, letting their envy wash over me. I couldn't help it; I was beaming.

"Quit showing off." Grandma pulled off my hat, ruffled my hair, and slapped my hat back on so hard it covered my eyes. I fixed it and grinned up at her. Her smile twice the size as mine. I followed her up the gangplank, the steel railing cold under my grip.

It took five minutes to reach our quarters. They weren't anything luxurious: a small sitting/dining area, sleeper bunks, and a refresher station. A closet of a bathroom in the back. Metal rivets the size of my fist lined the walls and ceilings. Everything was painted a gray-primer.

Cold in design and temperature. I rubbed my arms, already missing the Arizona sun.

"I almost forgot," Grandma said as she squeezed her clothes onto the shelving units. There weren't any dressers in this cabin. "Remember to pay attention during the slingshot jump."

"What do you mean?" I asked.

"Well, they'll have us strap in, that you know. Not really necessary, but a precaution. Anyway, they'll do the countdown and you can actually feel a difference at zero."

"What kind of difference?"

"I've never felt it, but I heard it's an eerie, dreamy type of feeling. It has to do with the fact that your molecules, as well as this ship's, must leave our universe to enter a different thread of the multiverse, and return again."

I tried to understand, but it was clear she had lost me. I squinted at her.

She laughed, "I'm no astrophysicist, but think of it this way. Our universe has the same number of atoms since the beginning of time."

I nodded although I didn't get it.

She went on, "So, if we leave this universe in order to space-jump, our atoms are being added to another universe and taken away from this one."

"Yeah," my tone implied I understood, but it was clear I didn't.

"Supposedly, there's an exchange. A fraction smaller than a split second where the other *you* slips in and shares that space."

"And you can feel him?"

"Him? Who?"

"The other you," I said.

"Yes, just before you return to our universe. Some say they felt it. I never have, but it gives me a sense of peace knowing there's another Etta Thain out there." She gazed at the steel wall.

I sat back and thought about this as the countdown started nearly two hours later. The jump happened, but I didn't feel anything different. Just the subtle jolt of the transport and then the second jolt as it settled.

After the space-jump, I realized Grandma had told me all that mumbo-jumbo just to distract me. Mom must've told her about the nightmares I'd had as the trip approached. Spending three days on a freighter didn't bother me, the opposite actually; I was excited. Something else had been nagging at me. Something I couldn't figure out. Maybe it was because I was the only grandkid who opted to accept Grandma's invitation. That made me wonder if I wasn't grasping something that everyone else understood. Why wouldn't they want to come along?

"You got the schedule down?" Grandma asked me over breakfast. We ate oatmeal with dehydrated blueberries and craisins. She frowned at the cupfuls of sugar I added, but didn't say anything. She had woken me up two hours earlier than normal. The sugar was a necessity.

"Our schedule? Yeah, pretty much got it." It wasn't a strict schedule. We had three days of space-flight as we approached LePhan. Plus, I counted on Grandma to just tell me what she needed.

"There's uhm, something we've got to add to the schedule," she said hesitantly. "Probably during the early morning rotation, couple hours a day." She looked me up and down, as if making some final consideration.

"What is it?"

She took a breath and then said, "Follow me."

We ended up in the cargo-hold. Most mountain cats slumbered in their cages, others circled restlessly.

"Poor things," she muttered, "They're not made to be cooped up."

Weird, Grandma sounded as though we had nothing to do with it. The cargo-hold was even colder than our quarters.

I followed her to the back row of cages. She brought up her sIdekIck, checked the barcode and recorded the number. The mountain screamer had sensed us twenty feet away, and now eyed us suspiciously.

"Would you mind grabbing a meat-brick?" Grandma asked and pointed to the dispenser.

I hit the switch and a block of ground beef the size of my hand dropped down. A film of icy-mucus covered the cold meat. After handing it to Grandma I simply stood back and watched.

The meat-brick remained at her side while she punched in a command into her sIdekIck. The mountain screamer's head snapped toward its haunches and then it scratched its side furiously.

"Normally, mountain cats are put under a minor sedative when the tracker-tag is removed. However, doing that would notify the mainframe that the tracker-tag needs to be refilled after the sedative is dispersed."

I just watched silently. Unlike the old tracker-tag, newer tracker-tags could be programmed to self-eject.

The cat's scratching flung the tracker-tag to the center of the cage.

"Dang, I was hoping it would land closer to the side." She broke the meat-brick in half and handed me a chunk. "Would you mind taking this to the other side of the cage?" she asked innocently.

The mountain screamer followed me as I walked to the opposite side of the ten-by-ten cage. Grandma keyed in the pass-code, opened the cage, and ran inside to retrieve the tracker tag. The mountain screamer heard the door open and turned, so I quickly stuck my arm in and shook the meat-brick, clicking my tongue loudly. It worked, the mountain screamer was too tempted by the extra breakfast to notice Grandma.

Grandma exited and the door shut. The mountain screamer licked its lips, barely noticing.

She placed the tracker-tag in her pocket and waved me over to follow as she approached the next cage.

"Well, one down, over two hundred more to go." She handed me the remaining meat-brick. "Without getting caught."

"Cameras," I said, pointing to the beams overhead.

She pointed to a box high in the corner of the ceiling. She brought up a new window on her sIdekIck and showed me a diagram. "Those wires run to the video-feed. I've set up a recorder for the nighttime hours. It records in two hour intervals. I can switch it here. Then when we leave, it goes back to a live feed."

"A loop," I confirmed.

"I helped install the monitoring system. Besides, this isn't a high security risk project. Not-for-profits are like that, no need for oscillating feeds or tripwires. Plus, it's not like someone's going to try and steal a mountain cat in superluminal space."

I held up the remaining meat-brick. "So you want me to distract them?"

"That and keep your eyes and ears up. Let me know if you hear someone come in. You never know who might be suffering from insomnia and come visit the cats."

"Okay."

"Don't worry, William, I won't let you get in trouble. If we get caught, I'll tell them I told you it was part of the procedure."

"I wasn't worried," I said. "But why exactly are you removing the tracker-tags?"

"A promise to Professor Munoz. One of the conditions set up long ago was that all the animals had to have tracker-tags installed once on LePhan. The debate went back-and-forth, but finally the department had to give in. You see, Munoz wanted the animals to finally be free. You can't have that if some poacher can hack into the system and tranq you. Eventually, the suits argued that people have Life-Chips and are free—animals are just as free with tracker-tags."

"Poachers on LePhan?"

"Bad guys know no bounds. Setting up LePhan is only the first step in a long journey. Next, is making sure the preservation stays safe."

I surveyed the cages stacked across the cargo-hold, finding it difficult to think of this stage as the *beginning*. For years, all we had heard about was Grandma's preparations for the LePhan Planetary Wildlife Preserve. The implementation of the final wildlife specimen didn't feel like a "first step."

Grandma insisted that we eat our lunch an hour after everyone else. I thought it was because she hated crowds, but the cafeteria was large and hardly crowded, even at lunch hour.

It didn't make sense, so I decided to ask her why.

"Your grandpa used to say it was because I thought a lot about myself. Like I thought I was Mrs. Popularity or something, but he learned soon enough I was right," she said as we set our trays down. She had grabbed one pork tortilla and two bulbs of milk. I grabbed two pork tortillas and one bulb of milk. I also threw on two pieces of cheesecake.

"Growing boys," she smirked.

I ate quietly for a moment. She didn't talk about Grandpa often. I was four when he died, never knew him.

"What do you mean?" I eventually asked.

"My 'unorthodoxly lengthened' tenure at the university had me between many departments." She wasn't going to talk about him. Not this time. She continued: "I didn't mind covering so much ground, it just meant I had to keep track of more people. It seemed every semester I was meeting someone new. As the years piled up, I soon learned I was somehow associated with everyone in some way or another. I'm not antisocial or anything, but more times than not, I ended up with a cold plate of food because I'm caught up visiting."

I realized it was true. Everywhere we went, someone was always nodding a "hello." Usually, it was a simple wave, but other times they'd call her over. Some were complete strangers, and would introduce themselves as a son or daughter of a former student or colleague.

"I dunno," she shrugged. "Guess I just got one of those affable faces."

But I could tell it was more than that. Whether a quick nod or a flick of a salute, Grandma at least said "hi" to most people in some form. Every once in a while, she'd stop and chat, genuinely curious how they were doing.

Grandma ended up leaving half her meal that day. She tried drinking more water, but it wasn't enough. We hurried back to our quarters. She rushed to the bathroom and hunched over the sink. I pretended not to hear as I sat on the edge of my cot, my fingers flicking the springs.

"Sorry 'bout that," she said as she came out.

I shrugged. What was I supposed to say? "That's okay." Or "I don't mind." Both sounded stupid.

She dropped and sat on the floor across from me. "It's not going to stop."

Again, I just remained silent.

She waved it away and changed the subject. "I don't know if you realized, but I have access to the tranq in your Life-Chip."

"Really?"

"Yep, one of the criteria for you to come along."

"I guess that makes sense," I muttered. I knew access to a minor's tranq was always kept with the parents or legal guardian. A chill ran over the back of my neck.

She glanced at the bloodied paper-towels. "Fear and weakness play havoc on any person's mind." Grandma looked ashamed as she explained, "My original plan was to tranq you as we landed on LePhan and say you came down with something. But I've decided not to."

"Tranq me?"

"No, not now." She shook her head. "I can't believe I didn't think to tell you from the get go."

"Tell me what?" I asked.

And for the next hour she laid it all out.

The next day, two days out from landing and making the drop-off on LePhan, Grandma became more reflective. We were in the back cargo-bay that served as the bird sanctuary. Not really much of a sanctuary though; the birds were individually caged and kept quiet by heavy tarps that covered them.

We removed one of the tarps to watch one of the hunter hawks. It didn't cry out; just jumped from each side of the tall cage. Grandma explained that this wasn't a hunter hawk, but a peregrine falcon. The fastest bird on Earth, it can reach speeds of 200 mph when diving. The bird's black cap trailed down the side of its head like sideburns. Its chest reminded me of chocolate-chip ice cream.

After listing random facts about the bird, Grandma's tone changed.

"Why don't you think anyone else came along?" she asked. "You know, your brother, sister, or cousins." There was disappointment in her voice.

"The heat?" I shrugged. "And many people don't go camping the way you do, in the dirt and all."

"Suppose so." Her tone distant.

"Summer Hiatus," I tried again.

"How's that?"

"Well, Jerm's got credits to make up because of last quarter. I think Veronica has band reviews."

"Why'd you come?"

Looking around the large cargo-bay, picturing the transport moving through superluminal space, the answer was easy. "I wanted to ride another transport. Especially a   freighter."

She perked up. "How many have you been on?"

"None like this. Not this cold." I laughed. "Normal passenger crafts . . . three of those. Once when I was four, because Dad wanted to see properties at Mussa. I don't remember that one too much. Then when I was ten on a fieldtrip. We jumped to Saturn, drew pictures, took vids, and returned."

"I remember the fundraiser your school had for that. Some type of reading contract thingy." She gazed at the ceiling, searching for details. "You hated reading. Your mother called to say you were entering some reading marathon thing. She said you'd have to do reports every week, take tests, and that they'd keep a chart of everyone's scores."

She went to the dispenser and returned with a small chunk of meat.

"I barely read at grade level back then, and the upper-grade books were worth way more points. I didn't think I stood a chance."

"I knew you would," she grinned, handing me half the chunk. "Once I heard the prize was a space-jump. No matter how many books it would take, I knew you'd do it."

"Other kids didn't care so much. Their families go all the time." I tossed the meat in the cage. The bird snagged it before it hit the ground. It'd been eyeing the morsel the whole time. "Guess I lucked out that way."

"Eh, don't downplay it. You earned it."

She was right, of course. The school quizzed me orally on two of the tests at the end of the contest, doubting that such a low reader could have scored so high.

"Do you think your cousins were scared to be on a ship with mountain screamers?"

"Uncle Keith's kids probably. 'Cause they're little."

"I should've been clearer about how safe it is."

"Well . . ." I trailed off.

"What?"

"I don't think anyone knew you'd care."

She waited for more of an explanation.

"I guess it seems like going to work with you," I tried. "When Mom first told me, I didn't quite get what she meant. She said something like, 'Grandma left a message seeing if any of you want to go with her on a transport.' For me, the mountain screamers made it more fun. But maybe it's not that way for everyone. Maybe everyone else felt like that. Or maybe they thought they'd be in the way."

She got up, "Well, you're here now, and you're not in the way."

Grandma woke me around three in the morning the day the transport was scheduled to land.

"Need your help with a little something." She sat at the edge of my bed holding a bio-strip.

"Your Life-Chip?" I asked, rubbing my eyes as I yawned

"Yep, it's time." She lifted the bottom of her shirt and wrapped the bio-strip around her stomach. She hesitated. "A friend said this is going to hurt like the dickens, shouldn't make a mess, but have a couple med-patches ready anyway."

I grabbed two from the first aid drawer and pulled the tags off the ends of one.

Grandma leaned back and pressed a command on her sIdekIck. Removing your Life-Chip was a felony. An internal alarm is set to notify the nearest authorities.

Fortunately for Grandma, the nearest receiving station was twenty-two light years away. The irregularity wouldn't register for quite some time.

"Sorta stings," she winced. "But not too bad."

She was lying. Her cheeks glowed red and a sheen of sweat started on her forehead. Gray strands of hair stuck to her neck. Soon she was doubled over, clutching the covers on my cot.

"It's out," she mumbled, unstrapping the bio-strip.

"Here." I handed her the med-patch and turned away.

"Ah, the stasis-gel is kickin' in." She exhaled heavily. I set the second med-patch down and covered her Life-Chip in a paper-towel. It was twice the size of a tracker-tag. A wave of nausea passed over me as I thought about the pain it must've caused.

"No worse than my coughing fits," she sighed. Her clammy hand patted mine. It felt as cold as the room.

After a few tense moments, she rose, grabbed her covered Life-Chip from my hand, and went to the bathroom. She hunched over the sink, washing her shaky hands and splashing her whitened face.

"Gotta go feed the cats," she called from the bathroom.

"Don't they have automatic feeders?"

"We've got to feed them *back* their trackers." She reached into a plastic bag and pulled out a tracker-tag. "The overseers haven't been running checks since the mountain cats have been caged up. Once they set them free, they'll run a quick-check to make sure their locations can be clocked."

"How are we going to feed over two hundred mountain screamers?" I asked. "Will there be enough time?"

"If we don't dilly-dally." She gingerly stepped out of the bathroom.

It was early, and I wasn't getting it. The confusion was clear on my face.

She explained, "The tracker-tags'll be in their stomach or intestinal track when they run the check. The transport'll be halfway back by the time the mountain cats crap 'em out."

261

"Grandma!" Sometimes her word choice surprised even me.

She shrugged, "What? That's what'll happen." She coughed a weak laugh.

A giggle bounced up from my throat.

She winked and left for the shelves, "I'll grab us some grub, you get dressed." She stopped and stared straight ahead. "I'm lucky you're here, honey."

After our quick breakfast—us and the mountain cats—we returned to our quarters to await the official start of the day. Today was the day I had prepared for the most. Each team would drive a Drifter to a predetermined location and drop off ten mountain cats via a hitched flatbed. Cages would be opened at least two miles apart from each other. The mountain cats would be anxious, so remote openers would be used on each cage. Tranqs were discouraged since it would leave the mountain cat groggy in its new terrain and that could mean the difference between life and death.

Our team consisted of Grandma, me, and some assistant named Cedric. We were the only team with three people. Two adults were needed in case the remote opener on the cage locked up: one to open the cage, the other to leash the mountain cat.

"Will the tranqs work in the stomach?" I asked. "In case someone freaks and some team would rather put one down for a nap."

"Yep."

"So everything's set?"

Grandma just nodded. Something still nagged at me, but I didn't want to worry her.

We met Cedric at the Drifter. He pressed his skinny arm into the plush tire of the Drifter. The material swallowed his forearm. He grinned and pulled it free.

"Try it," he said, waving me over.

I did.

"You must be Billy Thain, Etta Thain's grandson." His smile was as warm as the air that rushed in from LePhan.

"Yep." I pegged him for one of those cool college professors. Young; so he was probably a genius.

Enthusiastic; so he hadn't been burned by the system. He bounded around with the unbridled enthusiasm of a puppy.

The landing ramp dropped down. We were third in line to depart.

"You all set, Cedric?" Grandma asked.

He ran his hands over his gear quickly and checked the specs on his sIdekIck. "Yes, ma'am," he said, nodding emphatically. "And I just want to say how awesome it is to be part of your team." We climbed into the bench-seat of the Drifter. I sat in the middle.

I glanced at Grandma and back at Cedric who was now leaning on the dash and gazing out the windshield toward the LePhan wild-lands. He just kept nodding. *Poor Cedric*, I thought, *he has no idea.*

If Cedric's constant yammering bothered Grandma, she didn't show it. She just shrugged when necessary, shook her head when necessary, nodded along when necessary.

We dropped off the first of our mountain cats without a hitch. The back cage opened and the animal took its first steps upon new land. We watched the view-screen safely from the cab of the Drifter. LePhan's atmosphere had a red tint to it. The sun glowed orange as if setting even though it was overhead.

Grandma put the Drifter into drive, and we left the mountain cat to its new world. Cedric told us about entering his name in the lottery to ride with *the* Etta Thain, but how he didn't think he'd actually be chosen.

"This whole trip's been better than I ever imagined," he said.

That made Grandma smile.

Cedric kept his enthralling one-man conversation going as we dropped off the second, third, fourth, and fifth cat. I was so distracted by Grandma's ulterior plan that I forgot how amazing this venture truly was. As if to emphasize the exciting tone, a herd of antelope crossed our path and took our breath away.

263

"Pronghorns," Grandma said, carefully driving into the herd.

"You're not going around?" Cedric asked nervously.

"Can't," Grandma nodded toward the tail-end of the herd, "this bunch'll take nearly half the day to finish."

"Amazing," I commented.

"Yep, LePhan's the perfect breeding ground for Earth's unrestricted invasive species."

Grandma had mentioned how all the plant-life and herbivores were basically like the rabbits introduced to Australia over three hundred years ago. Fortunately, LePhan didn't have any indigenous species to overrun besides the native plant-life. Any Earth creature able to adapt would have free reign to "feed 'n' breed" unhindered by hunting. Well, until the mountain screamers and other predators were dispersed.

The herd picked up the pace as the mountain cats hissed and spit from their cages. Being far past the first generation, these pronghorns were encountering predators for the first time. Ironically, the threat of getting caught in the Drifter's driveshaft didn't worry the pronghorns as much as the passengers on the flatbed.

"Will they stampede?" Cedric asked.

"Possible, but not likely," Grandma answered. She didn't look worried. "They haven't been attacked so their instincts keep 'em from breaking out into a run. Cluster travelers like these pronghorns allow larger animals through as long as they don't attack."

We kept the windows up to keep the dust out. I could still smell the sharp tang of their hide. It reminded me of horses, although I hadn't been around many.

Finally, we were through. Cedric and I turned to watch the giant herd of pronghorns. The mountain cats examined the creatures thoroughly. It came as no surprise that the sixth, seventh, and eighth cat each darted off in the direction of the pronghorns once released. Even several miles apart, they knew where to go.

The ninth cat, our second-to-last, had a little trouble upon release. Not the cat, necessarily, but the cage.

"Cage is jammed," Grandma said, stepping out and grabbing the pole-leash from the rack. "Should be alright, Cedric, just pull the door open after I snag the poor missus. Be ready to zap her if she charges."

Cedric took a couple deep breaths and joined Grandma at the flatbed. "Okay, ma'am, got it." He brushed his hands across his thighs as he walked.

"You stay in the cab, William," Grandma shouted. "Holler if anything approaches." Basically, she wanted me to make sure Cedric was properly distracted.

I did as told: waited until Cedric's full attention was diverted, and got to work. I pulled up the loose cloth covering the cushion on his side of the seat. After grabbing a tranq-cartridge from the box, I set it in his seat, needle sticking straight up. Grandma had cut open a crevice in the cushion to hold the cartridge snugly.

I was facing forward when they returned.

"You did great, Cedric," Grandma said rather cheerfully as she entered the Drifter.

"Thanks, I have to admit I was a little—YOWEE!" Cedric bolted from his seat, clutching his rear. He nearly fell out face first; he was bouncing so frantically. Grandma darted out and rushed around the front to gather Cedric.

"Watch that screamer!" she called to me. I grabbed the tranq-rifle, made sure my pulse-shot was charged, and dropped from the Drifter. The commotion only encouraged the mountain screamer to run away quicker.

Cedric's speech was already slurring as Grandma caught up with him and put an arm under his shoulder. I hurried back to the Drifter to fish the cartridge out from under the seat and set it in clear view.

Grandma waved me over to help hoist Cedric into the cab.

"Looks like you snagged yourself on a tranq," Grandma said reassuringly as she pointed at the tranq-cartridge. I grabbed it and held it up for emphasis.

"I," he sighed heavily. "Didn't see . . . sat on it?"

"Yep," Grandma and I said in sync.

"Oh, I, but the messta gone to-ah," Cedric explained . . . er, tried explaining.

We laid him flat on the rear-bench in the extended cab.

Grandma set a folded blanket under his head. "Poor guy. Guess winnin' that lottery didn't work out as he dreamed." She readied the adrenaline shot as she checked his pulse. She'd bring him back to the land of the living if the tranq had left him with too weak a pulse. "He's fine," she confirmed. "Might have a bit of a headache when he wakes."

I didn't feel too bad for Cedric. He's lucky Grandma didn't go with my suggestion from earlier that morning: a pulse-shot. Less room for error, and guaranteed to knock him out.

I glanced back at the last mountain cat. We were close to the end. My heart pounded: part excitement, part worry.

Grandma started up the Drifter and drove us the required mileage.

"Pretty impressive," I commented.

"What's that?"

"How you made it happen."

"Lotta people made it happen."

"Not LePhan, this last bit," I clarified. "I mean, how you set it up yourself. I think Cedric would've gone along with it. He was like a fan of yours or something."

"Couldn't do that to him. Or anyone else. Getting them involved would've also made them accountable." She looked down to the bandage wrap at her stomach. "Felonies are not something you want to drag people into."

"You told *me* about it."

She drove on quietly for a moment, pulled over, and then said, "William, there's something I've always noticed about you. You're gonna be alright." She pulled my hat off, ruffled my hair, and shoved it back on. "Plus you're a minor . . . a minor who aided his crazy ole Grammy. Any court would be very sympathetic."

"Yeah," I said, deciding not to press the issue. She had included me for reasons I'd never get to know.

"Well, let's get this last feller out." She pulled up her sIdekIck and tapped in the command.

The mountain cat took a tentative step out of the cage. The rear mounted camera gave a close-up, but I turned around to watch out the back window. It jumped off the flatbed and took a few cautious steps. This one was different from the others, not quite eager to run off into the distance.

Once the large cat was clear from the cage, Grandma turned the Drifter around so we could watch it straight on. She gave the horn a honk to coax the cat into the wild unknown.

The mountain screamer sat rigid and cocked its head, ears twitching. Finally, it darted off for the nearest tree. Grandma drove the Drifter slowly in reverse. Once we were a safe distance, she threw the Drifter in park. Cedric's snores were the only sound as the Drifter idled.

"William." Grandma stepped out of the driver's seat. "Let's get going on with it."

I joined Grandma just outside the Drifter.

"Did you recognize him?" she asked as she gathered her gear.

"Who?"

"That old fart out there." She nodded to where the mountain screamer had disappeared. "That's the sixteen-year-old."

"Really? How could you tell?"

"There was a nick in his left ear. Also a patch of fur that grew differently near his right haunch, a scar."

"How'd you get him on the transport?"

"Remember when I told you about poachers being able to hack into the system and get information?"

"Yeah."

"I'm the one who ran code for the initial database. Know a few keystrokes myself. Let's just say the old fart got a break."

I didn't know if Grandma meant herself or the cat.

For several moments we stood there and breathed in the dry air. LePhan's average humidity was lower than most places back on Earth. However, the air felt crisp due to the higher oxygen content. Fifty percent versus twenty percent makes a big difference. It was said that fires burned twice as hot and twice as quickly on LePhan.

"That's the last of 'em," Grandma's sigh broke the silence.

"Pretty neat." I forced myself to concentrate on random LePhan facts. I refused to think about the end creeping in.

"Yep, pretty neat."

We stared out into the distance. Neither one of us ready to say goodbye.

I scrutinized the eucalyptus nearest us. Strips of bark flaked down the large trunk. Planted nearly half a century ago, the leaves grew broader on their new home. I refused to look at Grandma. Instead, I continued my thorough examination of that eucalyptus.

Eventually, she turned toward me. Pulling me into a fierce hug, she said, "You know what to do."

I nodded, my face resting on her flannel shirt. A button pressed roughly into my cheek, but I didn't complain.

She broke the hug and handed me her Life-Chip.

"I hate to say it William, but you better get. Can't dilly-dally out here too long. They've got that schedule to keep."

Again, I just nodded silently.

"I'm glad it was you. I shouldn't say something like that, but . . . I'm glad it was you that came along."

"Grandma," I mumbled.

"Nope, no more," she turned me and walked me to the Drifter. "You head out." She lifted my hat, kissed my head, and gently put my hat back. No ruffling my hair this time.

She was already moving at a quick stride when I turned around. Her back facing me, pack swung over her shoulder.

I wanted to run to her, convince her to stay. She had warned me earlier that she was "set" on living her last days out here. I would've camped with her if she had asked.

But she didn't.

Cedric didn't say much after he awoke on the way back to the transport. Just the quiet hum of the Drifter for half an hour. He was embarrassed. I told him Grandma had left to help another team and I was asked to drive back.

He asked if *he* could drive the Drifter up the ramp to the transport. It wouldn't look good having some kid driving while he sat in the passenger's seat. I agreed.

The phrasing repeated in my head as I rode up the boarding-ramp; "*My grandma's probably already back. We're a little late because I didn't know the route and had to keep checking my sIdekIck.*" No further explanation. Besides, no one would ask. That was the plan.

"Can't believe I sat on a tranq," Cedric sighed.

I nodded.

He stopped me just as I was about to step out. "Um," he smiled solemnly, "don't go telling anyone, eh?"

"Nah, Grandma said it could've happened to anyone." Which was technically true: anyone who was unlucky enough to ride with us. We both let out a deep breath, but for different reasons. I made a beeline for the exit of the loading area.

Soon, I was in the passageway marching straight for the cabin. The cold air of the transport made my hands shake involuntarily. My shin banged on a bulkhead lip, nearly tripping me.

Stop! Calm down, I admonished myself. No one had noticed.

I waited nervously for the intercom to ask where Grandma was. Maybe Quintos or some random worker would notice us separated. But no one said a thing. Before I knew it, I was sitting in our—my quarters, rolling her Life-Chip in my fingers as pre-flight started.

LePhan would begin shrinking outside our porthole window, but I didn't look. Instead, I packed her Life-Chip away.

The intercom chimed, breaking my reverie.

"Henrietta Thain to the main control room." It was Quintos.

My heart jumped. I calmed myself, rehearsed the script, and left.

"Believe the lie," Grandma had said. I checked my sIdekIck as I strode down the corridor. We were ten minutes out from the slingshot. *The point of no return.* Hit that and it'd be months before another transport was sent to LePhan. Even then, it'd be unlikely they could find Grandma without her Life-Chip. I blew warm air into my hands.

"Henrietta Thain, report to the main control room immediately," Quintos sounded annoyed. He was using the all-call over the ship's intercom.

No more stalling.

I took a deep breath and stepped into the control room. Quintos hovered over the shoulder of a crewman. Five other crewmembers worked various stations.

"Dr. Quintos," I said, announcing myself.

He turned, frowned, and asked, "What're you doing up here?"

"My grandma's not feeling well. She sent me to see what you needed." I realized I hadn't changed my gear after coming in from LePhan.

He gazed at me and then turned to face the crew. "Captain, something's wrong, halt start-up," Quintos commanded.

Each person paused and looked at Quintos as if he'd just asked them to bake a cake.

"We can't just stop," one of them spoke up. "We have tugs on standby, a slingshot waiting for the order to start initial charge."

Quintos's cheeks glowed. If I didn't know better, I'd say he looked angry. "I understand your procedure, but let me remind you that I am director and I can alter the schedule, should I need to."

"What's wrong with our current schedule?" the crewman asked.

To answer his question, Quintos waved me over to a separate console and pointed. "I need your grandmother to explain this."

A readout labeled, "Henrietta Thain" took up most of the monitor screen. All body systems displayed a flat line.

He monitored our Life-Chip data? My stomach lurched. It was possible that he would use the Life-Chips to verify locations of staff members, but accessing personal data was an invasion of privacy. That was like accessing someone's bank account or medical records.

"You accessed my grandma's personal data?" I said it loud enough for the crew to hear.

"Ahem, yes," he sputtered, and then quickly regained his composure. "And I'm glad I did because this anomaly would've gone unnoticed."

I stared at Grandma's readout. This was not part of the plan. I didn't have anything to say. Her Life-Chip showed she was onboard, but didn't register any life signs.

Quintos stood rigid and crossed his arms, examining me. The crewmember who had spoken up joined us at the console. He verified what Quintos was claiming.

"Can you explain this?" he asked. He was obviously their leader. The rest of the crew waited, curiosity written all over their faces. Like an idiot, I just stared at him. My chest went shallow. I felt cornered.

"It was no secret she was sick," Quintos said more to himself than anyone else. For several seconds he stared past me.

I coughed, trying to say something . . . anything.

"What's going on? What has she done?" Quintos loomed over me. The lead crewman just looked at me with a mix of disquiet and expectancy.

"I don't know what you mean. My grandma's resting in our quarters."

He shook his head and pointed to the readout. "I barely caught this recently. I was doing a final check before debarking," he sounded as though he were justifying it to the crew. "According to the readout, the Life-Chip's been reading empty for several hours."

I shrugged.

"It's unlikely you would've gone all that time and not reported anything." Quintos slapped his hand on the console. "If she's got others involved . . . I *will* figure out what's going on!"

Don't let him bully you, I heard Grandma whisper, *he thinks you'll run away bawling like a baby.* I stared right back at Quintos and didn't say anything.

"Who else is involved?" he asked, glaring down at me.

"Involved?" I asked. "Involved in what?" I took a harder look at Quintos. He wasn't angry, but worried. It made me wonder why he cared so much about Grandma's Life-Chip. Why he cared about her whereabouts.

He leaned in and whispered, "Is she down there?"

How's he know that? I gaped up at him.

Quintos stepped away, nodding to himself.

"Are we back on schedule?" the lead crewman asked. He was a smaller fella, but he put some authority behind his question.

Quintos put up a hand. He must've figured it out shortly after discovering Grandma's Life-Chip readout.

But why did Quintos care?

Grandma had warned me that the higher-ups would grill me once we reached home and saw she wasn't onboard—they'd be worried about liability and such. She prepped me on what to do if anyone went looking for her before we debarked or during the trip, but she didn't give me a story that would prevent Quintos from storming into our quarters because he had hacked her Life-Chip.

Quintos turned and examined LePhan on the nearest view-screen.

Why's he gotta get me off the planet? Grandma's voice asked in my mind. *He doesn't like animals, hates his job.*

Not as profitable as he had hoped.

"Poachers," I blurted. The word shot out of my mouth as it hit my brain. "It has to do with poachers."

Quintos snapped around, his eyes wide.

"What're you talking about son?" the lead crewman asked.

I don't know why the word popped in my head like that, but the shock on Quintos's face gave it away.

His pencil-neck went red. The blush crept to his ears. I recognized the sudden change in demeanor; the same agitation a mountain screamer shows when it senses a presence nearby. I had struck something in Quintos with that one word: "Poachers."

"Poachers here?" the pilot turned in her seat to ask. "On LePhan?"

"That's impossible," a different crewman added, scrolling through his display-screen. "No ships have passed through the Fornax Slingshot besides us. Not in the last three months anyway."

Time to hunt.

"No," I said, "not yet. They need someone to feed them coordinates. Send them schedules, safe times to hit LePhan."

Quintos stammered, "This is ridiculous. We have a passenger M.I.A., and you're conjecture—ahem, hypothesizing about poachers."

"You're saying Henrietta Thain's a poacher," someone asked playfully. A chorus of soft chuckles drifted across the bridge. Even here, Grandma's reputation was solid.

"Hold on." The lead crewman barked, silencing everyone. "What's the deal here? Why are we postponing our superluminal jump?"

I sucked in a deep breath, held it, and then took my shot: "Dr. Quintos hacked not just the Life-Chip intel, but other key systems as well, to coordinate with poachers."

"Ridiculous," Quintos said dismissively, but his body language said otherwise. His pale lips squeezed tight.

I may have missed the bull's-eye, but something connected.

"Not so ridiculous," the pilot commented. "You *did* hack a civilian's Life-Chip. The one we know about."

"I didn't hack it. I have authority to—"

"No you don't," I said.

Quintos surveyed the crewmen for support. He scoffed, "You know what, go ahead and proceed with start-up. I've got work to do." He marched out of the control room, throwing his arms up demonstratively.

The lead crewman stepped in front of Quintos and grabbed his arm. "Head to your quarters," he said. "And stay there."

"What?" he asked.

"You're confined to quarters pending an investigation."

"You can't," Quintos muttered, "you don't have the clearance. You don't have a bit of evidence."

"As chief helmsman on this route, maritime law grants me the authority to confine any passenger to quarters should I see fit." The lead crewman didn't release his iron grip on Quintos's arm.

"There's no evidence," Quintos said, his voice rising. "It's a boy saying whatever he can to mislead you, all of you."

"Maybe, but there's not a complete lack of evidence. There's enough to warrant an investigation." The chief helmsman let go and turned back to the main console. He swiped away Grandma's readout. "I'll be monitoring your whereabouts on this vessel—I *do* have the authority to monitor my passenger's Life-Chip's. Don't make me waste time with an escort."

"It'll be your job," Quintos said as he left the bridge.

"Doubt it," the chief helmsman said absently. "Alright everyone, let's not waste any more time on dramatics. We got a place to be." He watched the door shut and then turned to face me. "So, she's really down there, huh? Old Etta Thain decided to stay dirt-side."

I didn't say anything. Instead, I took a breath and sent my brain into overdrive, readying my next yarn.

"Relax kid," he said, patting my shoulder. "I knew it was a bluff the whole time. Well, up until Qunitos started jarring all over the place. Guy's wound tight."

"He's an odd duck."

The chief helmsman was quiet for a moment. He shook his head, "Sure do wish I could've said goodbye. Tell her how her little speech about me and my caliber back during my cadet days pushed me through some uncertain times."

"You knew her," I said.

"Why the hell you think I asked for this gig?" He smiled warmly. "Now, get outta here."

My heart was still racing as I stood outside the control room. There was a soft jolt as the freight-transport debarked for the slingshot jump.

I headed back to my quarters.

An automated message announced that the jump was just minutes away, and passengers needed to secure themselves. Wall straps were available in the corridor, but I hurried to my quarters.

For a second, I expected to find Grandma sitting on her cot. I had to remind myself that she *really* was back on LePhan.

I would concentrate this time during the slingshot jump—try and focus like she had mentioned.

Maybe somewhere, in some other universe, another Grandma was able to come back and ride alongside another William.

Either way, it felt like she was there, right next to me, when the jump hit.

Doug C. Souza wrote "Mountain Screamers" because he wanted to see how cougars might fare in the future. He imagined they'd be marveled by society while battling extinction. He was pleasantly surprised when the characters took over the story. His grandparents—one set a pair of teachers, the other dairy owners—edged their way in, and he is grateful for this.

Recently, Doug C. Souza won first place in the 2nd Quarter 2016 Writers of the Future Contest. He will find out in April of 2017 if he wins the grand prize. His story, "The Biting Sands" will be featured in The Young Explorer's Adventure Guide. *He also has a story, "Tenth Life," coming out in the anthology* In a Cat's Eye. *You can read "Claim Jumpers" in* Visions V: Milky Way. *Doug C. Souza can be found at: dougcsouza.com.*

A courageous crew follows their colorfully outrageous captain on a mission of rebellion, danger, and discovery. This offbeat, irreverent parody will appeal to fans of a certain beloved science fiction television series.

SPACE OPERA

Amos Parker

"Now!" Captain Valiant shouted to his navigator, as he clung to the smoking console.

He coughed and tried to gather his thoughts. Through the smoke he saw her. Angelica Spacey. His ears rang from the violent explosion that threw him against the console. His heart rang in the same way, from memory. But he couldn't hear her screams. He only saw her fine lips move. Memories pushed into his shocked brain, battling with the deep space battle in the present.

"Just . . ." But his lungs coughed on smoke.

Incoming weapons fire smashed through the shields to the hull. Hard and fast. Valiant slammed again against the console. Unable to see it on the viewscreen, he pictured the long, angular form of the pursuing *Vindicator*, the Empire flagship. His mind, deprived of real sound, heard the Emperor cackle with ironical glee at the name he'd given it. How far away the core worlds seemed.

". . . Go!" Valiant shouted to Angelica, breath returning.

The rest of his *Nautilus crew* shouted orders, coughing. Smoke spread. And panic.

On *his* bridge. Fucking *his*!

Impotent, Valiant watched Weapons Officer Chance Ripcord howl and kick at his flaccid controls. With his booted foot he stomped with metallic bangs. He'd drawn his laser pistol. To fire on the *Vindicator*? His flashing red console lights gave him no alternative. Valiant pictured

Ripcord standing atop his *Nautilus*, without a suit, firing with a handgun.

"What?" Angelica shouted. She smashed a fist into her controls, dodging shrapnel.

Communications Officer Delta, flesh shining silver under its torn black uniform, held one transfigured hand jammed into its interface socket. Valiant saw, hoping the shattered onboard systems could still understand Delta. As Valiant watched, and waited, its lips moved in tune with its voice, an affectation designed to calm humans. Its disturbing, unmodified eyes glowed like bright emeralds.

Valiant winced, desperation fixing his eyes on Angelica.

The smoke thickened. Sirens blared. The *Nautilus* shook.

A defiant sector of his mind howled, *the Rebellion's doomed!*

But Valiant raged back, gasping for breath. He wanted to repeat his command, but he felt dizzy, thoughts congealed and cloudy.

He had to *stand up!*

"Sustained bombardment," the computer's neutral, robotic voice echoed. "Retaliate."

Angelica, long, obsidian hair drenched in sweat, wiped blood from her eyes. The deep gash in her forehead oozed blue. She stabbed at her console with long, elegant fingers, trying to obey her captain.

"Now! Go!"

But the alarm sirens, the flashing red lights and the smoke, threw her stabbing fingers off. And his beloved *Nautilus* had taken heavy damage. The spinning in her head made it even worse. How much, she asked herself, could she blame the malfunctioning artificial gravity? She'd *earned* this post! How weak was she? How... powerless?

Near Valiant, the vents kicked on. The smoke cleared.

He stood. Screaming. To protect his turf.

"God damn it, *now*, Angelica!" Valiant shouted, louder than before, eyes heavy and closed. "Go to fucking warp before those rail guns breech the *fucking drive!*"

That woke something in her. She focused.

But a blast shook the ship. The lights flickered. He heard a sharp clang and a dull thud through the din. Then the siren wail pierced his eardrums. He clutched his head, wincing and moaning, slumping again to his knees.

When he recovered, he saw her. His heart broke, like an atom in fission.

"No!"

Angelica had passed out, her azure blood pooling on the floor into bare, sparking wires, her body twitching. He forced his eyes to stay open, watching with terror as her open eyes lost their glimmer. He tried to run to her, but stumbled and fell, his mind exploding with colorful memories. Of Shiraz. Of leave time in The Jungle. Bare flesh. Love.

Clenching his jaw hard against the vomiting memories, he watched the tiny medical droids crawl toward her like spiders, inside her body to probe and work their bioengineering magic.

"*Shields at twenty-one percent,*" the ship computer's voice said in its strong, male, emergency monotone. "*Reactor containment failure imminent. Retaliate.*" The voice paused. Then it wove in the soothing Rebellion tonality. Female. Almost motherly. "*This mission cannot fail.*"

The deteriorating shields absorbed another vicious railgun shot, rocking hard from the stern. The emergency lights dimmed for a moment.

Time slowed. To Valiant, smoke seemed like morning mist.

Then the voice of the pursuing vessel's captain spoke, from out of nowhere, on the waves of the empire's advanced supertech.

"*Surrender now and return the plans,*" a disembodied, effeminate male voice said.

It sounded almost bored. Valiant, sleepy, wanted to punch its imaginary face.

"*I'm done with this chastising game, little ones,*" the voice continued. "*But I promise I'll put my belt back on, if . . .*" And then he yawned! "*. . . if you stop* making *me punish* *you like this. I can promise you it hurts me more than you, children."* He yawned *again. "Or maybe keep it up. We do, you know, have too many torpedoes. A plethora. A veritable million. A vermillion! Perhaps you can feed the muscle of our homeworld industry? Think of the jobs it costs to close factories. The military industrial complex! Empire families. Empire children. Empire . . . dogs and cats. All going hungry, and fighting after. . ."*

"Delta!" Valiant shouted, standing again. He gripped the wall's ripped plasteel with bloody hands. "Get me engineering! Now!"

Delta nodded. The flashing lights overhead danced down onto its bare skull. Hypnotic. Alien.

It keyed the button. A moment of static.

"I think I've almost got it, Cap," Chief Engineer Dolly Brickwell returned over the speakers, through the static haze. *"Five seconds to miracle."*

She sounded lost in thought. Unperturbed.

Valiant remembered how her best assets had saved them in the Gamma Quadrant. He remembered The Vacation Planet. And her flesh. He almost smiled as another rail gun blast rocked the ship, rocking the past away.

"Twelve percent," the computer boomed.

A third yawn from *Vindicator.*

Then the effeminate voice said *"Aw. Are you waiting for a Brickwell miracle, Valiant? Are woo jus waitwing for a boo boo fix from mummy, baby Valiant?"*

Reddening, Valiant forced himself to remember their just-completed mission.

He grinned, pointing to air, and retorted. "Are you waiting for your teeth to grow back, Captain Asshat?" Valiant snapped. "You know I'll just punch them right the fuck out again, in any bar, wearing any disguise. You craven, skinny tool bag."

"My plan still worked," the voice answered, still yawning and bored. *"Captains like us should have the courage to stand on the front lines and fight. You think we should leave it to the pawns? Pass off the true glory? Ha!"*

A cackle before continuing.

"I know, Valiant, that you have your rebel base coordinates in your computer. I almost feel bad telling you the data you stole in that staged brawl is phony. But it's the same way I feel badly about moving from planet to planet, stripping them each bare in the name of Civilization. You and I are king and queen! Sure I could have run away and let you fight a pawn. *And maybe you would have bought it! But if you want something done right . . ."*

Yawn!

"You said five seconds!" Valiant shouted to Brickwell, red rage flooding him, beads of sweat streaking his temples. "I need that patented miracle, Dollface! Now!"

"Oh, Valiant," the effeminate voice continued, oozing fake pity. *"Do I really have to tell your infantile mind that Brickwell's our double agent?"* Valiant heard a subordinate *Vindicator* officer say something unintelligible to Captain Asshat before Asshat continued. *"Prepare . . ."* Another yawn—the *gall!* *". . . to be boarded. Loser."*

Inside Valiant, in that secret pressure cooker place where he always kept his raucous noise of blustery confidence, silence fell. It dropped hard. A deadly, plugging landslide. He wiped blood from his face. Silence terrified him. Confidence and power never, ever, fell silent. Not even in dreams on a planetary scale.

"D-dolly?" he stammered.

"Seven percent," the computer said, before hybridizing a new voice. Half feminine now. *"Succeed, Captain."*

The lights came on. The bridge brightened. And deep in the bowels of the ship, the rising, familiar hum of the warp drive's quadlithium chamber started up and rumbled like a roaring wave.

The confident noise of the frat party inside Valiant returned, clearing out the intruding, stifling debris. Brickwell was his. Had to be! He'd checked, double checked, and triple checked her! And she'd let him!

"Triple agent," Brickwell said over the intercom, dry as a professor brushing off a stupid question.

Valiant forced himself to take a few oxygen-deprived steps. He made it halfway to Angelica, and right into the midst of the sea of Brickwell's everywhere honey voice. But then, weakening, he staggered back to his captain's chair and sat. He grinned and punched a big fist into his palm.

"Fucking right," he murmured. "Triple."

"*What?*" Asshat screamed. "*No! You traitorous* bitch! *You can't be—*"

And then Valiant felt his body thrown back into his high, padded seat. View screen stars stretched miraculously to star lines as the *Nautilus* went into warp, streaking like a laser toward life in the Dead Zone.

What felt like eons after, the *Nautilus* dropped out of warp. It did so, hours after the battle, into steady, smooth orbit over an uncharted blue water world three times the size of the Rebellion's massive forest home world of Ceti Alpha V. The crew? Even in emergency stasis, adrenaline fatigue still plagued each member.

Nautilus herself suffered in much the same way. Her energies spent, the bridge lights remained out. Overloaded. Drained. A kind of exhausted moan sounded from deep inside the ship's core. None of the crew stirred in their nooks.

Onboard systems had extinguished the flames in transit. Vents had pumped out the smoke, after pumping in the insta-hibernation gas necessary to protect the crew from warp's traumatic effects. As they had not had time to prepare, droids had stripped and moved their necessarily naked bodies to harbor beds extruded from the walls. Outside those walls, swarms of zygotic nanobots had toiled to repair the ship prior to the pump-in of the hibernation insta-antidote gas. The master computer delayed this moment until the *Nautilus* could function at an effective, life-sustaining level. The future benefits of the mysterious Caribbean-colored water world could only help.

At least, the computer thought so. Its definition of "safety" blended with its definition of "holiday." And perhaps more.

This repair period, the master computer knew, would require three galactic standard days. But it also knew it might have to terminate the repair period early, should its long range scans pick up the *Vindicator* or any other vanguard Empire craft scouting for joyful "debris."

But then what?

Little. Had their escape been tracked by unknown tech, the vast *Nautilus* mainframe could do nothing but throw up the cloaking device—borderline useless against the Empire's insidious tech.

And yet, miraculously, they had not been tracked. And so repairs continued.

Half a standard day into the Nautilus' repair, a shattered moon orbited into view, as if rising up out of a small, scorpion-shaped continent. The moon, tinted green, carried the debris of its ancient near destruction, within the prison of its own orbit, like moons to a moon. Half a day deeper, a massive gaseous red moon emerged, a yellow storm staring out of its equator like a studious eye.

At the repair period's terminus, the mainframe finished mending the *Nautilus*. Then it pumped the antidote through the vents and into the lungs of the crew.

Valiant awoke first. "Angelica!" he cried, bolting upright and banging his head on the plasteel shielding.

"Ow!"

He'd dreamt about her. His drugged dreams had been crystal clear. He half expected to see Angelica lying in the grass across from him, sunlight making her body glow. But he only saw the cold metals of his bridge.

He writhed. But he remembered Angelica unconscious on the bridge floor. "Angelica?" Her blood made him see red. At Fate?

He remembered her falling. Had the medical droids saved her?

"God damn it, let me *out*!" he cried, twisting and half rising, beating his fists on the shielding that kept him safe and soundless.

"She is fine," he heard the ship's computer say, gentle and feminine. *"Relax, Captain."*

He relaxed. Drugs from an IV tube helped. But still his heart beat hard against his ribs. He focused on that, and slowed its heavy beating. Drugs couldn't do everything.

"I still want you to let me out," he said to the computer. "Please and thank you."

The shielding hissed away, sliding into hidden curvatures, IV tubes retracting. The bright lights of the bridge made him squint and cover his eyes. He grunted, wincing and fighting the urge to turn away toward the wall.

"You are safe, Captain," said the computer. "You all are. Come out and live. Rebel."

Valiant crawled out, naked, his bare feet hitting the cold floor, he first caught sight of the main display revealing the blue planet below. Donning clothing laid out by the bots, he nodded, drinking in the bridge like fresh water.

"Where are we?" he asked the computer, lifting his eyes to its glittering, orange eye staring down at him from the ceiling.

"*An uncharted system, far beyond the frontier, Captain.*"

"Status report." He rubbed hard at his numbed, post-hibernation flesh.

"Prepared for full return, Captain," the computer cooed.

The other bed shieldings began retracting. Chance emerged, and promptly pretended he didn't feel groggy. Then Angelica rolled out, safe and healthy. Beautiful. Valiant sighed.

Lastly, from a vertical door in the far wall, never having required sleep but having submitted for propriety's sake, Delta emerged and turned its emerald eyes to the waking crew.

Chance cleared his throat, lurching up toward a mounting nearby. He rubbed his eyes, before scanning the bridge. "Dolly?" he asked. "Where's Dolly?"

Without emotion, Delta sat down at its console, resuming its post. "At work in engineering," it replied. "Awoken two point one days ago. There is a stubborn crack in quadlithium containment requiring human creativity. She wished me to pass on a message." It paused, inclining its head, as it did when it did not understand a deeply human concept, and then continued. "She wished you all to know that she is not a quadruple agent."

The Captain chuckled. With a flourish he strode to and sat once more in his deep captain's chair.

"Food," he said, with a twirled hand.

"Replication capacity damaged, Captain," the computer replied. *"Selective damage—Heisenberg's Uncertainty Principal perhaps."*

"Well, at least natural selection left us caffeine," Angelica said with a sigh, pouring her own coffee.

"Solution?" Valiant asked the computer, face upturned. "It's not an Empire encryption virus is it?"

"No. Pure battle damage. Unlucky chance."

"Then how can we get a meal?" Valiant asked.

"There is live game on the continent below, Captain."

Everyone turned at that, eyebrows raised.

"Hunting?" Valiant inquired.

They all felt the computer, somehow, nod in the ether.

"I have the shuttle craft prepped and ready for departure," it said. *"On your orders, of course."*

Valiant's stomach growled. Hunting. Killing. Blood. Meat. Food. The distraction prevented him from inquiring about hostile, indigenous tribes.

Chance's stomach growled too.

"Marksman, first class," Chance said, aiming his pistol at the orange eye. "University."

Angelica rolled her eyes at the competitive, digestive, verbal sparring. Her jaw clenched. She felt her own competitiveness rise like bile. Memories of testosterone and hard muscle. Sweat and moans. She felt certain that Brickwell would have felt the same, had she not been stuck deep down in the hot world of engineering.

"Orders given, you silicone sycophant," Valiant said, with a wave of his mighty, rescuing hunter's hand.

The shuttle separated and distanced itself from the *Nautilus*, blasting white jets against the black of space.

Ahead, to the right of the blue planet, the fractured, green moon carried its broken debris closer. The fragments looked to Valiant like a god's severed hands knotted to invisible string. He imagined the string cut. Meteors in hibernation.

Shuttle controls in his hands, he took deep, cleansing breaths. Separation from his beloved *Nautilus* always jarred him. His bride. In a way. But predictable. Dependent and controllable. Infinitely beloved.

As he guided the bucking shuttle, using its long, retro, twin-stick controls down into the atmosphere and toward the scorpion continent, that old, awful sensation assaulted him. Like green meteors of envy.

How could he have left an ensign in charge. An ensign!

"Captain?" Delta asked.

The synthetic voice jarred Valiant back to reality. He looked at the thing.

It sat to his right in a leather seat, ahead of Navigator Spacey. Spacey, arms crossed, frowned at being denied by her Captain the right to navigate.

"Yeah, Delta," Valiant replied, aware of the thing's clean, logical lack of passion.

"You spoke before," it continued, "about progress in . . ." It chose its words with care, not wishing to impugn the Rebellion's computer scientists. ". . . progress in cracking the Empire's . . . intricate anti-espionage encryption."

The raising of the topic made the other crew members stir. Agitation

Valiant nodded, frowning. The quandary bothered him, too.

"We think we're close," he replied. He leaned the twin sticks to the right, for mere creative exercise. Artistry. Was it aimed at the women? "But we still don't fully understand how the transmission of the data can destroy the data. It shouldn't prevent . . ." He sighed, abandoning the phrase. "But it does."

"The Empire so loves its destruction," Ripcord said, from where he leaned against the back wall, beside the sealed narrow door into the weapons locker. The safety on, he pulled his pistol's trigger, one eye closed, the tip of his tongue clenched between his incisors, lips curled back.

"Like you?" Angelica said, turning back and staring at him, eyes narrowed.

"Defense is really what I'm after," Ripcord replied, not looking at her. But he retracted his tongue and clenched his jaw. "Not offense. All appearances to the contrary."

"Uh huh," Angelica replied, facing forward again. "Love your delusions. You don't have neurons in that head of yours. Just plasma nacelles."

"Powerful charges, babe," Ripcord replied, grinning. "But if destruction's what you have on your mind . . ." With his off hand he pointed a gun-like finger at her, "then let's talk about why we left Ensign Sincon in charge on the ship! You suggested it, toots. You want offense? Well, paint me offended."

"Sincon's not in charge," Valiant interjected. "The ship's computer is. He's just backup."

"Yeah, yeah," Ripcord replied, crossing his arms like Spacey. "I just don't trust anyone wearing that stupid red shirt with my noble captain's ship. That's all. He should be on this mission. The Captain should have stayed."

"Sincon could've handled this away mission, if I'd asked," Valiant said, voice calm.

Ripcord shrugged. "Is that opinion an order, sir?"

The shuttle craft hit the atmosphere like a bird of prey, smooth as pinion feathers.

The glow of entry heat lit the viewscreen. Far below, the clear, bright blue of the endless ocean sparkled in the sunlight. A patchwork of yellow and green, separated by sharp boundaries, decorated the arachnoid continent. One distinctive circular patch of black, uniform to a surprising degree and estimated by Delta to be hundreds of kilometers in diameter, seemed out of place to everyone. Suspicious. Alien.

They avoided it.

"You always did love your ancient scifi," Valiant said to Ripcord. "Strange to think of a weapon's officer as 'encyclopedic,' somehow." He smiled. "Now let's talk about where we should land, and our plan once we disembark."

"Wildlife nutrient analysis," Delta said. "A priority. Poisons, carcinogens, and human biology."

"To find a way to crack the Empire's encryption," Brickwell said, differing.

"Or a way to teleport ourselves to Talon IV, safe with the plans," Ripcord said, before remembering how those could well be only an illusory Empire trap.

"I'd settle for a rock-solid plan to kill Captain Asshat," Valiant added, ego grumbling like a stomach.

Then everyone, thinking about how they'd been tricked by the Empire, imagined driving their fists into the smug, bony face of the disguised little man they'd faced down in the Empire's home world bar. The same way that Valiant had, to the cheers of the drunks. They'd all heard the same smacking crunch, a sound well-remembered from that one mission to "the treasure planet." Every grand villain, it seemed, crunched with grandeur.

And then the atmosphere they'd disturbed erupted like a punched hornet's nest.

"What the . . ." Captain Valiant said, looking at the view screen.

As the shuttle neared the ground, a forest drew into hazy view and then into sharp focus. Up out of the trees, like a swarm of hornets launched from defensive missile batteries, shot a host of something the shuttle's computers could not identify.

"Hostiles incoming!" Chance hissed, punching the wall to pump himself up.

"Forty seconds to impact," the computer said, with perfect, unwarranted calm.

"Fuck," Ripcord said, lurching to the weapons controls and strapping himself in. "I swear on my mother's grave, Cap, when I shoot ourselves out of this shit, expect another formal complaint about our shuttle fleet's lack of high-end motherfucking weaponry. Goddamned crime it is. Mortal sin."

"Noted," Valiant replied, jerking the controls. "Taking evasive action."

"Let me—" Angelica began.

"Quiet," Valiant snapped.

Everyone else strapped in too.

Valiant began maneuvers, trusting his bond with Ripcord to sync his firing. The rising host, a terrifying hoard coming into clearer view, resembled horrifying prehistoric birds. Hundreds of them.

"One hundred thirty-nine," Delta counted aloud, as calm as the computer. "No sign of reinforcements. No sign of ballistics. Expect melee combat."

"Time to spare then," Ripcord said. "Gives Valiant a chance to be lazy." He vented a sharp, manly cry. "I can tell you right now there are too many of them, coming on too fast. I'm a badass, but I got my limits. Maybe you don't have time to be lazy. Buy me time, or I might as well use our last seconds to write up that complaint now and send it off sub-space before we die."

"You do your job," Valiant replied, jerking the controls in a complex, backward pattern.

Blue lasers shot from the shuttle, lancing out on the view screen, approximately three per second. The creatures began vanishing in bursts of red flame, leaving little puffs of brown stratospheric smoke to fall behind the flocking remainder.

"Up your asses you flying fuckers!" Ripcord shouted. "All the way up, out your mouths, and then up the asses of your wing men! Two birds with every stone!"

"Your maneuvers are slowing them down, Captain," Brickwell said. "They're regrouping."

"Don't tell me what I already know," he replied, jerking the controls again.

Ripcord kept his aim, despite the evasive flight pattern.

"You call that unpredictable?" he chided.

"Ninety percent accuracy," Delta said, after nine seconds. "Human level. Perhaps I should—"

"Zip it or flip it!" Ripcord snapped, fingers dancing.

Valiant, impressed by the accuracy, but knowing the bloody, survivalist history that drove his weapons officer, threw a verbal reprimand.

"Focus, soldier. This mission cannot fail."

"Yes, Captain," Ripcord replied, through gritted teeth. Nine seconds later.

"Ninety-five," Delta said about the accuracy, almost sounding impressed.

Outside, the diminishing but still deadly host closed in. Its proximity revealed that the creatures were twice as large as the shuttle itself, and, bristling with limbs, claws, and fangs. Did they breathe? Despite the lack of projectile weaponry, it became clear that even one could destroy the shuttle with ease. They may even have fed on it.

"God damn it god damn it god damn it!" Ripcord screamed. His sweaty face reddened.

"Get it together, soldier!" Valiant shouted into Ripcord's ear.

"There are too many of them!" Brickwell cried. "Call Sincon! Use the *Nautilus'* battery!"

"No time," Delta said. "And too far."

"Ten seconds to impact," the computer said.

"Ninety-seven," Delta said, more and more impressed. "Fifty enemies remaining."

"Soldier!" Valiant shouted toward Ripcord. "One hundred and ten percent!"

"Five seconds."

Delta wished to criticize the mathematical impossibility. But it refrained.

"No!" Brickwell wailed, covering her eyes. "I'm too—" But she cut herself off.

Then, a miracle.

The remaining seventeen enemies broke formation and retreated toward the planet surface, melting into the trees like rainwater.

"Scans negative," the computer said, half a minute later. *"Threat eliminated."*

Everyone considered that last word. The very word mystified them.

Eliminated? No. And even had it been, what reason had they to believe the mysterious planet didn't have more in store? But sometimes, they all knew, the advanced programming of the computer just wanted to make its keepers feel better. For all they knew, it knew they were doomed, but wanted to keep order before the end came.

"That might serve," Valiant said, pointing to a wide clearing far from the flock's disappearing point.

Hovering one kilometer above the ground, the shuttle's small engine hummed against the unusually strong gravity, thirty percent above standard. The computer calculated the clearing as a good home base from which to hunt food, or from which to operate as they saw fit. That analysis had led to well-argued agreement about the clearing as a landing point.

"*Scans reveal fresh water and easy game,*" the computer said. "*Carbon based. Protein rich. Fat replete. And it is a clearing. Easy view of oncoming threats.*"

By then, having recovered, Ripcord had unstrapped himself and stood facing the view screen. He pressed his hands hard to his hips, his back straight. Slung across his broad back he already wore a sleek, high-efficiency rifle, loaded with standard-issue armor piercing rounds, ready and waiting for food or foes.

Valiant stood back from the view screen, ready to give the order for disembarkation. Behind him, rubbing his shoulders without acknowledgement, stood Spacey. Brickwell pretended not to care. To aid that end, she watched Ripcord's body language.

Ensign Sincon's nervous voice sounded over the speakers.

"Can I help?" he asked, sounding worried.

"Just do your job," Valiant replied.

"The computer up here is acting funny," Sincon said, his voice cracking. "I don't—"

"Just rub the computer's shoulders," Brickwell snapped.

"Shoulders?" Sincon replied. "But I'm not . . ." Audibly, he struggled with how to handle outranked comments. "What good would . . . You want me to put on a suit and crawl out onto the hull?"

Spacey let go of Valiant's shoulders. Valiant accepted a rifle from Ripcord and examined the ammo clip.

"Just watch for Empire craft on our tail, Ensign," Valiant said. "Don't leave the bridge."

"But—"

"If it makes you feel better, just rub your own shoulders."

"But what if there's . . ."

His voice trailed off. Everyone let it.

Spacey retreated to sit in a seat by the wall. She reached to a compartment beside the seat, opened it, and removed a sleek, silvery, standard-issue topographical scanner before pretending to check its functionality. Brickwell watched her, glanced at Valiant, and then looked again at Spacey. Then she glanced at Ripcord's muscles. Her facial expressions fought with her body language. She retreated to the engineering display, checked the engine functionality, and let the human stuff go.

"Don't . . . do . . . anything," Valiant said to Sincon.

"All right, Captain."

"Unless you want to send *another* redundant request for reinforcements to base," Valiant finished.

"No."

"Good. Over and out."

"Thank you, Captain," Sincon replied, his voice cracking as he cut the link.

Turning away, Valiant looked at Spacey, smiled, and pointed to the navigator's chair. With the other hand, he pointed to the clearing on the view screen, over Ripcord's shoulder.

"Take us in, Navigator."

Straightening and smiling back, Spacey nodded, sat, and took the controls.

"Thank you . . . Captain," she said with a wide grin.

The shuttle landed, its jets burning various strains of colorful vegetation to black ash. Only the scientific portion of Delta's "mind" objected to the destruction.

"Uncharted territory," Valiant whispered, Brickwell watching him closely.

"You're trembling," she said, one corner of her mouth rising. "Something wrong?"

Valiant coughed and stiffened.

"Excitement," he said. "I'm not scared."

"I didn't say you were scared." Dolly said, her mind working on a new kind of engineering problem. "I said you were trembling. Delta has medical training. After that battle you could be in mild shock. You're shaking—"

"With excitement!" Valiant, frightened all of a sudden at his own reaction, cut himself off. "It's not . . ." He closed his eyes and sighed. Then he opened them again, looking at the view screen and the idyllic grassland. "It's not every day a captain gets to set first foot—his best foot forward, of course—on an entirely new world. It's monumental. You know the old TV shows. To go where no man . . . er . . ."

"One?" Brickwell interjected. "I know you, Captain. You forget too easily."

Valiant rose, turning from Brickwell and avoiding eye contact with Spacey. He holstered a pistol, the weapon making a smooth, almost hissing sound as it slid into the leather hanging from his waist. He watched Ripcord check and re-shoulder his much larger, much more manly weapon, chin thrust out. Valiant pretended not to notice as he straightened, nodded at Delta, and slapped the external door controls. They hissed as they opened, like snakes guarding dangerous knowledge.

"Childhood dreams start early," he said over his shoulder to Brickwell.

"There!" Valiant cried, pointing through the dry grassland air and beyond a cloud of tiny red insects. They hummed, half blocking the beast Valiant pointed at.

Valiant managed the first shot.

Ripcord's shot following a fraction of a second later. Both blasts missed the lithe, black beast as it leapt toward its distant herd. It seemed to vanish into thin air like smoke, or into the green of the grass like rainwater.

"Stupid gravity," Ripcord muttered. "Would've hit it otherwise. Sure as shit."

Their bones felt heavy in the new gravity. All of them, but Delta, felt a curious, multidimensional hunger in their bellies, the feeling as heavy as their bodies.

"You see that?" Valiant asked, turning with a smile toward Ripcord.

"How it vanished?" Ripcord replied. "Or how you missed?" He looked up, scanned for the fragmented moon, and narrowed his eyes. "I hope this isn't a whole planet full of bloody cheaters . . ."

Dolly and Angelica, walking apart from each other and separated from the men by Delta, glanced at each other. They wrestled privately with their own thoughts and suppressed feelings, but they both shared a knowledge of the men's strutting insecurities. Each, on making eye contact, felt the tenuous, old bond and almost grinned, though their own, different type of competition prevented it.

"Assume it moved directly away," Valiant said. "Follow it."

The group walked through the grass, toward an outcropping of grey rocks. Ahead a distant, white-capped mountain range concealed the vast ocean. Behind them, perhaps half a kilometer away, lay the shuttle craft, their lone link to the *Nautilus*.

"I've been thinking about that vast, black circle we viewed from space, Captain," Delta said at last. It carried a weapon too. But it remained holstered.

"Yeah?" Valiant replied.

The sounds of their footsteps in the grass made them all think of crinkling paper.

"Too circular to be natural," Delta continued, regarding the black circle. "Too perfect. I believe it to be an impact site. Meteor, perhaps. Not very old. An object with a mass of perhaps a million kilograms. Curious that the atmosphere is clear of ejected dust."

"There!" Brickwell cried, pointing ahead.

Another of the black beasts appeared, as if from nowhere, but more visible this time. Nearer. Like the others, its curved horns ran down its back on both sides of its spine. It almost looked curious.

Ripcord took the first shot that time, just as the creature leapt away. His blast struck the agile prey animal mid leap, felled it at a distance of twenty meters. It vented a horrible, unearthly howl as it died, white blood spraying in an impossibly high fountain. The remains of its suddenly visible, but more distant, herd scattered and vanished.

"Dinner," Ripcord said, hurling a wry smile at Valiant. "Credit me."

"Drink," Valiant replied, frowning, the first to notice the blue sparkle of water nearby. A stream curled like a snake off to their right. "You hit an ugly, weak, and old one."

He ignored the carcass and walked like a parched man to the water. He knelt, drinking with both hands cupped.

Everyone else, ravenous, walked to the dead body. Yet not even Ripcord seemed to know what to do with it. Something beyond a replicator had created it, and no computer had prepared it. Each of them, in their own way, feared what might be inside.

"I will take care of it at the ship," Delta said, kneeling and laying a hand over the dying white geyser. "Conducting nutrition scans." Its eyes lanced out a clear blue light. "Adequate. Edible. I cannot tell about the taste."

After the women suggested flying the shuttle to the body, and after the men refused to "wimp out," all five of the crew members ended up assisting in carrying it back. Leg, leg, leg, leg, and head. Overhead, bright-white, four-winged carrion creatures wheeled and shrieked. By carrying an alien and unappetizing thing, each member of the crew, save Delta, built up a fresh appetite for the unknown.

The creature's herd appeared around the large white puddle, when they'd gone. Dropping their snouts, one after another, they each paid homage.

At the shuttle, the shattered moon looming high overhead, Captain Valiant keyed in the shuttle's ignition sequence via a tactile holographic display.

"Sincon?" he said, into the microphone.

No answer.

Only Delta, his hands on the alien corpse, as if reading it like a crystal ball, did not look at Valiant. Ripcord grunted. Spacey's eyes widened. Brickwell stepped forward and tapped the hovering red activation dot herself. Valiant glared at her from his seat.

"Please don't touch that," he said, head inclined. "I gave no clearance for liftoff."

The onboard computer spoke, out of turn.

"Intruder alert," it said, agitated. *"Intruder alert."*

The monitor lit up with a wide-angle exterior view, revealing at least a hundred humanoids approaching. Each one bore a single, long, sharp-looking and yet somehow un-primitive weapon. To a creature, they wore sleek, spare, black, un-primitive clothing. They approached the shuttle craft without fear.

Everyone but Delta froze. Delta, hands white with blood from the kill, strode to the communications array and flipped on the universal translator.

"Identify yourselves," it called to them.

The eerie weapons of the invaders waved side to side, like the grass, in unison, tips over their heads. Like a choreographed dance. The mirrored motion lasted three seconds.

"Like . . ." Ripcord whispered, "a head shake."

Then he strode to the weapons controls. He flexed his fingers, agitated. He looked at his captain, awaiting approval. Valiant looked at Delta, who shook its head, like the shake of weaponry outside.

"Do you come from the crater?" Delta asked the hoard, over the external speakers.

The invaders then reached the ship. One of them, the tallest and most muscular, his bare arms glistening with sweat, stopped. He stood right in front of the ship, taking up most of the view screen, looking up, down, and side to side, and then, it seemed, right into Valiant's comparatively tiny eyes. Valiant felt pale and insignificant. Against his will he shrank back.

"Do you come from the Empire?" the leader asked, in a startling, deep, and yet feminine voice.

Spacey and Brickwell, eyes wide, glanced at each other and tingled.

"Don't let them in," Valiant said, to Delta who stood by the door.

Delta, doing nothing, only looked at the door, feet wide, as if in a defensive stance.

But the door opened, forced open by some power originating from outside. A wave of warm savannah air flooded in, carrying with it the powerful scent of active, alien bodies. Valiant and Ripcord aimed their weapons, each taking a step back.

"Hey!" Valiant cried. His voice came out weak. Tremulous. "Get back!"

Only the leader of the invaders entered, unafraid, and in command. He looked at Delta, as if certain Delta commanded the shuttle.

"You fired on our planet's tertiary defenses," he said. "I ask again: do you hail from the Empire?"

The alien leader then looked at the herd creature the *Nautilus* crew had killed for food. With a silent stare he looked back out at his tribe, as if communicating by telepathy with all of them. Then he looked back at Delta.

"Consider it a gift," the leader said.

He resumed waiting for an answer.

"We do not," Valiant replied, eyeing Delta, confused. "We're Rebellion."

After narrowing his eyes at Valiant, as if at some affront, the leader looked again over his shoulder at his warriors outside. He nodded. Something that might have been the ghost of a smile appeared on his face.

"At last, there *is* one," he said.

Delta stepped forward. The leader nodded.

Delta asked, "Just how prepared is this world? Are there other worlds? Are you in contact? Will they follow? That I can even ask such questions so soon is a surprise, but you do not appear to be in the deep disorder we expected."

This response from his officer proved too much for Valiant. He felt unmoored. The string connecting him to command severed by some higher power. So he rose, lifted both hands like a man pleading for peace, and spoke to a point between Delta and the leader, a leader who had so easily forced his way onto this shuttlecraft extension of his beloved *Nautilus*. And he asked his own question.

"What the *hell* is going on, Delta?"

Delta said nothing.

The leading intruder smiled, fully at Delta, before answering Delta's question.

"And just how prepared is *this* world?" he asked, indicating Valiant. "He seems to me, and us, to be poor in that regard."

More of the warriors, ones appearing to hold high rank, entered the shuttle without Valiant's permission, flanking their leader. Ripcord's hands twitched, craving a firearm, but something, or some things, held his hands back.

Dolly and Angelica, allegiances split, glanced at each other for support.

"Easy, Captain," Dolly said. "Easy."

Brickwell, catching Ripcord's eye, shook her head, her open palms pressing toward the shuttle craft floor.

"Seeds," Delta answered Valiant, and to everyone from the *Nautilus*.

Everyone stood outside in the grass, surrounded by the dark leader's warriors.

"Seeds," Valiant echoed.

"Planted on many uninhabited M-class worlds years ago by the Rebellion," Delta added. "It was hoped that, through new technology developed in secret, the full power of planets unknown to the Empire could be—"

"Communicated with and brought to bear," the leader interjected, his spear pointed toward the shattered green moon above. "All life. All."

Valiant and the rest of the crew, save Delta, sat down on the soft, green carpet of grass. They felt too overwhelmed to stand.

"And not just the life," Delta continued. "The planets themselves, conscious in previously undetectable ways. It was theorized that, were the living planets made aware of how sentient humanoids could be more than a cancer on and inside them, and of our wiser sentience, they would side with us, and help destroy the Empire. And then . . ." Delta waved a hand in a half serious, half comic motion. "A new galactic epoch, and so on."

"Uh huh," Valiant said. His voice came out dead, indicating his short circuited mind.

The alien leader led Valiant and the others inside, and, like a crew member, moved to the shuttlecraft controls. He keyed numbers, with surprising speed, into the onboard computer. Then he exited, calling back over his shoulder as the shuttle door closed.

"Fly to these coordinates," he said, eyes narrowed at Valiant.

Spears clacked in a ritual of unity. The Rebellion members, the civilized ones at least, felt dwarfed.

And then the crew of the *Nautilus* found itself alone.

It took a full minute before the humans could collect themselves enough to turn their heads to stare at Delta. But Delta, wearing a mysterious, thoughtful look on its metallic, inhuman face, did not bother to meet their gazes. Not even halfway.

Interminable time passed, for the humanoid crew.

Delta flew the shuttle low over the grassland, the distortion in the atmosphere caused by the shuttle jets throwing the alien grass blades outward like pawns.

When the craft reached the borders of the forest and its giant trees, Delta altered the trajectory to an angle that pressed the humanoid passengers' bodies down with the force of three Gs. No one spoke. Something had stripped all humanoid rank away, all force of action. Like paying customers in a dark theater, Valiant, Brickwell, Spacey, and Ripcord only watched Delta and waited, minds blank in a way meant to invite the scribblings of fresh stories. Their bodies begged for food and water. But their minds paid their bodies no more attention than the hardening, flesh and blood corpse of the creature they'd combined their simple efforts to kill, such a short time before.

Sometimes the shuttle passed so close to the new treetops that the jets set the needles aflame. Valiant expected retaliation. But something unknown, something powerful out of the secret darkness extinguished the fire the shuttlecraft ignited. Valiant felt weak. Tiny. He looked at Ripcord. The security officer looked equally weak.

Then the grassland ended, as abruptly to their human eyes as an eclipse is to Time's, and the blue ocean began. It shone, sparkling with a far brighter shade of blue than the old oceans of the long-dead Terran home world. Delta flew the shuttlecraft low, the Rebel jets throwing harsh saltwater upward and outward in high, curving sprays, as if the shuttle were a water craft splitting the azure fluid like the tip of a racing blade.

"There," Delta said, lifting a silver hand to point ahead with a long silver finger.

Valiant and the others raised their eyes to look.

The shuttle approached the border of the circular black land they'd previously seen from above, from a safe distance. When the shuttlecraft breached the border, freed from the forest, Delta angled the shuttle down hard and the engines screamed in protest. The Gs pulled up on the bodies of the crew, thrusting them against their safety harnesses. The body of the hunted, killed food, the prey, separated from the shuttle floor, flew upward, and struck the ceiling with a dull, bloody, smacking thud that drew all eyes to it in confusion.

"No," Valiant whispered, shaking his head.

He, along with the others, saw that the black land was not the uneven charring of some forest fire. Rather, it lay on the ground, smooth and hard, glowing with a dull sheen that carried bright waves of sunlight across it like waves across an ebony ocean.

In front of the settling shuttle, stood the alien leader, his tribe behind him, long weapons still at the ready, with no sign of the vessel that had transported them to that spot, so much faster than the *Nautilus* crew.

Seeing them, Delta brought the shuttle to a gentle stop, leaving it hovering one meter above the ground, like some wind-pulled, stringless balloon belonging to the leader below. Valiant looked impotently at Dolly and Angelica.

The leader raised his free hand, palm down. As he lowered it, Delta lowered the shuttle and landed it on the strange surface. Extruded landing gear clanked against the black, hard ground.

Delta activated the communications link with Valiant's *Nautilus*.

"Ensign Sincon," it said.

The crew sitting behind Delta heard a crackle. Some sort of interference.

"Um, yeah?" the boy's voice returned. "Delta? Is that you? Is the Captain okay?"

Delta hesitated, as if unsure, though Valiant sat comfortably and intact behind him. Valiant felt no desire to interject with an answer.

"Your Captain is . . . fine," Delta replied, seeming unsure about its choice of words. "He and the others are behind me. Do you have any indications of encroachment by Empire craft, Ensign? Be honest."

"Uh . . . no," Sincon grunted. "Why isn't the Captain calling?"

"Complex," Delta said. "Hold steady." Then it cut the link.

The main shuttle door opened.

The alien leader strode in, flanked only by two glistening, muscular women who stood even taller than he did. The women wore nothing but long wavy hair hanging to their hips. With two snaps of his fingers followed by pointing fingers, the leader directed the tall, powerful women to Valiant and Ripcord. Obeying with strong, striding confidence, they lifted the oddly docile men over their shoulders, carrying them through the doors to the shuttle's storage room behind. Spacey and Brickwell, watching with wide eyes, struggled against disorientation.

"Dolly Brickwell and Angelica Spacey," the leader said, inclining his head. "Please step outside with me. I wish to explain."

He only disinclined his head when they agreed. Then he led the way outside.

"What is this place?" Brickwell asked, eyes taking in the obsidian land.

She did her best to ignore the lithe warriors who watched from a safe distance. To her right, Spacey knelt and ran one hand along the dark, hard surface underfoot as she murmured to herself about theories derived from half recalled Academy engineering classes. To her left, Delta stared up at the broken moon, hands at its sides, frozen in inhuman contemplation.

"The top of a craft manifested by the planet," the leader said.

"What?" Brickwell replied.

The leader rapped the base of his primitive weapon on the ground. The impact created an almost musical ringing sound that vibrated hard through the air.

"This planet," the alien continued, "like others, everywhere, absorbed by the true Rebellion, has been brought to the point of seeing the threat posed to the galaxy by the Empire, a threat that could devour its kin like cancer in mere thousands of years." A moment of visible fury overtook him. He soon controlled it. "But it has been prevented, with great effort, from seeing the Rebellion as a close relative of the Empire. That," added the leader, his brow furrowed, "proved to be the greatest challenge. Just imagine how alike we sentient humanoids must appear to such a different, feminine form of life, one operating and existing on a so much higher plane. How much like identical cells bent on overtaking the diverse unity of the whole!"

Spacey rose from the ground, having heard the explanation. She walked to stand beside Brickwell, formulating words as she moved.

"Feminine?" she asked, tentative.

"Worlds," the alien leader responded, "seeded with life, give birth to life while they live." He gesticulated, most of all toward his tribe, all of whom stood still and monolithic. "The planetary men, in the way of many men, have vanished. The women do not even recall if they were destroyers."

Brickwell felt thirsty all of a sudden. She wanted alcohol, to scratch the old itch.

Spacey covered her eyes with the palms of her hands. She shook her head, her mouth moving as she looked deep inside herself, for a lost ability to process overpowering and terrifying data.

"Does . . . this planet want the plans we captured?" she said at last, uncovering her eyes to look at the alien.

Blinking and pausing for a moment, the leader only laughed.

"The trap you fell into?" he replied.

His warriors, arrayed like sentinels behind him, laughed too.

"Such things are not required," the alien said, with a fast slash of his wide hand. "You, all of you, were only needed as a lure. This planet is the starting point for . . . a new infection." His face distorted with a kind of dynamism. "Simply give your *Nautilus* the signal," he said at last

"Signal?" Brickwell replied.

A part of her yearned for Valiant's input. But her captain had been compromised.

Behind her and Spacey, out of the shuttle, emerged Valiant and Ripcord. They wore no clothing, only fingernail scratches all over their bodies, and gigantic, insipid, stupid smiles. The vast alien women who had taken them away did not emerge with them.

Delta turned to face the emerging men. It strode up to Valiant.

"Captain," it said. "Please signal the *Nautilus* to send out a distress signal, one traceable by the *Vindicator.*

"By . . . Captain Asshat?" Valiant replied, baffled. He sounded like a man half asleep, inebriated on a sandy beach, baked into submission by equatorial sunlight. "Of course, Delta. That's a wonderful idea. I should have thought of it myself."

And then two of the leader's warriors, the tallest and strongest, stepped up to Spacey and Brickwell.

But they did not take the women over their shoulders. Rather, they knelt on one knee, the action lowering their heads to the level of the heads of the women. Then they looked at the ground in the manner of men awaiting a benediction. It took some minutes before Spacey and Brickwell discovered the means of reply.

"Maximillion, by the way," the warrior leader said to Spacey and Brickwell, all of them now standing on a small island far off in the vast ocean, sometime later.

They all sat, comfortable in the hot, ivory white sand of a fine beach, looking out into the blue aquatic. In the distance, gigantic creatures with shining sharp fins breeched the surface to pull low-flying grey prey from the air. As if envious, the unclaimed birds, rather than flying away, flocked around the capture points, as if awaiting their turn to be sustenance.

Delta, standing rigid some distance off, watched the scene without expression. Sometimes it spoke into a communicator to Sincon, currying updates.

"Strange world," Spacey said. The sandy, soft grit under her soothed her nerves.

Maximillion nodded as Brickwell examined an intricate seashell held gently in her hands, her fingers caressing its prongs and curves. Sometimes she lifted its canyon to her ear, every time appearing startled at the vast ocean she seemed to hear inside.

"Fine world," Maximillion replied. "Unified. Possessed of the full perspective. Lacking in illusion." He examined a scar on the back of his right hand, fingers flexing. "Healthy."

Spacey studied the scar as well, out of the corner of her eye.

"The Rebellion—" she began, before her voice broke.

Far out in the waves, an alien shriek transmuted into an ecstatic wail. She looked from the approximate source and up toward the green broken moon above. She thought of Delta's eyes, seeing the moon half obscured by a thunderhead. Then she looked down at the unmarked back of her bare right hand.

"My parents brought me into it," she continued at last. "The way they always spoke about the Empire and the fight against it made it seem like a battle against the awful swirl of a hurricane. I always imagined that if I could . . . find the eye of the storm and attack outward . . . it might be possible to emerge victorious. Upward, somehow. Outward."

She looked over, toward Maximillion.

"How did you bring us here?"

"To this water world?"

"Yes."

"Deep code in the *Nautilus*. Passed on like a virus, from previous vessels. A tactic borrowed from the Empire itself. From that strain of Humanity."

"Why now?"

Far out to sea, the high thunderhead broke open, pouring a localized torrent of drenching rain into an already salt-drenched landscape. New, gigantic creatures emerged and rose into the downpour like deep water gods, their variegated forms obscured by the distorting sheets.

"The planet is ready," Maximillion replied. "And the planet's family is ready. Adequate preparation has been undergone."

"But if—" Spacey began, cut off by Delta, who approached with purpose.

"*Vindicator* ETA one hour forty-nine minutes," it said. "Mark."

Maximillion, seeming not to have heard the beginnings of Spacey's incipient question, rose and pointed toward the distant, invisible continent they had flown from. Spacey looked at his finger, and not out to sea.

"There," Maximillion said, his feminine voice bearing the hallmarks of excitement.

Spacey turned to look, and saw a supermassive black form rise up out of the blue. Her eyes widened, growing as if to match its bulk.

"Fly your shuttle back to Valiant's *Nautilus* now," Maximillion said.

He touched her then, too fast for her to stop him. And he transmitted something deep.

Spacey jolted, and then looked to the black form for just a moment. When she looked back to the place where

Maximillion had stood before the moment had begun, he had vanished, like one of the swallowed sea birds, far distant and irrelevant out over the waves.

"Shuttle to *Nautilus*," Delta called over an open channel as the shuttle returned home.

"Delta!" replied Ensign Sincon. "What the Hell is that thing, that big ass thing that just tore up out of the planet?"

"Aid," Delta replied.

"Aid?"

"Help. Support. Assistance."

"Oh. So . . ." Brickwell could almost hear Sincon's hand wringing. "So you're not being chased?"

"No," Delta replied. "Prepare to receive."

"Okay."

Clearing the atmosphere, Spacey saw that the shuttle needed to alter course to circle toward the far side of the fractured moon. But rather than going around, Delta plotted a course through the fragments. Spacey felt the gravity of the shards pull at the small craft as they ran the gauntlet.

"Initiating docking procedure," Delta said as the shuttle cleared the ocean planet's atmosphere, its inhuman hands keying in precise commands.

Spacey looked back over her shoulder, at the shuttle's rearward storage room. She wondered, with an air of strange detachment, how Valiant and Ripcord fared inside. Men, kept secure via Amazons. Were she sitting at a console with more access, Spacey would have done a scan of the rearward storage. And she would have done it despite a deep unease at what the scan would have revealed.

"Welcome back," Ensign Sincon said, rising nervously from the captain's chair the instant his crew members emerged onto the bridge.

He looked over their shoulders, expectant hands wringing.

"Where are Captain Valiant and Officer Ripcord?" he asked.

"Indisposed," Delta said, taking the captain's chair. The silvery creature seemed odd.

"Oh."

"How long to contact?" Delta asked. Its instruments already gave the answer. It seemed to ask Sincon for another reason than to discover the answer. "Did you make the necessary alterations to our scanning signature?"

"Yup. But I don't understand."

"Nor do you have clearance to," it muttered. "Yet."

Far below, the image of the supermassive black vessel separated itself from the planet below. Breaking clear of the atmosphere, it became apparent that it could not be seen against the blackness of space.

"That thing's not giving off any reading!" Sincon cried, eyeing the holographic readouts above Delta's head. "Our scanners must be broken!"

"Sit down and seal your orifice," Delta said.

Sincon sat in a seat against the wall. He bowed his head, strapped in, and looked at his feet. Spacey heard him mumbling to himself.

Time passed.

A holographic countdown appeared. Ten minutes. Delta made adjustments to the ship and its course.

"Can I help?" Brickwell asked Delta.

Delta only shook its head.

A bright flash exploded, lighting the darkness outside the *Nautilus*.

Spacey's mouth fell open, taking in what dropped out of the flash. An Empire fleet, twenty strong, fronted by the *Vindicator*. Static roared on the *Nautilus* bridge for three full seconds. And then the crew heard Captain Asshat's bored, effeminate voice.

"Quite an error of judgment, Valiant," the voice said. "Were you trying to seal your doom with that signal? God I hate it when my enemies bore me to tears."

Delta made no response.

"Communications breakdown, Valiant?" Asshat continued. "Sadness! I'd call your ship a sitting duck if you'd landed. But you're more standing now."

Delta again made no response. Instead it keyed something into its console.

Out beyond the moon, Spacey saw a shimmering where the black, planetary craft had vanished from sight. She looked down at the planet below, to the glitter of the blue ocean, and memories of the leviathans rising up out of the waters for food. Then she looked at the Empire fleet as it split formation to flank the *Nautilus*.

"Don't hope for help, Valiant," Asshat chuckled. "We've cut off your reinforcements. Their bogged down in a losing battle three systems away." He cleared his throat with an effeminate cough. "If you hand over the base locations I suppose we won't torture you." The voice snickered. "Much."

Spacey watched Delta, who made no response. She heard a sound behind her. Valiant, wearing civilian's clothing, emerged from the rear door.

"Pretty," Valiant said, pointing as he sat in a seat against the wall.

Spacey looked at Brickwell, who stared at another shimmer from where the black ship had vanished. Then she felt her gaze drawn to the fragments of moon, which began to vibrate as if gathering electrical charge.

"No dice?" Asshat said. "Good! I love torture. Very not boring."

One fragment of the moon, with impossible speed, launched from its godlike place, crossing the sharp distance separating it from the Empire fleet. It struck one of the auxiliary warships, vaporizing the enemy in a brilliant explosion.

"What the . . .?" Asshat exclaimed, his effeminate voice rising an octave.

Another fragment of moon lanced out, abandoning place, and another Empire warship vaporized. The causal fragment, deflected, struck and cleaved an enemy, sending the broken vessel spinning out of position to explode at a safe distance, in a shower of rainbow sparking shards.

"Evasive action!" Asshat cried, as the *Vindicator* began swerving to starboard.

Then another fragment of the green moon hurtled into the fleet, destroying three warships, as if the governing weapon master were learning on the fly.

"Get us the fuck out of here!" Asshat shrieked, all empirical composure gone.

Then the rest of the fragments of moon, in unison, hurled themselves into what remained of the Empire vessels. A silent cacophony of explosions lit the darkness, and when the light faded, only the *Vindicator* remained.

"What do you mean you can't go to warp?" Asshat's voice shouted. "We weren't hit. Stop faffing about and go to bloody warp! Get us back to the core systems or I'll personally strangle all those puppies you have in your room, you motherfucking pansy!"

Spacey turned her head as Valiant walked by her and up to Delta. She watched as her captain knelt beside the silver crew member.

"Well done," Valiant said, patting Delta's hard shoulder.

On the view screen, a circle of bright azure light opened behind the drifting *Vindicator* in the starlit darkness. The circle spanned twice the distance of the Empire flagship, and its light glittered just like the blue waters on the planet below.

"I hear the . . . ocean?" Asshat's voice said, sounding confused.

Then the blue light vanished. When it disappeared entirely, no trace of the *Vindicator* remained.

Only silence.

Moments later, Maximillion appeared beside Spacey. She jumped, yelping.

"How long before you let it escape back to the core systems?" Delta said, without turning around.

"Planting the seed should take twenty-one of your hours," Maximillion replied. "In the meantime, the sister planets in the Empire territories are continuing what we've begun here. It is now only a matter of time."

Delta nodded.

"What the Hell?" Sincon cried. "I mean seriously! What the *Hell*, Valiant?"

Ripcord emerged from the rear door, dressed in civilian clothing, just like Valiant. He placed a fist to his mouth, yawned, and seated himself against the back wall beside his captain, who'd returned to his seat. He winked at him, and playfully punched his mighty superior's hard shoulder.

Spacey, seeing Sincon begin to shake uncontrollably as he went into shock, ran to him, and sat beside him. Wrapping both arms around him, she held him as he buried his face in her chest. She comforted him, staring at the view screen over the heads of Delta and Maximillian.

The black form of the supermassive ship came again between the *Nautilus* and the planet below, once more in clear view. It descended, sank into the green, and gave the planet free reign to work its magic.

"There, there, Ensign," Spacey said, resting her chin on the crown of Sincon's head. "Everything will be all right. I promise."

"But . . . how?" Sincon whispered.

"Because now we know," whispering back, so that the others wouldn't hear. "Humanity is only an organ. Cells. Now? Power is back in the hands of the bodies that built us. The planets. It's almost . . . astrology." She sighed. "We are . . . the Rebellion is . . . trusting in the gods again. In the forces Evolution built us to trust, using its one and only tool: the mistake." She sighed again. "And we've taught it and its gods all we can with our primary failure."

"What failure?"

"False kingship," she finished. "Hubris. The stolen, unpalatable knowledge of good and evil, I think."

And they both stared silently out into the star-spangled darkness of space.

Amos Parker has believed he should be a "real writer" since high school in the early 90s. But it wasn't until getting fired from a job, in 2007, that he finally found (and flipped) the switch in his body/mind/soul necessary to become more than an email and journal writer. He got fired early on a Monday morning, round about September 3rd, on a lovely, early fall day, and spent the day wandering around the nature paths in East Burke, Vermont. The first half of the day was spent wondering what the Hell to do next: the second half, after flipping the switch, was spent mentally hammering out a fantasy book plot, terrified that if he didn't lock it in hard, the switch would un-flip. But, in spite of some bumps along the way, it never has. Since then, a space currently of almost 8 years, he's written about 10 novel manuscripts, 6 books of short stories and novellas...and failed utterly to find the 'switch' in his mind/body/soul necessary to care much about fighting to be published and make money off his writing.

About the Editor

Carrol Fix writes and edits for Lillicat Publishers. She is the editor of the *Visions Series*, science fiction short story anthologies describing human exploration of space, including *Visions: Leaving Earth, Visions II: Moons of Saturn, Visions III: Inside the Kuiper Belt, Visions IV: Space Between Stars, Visions V: Milky Way* and the current *Visions VI: Galaxies*. She was an editor for *The Future is Short: Science Fiction in a Flash, Vol. 1*, and for a biography, *Sunshine & Shadow: Memories from a Long Life*.

Carrol is a short-story author and novelist whose science fiction work includes the award-winning novel, *Mishka: Book One of the Quadrate Mind*. She is currently writing the second book in the *Quadrate Mind Series*, while working on a young-adult fantasy novel, *Worlds Apart*. Her most recent short stories appear in *Visions: Leaving Earth, The Future Is Short: Science Fiction in a Flash, The Future Is Short 2: Science Fiction in a Flash, Twisted Tales IX: Wunderkind,* and *Perihelion Science Fiction Online Magazine*.

A former computer consultant who has lived in six different states, Carrol currently resides near San Diego, California, USA, in a household containing three generations of grandmothers, of which she is one. Her brother, W. A. Fix, a frequent contributor to the *Visions Series,* occupies a well-deserved spot on her list of favorite authors.

http://www.lillicatpublishers.com
http://www.mishkabook.com

VISIONS V: *MILKY WAY*

VISIONS V

MILKY WAY

EDITED BY CARROL FIX

VISIONS IV: *SPACE BETWEEN STARS*

VISIONS III: *INSIDE THE KUIPER BELT*

VISIONS II: MOONS OF SATURN

VISIONS: *LEAVING EARTH*

READ

THE FUTURE IS SHORT:

SCIENCE FICTION IN A FLASH

An Anthology by 31 Authors

The Future Is Short

Science Fiction in a Flash

Edited by Jot Russell, Paula Friedman, and Carrol Fix

Cover Image by Chris Leib

. . . and coming soon!

VISIONS VII: UNIVERSE

www.ingramcontent.com/pod-product-compliance
Lightning Source LLC
Chambersburg PA
CBHW070539260626
47161CB00002B/451